TENETS

VAGABOND BOOK 1

A.O. AMBALI

CONTENTS

Content Warnings:

This book contains material that may be sensitive or triggering for some readers. Please be aware of the following themes and topics included in the story:

- **Violence:** Descriptions of physical confrontations, injuries and violent scenes.
- **Sexual Content:** Scenes of a sexual nature, including explicit descriptions.
- **Abuse:** Mentions or depictions of physical, emotional and/or sexual abuse.
- **Mental Health:** Discussions of mental illness, self-harm and/or suicide.
- **Language:** Use of strong or offensive language.
- **Trauma:** Depictions of traumatic events and their aftermath.
- Readers are encouraged to proceed with caution and to prioritise their mental and emotional well-being. If you are sensitive to any of these themes, please consider whether this book is right for you.

Legal Disclaimer:

This is a work of fiction. Unless otherwise indicated, all the names, characters, businesses, places, events and incidents in this book are either the product of the author's imagination or used in a fictitious manner. Any resemblance to actual persons, living or dead, or actual events is purely coincidental.

Copyright Disclaimer:

Prologue

A NEW BEGINNING

Flowers blossomed, trees dressed in new leaves, and the endless blue sky held wispy white clouds. Sunlight poured down, bathing the world in golden light, illuminating the green grass. Birds sang sweetly as they hopped from branch to branch.

A high-speed train raced through Flora's picturesque countryside. Among the passengers, a young woman in her late teens gazed out the window. Her eyes traced the rolling green hills dotted with bright yellow flowers.

As the train sped past, she caught a fleeting glimpse of a quaint village – the charming houses nestled along the tranquil lake.

Her gaze shifted from the landscape to the people around her. Families chatted animatedly; children giggled, absorbed in games on their phones; a couple in their mid-thirties shared a quiet moment, fingers intertwined.

The young woman rested her arms on the table, cradling her head gently. In her posture was an unmistakable loneliness, a quiet sadness. A soft sigh slipped from her lips, and her face wore an expression of silent sorrow and emptiness.

She sat like that, lost in her thoughts, a solitary figure amidst the bustle. Every gesture, every detail – her slumped shoulders, the faraway look in her eyes – spoke of a silent plea for connection, for something to fill the aching void inside.

She remembered a conversation – every word etched into her mind:

'Elisa, are you sure about this?' David had asked, concern shadowing his features.

Elisa had met his gaze, her eyes calm but resolute. *'I am. I cannot, in good conscience, stand idle, David.'*

He exhaled slowly, the weight of the letter evident in his furrowed brow. *'This message holds great significance for Lance. If it's lost ... the consequences could be catastrophic. Are you truly prepared to take that risk?'*

A flicker of doubt had stirred within her then – quiet but insistent. What if something went wrong? What if she failed? But no – she would not allow fear to rule her. Not this time.

'I understand,' she had replied softly. *'But I shall not allow any harm to befall it.'*

David's expression had hardened into something like reluctant approval. *'You're really determined, then ... Just remember, I can't go with you. We've lost too many already. I can't risk being caught.'*

She had nodded, her heart heavy with the shared burden of their past. They had endured so much – loss, grief, moments of hope. And now, the road ahead was hers alone.

'I know,' Elisa had said gently. *'But I must do this – for Archer. It is the least I can offer him.'*

Archer's name echoed inside her, a quiet drumbeat steadying her. She owed him more than words could say, and she refused to let his sacrifice dissolve into nothingness.

For Archer's sake, she repeated to herself, clutching that thought like a lifeline.

She treasured every moment with him – each evening when the world felt heavy, she found solace in the simple certainty of his return. No matter how dark the day had grown, the familiar creak of the front steps and the soft jingle of his keys breathed warmth back into the cold corners of her mind. His presence was a tether, anchoring her when the shadows threatened to overwhelm.

When sadness pulled at her, Archer's quiet attentiveness was a balm. His eyes held a patience that soothed her restless thoughts, and his gentle words slipped through the cracks in her defences. He never rushed to fix her; instead, he offered space.

And when joy stirred inside her, she longed to share it with him first. His laughter was a bright melody that lifted her spirits higher, whether they were cooking in the kitchen or lounging side by side on the sofa. Those small, unguarded moments felt like sunlight spilling through the gloom.

Even her anger, fierce and sudden, found refuge in Archer's calm steadiness. He had a way of tempering her storm with a soft word or a sly joke, defusing the fire before it consumed her entirely. With him, she did not have to fight alone.

When emptiness crept in – those hollow, directionless moments – Archer was her compass. His steady faith in her strength reminded her she was more than her fears and doubts. He helped her find purpose again, even when it felt impossible.

Their bond was deeper than protection. It was a rare friendship, threaded with trust and care. She was lucky – no, *blessed* – to have him beside her, the constant light in a world that often felt dim.

And then one day, he was gone.

The news hit her like a crushing blow, the weight settling in her chest so heavily it was hard to breathe. The world tilted, colours draining from everything around her. Archer – the anchor of her heart – was lost.

Tears welled unbidden as she clutched her chest, as if sheer will could staunch the ache. Grief crashed over her in waves, raw and unrelenting.

Her hands trembled, grappling with the hollow silence that now filled the room. The world outside carried on, oblivious to the gaping absence in her life. And in that unbearable quiet, Elisa felt utterly alone.

Suddenly, a voice from the train's speaker system interrupted her trance.

'*All passengers, we are approaching the next stop.*'

With no time to grieve, she focused on delivering that letter. Wiping away her tears, she steeled herself for the task ahead.

As the train doors opened with a hiss, Elisa stepped onto the platform, her luggage rolling lightly behind her. She felt the usual flicker of eyes on her – the quiet assessments, the silent guesses. They always saw the same thing: a well-mannered girl with kind eyes and careful poise. No one ever looked deep enough to see past it.

Elisa's eyes gleamed a luminous crystal blue, striking and serene even in sorrow. Her lips, soft and full, shimmered faintly with a delicate pink gloss. A dusting of freckles adorned her nose, adding a gentle charm to her otherwise radiant beauty.

Her navy coat hugged her frame. A breeze stirred the hem of her white skirt, patterned with soft blue flowers. The heels of her brown boots clicked faintly against the concrete. Vibrant red hair spilled softly beneath the brim of her blue newsboy cap.

Elisa wandered through the busy train station, her eyes scanning every corner. She blended with the crowd, unnoticed – people engrossed in their phones or chatting, paying her little mind. She preferred it that way. Invisibility meant no questions, no forced smiles, no one seeing the hollow in her eyes.

As she moved through the throng, each passerby was a quiet reminder of a world that had moved on without her. She no longer felt part of it.

At last, she found an exit and stepped outside. She drew in a slow, steady breath and took in the unfamiliar surroundings.

The sun warmed her face, and her eyes adjusted to the natural light. After spending such a while on the train, it felt like she had almost forgotten how it felt to be outside. The cool breeze on her skin was a welcome change from the stuffy air inside. But even the refreshing air couldn't lift the weight from her chest. Once Elisa had got used to being outside, she went for a wander.

While walking on a narrow country road, she came across a military checkpoint – it was positioned where the road curved. A group of people stood in line, handing their IDs to soldiers. The soldiers in the checkpoint wore red armbands with a gold lion emblem: they were part of the Floran military known as the Red Lions.

Should she go through?

The checkpoint loomed ahead, soldiers stationed like statues, rifles slung across their shoulders. There was a chance they might find the letter – and if they did, everything could fall apart.

Elisa hesitated, fingers clutching the fabric of her coat. The trees beside the road swayed gently, a quiet invitation to disappear into the woods.

Then the voice came.

Do it, you coward.

Her lungs seized.

That word.

Her throat tightened as if the syllable itself had claws.

Coward.

It echoed, not just in her mind, but from somewhere deeper – something old, buried, sharp as broken glass.

Her fingers curled. A dull sting flared in her palm. She'd clenched so hard her nails bit skin.

Heat surged in her chest.

The faint crackle of fire. The iron stench of blood. A girl's scream – *May*. But that couldn't be right. That was years ago.

No. No. Not now.

She squeezed her eyes shut, but the flames still licked at her memory. Smoke coiled in her throat. Her hands began to tremble – lightly at first, then harder, as if they couldn't decide whether to freeze or run.

She took a step back.

Then another.

She was fourteen again. The gun was in her hand. May's eyes wide with panic. Elisa couldn't—

Stop.

She blinked hard, pushing the memory back where it belonged. Her breath came in shallow bursts. She pressed a hand to her chest, grounding herself.

No. No more. I shall not run. I shall no longer be a coward.

Without another glance at the road, Elisa turned towards the trees. Her legs were shaky, but they moved. She didn't care if it was brave or stupid – only that she wasn't running from this.

Not this time.

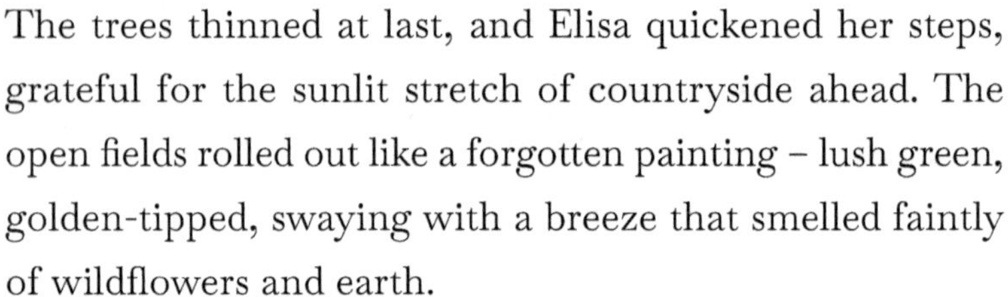

The trees thinned at last, and Elisa quickened her steps, grateful for the sunlit stretch of countryside ahead. The open fields rolled out like a forgotten painting – lush green, golden-tipped, swaying with a breeze that smelled faintly of wildflowers and earth.

For a brief moment, she allowed herself to breathe. To imagine peace.

A flash of movement caught her eye. A squirrel – small, alert – clutched an acorn in its tiny paws, cracking it open with fierce concentration. It looked so careful, so certain of its purpose. She envied that.

Her foot splashed.

She looked down – and froze.

The water was stained red.

Not wine-red. Not berry-red. But the thick, clotted kind that turned the stomach and tightened the throat.

Her breath hitched. Her gaze darted up, and there it was – *him.*

A soldier. Facedown. Still.

She staggered back a step, nearly slipping on the wet grass. The world narrowed to the emblem on his armband.

A Red Lion.

The words echoed inside her like a curse.

Her chest heaved. Hands trembled. The pulse behind her eyes pounded in waves. She could taste metal at the back of her throat, like blood – but it wasn't hers.

'Calm down. Calm down,' she whispered.

In. Out. In. Out.

Focus. Breathe.

She gripped the edge of her skirt, grounding herself in the fabric's texture. Her pulse slowed, though the dread remained, curling quietly behind her ribs.

She had to keep going.

The fields ahead gave way to ruin.

Burnt husks of homes lay scattered like broken teeth. Roads cracked and caved inward. Trees stood stripped bare, their limbs like bones thrust into the grey sky. Crows circled overhead in slow, silent patterns, as if mourning.

Elisa wrapped her arms around herself. The cold wasn't in the air – it was inside her now.

So much loss. So much pain etched into the soil. She could feel it underfoot, pressing against her bones.

Scattered bodies told the rest of the story – soldiers, yes, but civilians too. Children's toys strewn beside limbs. A woman's hand curled as if still clutching something. It was too much.

She turned away, unable to look anymore.

But she didn't cry. Not here. Not now.

She took another careful step, boots crunching over broken stone.

Then—

A sound. Faint. The snap of a twig.

Elisa froze.

Her gaze darted towards the treeline. Nothing. But the silence felt … loaded. Not the stillness of peace, but the pause before something ugly.

Her spine straightened. 'Who's there?' she called, her voice edged with steel.

No reply.

Only the wind. Only the whisper of crows overhead.

And then – movement.

Figures emerged from the bushes. Men, rough-looking, grinning in a way that made her stomach twist.

She took a step back, breath quickening.

One of them raised a knife.

Her heart slammed against her ribs.

She wasn't alone.

Chapter I

HER FEAR, HIS FURY

In a town damaged from war, everything showed the impact of conflict. Buildings were in ruins, walls crumbled and streets were cluttered with debris. Flickering streetlights cast eerie shadows, adding to the devastation of the surroundings.

He hated this part. The aftermath. The silence left behind once the screaming stopped.

Soldiers and civilians milled about, dazed or determined. Aid tents flapped in the cold wind, offering thin comfort to those caught in the crossfire. Children, ragged and wide-eyed, clutched warm bowls and bottles. One young boy's face lit up with a shy smile as he took a sip of water.

The mercenary's gaze lingered a moment longer than he meant to. Kids still found reasons to smile, even when the world gave them none. He looked away.

The soldiers wore red armbands with a golden lion – Flora's symbol of pride, justice, order.

The wind pushed against his navy blue jacket as he moved through the wreckage. No one paid him any mind. Just another man in a town of ruins. Blond hair tousled, jaw set, he kept walking – each step a quiet rebellion against the numbness clawing at him.

A low whimper drew his attention. A Rottweiler, ribs visible beneath patchy fur, padded towards him on shaky legs.

He crouched and pulled a bread roll from his pack, offering it silently. The dog devoured it with grateful urgency.

For a moment, something in him thawed. He scratched behind its ears, and the dog's tail began to wag. A soft smile tugged at the corner of his mouth.

'Good boy,' he murmured.

Then he stood and kept moving.

The next settlement was worse. Smoke curled from blackened timber. Corpses lay in the mud – soldiers, civilians, burnt-out lives. Flies had already gathered.

He didn't flinch.

From a hillside, he spotted movement. A group of thugs – scruffy, civilian clothes, makeshift weapons. And a girl.

Red hair. Slight frame. Cornered and shaking like a leaf in the wind.

He froze.

Something about her didn't belong there. Not just the way she looked – cleaner, finer – but the way she stood. Not begging. Not screaming. Just … trembling, like someone who still hadn't accepted what was about to happen.

His stomach twisted.

He knew what men like that did to girls like her.

He clenched his jaw. She wasn't a threat. Just a girl – frightened, cornered, completely out of her depth.

She looked so breakable. Too breakable for a place like this.

Didn't matter who she was.

What mattered was that those bastards thought she was easy prey.

He didn't stop to think. Didn't need to.

Men like that didn't deserve warning.

His hand was already on his hip.

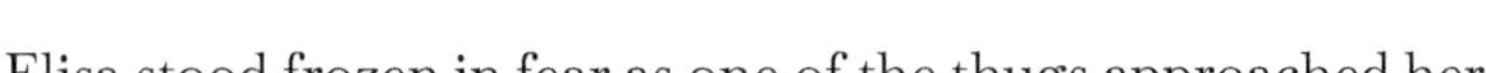

Elisa stood frozen in fear as one of the thugs approached her.

What was this man going to do?

The man, with black hair and a moustache, brandished a knife, waving it menacingly.

'Don't worry, love. We ain't doin' nothin' to ya. We just need some of that cash in the handbag you're carryin'.' He sneered.

Another thug, bald with a scar cutting through his brow, said, 'Hold on. We better not 'arm 'er. She's a pretty, this 'un.'

The black-haired thug then cast an appraising gaze upon her, scrutinising her appearance from head to toe. 'Yeah, you're right. We should 'ave some fun with the lass. Y'know me, I usually like 'em young.'

The remark sent a shiver down Elisa's spine.

Panic set in, and Elisa's survival instinct took hold. She ran, but coarse fingers curled around her wrist with bruising strength, yanking her back. She struggled, but more hands were on her, forcing her to the ground and keeping her there.

The first thug's voice boomed with aggression. 'Eh! Where d'ya think you're goin'!?' A twisted grin appeared on his face as he brought his knife closer to her cheek. 'You wouldn't want us to mar those pretty lips of yours now, would ya?'

Terrified beyond measure, Elisa's screams echoed through the air, a desperate plea for help that seemed to go unanswered. She thrashed, kicking wildly, trying to break free.

But it was useless.

The second man pounced, dropping to one knee beside her. His arm wrapped around her throat in a brutal chokehold, cutting off her air as he dragged her upright.

'Feisty little thing,' the black-haired one sneered. 'That's good – I like when they fight.'

Elisa clawed at his arm, gasping for breath. She writhed in his grip, trying to twist free, but he snarled and seized her wrists, wrenching them behind her. Pain shot through her shoulders.

'Hold 'er steady,' the first thug muttered.

With her arms pinned behind her and her balance stolen, Elisa couldn't stop him. He reached for the collar of her coat and yanked it downward – hard. The fabric slid off her shoulders, catching at her elbows, pinning her arms even tighter.

'There we go,' the second thug chuckled, shoving her forward into the other man's grip. 'Now you're nice and easy to handle.'

The first thug laughed, pressing the flat of his knife against her belly as his free hand grabbed the front of her blouse. He pulled. Buttons popped, fabric tearing open. The cool air bit at her exposed skin, sending a violent shudder through her.

The delicate purple lace of her bra was now visible, the thin fabric offering little protection from their leering eyes.

She screamed again – louder, more frantic – but the first thug clamped a filthy hand over her mouth. 'Ain't no one comin' for you, sweetheart,' he chuckled. He pressed the knife just below her chin, forcing her head up. 'But don't worry. We'll take real good care of you.'

Was this the end? Elisa's breath hitched as she stared at the blade. She had to get the letter to Lance – that was all that mattered. But even that conviction faltered as a bitter thought slithered in, uninvited.

Maybe it would be easier this way.

Her hands trembled. What was left for her, really? No home. No family. The ache in her chest pressed tighter, a slow, suffocating squeeze. The world could carry on without her. Perhaps it already had.

'Now then, just–'

BANG!

The dark-haired thug was silenced, and blood splattered over Elisa's face as his body fell on top of her.

'What the fuck ...!?' the other thug said, screaming. 'Where the fuck did that come from?!'

Amidst the chaos, Elisa remained on the ground bewildered, struggling to comprehend the abrupt turn of events.

Did someone come to rescue me?

The lifeless body of the thug still lay on her. With a surge of adrenaline, she pushed it off, struggling to free herself from its weight.

Abruptly, a new feeling stirred within her ... A desire to survive, a refusal to give up.

Why?

But there was no time to be asking herself that.

She quickly rose to her feet and scanned the immediate vicinity for any means to ensure her survival. Elisa spotted a gun tucked in the dead thug's jeans. Swiftly and quietly, she grabbed it, keeping her actions hidden from the thug who had held her.

However, before she could make her escape, the remaining thug became aware of her fleeing. 'Oi!'

Elisa gasped, her heart pounding in her chest as he grabbed her from behind.

'Please – please, let me go!' she cried, twisting in vain.

The thug ignored her pleas, holding her collar tightly, his gun pressed against her cheek. 'Shut your bloody mouth before I knock your teeth in!'

Overwhelmed by fear, she found herself being forcibly dragged away.

The mercenary reloaded with calm precision, raised the rifle, and fired. The bullet struck the bald thug square in the chest. He dropped instantly. The others froze, stunned by how quickly it had happened.

Good. One less.

'Bloody hell!' one of them shouted, already turning to run. 'I'm out! I'm out!'

Another spun around, wide-eyed. 'It came from over there! Behind the trees!'

The thugs ducked behind trunks. The mercenary remained composed. He folded the rifle's bipod, slung it over his shoulder, and slid down the hill, using a tree for cover.

Gunfire erupted. Bullets shredded bark, spraying woodchips around him. He jerked his head aside – instinct kicking in.

Then – silence.

He moved. Stepping out from cover, pistol raised, eyes locked on his target like a wolf stalking prey. Three quick shots. Each one landed clean.

The smallest thug collapsed.

The others hesitated – panic creeping in.

'Dammit!' shouted the tallest of the group.

Furious over his comrades' loss, the tall thug opened fire. The mercenary dodged the bullets, swiftly ducking and rolling behind a nearby log for cover.

'You'll pay for that, arsehole!' The thug screamed fiercely with his gun out. 'When I come over there, I'm gonna feed your dick to my dogs!'

He reloaded with quiet precision, thumb sliding the mag into place. His body crouched low, weight balanced. He studied the layout. Distance. Wind. Cover.

One breath. In.

Out.

'Come on out, you motherfucker …' The tall thug sneered as he pointed his gun towards the mercenary's hiding spot.

The thug prowled forwards, gun aimed at the wrong corner.

He had no idea.

The mercenary had already closed the distance, boots silent against the ground, pistol raised.

He stood just behind him now, breath calm, finger resting on the trigger.

The thug turned – and froze, eyes wide as they met the mercenary's cold stare.

Realising his mistake, he flinched, hands shooting up. 'No, wait, wait!'

The mercenary didn't wait.

He fired. Once. Twice. Again.

Each shot slammed into the thug's body, twisting him with pain. His screams tore through the air.

The mercenary didn't flinch. Didn't blink.

He watched the man fall, expression hollow. The stench of blood and gunpowder settled around him like smoke.

Elisa's breath hitched as the mercenary stepped into view. He was striking – wavy blond hair framing a face both rugged and handsome. His sea blue eyes were sharp and watchful beneath a faint touch of black eye make-up, lending him a fierce, almost theatrical edge. He looked a few years older, carrying himself with an easy confidence that made her pulse quicken, despite the tension in the air.

Her gaze flicked over his clothing – a blue blouson jacket with an archangel logo, a dark grey T-shirt with three wolves howling at a full moon, and well-worn jeans with black Converse shoes. A leather holster hugged his hip, hinting at the pistol he kept close. His olive green backpack completed the picture, giving him a look she couldn't quite read – equal parts soldier, vagabond, and myth.

Military, perhaps? Or just a sharp-eyed civilian with a knack for fighting?

The question lingered as she watched him move with a lethal grace that unsettled and fascinated her. Every gesture precise, every shot calculated – fluid, practiced, and unlike anything she had seen before.

Her heart beat faster, admiration and unease swirling inside her.

This was no ordinary man – dangerous, yes, but also strangely magnetic.

For a moment, she forgot where they were, caught in the silent pull of his presence – something wild and untamed beneath the surface.

As the tall thug's body collapsed onto the grass, lifeless and still, the sound of gunshots echoed in the distance, catching the attention of those who were nearby.

'Dammit, he got another one!' said an older thug, faltering.

'Just use her!' said another, his face heavily scarred.

The older thugs' face twisted into a sinister expression as he forcefully dragged Elisa towards him. 'Come 'ere!'

The helpless cries of the young woman cut through the air. The thug holding Elisa as a shield pressed a gun barrel against her cheek, his voice oozing with malice as he shouted to the mercenary.

'Come any closer and I'll put a bullet through her skull!'

Elisa's heart thudded wildly, her breath shallow against the cold press of the gun barrel at her cheek.

The older thug barked threats, spit flying from his mouth, but Elisa's thoughts were fixed solely on the blond man – the mercenary.

He stepped into view. His hands raised.

What is he doing?

He hadn't moved rashly. In fact, he looked ... composed. Unshaken. As if this situation – this life-or-death moment – was something he'd seen a hundred times before.

Her captor shouted again, louder now. 'Drop the gun and slide it over 'ere!'

The mercenary placed his pistol on the ground, never once taking his eyes off the thug. Not even for a second.

Elisa's breath caught.

Is he truly surrendering?

No. No, not quite.

There was a precision to it. Every motion was deliberate – calculated.

It wasn't submission. It was theatre. He was letting the man think he'd won.

Elisa's gaze flicked towards the shadows behind him – just in time to catch a flash of metal disappearing behind a tree. A rifle. Hidden. Within reach.

Her stomach twisted.

He was planning something.

She could see it now – the way his body had shifted subtly, weight balanced and ready. He was reading the field like a chessboard, measuring angles, anticipating moves. Not panicked. Not afraid.

He was waiting.

Elisa felt a strange calm begin to settle beneath her fear. It wasn't rational, not with a gun pressed to her skin.

But something in the way he stood – steady, watching, unblinking – made her believe.

He was dangerous.

Elisa saw the scarred thug's fingers creep towards the shotgun's trigger, tightening his grip.

He was about to fire.

You're just going to stand there? the harsh voice echoed in her mind. *Useless. Letting him do all the work while you do nothing. What kind of coward are you?*

That word.

Her breath hitched. Her pulse hammered in her ears. She had to act.

Slowly, she reached for the pistol hidden in her coat pocket, careful not to draw attention. Her hands trembled, her breath shallow.

She had never fired a gun before.

But there was no time to hesitate. Gritting her teeth, she aimed at the thigh of the thug holding her, closed her eyes, and pulled the trigger.

The gunshot rang out. The thug cried out in agony, his grip on her loosening as he staggered back. The gun clattered from his grasp, hitting the ground with a dull thud.

The pistol's recoil jolted through her, causing her to lose her grip on it. Elisa staggered and fell to the ground, wincing from the pain in her injured hand.

The thug's agonised scream pierced the air as he crumpled to the ground, blood gushing from his gunshot wound. 'My leg, my fucking leg!'

Witnessing Elisa's bold act, the mercenary's eyes widened, but he swiftly regained his composure.

From the ground, the thug shifted his attention to Elisa. He pointed the shotgun at her, his finger tightening on the trigger. 'You dirty bitch!'

Elisa gasped, horror in her eyes. She then saw the mercenary spring into action. With a single, well-aimed shot, the bullet hit the thug's hand, causing him to squeeze the trigger, unleashing a loud blast. The shotgun fell with a resounding clatter.

The mercenary swiftly closed the distance to the wounded thug, who clutched his own bloody hand.

With calculated force, he unleashed a series of rapid, devastating strikes, leaving the thug reeling in agony.

Elisa watched in stunned silence as the mercenary dislocated the thug's arm with a swift, brutal motion. The man cried out in pain, but the mercenary didn't stop. He followed up with a brutal punch to the stomach, forcing the thug to double over, then grabbed the back of his head and drove his knee into his face.

Elisa flinched. He was relentless. *Efficient.*

The mercenary then wrapped his arm around the thug's throat, locking him in a chokehold. The man thrashed, struggling for air, his hands clawing at the mercenary's grip.

Elisa's breath hitched as she looked at the other thug – the one who had taken her hostage. He was still on the ground, clutching his wounded leg, his face twisted in pain.

His wide, fearful eyes darted between her and the mercenary, realising he was utterly at their mercy.

The mercenary shifted his grip, pinning the struggling thug in place. Then, without a word, he raised his gun and aimed it at the wounded man.

The thug on the ground panicked, throwing his hands up to shield himself. His voice shook. 'Oh God, please don't shoot!'

Elisa's stomach clenched. *Would he really kill him?*

The mercenary hesitated for only a moment, his eyes briefly flicking to Elisa. Her breath hitched in her chest, unsure of what he would do next. Instead, he swung the handle into the back of the restrained thug's neck. The man crumpled to the ground, unconscious.

Then, without warning, another gunshot rang out. Elisa jumped, her ears ringing as she saw the second thug – the one had the shotgun – screaming in pain. Blood seeped from his newly wounded leg.

Her breath came in shaky gasps. The mercenary didn't hesitate. He didn't show remorse. He just ... acted.

Elisa's gaze shifted to the wounded thug on the ground, now trembling violently. His breaths came quick and shallow as he cowered under the mercenary's cold, piercing stare.

She wasn't sure what unsettled her more – the thugs' cruelty or the mercenary's efficiency. He showed no hesitation in inflicting pain, but she knew these men would never forget what had happened.

'By the time I count to ten, I want you and your friend out of my sight,' the mercenary declared.

The thug scrambled to his feet, hastily assisting his injured comrade as they both retreated.

The mercenary's eyes narrowed, a sharp and frigid glare. 'And you better be quick because I might skip a number if you irritate me.'

He began to count. 'One ... Two ...'

The wounded thug's fear seemed to spike, and he quickly rose to his feet. Grunting in pain, he limped towards his wounded friend.

'Three ... Four ...'

The injured thug dragged his wounded comrade across the ground. Each movement was a struggle, leaving a trail of blood behind them.

'Six!' the mercenary shouted.

'O-okay, okay! I'm leaving! I'm leaving!'

The mercenary stared them down, and the thug and his friend quickly limped away from the two of them.

Elisa was in complete shock, her wide eyes and unmoving expression revealing her turmoil. So many questions swirled in her mind. Who was this man? Was he a soldier or a civilian? How could he take down the thugs so effortlessly? Whoever he was, he was dangerous.

Chapter II

THE ROAD AHEAD

The mercenary's posture eased. A breath left him – slow and controlled – as he holstered his weapon and stepped forward with caution.

'Are you hurt?' he asked, extending a hand towards her.

Elisa flinched and instinctively stumbled back, her pistol snapping up between them. Her heart thundered in her ears.

'Do not come any closer!' she warned. Her arms ached from holding the weapon so tightly, but she refused to lower it.

'Alright, easy – easy,' he said, hands lifting in surrender. 'I'm not your enemy.'

She didn't trust him. Not yet. Her breath came shallow, and her eyes darted over him – watching for any flicker of deceit. The calm in his gaze unnerved her; he was far too composed for someone who'd just risked his life.

Then, slowly, he reached into his coat pocket.

Elisa tensed. 'What are you doing?'

'Just this,' he said gently, producing a card and holding it up between two fingers. 'I'm a professional. Not some thug. See for yourself.'

She hesitated, lips slightly parted. Her eyes narrowed as they scanned the card – then widened in realisation.

'Oh ...' she breathed, her voice barely audible.

He tucked the card away, taking a half-step back. 'You can lower the pistol now. Unless you're planning to shoot me for helping you.'

Elisa's arms dropped, the weight of the gun suddenly too much to bear. Her voice cracked with shame. 'Forgive me. I – I did not know what to think.'

'No harm done,' he said. 'You were scared. Understandable.'

Her arms hung limply at her sides. She swallowed. 'Thank you ... for intervening. Had you not—'

'I'd rather not imagine it,' he said with a tired shrug.

He ran a hand through his hair and sighed. 'Thugs, rebels, stray bullets ... and now this. Honestly, I didn't plan on spending the day wasting silver rounds on small-time scum.'

To him, the situation felt more like an unwelcome burden than a calling – a string of unfortunate events disrupting his path, rather than a duty to be shouldered.

Elisa quickly noticed her bra was showing, a few of her buttons torn open. Her face flushed with embarrassment, and she fumbled to button up the blouse as quickly as possible, hoping he wouldn't notice.

She watched as the mercenary examined the pistol he had taken from her. His hands moved with the assurance of someone intimately familiar with such weapons – fingers deft and practised, as though the gun belonged there.

'A Glock 17 ... how quaint,' he murmured, more to himself than to her.

Then his eyes shifted – sharp, unyielding – and fixed on her with startling intensity. The warmth he had shown only moments ago had vanished.

'What the hell are you doing here?' he asked, voice low but cutting.

Elisa flinched at the sudden severity.

'This area's dangerous. The safe zone is miles from here. So which is it? Are you lost ... or did you wander here on purpose?'

The question hung in the air – accusatory and cold.

Elisa hesitated. Her mouth opened, but the words caught in her throat. 'I ...'

He crossed his arms, brows drawing tighter. 'So? Are you lost?'

She shook her head. 'No,' she answered – soft but firm.

His expression darkened. 'Then you came here deliberately. Why? I need an answer. Now!'

She blinked at him, startled by the shift in demeanour. Moments ago, he had seemed almost kind – concerned, even. But now? Now it felt like she was being interrogated. Had he already forgotten what she had just endured?

What was this? Some form of judgement?

Elisa said nothing, frozen in place, her mind struggling to catch up – but the man's voice rose, sharp and unrelenting. 'Answer me!'

She recoiled as though struck, stumbling back a step. Her throat tightened, breath catching. 'I beg your pardon!?' she snapped.

He was terrifying.

Elisa's body trembled, the aftermath of the attack crashing down upon her. She wrapped her arms around herself, as if that alone might contain the panic building inside her. Everything – the shouting, the thugs, the sheer chaos – it was too much. Her composure, once carefully maintained, now hung by a thread.

She could barely think – barely breathe.

The man before her radiated a raw, feral energy – like a wolf sizing up a threat. She, in contrast, felt as fragile as glass. No – not even that. A trembling rabbit, backed into a corner, caught beneath the gaze of something that might devour her without a second thought.

The man bared his teeth – not in a smile, but in something wild and untempered. Fury twisted across his features.

Then, just as suddenly, he froze.

'Oh ... shit,' he muttered, the anger draining from his face as his eyes widened. 'Oh my God. I ... I'm so sorry. I didn't mean to shout – I just ... get carried away sometimes. Force of habit.'

Force of habit? Elisa's pulse quickened. *What manner of life must this man lead, that such aggression came so easily – so naturally? What does he do to those who truly anger him?*

The mercenary awkwardly cleared his throat, as if attempting to reset the entire encounter. 'Right. Let's start again, shall we? My name's Duncan. Duncan Saul.' He gave a small, sheepish shrug. 'It's ... a pleasure to make your acquaintance.'

Elisa blinked, uncertain what to make of him. Just moments ago, he had looked ready to tear her apart.

'Dammit,' he muttered under his breath, rubbing the back of his neck. 'I messed this up.'

Something shifted.

For the first time, the hardened shell around him cracked, and Elisa caught a glimpse of something unexpected – hesitation, perhaps even regret. The fierce, wolfish energy gave way to something more human. And strangely ... that made her pause.

There was someone underneath the harshness – someone she didn't quite understand, but couldn't entirely dismiss.

Elisa's lips parted as if to speak, but no words came at first. Her voice, when it finally emerged, was thin and strained. 'It's … nice to meet you, Mr Saul. My name is Elisa.'

He gave a small, awkward smile. 'Yeah … hey.'

The exchange felt surreal. Moments ago, she'd been shoved to the ground, her life hanging by a thread. Then came gunfire, blood, a pistol in her hand. And now – this man. Harsh, unpredictable, now trying to be polite.

She couldn't make sense of it.

Every part of her wanted to remain composed, to act as she'd been raised – to smile, to be civil, to converse like nothing was wrong.

But her body betrayed her.

Elisa shifted back a step, arms wrapping around herself as if to hold her insides together. Her throat tightened.

'I—I'm sorry,' she said quietly, almost choking on the words. 'I do not … I do not have time for this.'

Duncan frowned. 'What do you mean, time—'

'I mean—' she cut in, her voice taut with strain. 'Time is not my ally, Mr Saul. I … I took a shortcut. A foolish one, clearly. I need to get to my destination.'

He tilted his head, expression cautious now. 'And where exactly is that?'

Elisa shook her head, suddenly unwilling to give more. 'I cannot say. Forgive me, but … I need to leave. We may speak another time, if fate permits.'

Her words were still refined, still formal – but behind them, Duncan would see it. The cracks. The tremble in her voice. The sheen in her eyes. The sheer effort it took to stay upright.

Duncan frowned as he watched Elisa's hurried departure. He immediately called out to her. 'Wait.'

Elisa froze in her tracks, startled by Duncan's unexpected interruption.

'I *am* a mercenary, after all. I could escort you to your destination.'

Elisa's eyes widened in surprise at his offer. She hadn't expected help from a stranger. A wave of hesitation swept over her as memories of Archer – the only friend she had ever trusted – came flooding back. Could Duncan be someone she might trust now? Could he help her escape the loneliness she had carried since Archer's death?

'What's the matter? You staring at me like I'm some sort of bloody freak?' Duncan grunted.

Elisa flushed, embarrassed. 'Apologies, Mr Saul. I must respectfully decline. I require money for your services.'

'Look, I'm not here to play games. Usually, my services come with a price.' He folded his arms, his gaze steady. 'But right now, you're in no shape to pay or argue. You better accept help before whatever's on you festers.'

Elisa didn't answer straight away.

She lowered her gaze, her hands twisting at the fabric of her sleeves. Images of the attack flashed behind her eyes – grimy hands, shouts, that awful knife. Her body still trembled from the aftershocks, the taste of fear lingering on her tongue.

Could she really walk the rest of the way alone? Would the next street hold another group of men like them?

Her mind drifted to Archer, to how safe she had felt when he was near. But he was gone. And in his place stood this strange, gruff man who had – despite everything – saved her life.

Elisa took a slow, shaky breath. '… Very well,' she said at last, lifting her chin though her voice still wavered. 'I accept, Mr Saul. I do not wish to endure anything like that again.'

Duncan nodded once, serious. 'Good. Now, first thing – you need to clean up. You're covered in dirt and blood. That's how trouble finds you.'

Elisa grimaced as she looked down at herself. Her clothes were a mess – caked in dirt, sweat and blood. The sight made her stomach churn. She needed to wash away the remnants of the day's horrors.

Standing by the riverbank again, she stared at her reflection in the water. Her clothes were in a pitiful state, and her face was streaked with blood – not her own, but from the thug Duncan had shot. With a resigned sigh, she knelt and began to scrub her face, the cold river biting into her skin as she washed away the dried blood. Though the cool water stung, it helped clear her thoughts, if only for a moment. The once-clear surface became clouded with the grime she was washing away.

The day's events replayed in her mind – the sudden ambush, the struggle, the violence. She had seen violence before, but this was different – raw, brutal, chaotic. War, she realised, wasn't just about battles and strategies: it was about survival and facing the darkest parts of humanity.

What haunted her most wasn't the blood or the pain. It was the moment when the thugs cornered her, their intentions clear in their eyes. For the first time in her life, she felt truly powerless, vulnerable in a way she had never imagined. The memory of their leering faces and rough hands made her skin crawl.

She shivered, trying to push the memory away as she splashed more water on her face. She had to be strong, she told herself. There was no room for weakness, not now.

After a few more moments of scrubbing, Elisa stood, her hands trembling slightly as she wiped her face with the back of her hand. She couldn't bear to look at the ruined clothes she had been wearing, so she checked that Duncan was out of sight before discarding them on the riverbank. From her luggage, she pulled out a fresh white blouse and an olive green skirt – the fabric soft and clean against her skin. A small comfort, but one that helped her reclaim a measure of dignity after everything that had happened.

She slipped into her long, fitted coat. Then, with slow, deliberate motions, she ran a wooden comb through her damp hair, smoothing it back from her face. Finally, she reached for her worn newsboy cap, settling it atop her head with practiced ease – a finishing touch that made her feel just a little more like herself again.

As she dressed, her thoughts wandered to Duncan. He had been there, had fought off the thugs, had saved her from a fate she didn't want to think about. He was so different from anyone she had ever known – rough around the edges, unrefined, with a bluntness that was almost abrasive. Yet, there was a kindness in him, a protectiveness that she couldn't ignore. It made her wonder if she could trust him.

Elisa glanced at Duncan, who was checking their supplies nearby. Could he truly be her friend? It was hard to say. He wasn't like the people she was used to, but maybe that was a good thing. Maybe she needed someone like him right now.

With a deep breath, Elisa finished adjusting her skirt and walked back towards Duncan, feeling a little more composed but still uncertain of what lay ahead. There was so much she didn't understand, but one thing was clear – she couldn't do this alone. And for now, Duncan was the only one she could rely on.

Elisa returned to the path and joined Duncan without a word. Her hair was neater, and her face was free of blood and grime. The sound of her footsteps blended with the rustling leaves and the distant murmur of the river.

Duncan glanced up from where he was checking their supplies and raised an eyebrow.

'Well now – that's better. You don't look like you crawled out of a battlefield anymore.'

Elisa gave a small, polite smile. 'Thank you. I felt it was necessary to restore a semblance of ... dignity.'

Duncan chuckled, standing to meet her. 'Yeah, you clean up well, miss. Posh again, like nothing happened.'

She raised a brow at the word *posh*, uncertain whether it was praise or teasing.

Then, with a theatrical air, Duncan lowered his head and awkwardly hunched his shoulder forward, stretching one arm across his chest in what could only be described as a butchered attempt at a bow.

'Don't worry, Elisa,' he said, grinning. 'I'll try not to be an inconvenience on your noble quest.'

Elisa blinked, puzzled. Then frowned. 'That is ... not quite how one bows.'

'No?'

'No.'

Duncan straightened, wary now. 'Okay? What did I do?'

'It's not a complaint, I assure you,' she replied calmly. 'Merely an observation. Your gesture – that is, the bow – was executed ... incorrectly. The proper form lies not in the shoulders, but the chest. One must maintain upright posture and incline forward at a precise forty-five-degree angle.'

Duncan stared at her. 'You're joking.'

'I am not.'

He scratched the back of his neck, eyebrows drawn together. 'Forty-five degrees? What is this, a maths lesson?'

'I beg your pardon – I forget not everyone was taught these things,' Elisa said gently. 'I appreciate the effort all the same.'

'That's a bit much just to say hello.'

'It is not merely a greeting,' she replied, folding her hands in front of her. 'It is a reflection of respect, refinement ... and discipline.'

Duncan looked at her like she'd just started reciting from a maths textbook.

'Where I come from, people just nod or say "alright" and move on. Bowing at forty-five degrees sounds like a way to pull your back out.'

Elisa tilted her head, half-confused, half-amused. 'That is regrettable. Though I must commend your attempt ... however curious it appeared.'

He snorted. 'Yeah, I looked like a right idiot. Can't fake class, I suppose.'

There was a pause. Then, quieter:

'So, what's the deal with all this etiquette stuff anyway? You sound like you walked out of some noble court.'

Elisa hesitated, then spoke with her usual poise. 'My parents are of noble heritage. They ensured I was raised in accordance with proper decorum – speech, posture, presentation, and so on.'

Duncan blinked. 'You serious?'

'I am.'

Duncan raised both brows. 'Ah. So I was talking to a proper rich girl.'

'That is ... a rather crude way of putting it, but yes.' Elisa said, brushing a lock of hair behind her ear.

'Well, that explains it.' He laughed. 'Here I was thinking you were just pretending to be posh for the fun of it.'

She allowed a faint smile, then looked away. 'My circumstances, however, are no longer what they once were.'

Duncan tilted his head. 'How so?'

She drew in a breath, then let it go. 'It is a long story, and one I am not prepared to share – not yet.'

Duncan didn't push. Instead, he gave her a quiet nod. 'Fair enough. Everyone's got something they'd rather keep locked up.'

Duncan broke the silence first.

'Alright. First things first – where are we headed?'

'Gothenburg,' Elisa replied, her voice measured.

Duncan gave a low whistle. 'Gothenburg, eh? City of the Kingslayer. Same direction I'm heading, actually. But you – what's a girl like you doing heading into a war zone?'

She hesitated.

His question wasn't unkind – more curious than suspicious – but her instincts warned her to tread carefully. She didn't know him, not really. He had saved her life, yes, but that didn't make him safe.

'It is ... personal,' she said at last. 'A favour for a friend.'

Duncan squinted at her, unconvinced. 'Must be a hell of a favour. You nearly got yourself killed.'

She didn't respond.

'Don't take this the wrong way,' he added, glancing sideways at her, 'but back there? You handled yourself like someone who's never held a gun.'

Her silence persisted. He continued, gently probing.

'So you're not Red Lion. And I doubt you're Night Hawk either – they don't tend to send civilians on suicide runs.'

A pause.

'So what are you, then?'

Elisa hesitated. She didn't owe him anything – and yet, after what he'd done, a part of her felt … indebted. Or maybe just lonely.

'I am doing a favour for a friend,' she said finally. 'He served with the Night Hawks. His name was Archer.'

She glanced away, her voice tightening. 'He was entrusted with … something of significance. Something he was unable to complete. I am merely endeavouring to honour that.'

Duncan studied her. There was no bravado in her voice – no rehearsed patriotism, no militant pride. Just weight.

'You're delivering something,' he said.

She gave a quiet nod. 'Yes.'

He didn't press. Not yet.

'Risky move. The safe zone's miles behind us. Thugs, rapists, even worse out here. You didn't think to bring backup?'

'There was no time. And too many questions would have only hindered me.'

Duncan folded his arms, walking in silence for a few paces.

'You're brave,' he said. 'But reckless.'

'Is there truly a distinction?'

'Sometimes. Brave gets you remembered. Reckless gets you killed.'

She didn't reply.

After a moment, Duncan tried again.

'So what exactly are you bringing to Gothenburg? A message?'

Elisa looked at him, the question lingering between them. She felt her throat tighten. The words she *shouldn't* say were already forming – rising, swelling like a tide.

He'd helped her. Saved her. He was kind, in his own coarse way.

But this was a line. And lines mattered.

'You have been kind, Mr Saul,' she said softly. She paused, her hands curling into the fabric of her coat. 'But I have told you all that I am able.'

Her heart thudded in her chest.

That is quite enough, Elisa. Say no more. Allow the silence to bear the weight of what you cannot.

But then, the rest came – quiet, trembling, but firm:

'And ... and I do not intend to say more.'

There. It was done.

Her fingers twitched with the need to fidget, to retreat. She feared his reaction – feared that challenging him might turn him cold, or worse, angry. But to her surprise, Duncan only studied her for a long, thoughtful moment.

Then, he gave the faintest grin.

'Smart girl,' he murmured.

Elisa blinked. Relief rushed in, chased swiftly by embarrassment. She hadn't meant to sound defiant – only to protect something important. But maybe ... she'd earned a little of his respect.

Curiosity prickling at her thoughts, Elisa turned to Duncan, her gaze tentatively meeting his.

'So ... Mr Saul,' she began, her tone careful, 'may I ask – why are you escorting me?'

Duncan shot her a side glance, a wry smile tugging at his lips.

'Good question.' He scratched his jaw. 'Maybe I don't have a proper answer. Could be the perfume. Or maybe it's because your face doesn't scream "stab me in my sleep." Or maybe ...' He shrugged lightly. 'Maybe I just haven't seen a pretty girl in a while.'

Elisa blinked at him, her brows gently arching. 'Oh really?'

His smirk deepened. 'I'm being serious.'

She let out a soft, reluctant chuckle, the tension in her shoulders easing ever so slightly.

'Well ... regardless of your reasoning, I do appreciate it.'

Duncan's smile lingered, and for a moment, the atmosphere between them warmed.

'And stop calling me "Mr Saul". Just Duncan is fine.'

She nodded, her voice softer. 'Alright then ... Duncan.'

She tried the name out cautiously, as if tasting it on her tongue for the first time.

After a beat, she added, 'May I inquire where you're from? I imagine you've seen quite a bit of the world.'

'I'm Floran,' he said. 'Born and raised.'

Elisa brightened faintly. 'Ah. A fellow Northerner.'

Duncan glanced over at her.

'Yeah, well ... bit of Kingsgurian blood in me too. My grandfather was from the west – Syrida region.'

'I see,' she said, intrigued. 'A rather rich blend of roots, then.'

As they continued down the forest path, the branches thinned and the sounds of distant movement trickled in from ahead.

Elisa hesitated for a moment, then asked, 'So ... what brings you to Gothenburg?'

Duncan grew quiet, his earlier humour fading like smoke.

'Looking for somewhere to stay. Somewhere that needs help.' He sighed, scratching the back of his neck. 'I've been bouncing around – missions, jobs, clean-ups. War follows you wherever you go now. Dead families. Empty homes. Kids with no parents. Same old bloody mess.' A pause. 'Honestly? I just want it to stop. All of it.'

His voice had a tired weight to it – not bitter, just worn.

Elisa glanced at him, her expression softening. 'Yes,' she murmured. 'I can truly relate to that.'

Duncan looked at her, as if surprised by her sincerity, then offered a quiet smile – one with no trace of charm, only gratitude.

They walked the final stretch in silence, until the trees opened, revealing the stone roads and low, crumbling skyline of Gothenburg.

'We're here,' Duncan said.

Chapter III

GOTHENBURG

As they entered the city, Elisa was struck by the vibrant energy that pulsed through Gothenburg. The buildings were alive with colour – blues, greens, reds, pinks, and yellows blending into a vivid kaleidoscope across the skyline.

The calm cerulean sea cradled the city's edge, its gentle waves lapping beneath sturdy bridges that connected the bustling streets.

Her gaze settled on the Great Bridge, an impressive feat of engineering stretching far and wide, carrying both vehicles and pedestrians in effortless flow.

Then, towering above all, the clock tower stood as a proud symbol of the city's history – its intricate design whispering tales of a bygone era.

Elisa's lips curved into a quiet smile, a rare moment of peace washing over her as she drank in the view.

Duncan's voice broke the silence. 'Beautiful, isn't she?'

She nodded softly, the joy in her eyes betraying the heaviness she usually carried. 'Absolutely ... it's beyond words.'

Duncan glanced towards the city gates. 'Well, you'll get a proper look soon enough. Just a heads-up – the guards'll want to see ID. You got yours?'

Elisa's trance was broken, and she quickly retrieved her passport from her pocket. 'Yes, of course. I have it right here.'

'Perfect,' Duncan said with a faint smile, gesturing towards the gates. 'Shall we?'

They joined the slow-moving queue of travellers approaching the checkpoint. The gates of Gothenburg loomed ahead, bustling with life. One by one, people handed over their IDs to uniformed guards.

As they stepped forward, one of the guards gave a nod. 'Let them through.'

Elisa's eyes wandered as they passed beneath the archway. A vast network of bridges spanned the river that split the city in two, while sleek trams glided along overhead tracks.

The streets bustled with cafés, corner shops, and vendor stalls, each one brimming with life.

Upon entering the city, Duncan pointed out the display of the Night Hawks' symbol – the powerful, gold hawk – displayed on numerous posters and billboards throughout Gothenburg. Lance Sainglend's face also appeared in these advertisements.

Duncan directed Elisa's attention towards the pedestrians passing through the checkpoint. 'Alright, Elisa. Just keep cool and they should grant us entry.'

Keep cool.

Simple enough, in theory. But her heartbeat refused to cooperate, thudding with each step they took. Her fingers itched at her sleeves, a subtle compulsion to fidget – one she resisted.

As they followed the stone path towards the checkpoint, her eyes swept the crowd, trained to detect subtle shifts in expression and posture – a habit born of long hours studying diplomacy and human behaviour as a girl.

A girl with a red scarf whispered something to her friend. A boy clutched a paper flag. A mother stared too long at the security guards. Everyone was watching everyone.

Then she saw *them*.

The figure moved differently. Deliberate. Quiet. Elisa's gaze locked onto the individual immediately – perhaps it was instinct, or paranoia, or both. The person was draped in a black raincoat that hugged their frame like water over glass. Their face was obscured beneath a low hood and mirrored goggles that gave off a faint metallic gleam. She couldn't see their eyes, and that unsettled her most.

Are they hiding something? Or protecting themselves?

Their green cargo trousers were mud-stained and torn near the knee. A soldier, perhaps? Or just someone who'd learned to walk like one?

The scuffed black shoes added to the rugged, utilitarian look. They moved with deliberate, measured steps.

She glanced at Duncan, who had also taken note. He didn't speak, but the subtle narrowing of his eyes said enough.

The hooded person approached a palm scanner stationed near the gate – a rectangular device with faintly glowing lines etched across its surface. Elisa had only read about them in reports: they detected magical signatures, able to distinguish between practitioners and nulls. The person in front of the hooded figure placed their hand on it.

A small green light blinked.

CLEAR.

Curiosity pulling at her, Elisa trailed behind Duncan as he decided to take a closer look at the hooded figure. As they weaved through the crowd, she kept a watchful eye on the mysterious person.

Abruptly, they heard a man bark. '*You.*'

Duncan and Elisa's attention turned towards the voice. The hooded figure froze in their tracks, meeting the gaze of the man who had singled them out.

'Yes, you, right there,' the guard continued. 'I see you with that 'ood. No 'oods are allowed within these premises, 'specially under martial law.'

They watched as the figure shifted, clearly intending to slip away.

'Oi! Where d'you think you're goin'?!' the guard barked, already moving.

'Oi, skulk! Attempting to flee from security results in immediate prosecution!' the guard bellowed, his grip tightening around the figure's arm.

The figure writhed and wriggled, desperate to break free. 'Leave me be!'

'Wait ... your skin,' the guard uttered.

Elisa caught sight of the figure's exposed wrist – not the colour of human flesh, but something else. Elf.

The guard yanked down the figure's hood, revealing sharply angular features and grey skin.

Gasps rippled through the crowd as murmurs spread like wildfire. Phones were lifted. Some people leaned in with morbid curiosity, others recoiled. A few simply stared, frozen.

A Dökkálfar. Elisa's breath hitched.

She'd only read about them in books, but there – in the flesh – stood one of the elusive dark elves. Her pulse quickened as she pushed her way through the gathering onlookers, ignoring the phone cameras and whispered slurs around her.

Closer now, she could see him clearly. The bone structure. The unusual hue of his skin.

Her heart fluttered. It was like watching a legend step out of myth.

The Dökkálfar, a race of dark elves, were known for their angular features, grey skin, and striking golden eyes. Like the Ljósálfar, they had pointed ears that marked their otherworldly lineage. Taller than humans, with long, slender fingers and prominent noses, their appearance was unmistakable. They lived far longer than humans, with time flowing differently for them, and even their reproduction occurred at a slower pace – generations unfolding across centuries.

The Dökkálfar stepped forward, his golden eyes narrowed with frustration. 'Why am I being stopped? I've got AMOB clearance!'

He yanked a folded ID from his coat pocket and thrust it forward. 'Look – right there. I'm authorised to be here. So what's your excuse?'

The first guard – a bald, overweight man with a red face and a belly that strained against his uniform – leaned in close, his breath foul. 'Don't need one,' he spat. 'We don't want your kind 'ere, long-ears. You lot ain't welcome.'

The elf's voice rose. 'This is ridiculous. I have rights—'

The bald guard cut him off with a scoff. 'What rights? You think we've forgot what your lot did to us? Back when you an' the Ljósálfar thought you were better'n everyone else – lordin' it over us like gods. Long lives, fancy magic, smug bloody faces. You lot trampled on us for centuries.'

A second guard stepped forward – bony and angular, his uniform hanging off him like it didn't quite fit. He sneered, voice sharp and nasal. 'Think about it. Your lot used to run this place. Now look at you. Fadin' out like a bad smell. Dying off, just like all the old rubbish. How many of you even left now, eh?'

Elisa stood just a few paces away, her chest tightening as the words sank in. She didn't need to hear more to understand what this was. The tension. The hate. The centuries-old poison that had never truly been flushed from the veins of Flora. The elf's face had gone rigid – not with fear, but anger. It flickered across his features like firelight.

'That's enough!' he snapped, his voice ringing out. 'Don't give me that racist rubbish. I'm half-human! My blood's the same as yours!'

The bald guard shook his head slowly, his eyes narrowing. 'Don't matter. To us, you're still not one of us. Half this, part that – you're still Other. An' if things were flipped – if you were standin' here at this gate, and we were on the other side – you'd be sayin' the same shite to us. You'd look down on us just the same. So don't come cryin' now. We're just playin' your old game.'

The bony guard gave a low chuckle, jerkin' his thumb behind him.

'Now piss off. Back to the woods. Or wherever your lot sulks these days.'

The Dökkálfar stepped forward again, his tone defiant. 'I'm not going anywhere. You don't scare me.'

The bony guard tilted his head, grinning. 'What, "piss off" not in your vocab? Or did yer mum drop you halfway through growin' a brain?'

The bald guard's expression shifted – his tone suddenly softer, mockingly so.

'Last warnin', mate. Leave now ... or we'll make you join your ancestors.'

The Dökkálfar took a step forward, defiant, wagging a finger at the guard.

'I'm not going–'

The words were barely out of his mouth when the bald guard drove a fist straight into the elf's gut. The impact knocked the wind out of him, folding him in half as he crumpled to the ground, wheezing in pain.

'You fuckin' cunt!' barked the bald guard.

Elisa covered her mouth, eyes wide with horror as the assault escalated. The two guards laid into the Dökkálfar without restraint – kicking, stomping, fists raining down like hammers. He curled into himself, arms up, but it was no use. Blow after blow crashed into his ribs, his side, his skull.

'You like that, eh, pointy-ears!?' the bald one jeered, laughter twisted with cruelty.

Elisa's heart thudded in her chest. This wasn't just prejudice. This was a beating designed to humiliate – to remind the elf of his place.

Beside her, Duncan leaned in close, his voice low and tight with restrained fury.

'This is exactly what I was afraid of.'

Then, louder – measured, but firm – he said, 'Go on into the city. I'll handle this.'

He stepped forward without hesitation.

Elisa stared after him, her breath catching as she watched him walk headlong into the fray. There was something about the way he moved – purposeful, fearless – that struck her hard.

'Oh wow,' she whispered, barely audible, awe laced into every syllable.

'That's enough.' Duncan said.

'Keep out of this, blondie! It's not your concern,' the guard spat.

'On the contrary,' Duncan retorted with a witty smile, 'it *is* my concern, mate. Look at the folks around you. The townspeople are growing weary with the violence you're displaying. Scaring them off might leave a lasting negative impression on Gothenburg, don't you think?'

Duncan's gaze shifted towards the crowd, and he noticed a mix of emotions on their faces. Some were filming the incident on their phones, while others wore genuine expressions of concern. The guard seemed to take notice of their reaction, and his tense fists slowly relaxed.

With a deep, sadistic whisper, the guard leant towards the elf, his words dripping with malice. 'Consider yourself lucky for help arriving, you wretched fiend. But mark my words, I want your kind eradicated … burnt like withered branches from a tree while I relish the smell of ashes from your charred corpses.'

The Dökkálfar's eyes snapped wide with shock and fear as the guard spat on his shirt, a blatant act of contempt. Then, with a condescending look, the guard walked away, his nose held high.

Duncan glared at the man. As much as he want ed to kick his ass, he knew that it would lead to too many consequences.

The elf whimpered, face buried in his hands. Duncan crouched beside him and gently helped him up. The bastard guards were gone, but the crowd wasn't.

People had started to gather. Faces gawking. Phones out. Flashing screens – like flies to blood. The buzzing sound of photos being taken filled Duncan's ears, prickling his skin.

'Bloody hell ...' he muttered under his breath. 'As if the attention wasn't enough already.'

He shot a glare at a woman filming two feet away. She didn't flinch.

Without asking, Duncan grabbed the elf's arm – not roughly, but firmly. 'Come on, let's get outta here.'

The Dökkálfar's eyes were red and puffy, tear-streaked, but Duncan didn't pause to offer comfort. Not now. There wasn't time.

'You can cry later,' he said, voice low. 'Right now we move.'

'W–Wait–' the elf croaked, dazed.

Duncan didn't stop walking. 'You wanna sit here while they keep circlin' round like vultures? Or worse – wait for the guards to come back?'

No answer. None needed. 'Now let's book it.'

Duncan tugged the elf's arm and picked up the pace.

They ran.

Duncan spotted the edge of a wooded area just beyond the throng of onlookers – enough cover to disappear without a trace. Gripping the elf's arm firmly, he pulled him forward, pushing past the curious crowd buzzing with their phones raised. The noise faded behind them as they broke through the last fringe of trees.

They didn't stop until the trees swallowed them whole.

Hidden under the shadow of the leaves, Duncan finally let go of the elf's arm. His own chest rose and fell like a piston. He crouched beside a log and peered through the foliage – nothing. Not a soul in sight.

He exhaled. 'Okay. We lost 'em.'

Behind him, the Dökkálfar sank to the ground, still trembling. He looked at Duncan – not with suspicion now, but with something softer. Grateful, maybe. Scared, definitely.

'Why ... did you help me?' he asked, voice hoarse.

Duncan turned, brows slightly raised. 'What?'

'You know what I am. It doesn't make sense. A human wouldn't stick his neck out for someone like me.'

Duncan gave a small shrug, wiping sweat from his brow. 'Maybe I'm just built different.'

The elf didn't buy it. He shook his head. 'No. No one does anything without a reason. You're either paid, forced, or guilty. So what is it? Obligation? Or you work for them?'

Duncan's gaze sharpened. 'Who's "them"?'

Before the elf could answer, a voice echoed faintly through the trees:

'Mr Saul?'

Duncan froze. His hand instinctively went up, motioning the elf to stay quiet.

'Shh. Hold up.'

He tilted his head, listening closer. The voice called again – fragile, lost.

'Mr Saul!'

Duncan sighed. He recognised it immediately. 'Elisa?' he muttered. 'What the hell is she doing out here?'

He stepped through the underbrush and raised his voice. 'Elisa? What're you doin' here? You were supposed to go inside!'

'I know,' Elisa called back, stepping carefully through the brush, her heels sinking slightly into the soil. 'But I did not wish to enter the city unaccompanied.'

Duncan groaned and rubbed his face with both hands. 'Ugh … I could've handled this first – then caught up with you after. Now I've got even more on my plate.'

Elisa stopped a few paces from him, brushing a loose strand of hair behind her ear with a sigh. 'I suppose you're right …'

Her eyes drifted past him – and then narrowed. Seated beside Duncan, half-hidden in the undergrowth, was the very same elf from the checkpoint. Dishevelled, shaken, but unmistakably non-human.

Her posture stiffened slightly. 'That is a Dökkálfar, is it not?'

Duncan nodded, glancing towards the elf. 'Yeah.'

'I see ...' she said softly.

Duncan turned his head, catching the look in her eyes – polite restraint, but edged with fascination. She wasn't frightened, not exactly. Just curious. And perhaps unsure how close she should stand.

'Never seen one before?' he asked, brow raised.

Elisa shook her head. 'I've only read about them – the Álfheimr Empire and their civil war.'

The Álfheimr Empire ... That name always sounded too elegant for what it truly was. A shattered monarchy hiding behind ancient rites. Once, it spanned from the western isles of Eirøy, to the edges of Skardøy. Elven superiority had been law – until it collapsed into blood and ruin. Civil war had burnt through their forests like wildfire, brother turning against brother. Light Elves, the Ljósálfar, claimed divine right. The Dökkálfar demanded liberation. Neither side won. Only death did.

Duncan remembered reading that elven wars weren't like human ones. They didn't just burn towns or kill soldiers – they *scarred* the land. Magic that seeped into the soil and poisoned it for generations. Madness spread in the wake of their battles. Trees that whispered. Rivers that forgot to flow.

'Yeah. I've seen a few elves before. But this one ...' His gaze sharpened. 'There's something different about him.'

This Dökkálfar – Dark Elf, in common tongue – was unlike the others Duncan had encountered. Most elves he'd seen, both Light and Dark, shared the same unnerving traits: angular beauty that felt almost sculpted, and golden irises that glowed faintly in low light. But this one had *brown eyes*. Plain. Human. And his face lacked the otherworldly sharpness Duncan associated with elvenkind.

A half-breed? Or something else?

He studied the creature's posture – measured, alert, but not overtly hostile. The way the elf sniffed the air, cautious, almost feral. He was strange ... Though, not everything strange was dangerous – but most dangerous things were strange.

So what was *this one* doing here, alone, in Gothenburg?

'What's your name, Dökkálfar?' Duncan asked finally, his voice steady but firm.

The elf flinched slightly at the title, and Duncan caught the subtle tension in his shoulders – the way his nose twitched, sniffing the air like a hunted animal. Not fear. Wariness.

Duncan narrowed his eyes. *Yeah. He's seen things. Maybe worse than I have.*

And that unsettled him more than he cared to admit.

After a moment of hesitation, the Dökkálfar decided to share his name. 'It's – it's Ryonil ...'

Elisa saw the blood covering his face. 'You poor thing – let me clean those wounds.' She took a handkerchief from her pocket and stepped towards him. Ryonil instinctively moved back, meeting her with a wary stare. Elisa widened her eyes in surprise.

Observing the scene, Duncan couldn't escape the surge of anger welling up within him. He pondered the extent of the elf's suffering and abuse. As the elf drew back, Duncan's fists clenched tightly.

'I understand if you don't trust us – but we mean you no harm,' Elisa said.

Duncan watched as Ryonil slowly stopped flinching, letting Elisa dab gently at the blood on his face. The cloth turned red, but beneath it were just cuts and bruises. Superficial. Still ugly – but not life-threatening.

Didn't make it any easier to look at.

Something twisted in Duncan's gut – not just pity, but anger. He hated seeing anyone broken like that, especially over something they couldn't control. He frowned, folding his arms.

'Alright,' he muttered. 'What the hell happened back there?'

Ryonil exhaled shakily, his voice raw. 'I was just trying to go home. That's it. My face was covered – I know. But how could I not?' His hands clenched into fists on his knees. 'They didn't even ask questions. Just ... went straight for me. Like I was a threat. Like I deserved it.'

He looked up, eyes wet with fury. 'Is that all I am to them? A reminder of some war centuries ago? Something they get to punish because I was born the wrong kind of person?' His voice cracked. 'I didn't do anything. I didn't *do* anything.'

Duncan stayed quiet, letting the words sit heavy in the air. He didn't know what to say. No clever remark. No silver bullet to fix it. Just the sound of the wind stirring the trees around them.

'My father would've stood up for me,' Ryonil added quietly. 'And my mother ... well, she's not around anymore either. Feels like I've got no one left.'

Duncan looked away. The weight of it hit harder than he expected. It wasn't just the injustice. It was the *loneliness* of it.

He cleared his throat. 'This city ... people here don't change easy. You know that, yeah?' He paused, brow furrowing. 'So why stick around? Why not go somewhere you're not treated like dirt?'

'My father lived here before I was born. I guess I just wanted to hold onto that,' Ryonil said. 'And he was human, so technically, I'm part of your species.'

'But your mother was a Dökkálfar?' Elisa asked.

Ryonil placed his hands on his knees and stood up slowly. 'Yes, I'm a half-breed,' he said, voice steady, though his shoulders were tense.

Duncan blinked. 'A half-breed?' That explained the eyes – dull instead of gold. He'd never met one before. He stared, not out of malice, but curiosity laced with something else – something sharper.

'No wonder your eyes aren't golden,' Duncan muttered, half to himself. 'Didn't think I'd ever meet one.'

Ryonil sat back down, head in his hands, and Duncan recognised that look too well – worn-down shame. That raw, quiet frustration of being made into something you never asked to be.

Duncan folded his arms and leaned against a nearby log, his jaw tightening. 'It's ridiculous this still goes on. Even though I'm human, I hate the way they treat your kind.'

What he didn't say was that he'd seen it before – hatred masquerading as order. It had taken his father's life and left Duncan with scars no one could see.

Ryonil didn't respond. Just sat there, staring at the dirt like it might give him answers.

Duncan eyed the hood draped around Ryonil's neck. 'I'm guessing this isn't the first time it's happened, right? That you've had to hide.'

Ryonil looked up at him for a moment, then lowered his gaze again. 'My parents are gone ... My mother was exiled when I was a child. And my father ... he was murdered.'

The word *murdered* landed like a stone in Duncan's gut.

'They killed your father!?' His voice came sharper than intended.

Ryonil nodded, slowly.

A familiar heat rose in Duncan's chest – anger and something deeper, older. That same fire that had never gone out. He clenched his fists, forcing the memory down: the smell of blood, the sound of tears, the moment everything went dark. He'd been thirteen, too weak to stop it. But not anymore.

'Losing a parent's rough ...' he muttered, eyes shifting away.

He didn't say *I know*. He didn't need to.

But deep inside, the old vow stirred. *One day*, he'd find the heretic who did it. *One day*, he'd make them pay.

One day. One day ... I'll find you. And when I do ... you'll remember my name. The name of the boy whose father you took.

'It was my father who kept me in this city. Even after all the abuse they threw at me ...' Ryonil's voice tightened, his teeth clenched and fists balled. 'They pelted me with stones, spat insults, beat me down – yet he never abandoned me. They killed him because they believed he'd betrayed their kind.'

Elisa covered her mouth in shock. 'How awful ...'

'Since his death, staying here became a battle I fought alone. No one stood by me – not a soul. I've been utterly alone ever since ...'

Elisa looked aside sorrowfully and repeated his word. 'Alone ...'

Duncan's gaze fixed on Elisa as she spoke.

Is she truly alone in this world? What happened to her family?

She hadn't given him a clear answer when they first met. He noticed how attentively she listened to Ryonil's painful story. The dejected elf must have stirred something in her – as if she were looking into a mirror, reflecting her own past struggles.

Then she smiled softly and placed a hand over her chest. 'Maybe I could help you,' she said.

Ryonil frowned. 'How can you do that?'

'I can distract them. While they're focused on me, you can climb over the wall unnoticed.'

'With all due respect, Elisa, that plan's got a few issues. The wall's too high for him to climb, and it's broad daylight. People will likely notice you guys entering illegally. And if they catch us, you know what's gonna happen.'

'So, what are you suggesting?' Elisa asked.

Duncan rubbed his chin, lost in thought. 'Hmm ... I have an idea. Wait here.'

'Where are you going, Mr Saul?' Elisa said, calling after him.

Duncan waved his hand without looking back at them. He needed a plan to sort this out, so he walked off towards the city. 'I'll be back in about half an hour, don't worry.'

After some time had passed, Duncan returned, a carrier bag slung over his shoulder. 'Hey, I'm back.'

Both Ryonil and Elisa stood up from the ground, eager to see what he had acquired.

'Where did you go?' Ryonil asked.

'I went to a shop that sells the tools we need for this situation.' Duncan reached into the bag and pulled out a grappling hook and a tranquilliser pistol. 'I got us a couple of friends.'

Duncan continued. 'Tranquillisers are used mostly for animals, but that doesn't mean they're ineffective against people. So, I'm thinking ... when the guards are rendered unconscious, what I need you to do is sneak past them and use the grappling hook to climb over the wall. It's as simple as that. Elisa, you don't have to do this. It could just be Ryonil and me. You could enter the gate by yourself,' Duncan suggested.

Elisa shook her head. 'No, I want to help. I do not want to be a burden to you two.'

Duncan tilted his head. 'Are you sure that you want to carry out this task? You're putting yourself in danger, too.'

Elisa closed her eyes, taking a deep breath. When she opened them, she showed her resolve. 'I can do it. If the worst-case scenario is that the municipal police arrest us, I can explain to them that I wanted to deliver an important letter to Lance.'

'Yeah, that may be true, but it may not be enough to justify our actions. The police may just take the letter and lock us up regardless.'

Elisa paused momentarily. 'I ... You do not know how much help I can be. Don't you think that if we work as a team, we would increase the likelihood of success? Two heads are better than one, Mr Saul. The more people we have taking part in this plan, the more effective the outcome will be.'

As Duncan watched Elisa, he couldn't shake the question – why was she so desperate to prove herself? She had a vital letter to deliver, yet here she was, risking arrest for someone she barely knew. It didn't add up. He took risks because he had the skills to back them up. Elisa didn't. She was either brave ... or just foolish.

Duncan sighed, clearly showing his apprehension. 'That depends if that person doesn't mess everything up

…' But eventually, he relented. 'Fine, you can help if you want to – I won't stop you.'

'Thank you,' said Elisa.

Ryonil chimed in. 'Forgive me for being a downer, but are you sure this will work? I mean, I've seen how humans have evolved their technology. As you know, I have been in this city for a very long time – more than your lifetimes. The technology that you humans build is … no offence, bothersome.'

'You underestimate me – I know how to sneak by. I do stuff like this all the time,' Duncan said with a confident smile.

'Good, we're all set …' Ryonil nodded, his happiness evident. 'Þakka þér, Mr Saul.'

'Just call me Duncan – Mr Saul feels too formal.'

'Once again, Þakka þér, Duncan, for what you are doing for me.'

'I assume that's "thank you". If it was – don't mention it. I believe it's unfair for them to treat you in that manner for something you weren't responsible for.'

'I don't know what I can say about this. Initially, I had every right to distrust you two – but your actions and words have proved otherwise,' Ryonil admitted.

'That's good to hear,' Duncan said. 'Elisa and Ryonil, we're gonna do this when it's dark, so set up a tent if you need to. Also, make sure you avoid the streetlights when you enter the gates.'

'Okay,' Elisa replied.

'Understood,' Ryonil said, nodding.

Chapter IV

A HELPING HAND

As the hours slipped by and night wrapped the city in stillness, the streets emptied. Even the police patrols had thinned, reduced to the occasional flash of headlights in the distance.

Duncan sat just beyond the tent's shadow, phone pressed to his ear, voice low so as not to wake the others.

'Mm-hmm ... I need you to do this for me, Jénmar. Is that okay?'

He scanned the treeline, eyes sharp. After Gothenburg, he couldn't risk another mistake. The AMOB would've registered Ryonil's incident with the security guards. And once they flagged something, they'd start sniffing around. Maybe they'd harass them with 'routine inspections', or worse – try to trace the signature back to them. The AMOB didn't forget. And they never let things slide.

Their silence wasn't peace – it was patience.

'I just need you to wipe the traces. Our presence at the checkpoint, any pulse anomalies. Kill the flags and bounce the signal. You know the drill.'

There was a pause on the line, then a muffled, weary groan from the other end.

'Please, Jénmar,' Duncan added, softening his tone. 'Just this once.'

Another pause. Then, finally, a reluctant, *'Yeah. Alright. But you owe me.'*

'Okay. Thank you. Bye.'

He ended the call and slipped the phone into his pocket. His gaze drifted towards the camp, where movement stirred gently.

Elisa rubbed her eyes and sat up, blinking through sleep. Ryonil was already half-awake, his expression unreadable beneath the dim light.

Duncan cleared his throat. 'Alright – we need to move. The longer we wait, the more likely someone gets curious.'

Elisa nodded quietly. Ryonil gave a small dip of the head as he adjusted his hood and slid his goggles into place.

Duncan rose, checking the weight of his tranquilliser pistol, then clipped his grappling hook to his belt. He glanced at Ryonil. 'You good?'

Ryonil nodded again, wordless.

Then Duncan turned to Elisa. 'You ready?'

'Yes, I am.'

Duncan gave a tight nod.

Good. No hesitation.

He allowed himself a quick smile – confident, if only on the surface. 'Alright. Let's commence.'

At the city gates, two Gothenburg security guards were engaged in a conversation.

'This checkpoint duty is fucking terrible. Isn't there somethin' more enjoyable to do than standin' by the city gates all day? I'd prefer being in a bar with a bottle of whiskey than dealin' with this shit,' the bald guard began.

'Quit your fucking complaining,' the bony guard retorted. 'It's our duty. You should be thankful we're here, instead of out there fighting in that brutal war. Imagine it – all you'd find is the stench of corpses and blood.'

'Aye, you've got a point,' the first guard conceded.

'Well, to kill the time, let me tell you a tale. The Jötunn, Alvaldi.'

The bald guard's face tightened at the mention. 'Alvaldi? I've heard a bit about him. Isn't he the shadowy bastard that gives folks the creeps? Sounds like a tale meant to scare the wits out of people.'

'Yes,' said the bony guard.

'Okay. Sounds right interestin'. Could ya tell me more?'

'Believe it or not, the Jötnar are dangerous. We had to join forces with the elves to take them on. These giants can see into the future, shape-shift and be anywhere, even hiding as one of us or as a rat at our feet. They could strike anytime. *Loki's trick*, they call it.'

The bald guard seemed intrigued. 'Oh ...?'

'I must caution you, old chap. Keep your wits about ya, especially with Alvaldi.'

The bald guard stuck his finger into his right ear to clear the itching earwax, seemingly unaffected. 'Eh.'

'What do ya mean, "eh"?' the bony guard said in disbelief.

'Alvaldi don't sound that intimidating ... I'd just stick the barrel of my gun in 'is mouth so 'e could shit bullets – into the mouth and out from the arse, now that'd be a sight, wouldn't it?'

The bony guard responded with a raised eyebrow, folding his arms. 'Wow ... Such a confident mouth, considering what I just described. If you ever actually met—'

Interrupting his comrade, the bald guard lifted his chin and scoffed. 'If I ever encountered Alvaldi, I'd slice the guy's 'ead off and hang it on me door, sendin' a clear message not to fuck with me.'

'Oh, please! The only thing you're good at is sittin' on yer lazy arse an' whittlin' away at that lil' knife o' yours.'

The bald guard's glare intensified as he shot back, saying, 'Fuck you! Speak to me like that again and I'll make sure your finger becomes a snack for my mutt.'

As they exchanged words, a sudden disturbance captured the attention of the gatekeepers. A bottle was thrown, shattering as it hit the ground. The security guards' focus was immediately drawn to the sound, causing them to pause in their conversation.

'What the fuck?' exclaimed the bald guard as he stood up.

'Who's causing this ruckus?'

'I 'ave no idea, but it's likely just some drunk or kids messin' around.' The bald guard grumbled, showing more irritation than concern.

Then the sound of another bottle shattering reached the security guards' ears once more.

'What the bloody hell!?' the first guard barked, springing to his feet. His fists clenched as he stormed off towards the sound. 'I swear, I'm gonna break that fuckin' idiot's jaw!'

He spotted the broken glass glinting on the ground and snarled, 'Oi! Who the fuck d'you think you are, pissin' about like this? You think you're some kind of comedian, do ya!?'

As he approached the bushes, he heard rustling and quickly turned his head in that direction, yelling, 'Oi, come out of there!'

The guard stomped angrily towards the rustling and leant in, fuming. 'You crazy bastard, just wait till I get my hands on you–'

The moment the guard turned his back, Duncan moved. He raised the tranquilliser pistol, breathing slow and steady, then squeezed the trigger. The dart hit its mark – right in the neck. The man slapped the spot instinctively, eyes narrowing with confusion before his knees buckled. He staggered, wobbling like a drunk, then crumpled to the ground.

Duncan didn't flinch.

A dull thud caught the second guard's attention. He spun around fast, instincts sharp. 'What the fuck?!' he shouted, rushing to his fallen mate. Dropping to a knee, he shook him. 'Oi! What the fuck happened!?' Panic bled into his voice.

Duncan could see it in the man's eyes – he was about to call for backup.

Not happening.

The guard reached for his walkie-talkie, fingers trembling as he pressed the button. 'Shit, I better call the–'

Duncan tapped him on the shoulder.

The man turned. 'Huh?'

Before the guard could even register what was happening, Duncan's fist cracked across his jaw. Bone met flesh – clean and brutal. The man dropped like a stone.

Duncan stared down at him, jaw tight, breath steady. 'Arsehole ...,' he muttered under his breath.

No time to waste.

He turned to the others, slipping back into command. 'Alright, you two – move in.'

While they followed his lead, Duncan crouched, pulled the grappling hook from his gear, and gave the rope a quick flick. It coiled with ease – still strong. *Good.* He took aim, then launched it. The metal hook soared up and caught the gate's bars with a solid *clink*.

He tugged once. Firm and secure.

'Right. I'll drag these two outta sight – last thing we need is a patrol spotting them.'

'Understood,' Elisa said softly with a nod.

Elisa started to climb, but Duncan held up a hand. 'Wait, Elisa.' He pressed the tranquilliser pistol into her grip. 'You'll want this – just in case.'

She took it without hesitation.

'You comfortable with it?' he asked.

She nodded, steady.

'Good. Now, go.'

As Elisa ascended, Duncan moved quickly to hide the fallen guards. Years of covert ops had taught him how to erase traces – and that's exactly what he did, dragging the bodies into the shadows where no one would find them.

Meanwhile, atop the gate, Elisa came face to face with a municipal patrol officer, easily identified by his blue jacket, white shirt, and peaked cap – a sharp contrast to the state police's darker uniforms and side caps.

Her heart skipped a beat. The officer's torch beam sliced through the shadows as he walked closer, humming softly. Elisa held her breath – then her foot nudged the gate.

The clang echoed. The officer stopped, frowning, and turned the beam towards the noise.

Oh no. The officer must've heard that.

Elisa needed to get out of there before she got caught.

The police officer's torch illuminated the gate, revealing Elisa's position. The sudden burst of light startled her, causing her to shield her eyes instinctively, momentarily blinded by the brightness. She blinked rapidly, trying to readjust her vision and overcome the initial shock.

'Oi! What do ya think you're doin' up there?' the policeman immediately asked.

Elisa panicked, her heart racing. She gasped and gripped the tranquilliser gun, her hand trembling. Out of necessity, she aimed and fired. The dart struck the officer's chest, piercing his clothing and injecting the sedative. He froze, confused and disbelieving, before collapsing as the torch slipped from his hand and the beam faded.

With a heavy sigh of relief, Elisa allowed her tense muscles to relax, the adrenaline gradually subsiding. She reassured herself. 'Oh my gosh, that was so close.'

'Hey Elisa, is everything alright?' Ryonil asked.

Elisa nodded. 'Yes, do not worry,' she assured him, her voice lowered to a whisper, mindful of their surroundings. Determined to carry out their plan, she leapt from the gate, landing on the ground below. Her gaze darted in every direction, scanning the area for any signs of additional patrols or unwanted attention. 'Ryonil, I'm inside,' Elisa whispered.

'Okay, good. It's my turn,' Ryonil affirmed, preparing himself to follow in Elisa's footsteps. He began his ascent up the rope, making his way over the gate.

Elisa remained alert, scanning her surroundings for any lurking threats.

Finally, Ryonil managed to climb the gate and, with a leap, descended to the ground below. However, a slight misstep resulted in Ryonil wincing in pain. 'Ow,' he muttered, clutching his leg.

'Are you okay?'

Ryonil lifted his hand, assuring her that the injury was minor. 'Where is Duncan?' he asked.

Turning her attention back to the task at hand, Elisa glanced back towards the gate where Duncan's arrival was still awaited. 'He should be coming anytime now.'

Duncan efficiently repositioned the security officers, relieving the strain in his back with a quick stretch. He then joined Elisa and Ryonil. 'Okay, the security guards are hidden,' Duncan announced.

'Good, because we need you right now. Unexpected events have occurred,' Elisa explained.

A wave of concern washed over Duncan as he shook his head, hoping against hope that the gravity of the situation wouldn't be as dire as he anticipated. 'Oh no, what happened?'

'There was a municipal police officer. He ... kind of saw me.' She rubbed the back of her hair, a gesture of nervousness.

'Ugh ... Elisa.' Duncan growled, his frustration noticeable.

Elisa raised her hands in a swift, reassuring motion. 'D-don't worry. I quickly incapacitated him before he could see my face.'

A sigh of relief escaped Duncan's lips, his composure gradually returning. 'Okay ... That means we gotta move him away before anyone finds him.' Duncan swiftly descended the rope with agility, joining the two as they observed the unconscious police officer lying nearby.

'Okay, Elisa, you take Ryonil to his house. I'm gonna handle this situation.'

Elisa nodded. 'Okay,' she said before turning to Ryonil. 'Ryonil, let's go.'

Ryonil, ever obedient, nodded in agreement. 'Okay, right behind you.'

As Elisa escorted Ryonil to his house, Duncan took charge of the situation. He positioned the unconscious police officer against a nearby wall, arranging the body to create the illusion of a sleeping guard. Once satisfied with his work, Duncan retrieved the officer's cap and settled it back atop the unconscious man's head.

Good enough.

Leaving the guard slumped in place, Duncan turned away and moved on. It wasn't perfect, but it would buy them some time – just enough to get clear before anyone started asking questions.

Now all he had to do was find Elisa and Ryonil. His eyes swept the area, scanning for any sign of them.

'Over here,' Elisa whispered, grabbing Duncan's attention. He swiftly turned his head and spotted the two taking cover behind a parked car. Ryonil's hand waved in greeting, signalling their position.

Closing the distance, Duncan joined them, and without delay, he shared the result of his efforts. 'Okay, I hid the police officer.' Then he shot a glare at Elisa, his disappointment evident. He recognised the importance of precision in these critical moments.

Elisa couldn't help but flinch, her gaze averting in embarrassment.

'Elisa, when people's lives are on the line, there's no room for messing up. You do understand that, right?' Duncan said sternly.

Elisa's voice trembled as she apologised. 'Y–yes, forgive my inadequacy.'

'Whatever. Just remember that some mistakes can have severe consequences. Don't forget that.'

The words sounded harsher than he meant, but he didn't take them back. This wasn't about scolding her – it was about keeping them all alive. He needed her focused, not careless.

'I'm sorry to interrupt, but we need to keep moving,' said Ryonil, interjecting.

'Oh, right ...' Duncan inwardly chided himself for the lapse, almost smacking himself.

As the trio crept towards Ryonil's house, a police officer in the distance caught sight of them. His brow furrowed, but he looked away, returning to his duties – either unwilling to interfere or afraid to abandon his post. Still, he glanced back once more, briefly, before moving on.

The trio slipped ahead, undeterred. Soon, they reached Ryonil's modest, unremarkable home – a structure that blended easily into the neighbourhood.

Duncan looked around to see if anyone had seen them, but nothing caught his eye. 'Do you think anyone else saw us?'

Ryonil shook his head. 'I don't think so.'

'Okay, good,' Duncan said with a firm nod.

'Well, this is my home. I thank you two for escorting me here. I wouldn't have done it without you,' Ryonil said.

Duncan folded his arms, his voice losing all softness. 'Hate to break it to you, mate, but you need to leave Gothenburg.'

'What? I can't do that – I've lived in this house ever since I was born. My father fought hard for me to stay in this city – running now would be spitting on everything he stood for.'

'And if you stay, you'll keep getting treated like dirt. You saw what happened at the gate earlier – the guards, the stares. It won't stop. It'll only get worse. My advice? Find somewhere quieter. A village, maybe. Somewhere you can live in peace.'

'I–I don't know …'

'Look, the rumours appear to be spreading about you. You can't hide in this city forever. You may appear on the web. Once the secret's out that you're a Dökkálfar living among them, you'll become a target. And since people have taken pictures of you, it's going to attract the AMOB.'

'The AMOB?' Ryonil queried, his brow furrowing.

Elisa let out a sharp gasp. Duncan caught the shift in her expression from the corner of his eye – the way her face tightened at the mention of the AMOB. That wasn't just surprise. She knew something. More than she'd let on.

He didn't say anything, just filed it away. There was a connection here, something she hadn't shared. She was biting her lip, clearly lost in thought, and hadn't noticed him watching.

'Yeah,' Duncan nodded. 'I'm surprised they didn't come to the city and try to discover your whereabouts. Furthermore, I'm surprised that you remained hidden for so long, given our technology – unless I'm missing something.'

Ryonil paused for a moment, then spoke cautiously. 'The AMOB … yes, my father told me about them.'

'And what did he say?' Duncan asked.

'He mentioned something about a promise they had made to him,' Ryonil recounted. 'They said that no harm would come to me as long as he agreed to provide a sample of my blood.'

Duncan's eyes narrowed as he pieced together the puzzle. 'I see ... They likely sought to exploit your unique heritage, using your blood as an experiment. That could explain why you've been able to stay offline for so long – those guys must've hacked the internet.'

He didn't say more right away. Memories of Jénmar's reports and the classified files they'd once sifted through surfaced unbidden. Dossiers, lab scans, mutated genomes. The AMOB didn't make promises – they made trades. Temporary ones. They didn't want peace. They wanted assets.

Duncan continued. 'Regardless of their motives, I still believe in the necessity of my suggestion.'

Ryonil shook his head. 'I ... I can't ...'

Standing with hands on her hips, Elisa interjected. 'Ryonil, I agree with Mr Saul. As a Dökkálfar, you are a precious and rare being. There are few of your kind left. I implore you to heed his advice.'

Ryonil's face contorted with anger. 'It's not fair! Why must I be forced into hiding like the rest of my kind? Do I have to endure this suffering just because of my birth?'

As Ryonil vented his frustration, Duncan and Elisa stood silently.

Duncan countered. 'Think about it, Ryonil. Look at the reality of your current situation. You're already living in hiding, sneaking into the city with your hood up to avoid abuse. If the local police or the Night Hawks discover our involvement, they won't just come after us, they'll also come after you.'

Duncan's words caused Ryonil to pause. It seemed like he wanted to respond, but didn't. After a moment of thinking, he finally relented. 'Fine … I'll give it some thought.'

'Good,' Duncan replied. 'Maybe, we'll see each other again in the future.'

Elisa chimed in with a chuckle. 'And next time, try to avoid entanglements like the one we just experienced. We might not always have the means to free you from another challenging situation.'

'Thank you, Duncan. Thank you, Elisa. I appreciate your help. I hope to encounter more humans like you in the future.'

Duncan's warm smile grew wider. 'You're welcome, Ryonil.'

As the moment of parting arrived, Ryonil's gaze fell to the ground. 'Well, I suppose this is goodbye …'

'Yeah, I guess so,' Duncan replied.

'Goodbye, Ryonil,' said Elisa.

'Far Vel,' Ryonil said in his elven tongue. He extended his hand, shaking theirs one last time, and watched Duncan and Elisa leave his home.

Duncan then turned to Elisa and said, 'Thank you, Elisa, for being very brave during that time. Even though you messed up, things could've got a lot worse.' He paused and smiled. 'I believe you earned a bit of my respect.'

'Oh – thank you, Mr Saul.' Elisa blushed.

Duncan nodded and then looked up at the sky. He could see dark clouds and a half-moon. So much time had been taken by their plan. 'But more on that later, it's getting late,' he said.

Elisa grabbed her chin. 'Hmm ... We need a place to stay. A hotel would be nice,' she suggested.

'Good thinking. Sleeping out on the street is the worst. The stench, the rats, people's piss on the floor. Disgusting, if you ask me ...'

'I strongly agree, Mr Saul,' Elisa replied.

'Anyway, let's save our conversation for later. We'll talk when we're at the hotel, alright?'

'Okay.' Elisa nodded.

Chapter V

SAFE HAVEN, FALSE DAWN

Duncan and Elisa wandered the streets in search of a hotel. Eventually, they stumbled upon a place displaying a sign that read *Shangri La Ibis Hotel*. Duncan courteously held the door open for Elisa, who responded with a warm smile. Together, they entered the hotel lobby and began to survey their surroundings.

Inside, various people occupied the tables, engaged in casual conversations about everyday matters. Some were engrossed in card games, while others shared drinks with friends.

As Duncan and Elisa approached the hotel's concierge, their attention was momentarily drawn to a conversation at one of the nearby tables. Three men sat there, discussing an unusual topic. The first man initiated the exchange.

'Too bad we never saw any female Jötnar. I'd wager their elegant beauty would bring a tear to my eye.'

The second man replied with enthusiasm. 'True that. I'd pay you a hundred Livres that female Jötnar are just as attractive as the ladies in Flora.'

The third man, while inclined to agree, voiced a practical concern. 'Yeah, I hope you're right – but think about it. The difference is their size. Do you know how big those giants are? They're over, like, eight fucking feet. If we wanted to get intimate with them, we'd need a bloody ladder.'

The second man paused in thought, then said, 'I don't know, mate. That process sounds stressful as hell.'

The third man chimed in again. 'Oh, come on, David. Which one do you prefer – a giant one or a regular one?'

When Elisa heard the name 'David', she couldn't help but glance over at the man – only to realise it was the wrong David. It wasn't Archer's comrade. With a slight blush of embarrassment, she quickly averted her gaze.

'It depends,' David replied nonchalantly. 'If it's clean and not greasy, I'm down for it.'

Duncan scowled, unable to hide his disgust. 'Ugh. Conversations like that just make me wanna throw up in my mouth. They should do me a favour and shut the hell up.'

Elisa, however, maintained a more light-hearted perspective. She smiled and reassured him.

'Lighten up, Mr Saul. Disgusting as it may be, they're just having a harmless conversation.'

Duncan nodded, reluctantly agreeing. 'Yeah, yeah. Whatever you say ...'

With their minor detour behind them, Duncan and Elisa proceeded to the hotel's concierge where a friendly staff member greeted them with optimism. 'Ah! How may I help you two?'

Duncan stepped forward, saying, 'Yes, I would like to rent a room for two, please.'

The concierge immediately attended to his request. He began searching for the appropriate room key among the collection on display, finally locating it. 'Head towards Room 2A, the first door on the second floor. Please remember to remove your shoes before entering.'

'We understand,' Duncan acknowledged.

With a courteous smile, the concierge handed Duncan the room key. 'Make sure you enjoy your stay at the Shangri-La Ibis.'

Elisa froze for a moment, her heart racing. She felt the colour drain from her face, her mind immediately spinning with panic. *Wait ... we're sharing a room!?*

Her voice wavered slightly as she asked, 'Wait ... are we ... sharing the same room?' She glanced at Duncan, feeling her cheeks burn with embarrassment.

What does he think this is?

Duncan, oblivious to her rising anxiety, nodded casually. 'Yeah, seems like it.'

Seems like it!? How is this man so casual about this?

Elisa's mind went into overdrive. *No, no, no. This cannot be happening. What if he thinks I'm his ... no, no, he does not mean it that way, right? Right!?* She felt like she was going to explode.

She could already imagine the scenario. One room. One bed. An awkward, silent night where she'd have to sleep stiff as a board, gripping the duvet for dear life.

Or worse – what if Duncan was a sleep-clinger? What if he latched onto her in the middle of the night like some kind of oversized bear cub?

She forced herself to nod, even as her heart thudded in her chest. 'O-Okay ... thank you,' she stammered, her voice barely above a whisper.

The two made their way upstairs and reached their designated room. Duncan retrieved the room key and unlocked the door.

As Elisa stepped inside, her eyes immediately darted to the bed. *Please, please, please be separate beds,* she silently begged. Her heart was pounding in her chest as she nervously surveyed the room.

But then, relief flooded through her when she saw the two neatly arranged single beds, each with their own set of pillows and blankets. Her shoulders relaxed, the tension she hadn't even realised she was holding easing away.

The room was simple but comfortable. A cosy lamp stood on a small table beside the bed, and there was a white fabric chair tucked neatly into the corner. A small television sat on a shelf, and a cupboard was neatly positioned against the wall.

The blue-painted walls, adorned with delicate white patterns, added a charm to the space, giving the room a welcoming feel. The bathroom, clearly well-equipped, was stocked with all the necessary amenities for their convenience.

Elisa let out a quiet sigh of relief, feeling her nerves finally begin to settle. *Okay, this will not be so bad,* she thought, still trying to suppress the fluttering in her stomach.

At least she wouldn't have to worry about Duncan expecting anything awkward.

Duncan and Elisa entered the room, slipping off their shoes as they stepped inside. Duncan removed his jacket and hung it on a hook while Elisa carefully placed her coat beside it. She then took off her cap and settled onto her bed.

Duncan leant against the wall, crossed his arms and cast a thoughtful gaze at Elisa. 'Elisa, what're you planning to do once you've completed your task?' he inquired.

Elisa paused, her expression troubled as she looked down.

That was a good question.

She had no one to protect her or look after her. 'Frankly, I'm uncertain. I find myself without any alternative options ...'

Duncan furrowed his brow, concern etched on his face. 'Why's that? Don't you have a place to live?'

'No, I do not,' Elisa replied sadly, shaking her head. 'The place I once called home is long gone. I find myself without a place to reside. Archer was the only one who looked after me after my family's passing ... and now he's gone.'

'So, all this time, you've had no one by your side except for Archer,' Duncan mused. Elisa nodded slowly, and Duncan let out a sympathetic hum. He then took a seat on the bed beside her and spoke softly. 'That's rough. I'm so sorry to hear that ... I could never truly understand what it's like to lose everyone you love.'

Elisa offered him a reassuring smile and replied, 'Do not fret, Mr Saul. None of it is your fault.'

Deep in thought, Duncan scratched his head. Elisa watched him closely, curious about what was going on in his mind. She sensed he was wrestling with the idea of offering her a place to stay, knowing she was currently homeless. Elisa couldn't help but wonder what solution he might be considering. Then, suddenly, an idea seemed to spark in his mind.

'Don't worry, Elisa. I think I know the place where you could stay.'

Elisa furrowed her brow and inquired, 'Truly? And where might that be?'

'My mother's place. I haven't seen her for about a year, but she would be kind enough to take you in.'

Elisa paused and looked at Duncan with a glimmer of hope. 'Mr Saul, you would really do that for me?'

Duncan nodded his head with a small smile and replied, 'Of course, I ain't a heartless prick.'

Elisa gave a disbelieving shake of her head, caught somewhere between shock and relief. The moment felt almost dreamlike – too kind, too strange, too real.

'I ... I scarcely know what to say. Do you truly intend for me to stay at your mother's residence, Mr Saul? Please, do not feel compelled if it burdens you in any way.'

Duncan shrugged lightly. 'Don't worry about it. I've no issue helping someone out when they need it.'

His words struck something deep within her. That small reassurance, offered so plainly, unravelled the knot of fear and isolation she had carried since this dreadful ordeal began. The ache of solitude that had gnawed at her – quiet, constant – was suddenly met with warmth. A place to go. Someone who cared. She tried to steady herself, but the tears welled up regardless.

'Thank you ... Mr Saul. Truly. You're too kind.'

Duncan raised his hands awkwardly. 'Alright, alright – no need to cry over it ...'

She quickly dabbed at her cheeks, mortified. 'Forgive me. I do apologise, Mr Saul. It is all a bit much ...'

'It's alright. And you don't have to keep calling me "Mr Saul", you know.'

'Ah – of course ... I mean, Duncan,' she corrected herself, flustered.

He rose from the edge of the bed with a stretch. 'Alright, enough talk. We'll get some rest, then head to Lance's tomorrow.'

'Yes,' Elisa replied, a soft smile blooming on her lips – not one of politeness, but of true, quiet joy.

Elisa awoke to the hush of a cloudy morning, well-rested for the first time in days. The hotel bed had been surprisingly comfortable, and for once, her dreams had not turned to ghosts.

She and Duncan walked along the pavement, the wind tugging gently at her coat. Grey clouds pressed low over the skyline, casting the city in muted shades of steel and ash. Cars passed now and then, but the streets felt distant – like the world was holding its breath.

In the distance, beyond rows of shuttered shops and cracked signs, stone towers rose against the grey sky – the first markers of their destination.

The Valley of the Five Kings.

The name stirred something in her. A memory.

Archer had spoken of it once, in that bright, excitable way of his – describing how the valley had been named after five ancient rulers.

Elisa slowed, her gaze drifting to the horizon.

Five kings, she thought. *Five rulers.*

Their statues, Archer had said, were carved into the cliffs above the valley, gazing eastward as if still guarding the land they had once bled to unite.

His voice echoed in her mind, vivid and full of life:

'One for the Jötunn – the mountain king whose voice shook the sky.

One for the Ljósálfar – all beauty and order, so sure of their place.

One for the Dökkálfar – who ruled in shadows, cunning and cold.

And two for Man – a king and a traitor.'

She remembered how animated he'd been telling it, gesturing with his hands like a bard mid-performance.

'No one agrees which human was the traitor,' he'd added with a grin. *'That's what makes it fun.'*

Back then, it had seemed like a story.

Now, she was walking into the very place – the myth made stone – holding a letter that might tip the scales of a war.

'We are nearly there,' Elisa said, her voice quiet but steady. 'All we have to do is give the letter to Lance, and we are done.'

Duncan nodded, his brow slightly furrowed. 'Let's hope they let us in. Or at least accept the letter.'

'Indeed.'

They continued on, the wind stirring faintly, blowing bits of litter across the pavement. Elisa glanced at the broken windows lining the upper floors, her fingers tightening around the folded envelope inside her coat.

Something felt ... off.

The city had fallen too quiet. The usual hum – traffic, distant voices, even birds – had faded into a kind of hush that pressed in on her ears.

Duncan stopped, scanning the empty street. 'Elisa, is it just me, or are the streets too quiet?'

She paused too. 'You are correct. By now, we should have seen a patrol.'

'Where could they be?' Duncan murmured, his hand drifting towards his holster.

'I do not–' she began, but something metallic chimed sharply against stone.

A *clink.*

Her gaze dropped – a coin rolled lazily across the road, spinning once, then tipping over with a soft ring before settling beside the gutter.

Duncan stepped forward, eyes narrowed. 'What the–?'

He moved towards it, cautious but drawn.

Elisa stayed still, watching him.

Then – a flicker.

A motion – just there, to her right. At the edge of her vision. A dark figure, moving fast.

Before she could turn – *hands.* Rough. One clamped across her mouth, the other forcing a sharp-smelling cloth against her nose. The stench hit her first – chemical, cold. Her cry caught in her throat, muffled and useless.

Her eyes darted to Duncan – *still facing the coin.*

She thrashed. Kicked. But more hands grabbed her – arms seized, pinned back. The shock of it made her stumble. She tried to scream his name, but the cloth smothered everything.

The world spun, panic roaring through her chest. Her heels scraped the concrete as they dragged her backwards, fast, away from the road and into the alley behind them.

Duncan hadn't turned. Not yet.

Her vision blurred, the air running out. Her body slowed, her struggles weakening as they pulled her deeper into the darkness. The distance between them stretched further, and Elisa could only watch helplessly, unable to reach him.

Duncan ...

Her thoughts fractured. Darkness closed in, swallowing her whole. She closed her eyes, surrendering, and then the world went black.

Duncan blinked at the coin before picking it up, confusion flickering across his mind. *Who threw this?*

He snapped back to the moment. *Focus.* His voice dropped, low and urgent.

'We need to be cautious, Elisa – I think they're onto us.'

No response.

His eyes darted sideways. She wasn't there.

'Elisa ...?' His voice caught. His head jerked from side to side, scanning the empty street, the buildings, the doorways. Nothing.

'Elisa!'

Panic seized his chest like a vice. *No, no, no ...* She'd been right there.

He drew his gun. The silence around him was suffocating. Not even wind. Not a footstep.

Something's wrong. They're here. They've been watching us.

A shadow stirred in his periphery.

Duncan turned sharply – too late.

A figure lunged. A cloth flashed towards his face – inches from his mouth. Instinct kicked in. He recoiled, pivoted slightly, and drove his elbow back with brutal force.

It connected – nose, maybe cheekbone – hard enough to send the attacker stumbling.

Duncan spun and kicked low, sending the man collapsing onto the pavement. But even as the first crumpled, others emerged – five, six, more – rising from the alleys and corners like ghosts.

He raised his weapon – but hands grabbed him from behind. A boot slammed into his leg. Another fist clipped the side of his head. Then he was on the ground, his gun skittering away into the dark.

They swarmed him. Heavy boots thudded against his ribs. Fists pummelled his chest, arms, face. His body bucked under the assault, but they held him down with cruel precision.

Through the blur of pain, he caught it – the matching uniforms. Navy-blue tunics. Black ties. White gloves. Brass belt buckles flashing like teeth in the dark.

Then he saw the armbands. Blue, with the face of a hawk stitched in white thread.

Night Hawks.

The thought struck like a hammer to the gut. *They found us.*

'Fuck him up! Fuck him up!' The voices were jeering, wild, distorted.

He tried to roll free, but boots pinned his shoulders. Another fist cracked across his jaw. Something warm ran down his cheek – blood? Sweat?

His limbs slowed. The hits came faster, heavier.

Then came new footsteps. Measured. Official. A different cadence.

Duncan's vision swam. He tilted his head just enough to see the approaching figures.

Uniforms. Blue. *Municipal Police.*

Help ...

But they didn't stop the beating.

They *joined* it.

One officer drove a knee into Duncan's side. Another punched him across the face. A third raised a baton and brought it down.

Pain. More pain. He was slipping, fading.

They were watching the whole time.

Bystanders lined the far pavement, unmoving, their faces pale and unreadable. No one stepped forward. No one stopped it.

Among the onlookers, a woman gasped, her hands flying to her mouth. Beside her, a man stood frozen, wide-eyed, until instinct kicked in. He grabbed her arm, murmuring urgently, 'Let's go, let's go ...' and pulled her away.

Duncan, bloodied and barely conscious, was dragged to his knees by the Night Hawks and Municipal Police. His arms were pinned behind his back, boots on either side keeping him in place. His breath came in short, shallow gasps.

Then a familiar figure stepped forward – the security guard from earlier, now sporting a swollen black eye. A cigarette dangled from his lips as he slung a rifle casually over his shoulder. He took a long drag, exhaled, and brought the muzzle to Duncan's face.

'Careful now,' he drawled, voice oozing with mockery. 'I might just blow your bleedin' head off.'

He crouched to eye level, cigarette still smouldering between his teeth, and grinned.

'Did you really think we wouldn't be on your arse the second you laid hands on us? You and your little friend made a massive fuckin' mistake bringin' that grey-skin into our streets.' His tone darkened. 'This is what happens when you mess with the wrong–'

Duncan spat in his face.

The guard recoiled, blinking as saliva dripped down his cheek. For a moment, silence hung between them.

Then he chuckled – low, cruel.

'Oh-ho ... Big mistake.'

Without warning, he slammed the butt of his rifle into Duncan's face.

A flash of white-hot pain exploded behind Duncan's eyes. His head snapped to the side, blood spraying from his lip. Sound dulled. Everything wavered.

He barely heard the guard speak again.

'Lads, let Jeremy have him. He'll want a little one-on-one. And trust me ...' The man grinned. 'He won't be the same when Jeremy's done.'

'Understood, sir,' one of the other guards replied.

Duncan's vision narrowed, black creeping in from the edges. His body sagged. The last thing he felt was the cold concrete beneath him – then nothing at all.

Chapter VI

THE NIGHT HAWKS

The room was occupied by Lance Sainglend and his subordinates, seated around a large table. Lance was hard to miss – his long brown beard was braided in places, and a mohawk crowned his head. His piercing sea-blue eyes were striking, and his attire even more so: a violet suit over a white shirt and waistcoat, navy tie, brown dress shoes, and a white cloak clasped with a gold chain, a hawk's face emblazoned on the back.

He and his inner circle were deep in discussion, strategizing their search for allies in the civil war. But their reputation as terrorists made diplomacy difficult. Lance's infamous title – the Kingslayer – only added to the stigma, especially with someone like King Edward. Even if Edward agreed, he would need permission from Emperor Claudius, who ruled his lands.

Securing an alliance was proving no easy feat, and the group pressed on, navigating the complications ahead.

'Why not open secret talks with Emperor Claudius?' said General Secretary Rainer, his sharp grey eyes fixed on Lance. 'If we explain the war's context and ask for aid, even a fraction of his forces could crush the Floran army.'

Lance met Rainer's gaze. 'Claudius is biding his time. Once the Kingslayer or Red Lions fall, he will use it as an excuse to seize Flora for himself.'

'Still, our chances dwindle by the day. General Siegfried counters every move we make. It may be wise to explore an alliance – any alliance.'

Lance fell silent, weighing the suggestion. His instincts churned. Could they afford to risk it?

Reiman, his second-in-command, spoke next. His salt-and-pepper beard and worn coat marked a man seasoned by war.

'Rainer, few nations will back what they see as terrorism. And your plan's too slow. Two-thirds of Syrida answers to the Kingsgurian Empire – without Claudius's approval, we gain nothing. Finding an ally would take time we don't have.' He looked to Lance. 'What is your call, my lord?'

Lance pondered deeply. 'This situation is extremely critical ... I do not have a conclusive decision yet, but–'

Abruptly, four Night Hawks burst through the door, holding Duncan and Elisa captive in handcuffs.

'What is the meaning of this intrusion?' Reiman said, his eyes narrowing as he confronted the Night Hawks.

One of the Night Hawks slammed Duncan down hard, his body hitting the concrete with a sickening thud. Pain tore through his side, and a low groan escaped before he could grit his teeth shut. His vision blurred – stars mocking him in the dim bunker light. Nearby, Elisa's muffled screams stabbed the air, high-pitched and terrified.

He tried to push himself up, but his limbs trembled under his own weight. Every breath he took scraped against the bruised walls of his ribs. His face was already swelling, the metallic tang of blood pooling in his mouth.

Still, he lifted his head.

Elisa lay beside him, her delicate frame curled up, restrained, her eyes wild with panic.

Damn. I should've protected her. That thought hissed in his mind like poison.

What had I dragged her into? What kind of man leads a girl like her straight into a lion's den?

And in the back of his mind a quieter voice whispered:

This is your fault, Duncan. She's here because of you. If she dies, that's on you too.

The room around them bristled with tension. Rifles were raised, fingers twitching on triggers, eyes full of disdain. Duncan's instincts screamed at him – *don't move, don't speak, don't give them a reason.* The Night Hawks didn't look like men seeking truth. They looked like wolves salivating at the chance to rip something apart.

A new figure stepped forward – different. More dangerous.

He moved with the certainty of someone used to being obeyed, each stride sharp, deliberate, as if the ground itself had to make way. His uniform was cleaner than the others', almost pristine – an olive green military jacket pressed flat against his sturdy frame, the dark purple armband on his arm just a shade deeper than the others', like a mark of rank or something more personal. His trousers matched, tucked neatly into polished boots laced to the knee. White gloves covered his hands – not a speck of blood or dirt on them.

But it was his face that truly set him apart.

Curtain-styled black hair framed his pale, angular features. Cold, grey eyes cut through the room with surgical precision, the kind of stare that stripped you down to bone. He couldn't have been much older than Duncan – mid to late twenties, maybe – but there was nothing *young* in that expression. It was brittle, wounded, cruel. Not rage – something worse. Something *patient.* Duncan had seen eyes like that before, in men who'd been broken and never put back together right.

This wasn't some hot-headed rebel. This was someone who *believed* in what he was doing – and who'd burn the world down to make others believe it too.

'Lord Sainglend, I present to you the culprits that wreaked havoc around the city,' the man beside him announced, his voice crisp with duty. Then, turning with a sneer, he addressed Duncan and Elisa: 'You kneel before the true king and saviour of Flora, the leader and founder of the Night Hawk Rebellion. Identify yourselves!'

King? Saviour?

Duncan's blood ran cold. *What kind of fantasy had these bastards built around themselves?*

He tried to speak, but the words stuck at first, caught in the grit of pain and fear. His heart pounded so loud it threatened to drown out his voice. He forced it out anyway. 'What's going on? Why are we being held captive?'

The man's expression twisted into disgust.

'Don't play the idiot! You attacked our guards, smuggled that Dökkálfar in, and took out the city police without cause! And most importantly – why were you heading straight for Lord Sainglend's location? Planning to assassinate him? Speak up, or I'll put you down like dogs!'

The words cracked like a whip. Duncan felt his jaw tighten.

He tasted blood again. It filled his mouth like guilt.

'Assassinate him ...?' Duncan repeated, his voice shaky but resolute. 'What kind of ridiculous accusation is that? We only did what had to be done ...' He coughed, doubling over as sharp pain flared in his chest. 'Your guards – arrogant bastards – beating an innocent elf near to death just because of who he is. Clinging to a war they never even fought.'

He didn't know if they would believe him. Maybe they didn't care. But he had to say it. He had to own what they did – even if it cost them both their lives.

'Shut your bloody mouth, lout, before I ram a fistful of centipedes down your throat!' the Night Hawk barked.

'Wait, Jeremy. Before you do anything rash, I want to hear what the captives have to say,' Lance said calmly from his chair.

Jeremy turned towards Lance, bowing his head. 'Very well, my lord.' He then turned to face Duncan and Elisa. 'I'll ask again – no more delays, no more hindrances! Who are you two and state your purposes!' he snarled impatiently.

Duncan lifted his head slowly, glaring at Jeremy with exhaustion.

Infuriated, Jeremy raised his fist and punched Duncan on his left cheek. 'Answer me!'

Duncan grunted from the impact of the punch, and Elisa widened her eyes, attempting to scream, but the handkerchief muffled her voice.

Duncan hacked up blood, spitting it onto the floorboards. His fists clenched so tight his knuckles cracked, chains cutting into his skin like they wanted to bleed him dry.

Rage was boiling under his skin – raw, brutal, desperate to snap loose and tear that bastard Jeremy apart. If he weren't chained like some sorry fuck, he'd have already smashed his face in.

The ache in his cheek screamed, but it was nothing compared to the fire in his head. His mind was sharp as a blade, slicing through the pain. No way he'd give these assholes the chance to break him.

Duncan took a deep breath and asked, 'Why ... the hell do you think we're here? My friend wanted to ... deliver an important letter to Lord Sainglend. Maybe you should ... take that gag off her and let her talk.'

Jeremy peered at Duncan, suspicious of any sudden movements. He cautiously approached Elisa and untied the handkerchief.

Elisa's mouth was sore from the tightness of the binding. 'Argh ...' She quivered and nervously continued. 'Lord Sainglend, forgive my intrusion. My name is Elisa Evergreen, and this is my friend, Duncan Saul. We are here to deliver a letter penned by a man named Archer Norman, a close friend of mine. He was dispatched on an espionage mission at your behest, concerning Olav, your trusted officer. Regrettably, Olav was captured, and before Archer could escape, he was shot by soldiers. The particulars of the mission and Olav's involvement are detailed in Archer's letter.'

'That's bullshit!' Jeremy shouted viciously.

'No, Jeremy. What they speak is true ... I do recall sending a subordinate of mine named Archer on a mission.

However, mere words won't dispel my doubts. Show me this letter you speak of – let it serve as proof that you are not simply spouting nonsense.'

Lance then motioned with a click of his fingers towards one of his men who promptly nodded in acknowledgment. The Night Hawk approached Elisa and proceeded to search her body to see if she was indeed carrying the letter. He found it in her coat pocket and delivered it to Lance.

'Hmm ... Let's see here ...' said Lance as he opened the envelope and read the letter, his eyes falling upon the stained paper which was marked with bloody fingerprints.

Dear Lance,

The mission you assigned to David and me had mixed results. While we succeeded in our primary objective, we also faced significant setbacks. During the raid on The Red Lion camp, Olav uncovered critical information, but his entire unit was wiped out and he was captured. He is now held as a prisoner. General Siegfried is planning to execute Olav on 2 May at Stansted.

Although I couldn't fully grasp the importance of Olav's information, it appears to be vital for our war effort. After completing the mission, I attempted to report back to you but my cover was blown by the Red Lions. I was injured during the escape, so I write you this letter in case my condition worsens. I entrust it to David who has promised to deliver it to you.

Rescuing Olav will be extremely challenging: General Siegfried is a cunning opponent. Proceed with caution and plan meticulously.

It has been an honour to serve under your command. May God bless you.

Elisa, if you are reading this, I'm deeply sorry I couldn't keep my promise to be there for you. Please know that my final thoughts were of you and my hope that you'll find strength and purpose in our struggle.

Yours sincerely,

Archer

After reading the letter, Lance felt a mix of emotions. He was relieved about the mission's success but saddened by Archer's sacrifice.

'I see ... This is the punishment that I have to bear,' Lance said.

'What's the matter, Lord Sainglend?' Reiman asked.

'Olav has been captured. He possesses vital information that could tip the scales of the war.'

'So, what is your plan, my lord?'

Lance's expression showed sadness as he replied. 'I have made my decision. I will turn myself in and end the civil war once and for all.'

Jeremy was shocked and confused. 'What!? With all due respect, my lord, that doesn't sound wise. Why not send a few of our men or myself to rescue Olav? Why surrender to the enemy? It's absurd!'

Reiman looked at Jeremy. 'Hush, Jeremy! Watch the way you speak to Lord Sainglend.'

Jeremy saw the look on Lance's face and then heeded Reiman's words, silencing his complaints.

'Forgive me for my dissent, Lord Sainglend, but I must agree with Jeremy on this,' Reiman interjected. 'Your plan is nothing short of suicidal. You must reconsider this idea immediately. Surrendering yourself would bring an end to the entire war, and the sacrifices made by our comrades would be in vain.'

'You're mistaken, Lord Reiman. Our comrades' sacrifices won't be in vain,' Lance said firmly. 'You didn't let me finish. I plan to arrange an audience with the House of Royals. I'll send them a video message and do my best to convince them. If they agree, they'll leave our followers and members alone. I'm willing to exchange my life for theirs.'

'But Lord Sainglend, that might not work,' Reiman said with concern. 'They'll see it as merely a sign of defeat. If they capture you, they'll claim victory over the war. Then, they'll have the opportunity to hunt down the rest of us and execute us.' Reiman folded his arms and continued. 'I believe I can go and save Olav if you need me to because my position in this war is far less significant than yours.'

The memory of King Ivar, Lance's friend-turned-enemy, was on his mind. Lance recalled the moment of that crucial decision. He believed he had made the right choice then, but now – with hindsight – he saw the consequences differently. With his companions nearby, the burden of leadership felt heavy. He valued their advice and respected their differing views, but he knew the responsibility rested on him to lead the way.

'No!' Lance yelled. 'Do you both know the reason why I killed my friend, Ivar? I killed him to prevent war and bloodshed in our country. I did not want him to start a resistance with the Kingsgurian Empire. He was willing to sacrifice his men, and even the innocent, to drive the Empire back. If I had let him live, all hell would have been set loose, and yet I created the very same thing that I wanted to prevent. Now I see the hypocrisy of my actions, and now it's time to take responsibility.'

'I beg to differ, my lord. Patience is the best method for now ... We could think of a plan to overcome this situation.'

'I have made my decision, Reiman, and I will proceed regardless of whether you two agree with me or not,' Lance replied firmly. 'Continuing to use evil to fight evil will only bring more conflict. Risking my men on a mission that may not even succeed will lead to more deaths and casualties. I cannot allow that. If death comes for me, so be it.'

'So, that's it then? You're just going to surrender and give your life away?' Reiman questioned.

'Lord Reiman, though I may be gone, the soul of the Night Hawks will live on. To the world, I might be seen as a murderer, but to the Night Hawks, I am Flora's saviour.

Perhaps someday, you or even Jeremy will take over and carry on our legacy in your own way,' Lance responded.

Reiman exhaled, trying to retain his composure. 'I understand ... I don't agree with it ... but I understand ...' Turning to Jeremy, Reiman inquired, 'What will you do with the prisoners?'

'Oh, forgive me, my lord. I nearly forgot,' Jeremy apologised.

Jeremy turned sharply towards Duncan and Elisa, his expression cold and merciless. 'You may have brought news of consequence,' he said icily, 'but that doesn't exempt you from punishment. Both of you will be confined in the Gothenburg prison, to be handed over to the municipal police. Men, remove these prisoners at once. The more I see them, the more they irritate me.'

Duncan struggled against the Night Hawks' restraint. 'You son of a bitch! Is this how you treat your citizens?!'

Elisa's eyes closed briefly as she collected her thoughts, her chest rising and falling with each deep breath. She couldn't bear this any longer. Why did they deserve such treatment? Why did Jeremy hate them so much? Why would he go so far as to punish them for a petty crime?

In that moment, she raised her voice. 'Enough ... I've had enough!' Elisa's proclamation cut through the air, commanding the attention of everyone present.

All eyes turned towards her, silence falling upon the room.

'You may view me as just an ordinary citizen of Flora, someone without a right to speak,' Elisa continued. 'But I implore you to think again! Ryonil, a Dökkálfar, possessed full citizenship within our country. He held a valid passport to enter our city and abided by every law in Syrida. The only thing he did was conceal his face to escape the abuse inflicted upon him by your fellow citizens. He did nothing wrong!' Elisa yelled, her eyes ablaze with righteous anger. 'For merely daring to speak out against the unfair treatment he endured, your gatekeepers ruthlessly assaulted him! And you all stand there and dare claim to be helping the people of Flora. It is a farce! My friend, Archer, served with honour under the Night Hawks, singing praises of their greatness. But witnessing your abhorrent actions has shattered my illusions. You people have the audacity to act as if you are morally superior to the Red Lions, yet you fail to comprehend the true meaning of equality!'

Elisa's movement matched the power of her words as she took deliberate steps forward, refusing to be confined or silenced. She stood tall, moving closer to Jeremy. 'You, Jeremy, are nothing more than an egotistical, callous, self-centred swine!' She spat.

Duncan opened his mouth in amazement: it seemed like he was impressed by Elisa's sudden display of courage.

Jeremy clenched his teeth in response to the insult. 'You better watch your tongue, bitch!' he snarled, delivering a hard backhand slap to Elisa's face, leaving a bruise on the side of her cheek.

'Argh!' Elisa cried out, instinctively moving her face to the right to escape the blow. With her stinging cheek, her eyes widened in shock as she stared back at Jeremy. The taste of blood filled her mouth.

Duncan became enraged; he broke free from the Night Hawks' control and head-butted Jeremy's nose, then watched him stumble back, holding his face in pain. 'You son of a bitch!' Duncan yelled in outrage. 'I'm gonna strangle you with these cuffs!'

One Night Hawk then punched Duncan in the stomach and he coughed in pain. 'Know your position, cockmonger!' The Night Hawk snarled.

'Take them away immediately, and I hope they'll rot in prison!' Jeremy shouted.

Elisa observed the intense situation, her heart racing with anxiety.

Are we going to end up in jail? And if that happens, who will come to our rescue?

'Stop! Stop at once!' Lance's voice boomed from his chair.

'But, my lord–!'

'You will heed me at once, Jeremy, or I will dismiss you early!' Lance's voice was firm.

Jeremy's eyes widened, and he lowered his head, submitting to Lance's authority and obeying his command.

Lance's voice dropped into a firm, serious register. 'We should be thanking these two for bringing this to my attention. Without them, who knows what might have happened? Release them. Immediately. They haven't killed anyone – and this war is far more important than a minor offence.'

A flicker of hope stirred in Elisa's chest. But Jeremy didn't move. His body was taut with resistance.

'If this is about venting your anger,' Lance continued, calm but cutting, 'do it with dignity. The young lady is right – how are we any better than the Red Lions if we've forgotten the meaning of equality? Look at how we treat our own people.'

His words swept through the room like a quiet wind, drawing uncertain glances from the Night Hawks around them.

'This isn't who we are. Or who we claimed to be. We were meant to protect Flora – not punish civilians for trivial missteps.'

Jeremy clenched his fist. 'Lord Sainglend, you don't understand. If they hadn't shown you that letter—'

'I do understand,' Lance interrupted, his voice steady. 'And if you hold a grudge against them, I'll be disappointed in you.'

Elisa watched him carefully. The shift in his expression was subtle – a softening at the edges. Grief, maybe. Or guilt.

'She's already lost her friend,' Lance went on, 'a man who served our cause with honour. Because of me. She's suffered enough.'

Something stirred in Elisa. Amid her grief, she found herself moved by the sincerity in Lance's words. There was real empathy behind them – not just rhetoric, but remorse. He wasn't simply a leader issuing orders. He was a man taking responsibility for his failings. For hers. For Archer's. And that meant something.

Jeremy stood stiffly, at a loss for words, until Lance stepped closer and rested a hand on his shoulder.

'I killed my closest friend,' Lance said quietly. 'And that decision has led to more deaths than I can count – comrades, innocents, people we swore to protect. I have to live with that. I must pay for it. If we're not willing to make sacrifices, then how can we claim to build something better?'

Jeremy's anger faltered. He looked away, jaw tightening, then gave a reluctant nod.

'Very well … I accept your decision, Lord Sainglend.'

'Thank you, Jeremy,' Lance said softly.

As Jeremy gestured to his men, the handcuffs that held Duncan and Elisa were finally released, granting them freedom.

Lance stepped forward. 'Forgive my subordinates. Their loyalty sometimes blinds them to the bigger picture. But rest assured, I will make amends for their behaviour. You both have my word.' As Lance looked at Elisa, he placed a gentle hand on her shoulder, offering comfort and sympathy. 'I'm truly sorry for the loss of your friend, Elisa. Please accept my deepest condolences.'

'Don't be,' she replied. 'But thank you for your kind words.'

'Thank you, Lord Sainglend, but we need to get going because we've matters to attend to,' Duncan said.

'I understand. We will not take your time any longer. May God bless you.'

Duncan and Elisa quickly left the mansion. Unnoticed by Jeremy, Elisa stuck her tongue out in a playful gesture. 'Ngh.' It wasn't ladylike, but she didn't care at that point. Duncan raised an eyebrow with a smirk.

Outside the mansion, Duncan checked on Elisa, concerned about her well-being following the encounter with Jeremy. She assured him with a nod, though her bruised cheek told a different story. But Duncan's anger surged as he examined the bruise. He expressed his desire to retaliate against Jeremy for his abusive actions. 'If I hadn't been bloody chained up, I would've made sure that arsehole couldn't chew for a week!'

'Please, Mr Saul, do not harbour any distress. In fact, I must express my gratitude to you for coming to my defence. You've done a great job in dealing with that' – Elisa cleared her throat – '... mind my profanity ... arsehole. He had no right to assault me like that.'

Duncan chuckled. 'I'm more impressed that you had the courage to call out that animal's bullshit. You really are something, Elisa.'

Elisa shook her head.

Duncan smiled. 'Come on, Elisa. You're tougher than you think.'

Blushing and still somewhat timid, Elisa insisted. 'No ... It's just that having you beside me made me feel more courageous. On my own, I'm uncertain if I could muster the strength to speak like that.'

Duncan rolled his eyes. 'Yeah, right ...'

'I'm serious,' Elisa said with a shy smile.

'Wait ... Oh no,' Duncan muttered, suddenly realising something with a sense of urgency.

'What?' asked Elisa, concerned by the expression on Duncan's face.

'Ryonil!' Duncan shouted.

'Huh?'

Without a second thought, Duncan sprinted away. 'Dammit!'

Seeing Duncan run off, Elisa didn't hesitate and called after him. 'Hold on, wait!'

Duncan's sudden departure left Elisa initially puzzled, but it didn't take her long to connect the dots. As the realisation sank in, her heart raced with anxiety about what they might find.

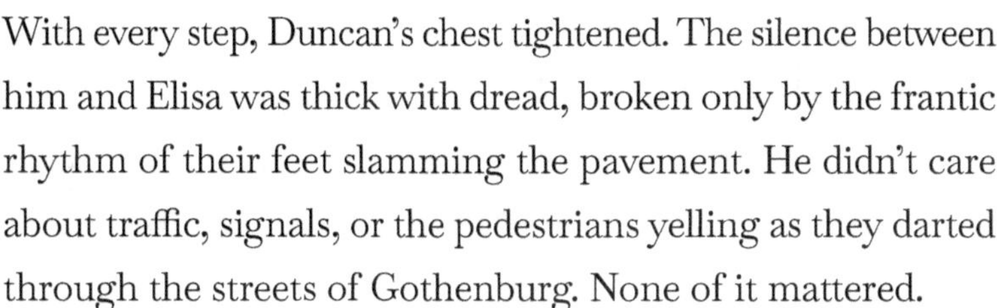

With every step, Duncan's chest tightened. The silence between him and Elisa was thick with dread, broken only by the frantic rhythm of their feet slamming the pavement. He didn't care about traffic, signals, or the pedestrians yelling as they darted through the streets of Gothenburg. None of it mattered.

Only Ryonil did.

He should've never left him alone. *Bloody idiot.* Things went wrong – *fast* – and now that old familiar knot twisted in his gut. The one he'd known since he was a boy, waiting for someone who never came back.

'Oh God,' Duncan muttered under his breath, barely audible. 'Please be alright ... please.'

Ryonil's house came into view – and with it, a jolt of pure panic. The door – battered in. Hanging open.

Duncan didn't wait.

He stormed up the steps and threw the door open with a crash. 'Ryonil!?'

His voice echoed off the walls.

He bolted inside, heart hammering like mad. The living room was in chaos – drawers yanked out, shelves emptied, curtains flapping in a cold gust through a shattered window.

No blood. No body. Just silence.

'Ryonil!?'

He moved like a storm through the house, flinging open doors, shouting like maybe the elf had just fallen asleep under a bed or something. But the emptiness pressed in like a weight.

Elisa caught up, out of breath. 'Ryonil!? Where are you!?'

Still nothing.

'Dammit,' Duncan muttered. His voice cracked with disbelief. 'He's not here ...'

Elisa called Ryonil's name again, but the house gave no reply. Her expression shifted as dread sank in. 'If he isn't here, that must mean ...'

Duncan's head dropped. His fists clenched. He stood shaking, fury and grief fighting in his chest. *Not again.*

With a shout, he kicked a wooden chair clean across the room. It splintered against the wall.

'No! No, no, no!'

The words tore out of him, hoarse and ragged.

'This is fucking *bollocks*! All this – because of what his ancestors did hundreds of years ago!? Ryonil didn't *do* anything! And now he's probably cuffed, locked up, maybe even worse – just for being born an elf!'

His chest rose and fell, eyes wide, voice breaking.

'What kind of sick world is this, huh? Why can't they just let the past *go*? Why's it always the next poor sod paying for sins they didn't bloody commit?'

'Mr Saul,' Elisa said softly.

He didn't hear her.

'Every time ... Every fucking time—' his voice cracked, a tremble in his throat '—you do your best, you think you've done enough, and then – *gone.* Just like that.'

'Mr Saul!'

He whirled on her, raw. '*What!?*'

'Please,' she said gently but firmly. 'Calm down.'

He stared at her. Eyes red. Shoulders trembling.

'How can I, eh? This is *our* fault. If we'd been smarter – if I'd come up with a better plan – we wouldn't have been caught in the first place. Maybe Ryonil wouldn't have ended up like this. I should've known the Night Hawks'd tip off the coppers – should've known better.'

'Mr Saul, I know,' Elisa said, raising her voice. 'He was my friend too.'

She folded her arms, exhaling shakily. 'But alas, we cannot return to the past. We must move forward, as painful as that may be. We are alive, are we not? That, in itself, is something – something to be grateful for. And surely that must give us hope that there remains a chance for us to rectify what has been broken.'

He looked at her, then to the floor. Words failed him. For a moment, he stood perfectly still – only the slight tremble in his jaw betraying him.

She was right. And still – it didn't stop the ache in his chest, that familiar, hollow ache he hadn't felt in years.

He shut his eyes. A memory tried to claw its way forward – but he shoved it down.

Later.

He opened them again.

'Let's just ... let's get to my mum's place,' he muttered. Voice low. Hollow.

Chapter VII

FAMILY REUNION

Feeling low after leaving Ryonil's wrecked home behind, Duncan and Elisa spent the next couple of days on the road. The journey was quiet, weighed down by guilt and fatigue, until they finally reached Lancefield – a sleepy village tucked in the lush countryside of Flora. The sort of place where the roads weren't paved properly and the air smelt of soil and smoke.

They stopped in front of a modest house made of old cement and tired wood. A thatched roof rested unevenly atop two floors, and the glass windows were just clean enough to let in the sun. There wasn't much to say about the house – it didn't stand out, didn't try to. Just ... home.

Duncan turned to Elisa. 'Elisa, this was once my home. I left when I was about twenty, wanting to make things easier for my mum. Fewer mouths to feed, less money stress. Seemed like the right choice then, given our financial struggles. After that, I got into freelancing as a mercenary,' he explained.

Elisa gazed at the house and nodded thoughtfully. 'I understand ... This house seems perfect for a small family.'

'Yeah,' he said. 'We were a regular, working-class family. Now, it's just my mum here. She doesn't have many visitors, except for the old postman, Norman. Nice bloke. Bit too cheery.'

'Loneliness must be frequent with her.'

Duncan pursed his lips. 'Not really. She has friends at work. But that's not the main point. I usually check in with her over the phone, at the very least. She's a kind person, but please, be on your best behaviour. She can be a bit ... embarrassing when she gets carried away.'

Elisa raised her right hand and smiled reassuringly. 'Do not worry, Mr Saul. I will make sure to be on my best behaviour.'

Duncan chuckled faintly and nodded. Then, with a deep breath, he stepped up to the door and knocked. His hand lingered a moment longer than it should have – frozen not from fear, but from the weight of absence. A whole year, gone in a blink, yet heavy on the chest.

The door creaked open.

And there she was.

His mother stood before him, still with that same black ponytail, her fringe brushing her brows, and those unmistakable sea-blue eyes that mirrored his own. She wore a checkered blue shirt with the sleeves rolled up, a loose skirt fluttering just past her knees, and her comfy old brown loafers that never quite matched anything. Her silver wedding ring still glinted on her finger, though time had dulled its shine.

She seemed older to him now, time leaving its gentle marks yet her core was the same.

Their eyes met.

And something broke open in Duncan's chest.

He hadn't realised just how much he missed her.

'Hello, Mum ...' he said, and his voice cracked slightly despite himself.

'Duncan ...' she breathed, before pulling him into her arms with no hesitation. She clung to him, as if afraid he'd vanish again. Like he'd always been her boy, and nothing had changed.

He held her just as tightly, his arms wrapped around her shoulders. A rare, genuine smile bloomed across his face – something unguarded, vulnerable. He shut his eyes for a moment, letting himself be small again, if only for a heartbeat.

Her hand gently patted his back. 'Wh–why did you decide to visit after so long? I missed you so much.'

There were things he wanted to say. Things he couldn't. Things about where he'd been, the blood he'd spilled, the people he'd failed to save. And other things – things older than mercenary work, things tied to a man whose name hadn't been spoken in this house for years.

Curiosity sparked in his mother's eyes as she turned to Elisa. 'Who's your friend, Duncan?'

'This is Elisa,' he explained.

Elisa, ever respectful, extended a hand politely. 'It's nice to meet you, Mrs Saul.'

His mother reciprocated the gesture, reaching out for a handshake. Elisa graciously accepted it with both hands, her elegance meeting Sara's cheerful warmth.

'You could just call me Sara,' she said kindly, 'and it's a pleasure to meet you, Elisa.'

Duncan stood just behind them, arms folded loosely, eyes lowered but listening closely. It was strange – watching two parts of his life, his past and his present, collide in a hallway that smelt like laundry detergent and old wood. This house still creaked in all the same places, still had that faint scent of his childhood clinging to the walls. And yet, he no longer felt like he belonged in it.

As the pleasantries passed, Sara turned to him once again, her expression softening. 'So, Duncan ... why did you decide to come and visit after such a long time?'

He tensed. The question didn't surprise him, but it hit harder than expected. There was a thousand different ways he could've answered. Guilt. Exhaustion. The ache to feel something warm again. A part of him wanted to say *Because I missed you* – but the words caught behind his teeth.

He glanced at Elisa beside him. She was standing quietly, a little guarded but holding herself with grace. She had no family left. No safety net. And she'd been through hell. Duncan knew what it felt like to have nowhere to go. No one.

His gaze returned to Sara. 'I actually came regarding Elisa,' he said, his voice a touch heavier now. 'She has ... nowhere to live. Her guardian – he was killed during the civil war.'

Sara's hand flew to her chest, her eyes wide with horror. 'Oh my God.'

Duncan nodded, jaw tight. 'Yeah. She's got nowhere else to go. I hoped ... I hoped you could help.'

He didn't like asking for things. Especially not from his mum. It felt like a weakness. But this was different. He wasn't asking for himself.

Still, the words tasted like vulnerability. And that was harder to swallow than he expected.

'I see ... That's why she's holding her luggage,' Sara said.

'Yes.' Duncan hesitated, then added quietly, 'Can you do that for me, Mum? You're the only one I trust.'

He meant that.

In a world where people lied, betrayed, and used each other like tools, Sara was the one constant in his life who had never asked him to be anything but her son. Even if he didn't always know how to be one.

Sara's eyes softened further. 'Of course, Duncan,' she said, without missing a beat.

A breath escaped him he hadn't realised he'd been holding. 'Thank you, Mum.'

He turned to Elisa, offering a small smile. 'Good news. You can stay at our home.'

Elisa's eyes widened. 'Really, Mrs Saul? Thank you so much. Your generosity is ever so kind.'

Sara chuckled, clearly charmed. 'Aww, no need to thank me. Now, don't just stand there,' she said, stepping back with a welcoming gesture. 'Come on in.'

As they crossed the threshold, Duncan felt something shift – like he was stepping back into a version of himself that hadn't existed in years. The boy who used to run down these halls. The one who still dreamt about a different kind of life, before it all went wrong. Before war. Before blood.

And somewhere in the back of his mind, the thought flickered –

He would've never come back here, not like this. But here I am, Mum. Without him. Without the truth.

But that truth would come. Just not today.

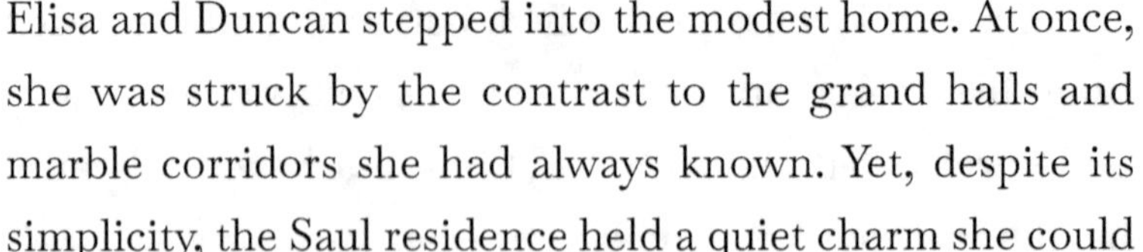

Elisa and Duncan stepped into the modest home. At once, she was struck by the contrast to the grand halls and marble corridors she had always known. Yet, despite its simplicity, the Saul residence held a quiet charm she could not easily define.

Warm brown pallet-wood creaked softly beneath her boots, and the cream-coloured walls – immaculately kept – were adorned with framed photographs that whispered of laughter, milestones and memory. A window lit the small kitchen, its view opening onto a quaint garden, while the dining table, set with three chairs, stood as an unspoken invitation to something far rarer than opulence: togetherness.

In the living room, a well-worn sofa faced a modest fireplace beside a smaller armchair. Between two tall dracaena plants stood a television – an arrangement more thoughtful than lavish.

'Right then, this is the living room,' Sara said with a cheerful gesture, clearly proud of the home she'd made. 'Kitchen's through there – north end. Bedroom's upstairs. Come on, I'll show you.'

Elisa inclined her head politely. 'Thank you, Mrs Saul. You are most gracious.'

There was something theatrical in Sara's cheer, yet nothing about it felt false. Elisa followed her upstairs, Duncan silent behind them.

At the end of the hall, Sara opened the door to a small room. It was bare, save for a lingering scent of wood polish and a window that cast a soft, golden light across the floorboards.

'This used to be Duncan's room,' Sara said with a faint smile. 'Cleared it after he left. No bed yet, I'm afraid, so it's the floor tonight. But we'll get something in here for you tomorrow – hope that's alright?'

Elisa turned to her with a gentle smile. 'It is perfectly acceptable, Mrs Saul. I am truly grateful for your hospitality.'

'Ah, don't be so formal, love. Call me Sara.'

Elisa hesitated, then gave a small nod. 'As you wish ... Sara.' The name felt strange on her tongue – familiarity was not something she offered lightly – but there was a warmth to the woman that made it easier.

'Just leave your luggage here,' Sara added, stepping aside. 'You can sort your things later.'

Elisa placed her luggage by the wall. Her hand lingered on the handle a moment longer than needed before she let go, as though setting down more than just her belongings.

'We're really pleased to have you here, Miss Elisa,' Sara added kindly. 'You're our guest of honour – make yourself at home, yeah?'

Elisa gave a soft laugh. 'I hold a hopeful anticipation that my stay shall be most agreeable.'

Sara grinned. 'I've no idea what that means, but it sounded lovely.'

Elisa went along with Sara downstairs. As they re-entered the living room, Elisa's gaze fell upon Duncan seated on the sofa, checking his smartphone for news updates.

'All in all, this place has a certain charm. I believe I'll enjoy my stay here,' Elisa said.

'Thank you, Miss Elisa. Your praise is lovely.'

'By the way, Mum.' Duncan approached his mother. 'Can I stay here tonight? I wanna help set up Elisa's room tomorrow.'

'Sure, that's great. It warms my heart to have you here longer after not seeing each other for a while,' Sara responded, smiling.

Duncan grinned. 'Yep. It would be rude to leave soon after reuniting with my lovely mother.'

'You're adorable when you give compliments.'

'I'll sleep on the sofa, but don't expect me to stay long. A job might pop up,' Duncan added.

'I understand. I'm just grateful that you are staying here.'

Curiosity piqued Elisa's interest. She noticed a collection of pictures on the table and approached to examine them. She first studied a picture of Duncan with a group of men. They stood tall and proud, arranged neatly for the photograph. They wore olive green T-shirts, camo cargo pants and Desert boots. It seemed the photo had been taken during Duncan's late teenage years.

Duncan glanced at the photo Elisa was looking at. 'This was when I graduated from recruit training. That's Adam, Abraham and Barny. And of course, that's me.'

'I see ...' Elisa shifted her attention to the next picture. Duncan was now in the law enforcement agency. Similarly to the previous photo, the team stood in a proud and organised manner but the uniform had changed. Duncan smiled alongside his colleagues, his hands behind his back, and head held high – the resemblance between the two pictures was striking. 'You were a part of law enforcement, too, Mr Saul?' Elisa asked.

Duncan nodded. 'Yeah, I joined the police force after my time in the military. I had my sights set on becoming a detective and solving crimes. But the pace of police work just didn't suit me. It's a shame, really. I did well in my coursework and exams, but policing wasn't taking me where I wanted to go. So, I resigned – simple as that.'

Elisa's eyes settled on a family photo of a younger Duncan. He sat on Sara's lap, beside a tall man with a hand resting on her shoulder. All three were dressed elegantly – the man in a finely tailored black tuxedo, Sara in a blue dress, and Duncan in a tiny suit. While the parents smiled warmly, Duncan looked lost in thought, lips slightly pouting.

Elisa studied the man – shaved head, light blue eyes and a golden beard matching Duncan's hair. The resemblance was unmistakable: Duncan's father. His serene smile left a lasting impression, and the photo captured a picture-perfect family moment.

As Elisa examined the picture frame in her hands, Sara met her gaze. 'That's our old family photo,' Sara remarked, her tone nostalgic. Closing the distance, Sara's finger directed Elisa's attention to the young Duncan in the image. 'This is Duncan as a tot,' she explained. 'Look at those cheeks – isn't he cute!'

Elisa readily concurred with a nod and a light-hearted agreement. 'Absolutely.'

Duncan cleared his throat to get their attention. 'Yeah, show my baby photo in front of her, it isn't *embarrassing* or anything,' Duncan remarked sarcastically.

'Don't mind him.'

Elisa noted Sara and Duncan's dynamics beyond the façade. Sara playfully mentioned Duncan's childhood cuteness, calling him a tot with amusement, and her expressions and gestures were natural, her interactions warm and welcoming. Elisa sensed that Sara often started conversations, creating an open and laughter-filled atmosphere. Duncan was, well ... *Duncan.* Their personalities were opposite but complementary. It was as if they were two puzzle pieces that fitted together perfectly.

Elisa gazed at Sara and indicated the man in the family photo. 'This is your husband, correct?'

Sara fell silent.

'Where is he now? Do you still live together, or are you separated?' Elisa inquired.

Duncan and Sara exchanged a silent look, and Duncan's face showed unease.

Elisa was surprised. She hadn't intended to uncover hidden pain, but her question seemed to touch on a sensitive history. Duncan's discomfort was evident, reflecting the unexpected shift in the conversation.

'He left a while back ...' Duncan answered.

Elisa felt a touch of sadness. She noticed how he spoke, his cryptic answer leaving her uneasy. A part of her wondered about their past, what led to Duncan's father leaving and how it affected their relationship. Elisa felt that Duncan's cautious behaviour was a defence mechanism, protecting himself and his mother from the full story. He clearly wasn't ready to share more. Elisa respected that and decided not to press further. She understood the topic was sensitive.

'I'm sorry, I should not have asked. It was foolish of me to dig into personal matters,' Elisa apologised sincerely.

'No worries, Elisa. We all get curious sometimes,' Duncan said.

Sara glanced out the window. 'It's getting late, and I need to prepare dinner soon,' she said. Sara playfully bowed. 'Tonight, I have something special planned. Especially for our guest, Miss Elisa.'

Elisa chuckled in response. Then she remembered that she hadn't mentioned her dietary preference. 'Mrs Saul, I must apologise for not mentioning earlier, but I am a vegetarian.'

'Got it. I'll make fried fish with lemon slices, freshly baked potatoes and garlic herb seasoning.'

'That sounds truly delectable, Mrs Saul.'

Sara smiled. 'It really is. You'd have to be crazy to resist my cooking.'

Duncan folded his arms. 'Ah, that's Mum for you – always keen to please the new people she meets.'

'And what's wrong with that?' Sara asked.

'Nothing, just making an observation.'

'I would be truly delighted to savour your exquisite meal, Mrs Saul. However, if you would permit, I would also be pleased to offer my assistance in the kitchen.'

Sara waved her hand. 'Oh, no need. You can relax and wait for the mouthwatering smell to guide you.'

Elisa stood confidently. 'I would be more than willing to assist, Mrs Saul. This visit is not merely a leisure escapade for me. As a guest bestowed with the privilege of residing within the Saul residence, I deem it entirely appropriate to adhere to the established norms.'

Sara frowned and looked at Duncan with confusion. 'What?'

Duncan shook his head. 'She likes speaking that way. Get used to it.'

Elisa's attention refocused on the practical aspects. 'Anyway. Mrs Saul, might you have an extra apron I could borrow? I would prefer not to soil my blouse.'

'Sure. There's one in that cupboard,' Sara said, pointing.

'Thank you.' Elisa took a pink apron from the cupboard and tied it around her waist.

Duncan joined his mother and Elisa, offering his assistance. 'I'll help, too. Elisa, just be careful not to break anything. My mum has enough to deal with.'

Sara raised her finger, scolding. 'Duncan, mind your manners. Elisa might be younger but she's a guest. It's her first time here.'

'Right, sorry, Mum,' he said, rubbing his neck.

Elisa nodded. 'Please, fret not, Mr Saul. I shall be careful.'

'Good.'

The trio soon settled into the rhythm of preparing dinner – Sara leading with cheerful energy, Elisa following her instructions with poised attentiveness. Duncan lingered on the periphery, offering help when needed but mostly observing.

They prepared three whole fried fish, each laid out with lemon slices that shimmered against the golden skin. The roasted potatoes – fragrant with herbs, smoked paprika and a touch of ginger. Elisa worked with calm precision, sleeves neatly folded, movements careful and methodical. Even Sara paused to watch her, visibly impressed.

'She's a natural,' she whispered to Duncan.

He said nothing, only watching as Elisa delicately arranged the final garnish.

When the meal was done, the kitchen bore the marks of cheerful effort.

Elisa stepped back, wiping her hands on a tea towel as she surveyed their work. The sight of the finished meal – humble though it was – stirred something deep within her: a quiet contentment she had not felt in what seemed like an age.

For a moment, she thought of Archer. His laughter echoing – the way he used to sneak far too many bites under the guise of 'taste-testing'. And the time when his sleeves were rolled up, face comically serious as he tried – so earnestly – not to weep while slicing onions.

This kitchen was different – smaller, more worn – but the feeling was achingly similar. Not comfort, exactly. But the shadow of it. A memory of something safe. Something lost.

And perhaps, just perhaps, something she might find again.

Chapter VIII

WHERE THE PAST SLEEPS

Duncan watched Elisa move deftly around the kitchen, a quiet admiration growing with each careful chop and stir. When she finally placed the last dish on the table, he couldn't help but smile.

'Wow, Elisa, you've really amazed me. You're an incredible cook,' he said, genuine awe in his voice.

Elisa was content with his response. 'Thank you, Mr Saul. Your praise honours me greatly.'

'Right then, enough of the pleasantries,' Sara said. 'The food won't eat itself.'

'Oh, you're right. Elisa, please have a seat.'

They all sat down and began to eat.

Duncan tasted his fish. 'Mmmm ... Elisa, Mum, this meal is fantastic. It's really lightening the mood,' he remarked.

'Your appreciation is most gracious, Mr Saul.'

Sara smiled. 'Elisa deserves most of the credit. She perfected the seasoning.'

Elisa chuckled at Sara's comment.

Sara leant on the table, intrigued. 'Anyway, Elisa, tell me about yourself. Your family, how you grew up?'

'My family? They are the Evergreens.'

Duncan scratched his chin. 'I know of the Evergreens. Weren't Herald and Amy assassinated six years ago?'

Elisa nodded. 'Yes, hitmen killed them. My sister and I were there when it happened.'

'You were there?' Sara asked.

Elisa twiddled her thumbs, explaining sadly. 'Yes, we witnessed it. I'm the last surviving member of the Evergreen family.'

Hearing that made Duncan clench his fist under the table – his jaw tightening. He met Elisa's gaze, the weight of her words settling heavily in his chest. The thought of Elisa – a young girl, standing helpless as her parents were murdered – sickened him. No one should have to live through something like that.

Sara gazed at Elisa with sadness. 'Oh, goodness ... How could you go through something so tragic at such a young age? I don't know what to say. I'm really sorry, kiddo.'

'Your compassion warms my heart, Mrs Saul. Please understand that I've managed to find solace with time. What transpired is now a part of my history, and I've made my peace with it. There's no use dwelling on the past.' Elisa rested her arms on the table and asked, 'So, what about your father? Any interesting stories?'

Duncan took a sip of tea. 'My dad worked as a mechanic. When I was little, he started investing – small stuff at first. Corner shops, local garages, places like that. We weren't posh, but we got by alright. Working-class, y'know? He wanted to build something long-term ... something stable for us.'

'I see – a clever plan. Did you benefit from it?'

Sara nodded. 'Yeah, we did get some money from his investments, but things shifted after the split. Money became less reliable. Juggling work and Duncan was tough. Luckily, Konrad stepped in to help out with Duncan while I was at work. Without him, I doubt I could've managed raising Duncan at all.'

Duncan grinned. 'Uncle Konrad was great. He taught me a lot, especially about fishing and baseball.'

Elisa's frown persisted as she reiterated, 'Baseball? It is not a widely popular sport in Flora.'

Duncan's smile remained as he revisited cherished memories. 'True, in Kingsgury, baseball had its own following. We'd gather at the park with makeshift bases. Uncle Konrad would pitch, I'd swing the bat or catch with a glove. Sometimes, I'd pretend to score a home run, Konrad chasing. We had comical moments, too. Once, we collided, ended up laughing. Good times.' Duncan chuckled softly.

With a touch of longing, he went on. 'Uncle Konrad gifted me a baseball with his signature. It's special to me, though I regret not having it here to show you. It's at my house.'

'Ah, how fascinating ... It's evident that you held a deep fondness for Konrad.'

Sara explained, 'Konrad and my husband, Jon, were best friends. That's why Duncan calls him "Uncle Konrad".'

Elisa nodded, saying, 'I see. Sometimes bonds go beyond family ties.'

Duncan added, 'Yeah, but unfortunately, he left us later on. He wanted to make a positive impact on the world.'

'What did he decide to do?'

'He aimed to help with the Kingsgurian and Citran conflict. He went to Citra to work on a peaceful resolution with their government.' Duncan sighed. 'I just want the war to end ... It's been years since I've seen Uncle Konrad. I miss him.'

'Sometimes, we have to let go of those close to us,' Sara said sadly, holding her teacup.

'Yeah ...' Duncan responded, looking at his plate, lost in thought.

Elisa empathised. 'I'm sorry to hear that. Hopefully, you and Uncle Konrad will reunite someday.'

Duncan nodded.

Elisa then asked another question. 'I find myself pondering, if I may inquire ... what was the cause behind your parents' separation? Was there a disagreement of sorts?'

The question landed with a quiet thud in Duncan's chest.

Why would she bring that up all of a sudden?

His jaw tightened slightly, though he masked it with a calm expression. Inside, however, his thoughts churned. He had already given her a partial answer earlier, hoping it would be enough to satisfy whatever curiosity drove her. Evidently, it hadn't.

The remnants of his earlier conversation with Sara still lingered – a bitter aftertaste he hadn't yet managed to shake. Now, Elisa's persistence felt like she was peeling back a scab that hadn't quite healed – pressing into memories he'd deliberately buried.

Why couldn't she just leave it? Why couldn't she recognise the lines he'd drawn – gently, even politely – and choose not to cross them?

Sara, sensing the shift in the air, took a moment before answering.

'Well, it's a bit complicated,' she began delicately. 'We did have our differences, and at the time, it seemed like the best course of action for both of us was to take some time apart. My husband needed space to sort things out, and he felt that it was necessary for me and Duncan to be on our own during that period.'

Duncan glanced at Elisa, his voice even but tight. 'Does that answer your question?'

'To an extent,' Elisa responded, her gaze thoughtful. 'However, this doesn't quite elucidate the reason for his absence. It leaves me rather puzzled.'

He shifted in his seat – the air suddenly too still, too sharp. 'Elisa, I'd rather not dwell on that event, and I think my mum feels the same way. We'd prefer to keep it in the past.'

'Understood,' Elisa replied gently.

'By the way, Duncan, I forgot to mention. I have a new job,' said Sara.

'Really?'

Sara nodded. 'Yes, I'm now a receptionist at The Royalists, a postal service company.'

Duncan gave her a small smile. 'I see ... It's better than working at that café, right? You don't have to wipe the tables because of those tosspots spilling their beverages recklessly.'

'Watch your language, Duncan.'

'Sorry, Mum.'

'But you're right, people should clean up after themselves. Just because they're not employees doesn't mean they can leave a mess. I'm tired of cleaning up for them. I'm almost forty-five – they should think about my health.'

Duncan smirked. 'Looks like me leaving the house was a good call. Like they say, "You can't make an omelette without breaking some eggs".'

'It's not a perfect choice because I miss seeing my boy often. But as you said, it's like the omelette situation.' She continued. 'I should count myself fortunate, though, that they had a spot for me. Getting a job these days is tough due to the civil war in Flora. The employment rate is dropping, and the Floran army needs new recruits.' Sara sighed and turned to Elisa, asking, 'So, Elisa, do you have a job?'

Elisa gently shook her head as she chewed a bite of food. 'If you are referring to a full-time occupation, the answer is no. I did, however, engage in part-time employment for a local shopkeeper who is associated with a bakery establishment. But during my days with Archer, the demands of high school did consume much of my time.'

Sara's curiosity was piqued as she took another bite of her fried fish. 'High school? Did ya graduate?'

Elisa nodded. 'Indeed, I did – approximately a year ago. Archer, my guardian, was not affluent. After losing his position as a journalist, we struggled financially and moved frequently between rented lodgings. Still, he selflessly gave what little he had so I could attend high school. Regrettably, his resources could not extend to a university education. I had hoped to become a politician, to serve alongside the ministers of the Floran Government – but such a path demands a degree.'

Sara looked intrigued and said, 'Politician, huh? That's an interesting career – you wanna help manage the country?'

Duncan grabbed his chin. 'To enter a university, you would be required to pay the tuition fee.'

Elisa nodded. 'Yes ... Archer had been considering a way, but with his passing, I fear that shall not come to fruition – at least, not anytime soon.'

'So, don't you have any relatives, any friends?' Sara asked.

'Relatives? I know little about my parents' side of the family. I do not know where they are, nor do I have their contact details.'

'Then what about friends? You gotta have some friends who could help you?' asked Sara.

'Friends? Given the circumstances of the civil war, it has been difficult to place trust in others. Many people are preoccupied with their own struggles, and it's hard to trust strangers.'

Duncan stood from his chair and grabbed his plate. 'Well, I've finished my meal.'

Sara shot him a look. 'Make sure you wash those dishes. Am I clear?'

He scratched the back of his head, muttering under his breath, 'Yeah, yeah, sure. Even though I'm not the one who used half of them ...'

Sara's scowl was swift. 'What was that?'

Duncan froze, eyes widening. 'Nothing, nothing,' he blurted, his voice tight and sheepish.

Yikes.

He hadn't expected that sharpness in her voice – not tonight, not over something so trivial. There was always a line with his mum, and somehow, without meaning to, he'd just stumbled over it. For all her quirks and jokes, when she put that tone on ... she could still make him feel like a guilty ten-year-old. It was humbling. And a little terrifying.

Thankfully, her glare softened a moment later. She turned to Elisa with a warm smile.

'Elisa, after you finish your meal, feel free to settle in. I know it's not much for now, but you can rest while we sort out your room tomorrow.'

'Thank you, Mrs Saul,' Elisa said politely.

As the household quietened and everyone retreated to their rooms, Elisa turned her attention to the modest suitcase resting at the foot of her bed. She knelt beside it and unfastened the latches, unpacking each item with meticulous care. There wasn't much – just the essentials. Her handbag, a small mirror, her make-up box, digital camera, reading glasses, and a slim selection of books and magazines, among them a worn photo book whose pages had been thumbed through many times.

She then laid out her clothing with the same quiet precision: a straw hat with a fraying ribbon, a yellow jumper, a crimson blazer, an olive-green skirt, a pair of blue jeans, her light blue nightdress, and two pairs of shoes – brown leather flats and white sneakers. It was a simple collection, far from the extravagance she had once been accustomed to, but she found no resentment in that. In truth, she welcomed the simplicity.

As she smoothed the creases from the last garment, her hand brushed against something at the bottom of the case – a photograph. She froze. Carefully, she lifted it out.

It was a candid snapshot, faded around the edges. Two young girls stood side by side, their arms linked and smiles bright. The girl beside her had the same auburn hair, the same delicate jawline.

Her sister.

Elisa's chest tightened, a hollow stirring within her – not a memory, but its shadow. The girl's smile was too familiar, yet distant, like a borrowed glimpse from another life. The longer she stared, the more the memory blurred, like mist slipping through her grasp.

She stood there, silent, the photo trembling slightly in her hand.

A voice interrupted the stillness.

'So, how're you liking the place so far?'

Startled, Elisa let out a soft gasp, swiftly hiding the photograph behind a book. She turned towards the door. Duncan stood there, leaning against the frame of his old room, arms folded casually, his expression unreadable.

'I … It is rather lovely, thank you,' she replied, attempting composure. Her fingers twitched slightly as she set the book down. 'You both needn't have gone through such trouble on my behalf …'

Duncan shrugged. His voice was calm but firm. 'I did it because I wanted to. I can't just leave someone without a carer or a roof over their head, you know? It doesn't sit right with my conscience. My dad taught me, "Help those who are in need and do whatever you can to put their lives in front of yours. Do whatever you can to survive so that you can keep doing what you're doing."'

Elisa studied him for a quiet moment, her expression softening. There was sincerity in his words – not rehearsed, but lived.

'Your father's wisdom and intelligence are truly evident in his teachings,' she said gently.

Duncan's gaze drifted slightly, his posture shifting as though weighed by something unseen. 'Yeah, he had his moments,' he murmured. There was a flicker of something fragile in his voice – grief, perhaps, or nostalgia.

'Just so you're aware,' he added, 'helping people is what I do.'

Elisa offered a thoughtful nod. She believed him.

'Anyhow, I'll let you get settled in. You have a good night, Elisa.'

'Yes, indeed. Thank you,' she replied with quiet grace, watching as he disappeared down the hallway.

Only once he was gone did she turn back to the photo, her fingers brushing the edge of it. The smile in the image had not changed – but she had.

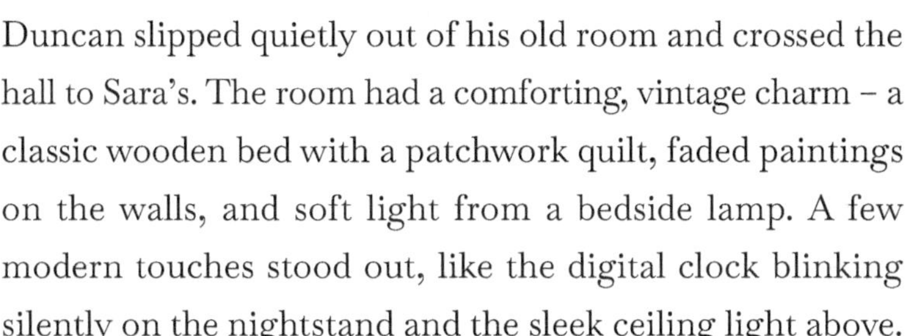

Duncan slipped quietly out of his old room and crossed the hall to Sara's. The room had a comforting, vintage charm – a classic wooden bed with a patchwork quilt, faded paintings on the walls, and soft light from a bedside lamp. A few modern touches stood out, like the digital clock blinking silently on the nightstand and the sleek ceiling light above.

Sara lay resting, her hair loose around her face, the yellow nightdress soft against the bedcovers. She looked peaceful until she noticed him standing in the doorway, then smiled gently.

'It's been a while since you dropped by like this,' she said softly.

'Yeah,' Duncan agreed, his voice low.

Sara shifted, propping her head on the pillow. 'Can I ask you something?'

Duncan nodded, waiting.

'Did you come to see me mainly because of that girl, Elisa?'

His eyes dropped. The weight of the question settled heavily in his chest. 'Mostly, yes ... I wish I could visit more often. Especially if Dad were still here.'

Sara sighed, her tone steady but firm. 'Even if he were here, it wouldn't fix everything, Duncan. It can't make up for the years we lost. You have to focus on your future, not the past. Jon is gone. And even if he wasn't, would it really change much?'

Her words hit a truth he'd lived with every day – no amount of wishing could bring Jon back. The absence was a hole that swallowed years and hope alike.

'Of course it would,' Duncan murmured, voice thick with longing. 'If he were here ... birthdays would feel like they used to. If I got married, he'd be there, proud, smiling with the guests.'

Sara sat up a little, eyes soft but firm. 'You say that a lot, but we've managed without him. You've done so much

– finished school, military training, the reserves, even the police. I'm working a normal job now, too. Jon would be proud, just like me.'

Duncan's gaze flickered away, caught between memory and doubt. He pictured his father beside him at those moments, the warmth of his smile, the pride in his eyes. But sometimes, he wondered if he was clinging to an ideal – romanticising a man who maybe wasn't perfect. Would things really be better? Or was it just easier to think that way?

Sara's voice pulled him back. 'Duncan, you're stronger than you realise. You've had to grow up faster than most. You don't need him here to take care of yourself.'

He met her eyes, trying to steady the swirl of feelings inside.

'It's time to stop putting your father at the centre of everything. What do you want? What makes you happy?'

Duncan's jaw set. 'I'm tired of feeling stuck. I want to be a hero – something more than just Jon's son. I want to find whoever hurt him and make sure they pay.'

Sara's concern softened her words. 'And if you don't? If you never find the culprit?'

He swallowed hard. 'Then ... I don't know. I'd feel like everything was for nothing. Like I have no reason to keep living.'

'Don't say that,' she said firmly. 'No matter what, never give up hope. It's what keeps us moving forward.'

Duncan fell silent. He stared at his hands – bruised knuckles, scars that never quite faded. *Hope.* He wanted to believe in it, but most days it felt like a story other people were strong enough to live. For him, there was just this – an empty space where his father should have been, a weight he had never learned how to put down. He wished someone would tell him how to stop hurting … how to stop feeling as if half of him had been buried with Jon. But the words never came.

His voice softened, a flicker of vulnerability showing through. 'I just wanted … to see you and Dad together again. To save him. To be a family again.' He took her hand gently, eyes pleading. 'Imagine that, Mum. Us, happy.'

Sara smiled, a warmth in her gaze. 'I'm already happy. Having you here, alive and well, that's enough for me. Don't live in the past. Keep moving forward – who knows what good things might come.'

Duncan said nothing more, the room quiet except for their breathing.

'Now, get some rest,' Sara urged.

'Alright. Good night, Mum.'

'Good night, Duncan.'

He left the room and made his way downstairs. Stripping to his underwear, he wrapped a blanket around himself and settled onto the sofa.

All was still, all was quiet.

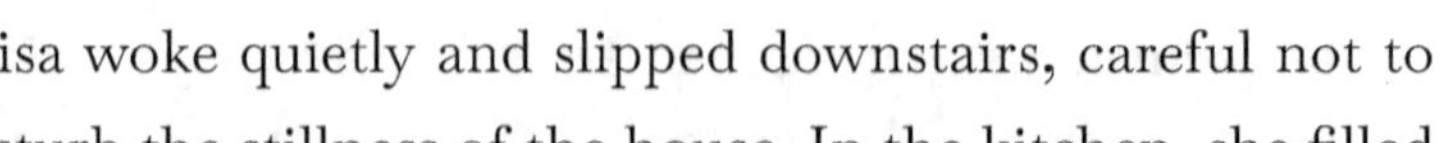

Elisa woke quietly and slipped downstairs, careful not to disturb the stillness of the house. In the kitchen, she filled a glass with water, her fingers trembling slightly as she brought it to her lips. Then, faintly, she caught the sound – a murmuring, breathless and broken.

'No … no … I'm so sorry …'

Drawn by the anguish in the voice, Elisa followed the whisper through the dim hallway. There, she found Duncan, tossing restlessly in his sleep, his brow furrowed in torment.

'I'm sorry I couldn't save you, Dad. I regret not being able to help.'

The words slipped from his lips, raw and haunted. Elisa's breath caught. Such a confession – so vulnerable – was not the man she had met during the day.

Her heart constricted. She had not expected this moment to reach so far beneath the surface of their acquaintance. Her mind raced, weaving his pain with threads of her own buried memories – echoes of grief she had long tried to suppress.

What had befallen his father? What horrors had shaped the man before her?

The questions weighed heavily on her. Feeling the chill of the night air, Elisa retreated silently to her bedroom, her eyes lingering on Duncan. The sorrow in his sleep clung to her like a shadow – and she knew that this fragile glimpse of his true self would not soon fade.

Duncan faced a terrible nightmare. He was drowning in darkness.

It pressed in on him like a living thing, thick and suffocating, pinning his limbs and stealing his breath. He tried to move, to speak, but fear held him fast. He was alone – utterly, violently alone – until a shape tore itself out of the void.

His father's head hovered before him. Jon's severed neck smouldered, his eyes burning like embers in a dying fire.

'You failed to stop me,' Jon hissed. 'The culprit is still out there. You have found nothing. Absolutely nothing. What kind of son are you?'

The words pierced him like blades. 'I am trying, Father,' Duncan choked. 'I *am* trying. I will find them – I swear I will.'

'Your efforts amount to nothing!' Jon's voice exploded through the darkness, shaking the ground beneath Duncan's feet. 'I am gone because of you. You swore you would rescue me. Ten years, Duncan. Ten years – and what have you done?'

'I … I …' The words dissolved on his tongue. His mind scrambled, desperate, ashamed.

Jon's voice pressed on, relentless. 'Who dressed you when you were small? Who kept you warm when you were sick? Who protected you? *Me*. And for what? A son who cannot even avenge me?'

The accusation crushed him. Duncan tried to speak, to defend himself, but guilt choked every breath.

'If you cannot finish what you started,' Jon thundered, 'then you do not deserve to live another day. Go. Avenge me. Or I cast you out as no son of mine.'

Jon's features cracked, splintered, and drifted away in a cloud of ash, his burning eyes the last to fade.

The darkness collapsed inward.

Duncan fell to his knees as the world quaked around him. His chest heaved. Hot tears spilled down his face as he struck the unseen ground, each blow a desperate attempt to silence the guilt clawing its way through him – guilt that felt more real than the air he breathed.

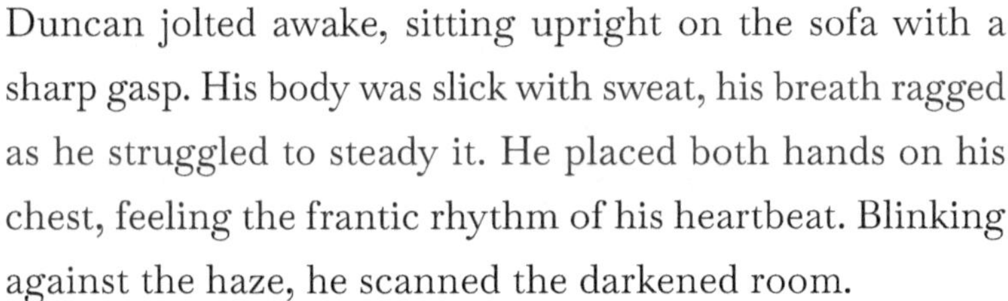

Duncan jolted awake, sitting upright on the sofa with a sharp gasp. His body was slick with sweat, his breath ragged as he struggled to steady it. He placed both hands on his chest, feeling the frantic rhythm of his heartbeat. Blinking against the haze, he scanned the darkened room.

Frustration surged through him. He struck the armrest with his fist, teeth clenched as he muttered under his breath, 'Every day, the same torment … Why did he have to leave? Why him? I don't deserve any of this …'

Tears streamed down his face, and he wept, letting out the pent-up emotions. He wiped his tears away, his expression hardening with determination.

'No more. Father, I'll find you, and that heretic will pay for what he's done.'

Chapter IX

SETTING UP

A man entered the Yellow Bull, his identity hidden beneath a long black overcoat, a brown check flat cap, and a dark green scarf that veiled the lower half of his face. He moved with quiet intent, eyes sweeping the lobby. At the reception desk, a woman was recording the names of arriving guests.

Hands tucked into his coat pockets, he slipped past unnoticed and entered the lift. He pressed the button marked '6' and waited in silence.

When the doors opened, he spotted a maintenance worker heading down the corridor. He followed at a distance. Partway along, the man removed a shoe – his motives unclear – and watched as the worker unlocked the boiler room.

Just as the door began to swing shut, he slipped his gloved hand between the frame and used the shoe to wedge it open. The worker, distracted while lowering his toolbox, was caught in a shaft of unexpected light and faltered.

The man struck. With a swift motion, he drew a metal wrench from beneath his coat and brought it down hard on the worker's head. The blow landed with a sickening crack, blood splattering the tiles as the man slumped to the floor with a groan.

Without hesitation, the attacker pocketed the keys, dragged the unconscious body to a nearby storage cupboard, and locked the door.

In the boiler room, he opened his briefcase. Inside was a glass jar swarming with peculiar, bee-like insects – their eyes glowing red. Locating the nearest air vent, he unscrewed the cover and released the swarm. The creatures vanished into the ducts.

He sealed the case, turned on his heel, and disappeared.

A lone staff member at the Yellow Bull was quietly enjoying a coffee. It seemed the other workers had either left for the day or were occupied elsewhere in the building. He sipped his coffee, pausing as a curious sensation tickled his neck. Frowning, he swatted it and found a crushed insect on his palm. 'A bee?' he said, perplexed.

This odd incident set off alarm bells in his mind. Suddenly, a sharp pain coursed through him and he began to cry out in torment. His body underwent a horrifying transformation: veins protruded and his skin turned a dark shade of grey. Seizures wracked his body as he collapsed, and white foam frothed in his mouth, as if his life had been taken.

Moments later, the victim's sclera blazed with a fiery red colour. He rose abruptly from the ground, no longer a man but a cannibalistic creature – a ghoul. Saliva dripped from the ghoul's mouth, its insatiable hunger for human blood and flesh evident.

Another employee, a woman, entered the room, calling out, 'Mr Ross?' But Mr Ross had now transformed into a ghoul. Swiftly turning his head, he emitted a vicious growl. The woman shrieked in terror, but it was too late. The ghoul lunged at her, forcefully bringing her down to the floor. In a grisly display, he bit into her neck, tearing flesh from bone. The woman gurgled blood, her life slipping away as the ghoul satisfied its gruesome hunger.

Another employee arrived at the scene, alarmed by the screams he had heard. He immediately noticed the woman on the floor being attacked by the ghoul. Shocked, he took a step back, his eyes widening. 'What the fuck!? A ghoul, here in this building?' he exclaimed.

The woman who had been attacked by the ghoul was transforming into one herself, confirming that the bite had caused this gruesome change. She stood up, a chunk of flesh missing from her neck, and staggered towards the man, hacking and shrieking.

Panicked, the employee fled, determined to call for help. He quickly dialled the emergency number, typing into his smartphone.

'F-one-one-two, what's your emergency?' asked a concerned voice on the other end of the line.

'Hello, there are ghouls attacking people in the building!' the employee said, his voice trembling with fear. 'You need to—'

Suddenly, the employee spotted another ghoul within the building. The ghoul moaned and slowly approached him. The two that had been chasing him closed in as well. The man was now surrounded, shouting at the approaching ghouls. 'Woah! Woah! Stay away from me, stay the fuck away from me!'

The woman on the phone repeated her question, sounding increasingly concerned. *'Sir, what's wrong?'*

The man's urgency grew as he screamed into the phone. 'Please help! You've gotta come to the Yellow Bull building, now!'

Amid the chaos, one of the ghouls pounced on the victim, sinking its teeth into his shoulder. The other ghouls joined in, tearing at his flesh. The victim's agonising screams echoed through the room until he could scream no more.

The woman on the phone kept pleading. *'Sir, please respond. Sir? Sir!?'* But there was no response. And thus, the scene of that night concluded, leaving a chilling sense of terror in its wake.

As the morning light filtered through the windows, Duncan stirred on the sofa, groaning softly as he rubbed the sleep from his eyes. His body ached from the awkward night's rest. Glancing down, he noticed he was half-dressed and reached for his clothes – his worn blue jeans and the familiar dark grey wolf T-shirt he liked so much.

Once dressed, he stretched with a grunt, loosening the stiffness in his back. A sound from the kitchen caught his attention – the clatter of utensils, the soft hiss of the cooker. Curious, he wandered over and pushed the door open.

Inside, Sara and Elisa stood at the stove, each wearing aprons and mismatched slippers. Something sizzled gently in a saucepan. The warm scent of butter and batter filled the air.

Elisa turned at the sound of the door, offering a graceful smile. 'Good morning, Mr Saul.'

'Good morning, Elisa,' Duncan replied, mirroring her smile.

'Good morning, Duncan,' said his mother.

'Morning, Mum.'

'Did ya sleep well?' Sara asked.

Duncan pursed his lips, his face showing the opposite answer.

'I made pancakes.'

'Pancakes? My favourite,' Duncan said, his mood lifting.

'With delicious golden syrup,' Sara added, beaming.

'Sounds scrumptious.' Duncan approached her and observing said, 'Elisa, working on the batter?'

Elisa, trying her hardest to mix the dough together, replied, 'Of course. I'm going to make sure to impress Mrs Saul a second time with my cooking.'

Duncan couldn't resist a playful tease, folding his arms. 'Doing whatever you can to help the Saul family? If we had you as our personal assistant, I would gladly pay you a fortune.'

Elisa blushed as she smiled and looked aside, tucking a strand of hair behind her ear. Seeing her cheeks turning a delicate shade of pink warmed Duncan's heart.

There was an endearing quality to her earnestness and the way she responded to his teasing. It made the morning feel lighter, offering a brief but welcome respite from his constant worries.

Breakfast was served, and everyone took their seats, picking up their knives and forks. As they ate their pancakes, the television played quietly in the background, tuned to a news broadcasting channel. The programme highlighted a pressing issue with bold on-screen graphics: *THE INVESTIGATION OF THE GHOUL OUTBREAK IN THE YELLOW BULL BUILDING.*

The segment opened with a middle-aged presenter in a sharp black suit and glasses.

'Good morning, people of Flora. I am your host, Howard Peterson.'

Howard continued, his tone steady. *'Breaking news. An incident occurred last night at the Yellow Bull Building. Twenty-seven individuals within the Yellow Bull Company were transformed into cannibalistic creatures known as ghouls.'*

At the word 'ghouls', Elisa's head snapped towards the television, her face frozen in shock. Her heart pounded, her hands beginning to tremble. That word alone had opened a floodgate – memories she had long buried came rushing back with brutal clarity.

'Twelve were employees and fifteen were civilians. Furthermore, during the event, a CCTV camera inside the building captured live footage. We will show it now. Viewer discretion is advised.'

The broadcast then played the CCTV footage, relaying the harrowing events of that night. Elisa braced herself.

A female reporter soon took over, delving into the finer details of the investigation. Duncan and Sara sat quietly, listening intently. When the segment ended, an uneasy silence hung in the room.

Elisa remained motionless, lost in thought. Duncan's voice broke through the haze.

'Hey, Elisa – you alright?'

'Y–yes, I'm fine,' she said, forcing a smile. She hoped it would mask the ache twisting inside her, but Duncan frowned and Sara's concerned gaze lingered. Her attempt at composure felt painfully thin.

Duncan stood and stretched. 'Alright, looks like there's work for me.'

Sara's smile dimmed. 'I'm guessing you've got to leave soon.'

He looked to her with regret. 'I know it's not what you want to hear, but I've got to do my bit for Flora. It's my duty.'

Sara nodded, pride softening her disappointment. 'So long as your heart's in the right place, I understand. I'm proud to have a son like you – someone who looks out for others. It truly means something.'

Duncan gave a brief chuckle. 'Thanks, Mum.'

Elisa, rising from her seat, glanced towards him. 'Will you be gone long, Mr Saul?'

Duncan, now shrugging on his blue jacket, looked back with a small frown. 'Maybe. Why d'you ask?'

Blushing, Elisa lowered her gaze and toyed nervously with the edge of her sleeve. She wondered whether he'd be open to knowing her better – perhaps even as a friend. Swallowing her nerves, she forced herself to speak. Her voice came out quiet, unsure.

'I was hoping that, perhaps, as friends, we might spend some time together – to become better acquainted.'

Her heart thudded in her chest. Since their first meeting, Duncan's warmth had cooled. He had grown more distant, and she feared she had misunderstood his interest.

Duncan regarded her, expression unreadable.

'I'll consider it,' he said evenly. 'I'll let you know when I've got some time.'

His answer made her blink. He hadn't refused. Her chest swelled with something close to disbelief. 'R–really?'

'Yes – but no promises,' Duncan replied.

Still, that was enough. 'Okay. That's good enough for me.'

Hours passed, and Duncan was prepared to depart, his backpack over his shoulder. Elisa and Sara stood by the house, preparing to say their goodbyes.

Sara began. 'So, you're leaving now?'

Duncan nodded, a hint of sadness in his response. 'Yes, I am.'

'Wait, before you go …' Sara said, interrupting his departure. She walked up to him and embraced him tightly, a small smile on her face. As she hugged him, she spoke sincerely. 'Please, Duncan … You're the only person left in my life, and I don't want to lose you. Please stay safe for me.'

'Mum, I won't die. I still have unfinished business to attend to. That heretic is still out there, and I won't rest until I eliminate him,' he replied, determination in his eyes.

Sara held his cheek, looking closely at him. 'Look … No matter how strong you are, you still have limits.'

'I'm aware of that. That's why I'll give it my all before I reach my limit,' Duncan assured her. Sara paused, and he offered a reassuring smile to cheer her up. 'Don't worry,

Mum. I'll be back before you know it. I'd like to have more of those pancakes you and Elisa made. They were delicious.'

'That warms my heart. It means you'll visit more often,' Sara replied, giving her son a kiss on the cheek before releasing him.

'Yeah.' Duncan smiled.

'Thank you, but I should thank Elisa for that. From the way it looks, I think she likes you.'

'What?' Duncan frowned, surprised by the revelation.

'Yeah, she blushes bright red whenever you're around or when you praise her,' Sara said playfully.

While Sara went on about Elisa's reactions, Duncan's attention began to drift. He couldn't deny the truth in her words, recalling the times he had been aware of the noticeable blush on Elisa's cheeks in his presence. However, his focus right now was on his duties as a mercenary, his responsibility for Flora's safety and the broader concerns that occupied his mind.

'Okay ...?' Duncan looked aside, his reaction rather impassive.

'I thought you'd have a better response than that. It would make up for that girl you had a crush on in middle school.' Sara pouted, sounding disappointed.

Duncan maintained a stern expression as he looked at his mother. 'Mum, I'm a grown man now and that girl's long gone. Besides, I'm not interested in dating people. Don't get me wrong, Elisa's a sweet girl, but I don't think we'd be a good match. I'm a mercenary and she's just a civilian.'

His point was valid. Duncan remained practical, recognising the clear distinctions between their lives. He was deeply involved in a dangerous profession, while Elisa was an innocent civilian entangled in the turmoil of war. Though she was beautiful, the question of whether they were truly compatible lingered.

'Yeah, but despite all that, she still seems to admire you, especially after you saved her life,' Sara reassured Duncan.

'That reminds me ...' Duncan's tone grew more sincere as he turned to his mother. 'Please don't tell her what happened to my father. I'm not ready to share that with someone I've only just met.' He looked away, unease written plainly on his face.

'What? Why?' Sara asked, perplexed.

'Because ... once you tell her, she'll bring it up – and it's something I'd rather not dwell on. It reminds me I failed to catch the culprit. My father's still missing, and that arsehole's likely still out there causing harm.'

'Look, none of that is on you,' Sara reassured Duncan, speaking sincerely. 'Why hold it in? Why not share it? Elisa has experienced loss, too – she might understand.'

'Mum!' Duncan snapped before quickly lowering his tone. 'I just ... I just need some time, okay.'

Duncan's attempt to shield Elisa made him question whether he was partly to blame. Her constant probing unsettled him – as if she had no sense of boundaries.

Sara recognised the expression on Duncan's face. 'Alright ...'

'Thank you,' he replied.

Once their conversation was concluded, Duncan walked over to Elisa and handed her his business card. 'Before I leave ... Elisa, here's my business card.'

Elisa accepted the card from Duncan, inspecting the details closely. The business card provided a clear overview of Duncan's professional identity:

CENTURION ARMS

Duncan Saul

Freelance Mercenary

Contact:

+555 871 790 330

Experience:

3 Years of Professional Service

Duncan took a moment to explain his purpose of giving the card to Elisa. 'If you need anything, just give me a call, and I'll let you know when I'm available.'

'Okay, Mr Saul. I'll keep that in mind,' Elisa replied.

Duncan smiled. 'Alright, I'll be on my way now. Take care, both of you.'

'Stay safe, Duncan.' Sara smiled back.

'Goodbye, Mr Saul.' Elisa waved.

With that, Duncan left the Saul residence, making his exit.

Chapter X

HELP FROM A FRIEND

After Duncan's departure, Elisa withdrew to her room. A subtle transformation had taken place – it was now a simple yet practical space, tailored for one. A functional desk stood against the wall, paired with a leather swivel chair. Upon it sat a small lamp, a neat stack of study books, a few pencil holders and a pair of blue wired headphones.

The bed – a modest white futon – completed the arrangement. Though the room lacked character, it felt far more inviting than its former emptiness.

Lying back on the futon, Elisa opened her book, allowing herself to be drawn into its quiet world. The silence was a comfort. She now wore glasses – a recent change – which, to the observant eye, lent her a softer, more studious charm.

As Elisa continued to read, Sara quietly entered the room. Elisa felt her presence and glanced back, spotting Sara at the doorway wearing a warm smile.

'Mrs Saul?' Elisa inquired, intrigued by Sara's excited expression.

With a playful smile, Sara beckoned Elisa to stand up. 'Come on, young missy, we're going out today.'

Elisa furrowed her brow, naturally curious. 'Very well, but might I inquire about our destination?'

Sara's arms spread wide, exuding joy as she explained her intentions. 'We're going on a tour of the University of Kate, and I want you to be my first guest for the ride.'

Elisa's confusion persisted. 'I appreciate the gesture, but may I ask why, Mrs Saul?'

Sara's confidence was noticeable as she held her hands on her hips. 'Because, my dear, we're setting you on the path to becoming a politician.'

Elisa couldn't help but feel bewildered by the unexpected response. 'That's quite a leap. But, Mrs Saul, what about the funds for the tuition fee?'

'Don't fret, I've got that covered. I'll head to the bank and secure a loan for half of the twenty-five thousand Livres. Once I have that, I'll kindly ask Duncan to contribute the other half.'

The notion that someone she had just met would go to such lengths on her behalf left Elisa blinking in surprise. It was hard for her to fathom the depth of kindness Sara was displaying.

Elisa's confusion lifted slightly, but she remained uncertain. 'Do you think he'll agree to that, Mrs Saul?'

Sara performed a raspberry sound and scoffed. 'I know my son. He would never say no to this. Alright, kid, let's go,' Sara declared.

Elisa's excitement bubbled over at the prospect of pursuing her dream role. Overcome with gratitude, she threw her arms around Sara in a spontaneous embrace. For a brief moment, joy eclipsed her usual reserve.

But Sara's body stiffened.

Elisa noticed the change at once and let go, a flush of embarrassment rising to her cheeks.

'I apologise, Mrs Saul,' she said with a nervous yet polite smile.

'It's alright,' Sara said with a soft smile. 'Now, let's get ready and change before we head out.'

'Okay, Mrs Saul.' Elisa nodded.

With that, the two changed quickly and then set off in Sara's car towards the University of Kate.

Duncan rapped on the door, and it swung open moments later.

'Jénmar, it's Duncan,' he greeted, a warm smile lighting up his face.

Standing in the doorway was Hendrik Jénmar, the hacker who could slip through firewalls like water through cracks. His dark brown hair, long enough to brush his chin, framed his face in a tousled, effortless style. The thick moustache and pointy goatee added a rugged charm, but Duncan knew there was more to him than the tattoos, gold earrings, and eclectic wardrobe that mixed street-smart with a touch of class.

Jénmar appeared older than Duncan, but their history was clear in the space between them – a quiet understanding built over years of working in the world's messier corners. To Duncan, Jénmar wasn't just a hacker; he was a reliable ally, someone who knew the rules of the game and when to break them.

Jénmar's face lit up with a big smile as he pulled Duncan into a warm hug. 'Hey, Duncan, great to see you! How's life treating you?' he asked, giving Duncan's back a friendly pat.

Duncan mirrored the warmth in his smile. 'Doing well, thanks.'

Jénmar stepped back. 'So, what brings you here?'

Duncan got right to the point, his expression focused. 'I'm here about the ghoul case, and I need your help.'

Jénmar's manner shifted, his face turning serious as he gave Duncan a thoughtful look. 'I had a feeling it might be that ... Come on in.' He opened the door wider.

In his cosy living room, Jénmar made coffee for both of them. The smell of the fresh brew filled the air as he put the mugs on the table and sat down, taking a sip of his own. 'What's your plan?' asked Jénmar as he leant on the sofa.

Duncan replied, 'I'll start at the Yellow Bull Company, gather info on the culprit. When I have leads, I'll share the suspects' names with you.'

Jénmar placed his mug down. 'So, you want me to research and find where these people are?'

'Yes, please gather any useful info you can. Once I've got the names and locations, we'll be able to interrogate them. But I'll start with the one who seems most suspicious to me.'

Jénmar raised an eyebrow. 'So, what method are you going to use? Torture?'

Duncan took a sip of his coffee and met Jénmar with a smile. 'You would like that, wouldn't you?'

Jénmar couldn't help but chuckle. 'You know me well.'

Duncan's tone shifted back to one of seriousness. 'Jénmar, I know you enjoy that approach, but we use it only when we're sure someone's guilty. I prefer the peaceful way.'

Jénmar got up from his chair, seeming content with the response. 'Alright, I respect that. It's settled, then.'

Duncan smiled with appreciation. 'Knew I could rely on you, Jénmar.'

Jénmar stopped and pointed his index finger in the air. 'Wait, before we continue. About your mother?'

Duncan looked at him suspiciously, not knowing where this conversation was going. 'Yeah, what about her ...?'

'I hope she's doing okay ...'

'Yeah, she's fine ...' Duncan folded his arms and replied, 'She gotta new job at a postal company.'

Jénmar also folded his arms and smiled, impressed. 'A postal company? That's wonderful to hear – it's good to know that she is handling herself well. But I was wondering if she was available because she needs a real man by her side ... I'm talking about me, of course.'

Duncan rolled his eyes. 'Ugh. If you're about to make flirty remarks about my mother, spare me, please.'

Jénmar chuckled. 'Alright, but I must say, she has some fantastic genes to look like that at her age.'

Duncan stood up immediately and narrowed his eyes. 'I'm leaving now.'

'Wait before you go, I have gift for you.'

Duncan raised an eyebrow. 'What kinda gift?'

'Stay right here,' Jénmar replied, heading to a storage area.

Jénmar returned with a sizeable briefcase, setting it on the table. Duncan approached cautiously, inspecting the briefcase before giving Jénmar a questioning look.

With a friendly grin, Jénmar gestured for Duncan to open it. 'Go on, take a look.'

Duncan proceeded to open the briefcase reveal a sniper rifle. He raised an eyebrow, clearly taken aback by the weapon before him. 'Oh?'

Jénmar couldn't hide his enthusiasm. 'Allow me to introduce the SVU sniper rifle!'

This was not any sniper rifle – it was a rare, finely built Dragunov SVU sniper rifle with a mil-dot reticle scope and bipod attached to it. Duncan picked it up, intrigued by its design and capabilities.

'It's a significant upgrade from that old Remington Model rifle. That thing's rusty and nowhere near as powerful as this beauty,' Jénmar said, a confident smirk on his face.

Duncan carefully examined the sniper rifle, feeling the weight in his hands. It was substantial but well-balanced, making it manageable for him to wield. As he inspected the rifle more closely, he noticed the high-quality texture, indicating the weapon's premium craftsmanship. It was evident that this rifle came at a significant price. He adjusted the scope, peering through it with his right eye. There, he noticed numerical markings alongside the scope's usual reticle, indicating precise measurements.

Jénmar nodded. 'Yes, it's quite versatile. The button makes it easy to switch between night and thermal vision, enhancing your adaptability in different scenarios.'

Duncan swiftly toggled between the two visions, experiencing the world through green-tinted night vision and purple-hued thermal vision. He noted the distinct colour change in the environment and even in Jénmar's figure, with the thermal view highlighting his body heat. He removed the magazine from the rifle, examining the 7.62×54mmR bullets loaded inside.

'Jénmar, do you think silver bullets could be used with this?'

'It's a possibility, but you might need to make the bullets yourself or go with Plan B and buy them from a store.'

Duncan sighed. 'I'm not so sure about that – I don't know anywhere that sells them these days. Crafting silver bullets might be my only option.'

'If you can manage that, the rifle could come in handy for dispelling magic,' Jénmar suggested.

Duncan nodded in agreement. 'Absolutely, it's perfect for dealing with those long-ranged magic users or those who prefer to hide in the shadows.'

The gun's intricate design and advanced technology spoke of its high cost. Duncan couldn't help but wonder at its worth. Glancing at the gun, he inquired, 'Jénmar, out of curiosity, how much did this weapon set you back?'

'Bigger than my fucking balls! Seven thousand fucking Livres, that shite cost.'

Duncan's expression turned to surprise, his frown deepening. 'Wow, that much? With that kind of money, I might as well buy an estate. But when I find the time, I'll make those silver bullets for this rifle.'

Jénmar nodded, folding his arms. 'No doubt heretics will think twice when faced with that thing.'

Duncan smirked as he held the rifle and glanced at Jénmar. 'Couldn't have said it better myself.'

Chapter XI

UNIVERSITY OF KATE

Elisa and Sara stood outside the impressive grand entrance of the University of Kate. The architecture exuded classic charm, suggesting a building with a rich history spanning centuries. The windows, each a masterpiece of intricate design, glistened in the sunlight, casting a vibrant array of colours. Posters showcasing the university's offerings adorned the entrance walls.

Both Elisa and Sara had dressed impeccably, intent on making a good impression. Sara wore a light grey trench coat over a crisp white shirt, paired elegantly with jeans and white trainers. Simple yet refined, her outfit highlighted her natural beauty. Elisa sported a fashionable straw hat, adding to her stylish look. She wore a pink-striped tank top beneath a perfectly fitted red blazer, a dark green box-pleated skirt, brown boat shoes and knee-high white socks.

'Welcome to the University of Kate!' Sara exclaimed energetically, spreading her arms wide with pride.

The two entered the university through a grand main entrance, revealing a modern Renaissance interior. The walls were painted in classic brown wood tones, while the marble floor tiles were a creamy hue. Paintings adorned the walls, each depicting ancient warriors and legendary battles.

Elisa admired one portraying the epic *Battle of Ragnarök* – a war against the giants who once ruled the earth. The central figure was the colossal giant Ymir, towering with grey skin, blue tattoos and a long white beard. The humanoid races appeared tiny, like ants, beside him.

Another depicted the elven civil war between Ljósálfar and Dökkálfar, with warriors clashing fiercely. They wielded shields, swords, spears and halberds; bloodstained masks revealing the intensity of combat. The Ljósálfar wore golden, shining armour, while the Dökkálfar donned lighter armour and masks.

A regal portrait showed the King and Queen of Erdite Island seated on their thrones. Both had blonde hair and golden eyes – the king's hair cropped short, the queen's flowing long – traits inherited from those near the magical Yggdrasil tree.

Another painting featured Fenrir the Ice Wolf, a mystical white beast with golden eyes, surrounded by a snowstorm and marked by a glowing magical symbol on its face.

The university bustled with students socialising, their conversations filling the air. Overall, the space was upmarket and creatively designed, with intricately crafted materials lending a visually appealing atmosphere.

Elisa surveyed the place, gently touching her chin. 'The design here is truly impressive, and the architectural creativity is striking. This environment is vibrant, and I'm confident I'll be able to study well here.'

As they stood in the bustling surroundings of the university, Elisa couldn't shake off the nagging feeling that had settled within her. 'Although, I must admit, I feel a bit uneasy visiting places like these.'

'What do you mean?' said Sara, slightly puzzled.

'I mean, being around so many people, it makes me feel out of place,' Elisa explained.

Sara frowned.

'When I was a little girl, I used to come to places like these all the time – birthdays, weddings, vacations, family gatherings, you name it. But after the tragic incident that happened with my family, I stopped being comfortable in crowded places. My social interactions dwindled, or I should say, became less frequent.'

'It's unfortunate, but that's how life goes, doesn't it? It's so unpredictable, anything can happen in the blink of an eye. That's why we must appreciate what we have in the moment, as it could always be better or worse.'

Elisa nodded in agreement. 'Yes, Mrs Saul, I completely agree.' Elisa's unease might not have vanished completely, but knowing that someone like Sara understood and cared made all the difference, gradually easing the weight of discomfort that had settled upon her shoulders. 'So, Mrs Saul, may I ask you something? Have *you* ever been to university?'

'I started a course, but I never finished it,' Sara replied. 'I was pregnant with Duncan when I was quite young, and I couldn't manage being a student and a mother simultaneously.'

'That is certainly challenging.' Elisa sympathised.

Sara shrugged. 'Well, it is what it is. I hope you never have to face similar challenges, though. So, make your choices wisely.'

Elisa took a moment to contemplate Sara's words, then her excitement for the university returned. 'Hmm ... I feel like if I start this course, it could also be a great opportunity to make new friends. I'm eager to see who crosses my path in the future.'

'I'm sure you'll make plenty of friends. You have such a wonderful personality, and I bet boys would be smitten with you,' Sara said warmly.

Elisa blushed, feeling flattered, and timidly responded. 'You really think so, Mrs Saul?'

'Absolutely,' Sara affirmed. 'You're beautiful, well-dressed and your personality shines. I believe any boy would be lucky to have you.'

Elisa hid her face from the flattery. 'Thank you for your kind words, Mrs Saul.'

Sara waved it off. 'No need to mention it, kid.'

'Elisa! Elisa!' A young woman's voice called out, abruptly breaking through the distance.

Elisa turned to see a familiar looking girl waving at her. She had short brown hair and round glasses and was wearing a hoodie, a student ID around her neck, and jeans along with a pair of blue sneakers.

The world seemed to pause for a brief moment as the girl closed the gap between them, taking Elisa's hands in a surprisingly heartfelt gesture. Elisa's heart skipped a beat, her mind trying to process the unexpected reunion with a friendly face from her past. 'Oh, hello, Emily ... What a coincidence.'

The girl's face lit up with happiness. 'It's so good to see you, Elisa.'

Elisa returned the friendly gesture with a warm smile. 'Likewise, Emily. It's a pleasant surprise.'

As they stood there, holding hands, Elisa felt a comforting presence. Amid unfamiliar faces and the uncertainties of starting university, having an old friend by her side felt like an anchor grounding her. This unexpected reconnection reminded her she wasn't entirely alone in this new adventure.

'So, what brings you here?' Emily asked. 'Are you transferring universities?'

'No, not quite.' Elisa shook her head in response. 'This marks my first year here, actually.'

A slight frown appeared on Emily's face. 'What? How come you didn't study last year?' she asked, shocked.

Elisa sighed, running her hand through her hair. 'It's a long story.'

With a smile, Sara folded her arms in a way that showed warmth. 'Ah, so you two know each other.'

Emily reached out for a friendly handshake. 'Yeah, we were friends in high school. Emily, by the way. Nice to meet you.'

Sara reciprocated the handshake, her smile genuine. 'Sara. Pleasure's all mine.'

Emily's curiosity shifted, and she turned to Elisa. 'So, how's everything back at home? Is Archer alright?'

Elisa's expression darkened as she grappled with how to broach the difficult subject. She knew this news would come as a shock, and her heart ached at the thought of revealing the painful truth.

'Oh, that ... He died.'

Taken aback, Emily covered her mouth. 'Oh my God, I'm so sorry to hear that. I don't even know what to say. How – How did he die?'

Elisa felt her throat ache as she found herself recounting the painful details. She took a deep breath, trying to steady her voice. 'He got shot.'

'Oh, I'm so sorry. Archer was a good man ...'

Elisa raised her hand, offering a reassuring smile to Emily. 'Please, there's no need to worry. I've been fortunate to have Mrs Saul's caring support during this time.'

Sara waved her hand, a gesture of comfort.

Emily responded with a warm smile. 'That pleases me. Don't worry, I'm here if you need me.' She checked her smartphone and realised the time. 'Oh, crap!' she exclaimed. 'I'm gonna be late for class. Well, I hope I'll see you at this university soon. And once again, sorry about Archer.'

Elisa nodded, maintaining her smile. 'No worries, and do not be late for class. By the way, may we exchange contact information at some point? It would be delightful to arrange a meeting for a more extensive conversation.'

Emily smiled. 'Definitely! Here, let me give you my number.' They exchanged numbers, and Emily waved to both of them. 'Bye.'

Sara folded her arms thoughtfully. 'Well ... at least you have a friend who recognises you. You won't be lonely in this place ... a great way to start afresh.'

'I agree,' Elisa replied. 'Being acquainted with familiar faces is a good start.'

Sara and Elisa arrived at the office of the Head of Department of Politics and Law, where a man with brown hair, a moustache and a distinguished appearance welcomed them. He wore a navy blue suit with a red-striped tie and rounded black glasses.

The man introduced himself, extending his hand. 'My name is Mr Darwin. I am Head of the Department of Politics and Law.'

Elisa shook hands with Mr Darwin, displaying politeness. 'It's a pleasure to meet you, Mr Darwin. My name is Elisa Evergreen.'

Sara also greeted him with a handshake. 'Sara Saul.'

'Please, both of you, have a seat,' he said, gesturing to a couple of chairs.

The two sat down, crossing their legs as they waited to hear what Mr Darwin had to say.

Mr Darwin placed his fingertips together and began with a question. 'So, Miss Evergreen, you wish to join this academy and study politics and law?'

Elisa nodded in affirmation. 'That's correct.'

Mr Darwin got up and searched through his cabinets, finding an application form and placing it on the table. 'Alright, please fill in this form with your high school qualifications and address details. Once completed, scan it and submit it through the university's website. We'll review your application shortly and inform you if we have an available space at the university.'

'May I ask a question?' Elisa asked.

'Of course, go ahead.'

'When does the academic year for this course begin?'

'The academic year starts at the end of this summer, provided you can pay the tuition fee before then. If you manage that, we'd be pleased to have you join the university,' said Mr Darwin.

'Alright, I understand,' Elisa acknowledged.

Mr Darwin stood up, shaking hands with both of them as they prepared to leave. 'Mrs Saul, Miss Evergreen. Hopefully, we'll be seeing you at the University of Kate.'

'Okay, thank you,' Elisa replied.

Exiting the university building, Sara turned to Elisa. 'That went well ... Now, all we have left to do is get the money for your tuition fee and then you are good to go,' she said.

Elisa's mind buzzed with a mix of appreciation, confusion and a hint of self-doubt as she held her arm, her eyes studying Mrs Saul's expression for any signs of ulterior motives. She couldn't help but be sceptical about the level of effort being put into helping her enter university. Could it be that Mrs Saul saw something in her that Elisa herself hadn't fully recognised? She felt the need to address this.

'I don't want to sound ungrateful, Mrs Saul, but why are you going to all this effort to help me get into the university?'

Sara held her hips confidently and proudly explained. 'Do you really needa ask? I see your potential, kid, and it would be a shame if it went to waste. You have dreams to achieve, and I believe everyone deserves a shot at their dreams.'

Elisa's scepticism began to waver as she absorbed Mrs Saul's words. The genuine faith this woman had in Elisa's abilities was both humbling and empowering. A small but sincere smile formed on her lips, and she felt gratitude welling up within her. It was a unique feeling being recognised for something she hadn't fully embraced herself. 'Thank you, Mrs Saul, for everything.'

Sara blushed slightly, humbled by the appreciation. 'No need to thank me. Now, I'm kind of hungry. Let's grab a bite to eat. Don't worry about paying – it's on me.'

Elisa couldn't contain her excitement, clapping her hands together. 'Oh, Mrs Saul, can we go to Hamlett Sandwiches? I've been wanting their tuna sandwiches.'

'Sure, anything you want, my dear.'

Elisa's smile radiated warmth. 'I'm sure I'll have a delightful time with you, Mrs Saul.'

Sara returned her smile. 'Yes, you shall, Miss Evergreen,' she said, agreeing wholeheartedly.

Chapter XII

THREADS OF INTENT

Elisa and Sara were sitting on a park bench, enjoying the sandwiches they had bought. The beautiful scenery of green fields, trees and a tranquil lake stretched before them.

Elisa started the conversation. 'Mrs Saul, may I ask you something?'

'Hm?' Sara looked up as Elisa continued.

'How do you feel about your son having the job of a mercenary? Do you approve of him having to get his hands dirty?'

Sara shook her head. 'Not really. I hoped he'd have a better job, like an accountant or a businessman. It's a bit unsettling for my son to have such a violent job. However, he's a man now and has the right to make his own decisions. As a parent, I must support him and allow him to choose his own path as he grows.'

'I see ... I do agree with that, Mrs Saul.'

'What about you, Elisa?' Sara asked. 'Why do you want to become a politician?'

Elisa stood up, determination in her voice. 'I want to fix Flora and rid the world of corruption. I've seen a lot of tragedy in my life, and I want people to avoid these kinds of events – especially what I've personally gone through. I want to achieve my dream for Archer and for my sister's sake. I want the world to be a happier and brighter place for people.'

Sara smiled and responded, 'I see ... that's very noble of you. University will give you the foundation, but there's always more to learn. I can pick up a few extra books from the library to help you along the way.'

Elisa nodded with approval. 'That would be helpful, Mrs Saul.'

Sara then looked at Elisa and tilted her head with intrigue. 'Another thing – you do seem to like talking about Archer, Elisa. You're obviously highly fond of him. What was he like?'

Elisa blushed as she thought of Archer. 'Archer was my hero. He took care of me when I was a teenager.' She winced, gripping her arm, her discomfort evident. 'He was ... a member of Lance Sainglend's Night Hawk rebellion.'

Sara's hand flew to her chest, her face frozen in shock. 'The Kingslayer?'

Her reaction to Archer's connection with the Kingslayer sent a wave of worry through Elisa. Though she deeply respected Sara and truly valued her kindness, revealing the truth about her ties to Archer – and the Night Hawk rebellion – was no easy task. Elisa didn't know how Sara would take it, and she feared it might change the way she was seen.

But the conversation had reached a point where honesty was no longer an option. All Elisa could do now was hope Sara would understand why she had stayed silent for so long.

Elisa nodded. 'Yes.'

'Why didn't you mention this sooner?'

Elisa looked aside with a sigh. 'I was scared you might see me as a nefarious person because I was working with so-called "terrorists". Keep in mind, I wasn't allied with the Night Hawks – I just wanted to fulfil Archer's wishes.'

Sara reassured Elisa, smiling to ease her concern. 'Don't worry, Elisa, I don't see you like that. After all, it was your friend's choice to join, not yours. He believed what he thought was right, and you're not guilty of just helping him out. You did what you did as a true friend, and I think Archer would be proud.'

Elisa agreed with a warm smile. She then asked Sara a serious question. 'Tell me, Mrs Saul, in your opinion, do you consider Archer's decision to join the Night Hawks to be a misguided one or do you think he genuinely believed he was doing the right thing?'

Sara then looked down, concealed in deep thought. 'Ultimately, I can't really judge him – it was his life and he made his own choices.'

Elisa sensed Sara's irritation growing as Sara thought about the situation.

'I'm actually quite annoyed that he'd choose to work with the Night Hawks, especially knowing he had a girl to look after,' Sara said. 'Didn't he realise the risks? Why didn't he refuse that mission? Didn't he consider that you were under his care?' She sighed, trying to ease her frustration. 'Well, I can't really judge without knowing Archer's intentions or reasons for joining. Another thing – if my son hadn't been there to rescue you, where might you have ended up?'

Elisa stood there, her mind swirling with uncertainty. *Where would I have ended up?* She couldn't help but think about the different path she might have taken without Duncan's help. A cold shiver ran down her spine as she imagined the grim possibilities that could have awaited her – the terrible things the thugs were about to do before Duncan intervened. Now, she truly understood the horrors of war: the lifeless bodies, the relentless violence and the terror she had narrowly escaped.

'I can't express how grateful I am,' Elisa said. 'Your son's bravery saved me from a horrific fate. The thugs intended something unspeakable – something I'm not comfortable discussing. Without him and the shelter you offered, I might have faced far worse. Mrs Saul, you were exceptionally kind to welcome me. I feel a strong need to repay your kindness.'

She recognised their compassion had given her safety and respect, and the desire to give back weighed heavily on her. Elisa was determined to show Duncan his compassion had not gone unnoticed.

Sara smiled. 'Don't worry about it. Saving people is what my son does – he'd never leave someone in need behind. He's like a superhero. He took those ideals after my husband was—' Sara stopped herself. 'Uhhh ... never mind.'

'Was what?' Elisa inquired, curious about the unfinished thought.

Sara quickly shook her head, evading the question. 'Forget it, Elisa.'

'What is it, Mrs Saul? You can tell me.' Elisa gently pressed.

Sara hesitated, then gently deflected the conversation. 'Let's not dwell on this, Elisa. Just finish your baguette, and we'll be ready to head back home.'

As Sara stumbled over her words and changed the subject, Elisa's concern grew. There was clearly pain behind her husband's departure. Though Elisa did not wish to pry, she sensed that sharing might bring some relief – sometimes, simply having someone willing to listen can be a comfort.

Elisa decided to respect Sara's wishes and stopped questioning her further. 'Okay, just let me know if you ever want to talk about it.'

Duncan was practising his kickboxing techniques at home with a punching bag. Focused on perfecting each strike, he began with a swift jab followed by a powerful right hook and a sharp left hook. Executing impeccable form, he gained momentum, initiating a swift right front kick and a powerful left roundhouse kick that landed with a resounding thud on the punching bag, causing it to shake.

Breathless and sweating profusely, Duncan paused, hands on his knees, to catch his breath. After a moment, he straightened up, reaching for his water bottle and gulping down the refreshing liquid. Putting the bottle down, his phone suddenly rang, interrupting his moment of peace. The ringtone filled the room, prompting Duncan to quickly answer the call.

'Hello.'

A familiar voice greeted him. '*Oh hey, Duncan.*'

Recognising the voice, Duncan relaxed, sitting back in his swivel chair and crossing his feet on the desk. 'Hey, Abraham. How're things?' he asked, a smile on his face.

'*Same old, same old,*' Abraham replied. '*Got a couple of kids to feed and a wife to support.*'

'I see ... So, I'm guessing that you're calling regarding the ghoul case at the Yellow Bull building, am I correct?'

'*Indeed, you are,*' Abraham replied. '*I need somebody who can get the job done, somebody who's swift. Somebody who can dispatch a target without causing a large commotion. If that 'somebody' could do that, I have five thousand Livres waiting for them in a briefcase.*'

Duncan chuckled. 'A fair compensation, Abraham. Even if you paid me less, I wouldn't refuse to help a friend.'

'*This is one of the reasons why I like working with you, Duncan.*' Abraham chuckled. '*Your admirable traits never cease to amaze me.*' Abraham continued. '*So, what's your plan, Merc? Are you gonna head towards the Yellow Bull Company's building and inspect the place?*'

'Indeed, there's a chance that the place contains valuable information to help with my investigation. I'm gonna arrive there and search for some evidence. It could help lead me towards the culprit.'

'Smart thinking. You always were one step ahead.' Abraham paused. 'Good luck, Duncan. Keep me updated.'

'Will do. Cheers,' Duncan said, ending the call.

He got up and moved to his desk, where his gear was laid out with near military precision – his M1911A1 pistol, .45 ACP ammo, a desk fan whirring softly beside them. Above the desk hung a wallboard crammed with maps, red threads, notes scrawled in half-legible handwriting – and photos.

His eyes landed on *that* one. The one he kept tucked in the corner but never really stopped looking at.

His father.

Gaunt. Sunken eyes. Skin like paper. There was something unnatural in his gaze – something hollow. He hadn't always looked like that. Before ... before *they* got to him.

Duncan's jaw clenched.

It wasn't an illness. Not a natural one, anyway. It was them. The *heretics.*

Outlaws who perverted the natural world for their own gain. Criminals cloaked in arcane filth.

These weren't misunderstood mystics – they were scum. Human traffickers with spells. Arms dealers who flung fire instead of bullets. Killers who didn't need guns when a single incantation could rip a man apart.

Unchecked. Unpunished. And one of them had done this to his father.

They didn't just kill. They corrupted. Twisted people from the inside out – body, mind, and soul.

They had done *this.*

They'd taken a proud, flawed, *real* man and broken him down into something barely human. Left him as a ghost of himself, and then ... vanished. No body. No grave. Just silence.

His hand drifted to another photo – a blurry still of one of *them.* Pale and monstrous. Not literally a leech, but that's what it reminded Duncan of: something that fed on others. Something that sucked the life out of good people and left nothing behind.

His knuckles tightened.

You people took my father from me. You turned him into something sick and lost. You left him like that – and you thought no one would come looking.

He stared at the pistol. Then the leech. Then the man his father used to be.

I'm coming. I don't care how long it takes. I'll find you. And when I do ... you'll wish you'd stayed in the dark.

Chapter XIII

SEEKER OF JUSTICE

Wearing a white bee suit that itched at the neck, Duncan approached the Yellow Bull headquarters. The company's glass-fronted tower loomed over the street like a silent witness to the chaos that had unfolded within. Even now, hours after the incident, the perimeter remained locked down by the Floran Police Authority. Yellow tape marked *POLICE LINE DO NOT CROSS* whipped in the breeze, stretched across parked patrol cars and the building's ruined entrance.

Duncan already knew what had happened. News clips, web reports, and a few leaked videos had made the rounds before the Authority scrambled to suppress them. He and Jénmar had sifted through the digital wreckage back at his flat. Between the distorted CCTV feeds and panicked livestreams from office workers, the truth had emerged – a cloud of weaponised bees had been unleashed.

The heretic's signature.

He tightened his grip on the badge in his pocket.

As he neared the outer cordon, a stern-looking officer raised a hand. 'Hold on. No locals past this point. I'll need to see ID or proof of clearance.'

Duncan stopped without argument and drew out his credentials. He held up his business card and, more importantly, the badge – silver and cold in the morning light. It was anything but ordinary. It bore the emblem of the Wings of Authority – an eagle in mid-flight, wings spread wide, twin swords criss-crossed beneath it. A rare thing to carry, and rarer still to flash in public.

The officer's posture shifted at once. Recognition flickered in his eyes – not just of the badge, but of what it meant. AMOB wasn't the sort of agency you asked questions about. If someone carried their insignia, you stepped aside.

'My name's Duncan Saul,' he said evenly. 'Freelance mercenary. I've worked with AMOB, the Floran military, and the Floran Police Authority. I'm here under clearance to inspect the building.'

The words came out clean and direct, but inside, Duncan felt a subtle unease. It had been years since AMOB handed him that badge – a cold, clinical meeting in some underground facility, with Jénmar present. They hadn't called it a reward. They'd called it a 'clearance upgrade'.

The officer gave Duncan a nod and gestured for him to follow. 'Understood, Mr Saul. I'll take you to someone who knows the place better than any of us.'

Duncan said nothing, falling into step beside him. The two moved past the crumbling barricade, their boots crunching over broken glass. The scent of burnt circuitry lingered in the air, mingling with something … acrid. Like fermenting syrup.

Ahead, the yawning entrance to the Yellow Bull complex loomed. Its security doors had been blasted open, edges scorched and warped. The building seemed to breathe faintly – windows cracked like fractured bones, shadows twitching in the corners.

The officer glanced at Duncan. 'Bees, right? That's what the reports said. But this wasn't nature gone mad. This was calculated.'

Duncan didn't respond. He already knew.

They turned a corner, stepping into what had once been the lobby – now littered with debris, scorch marks, and the remnants of panicked escape. In the centre stood a man in a full yellow hazmat suit. He wore the headpiece loose around his shoulders, revealing a lined, sun-reddened face with eyes like stormclouds.

'Mr Donnelly!' the officer called out. 'This is Duncan Saul. He's here investigating the incident.'

Donnelly turned, squinting. His voice was low, hoarse with age and cigarettes. 'The Heretic Hunter, eh? You don't look like much.'

Duncan stepped forward, arms crossed. 'And you must be the bloke who cleans up everyone's mess.'

Donnelly gave a dry chuckle. 'Aye, that's me. Chief of the cleanup crew – twenty years of scrubbing blood and black goo off government walls.'

He gestured towards the scorched stairwell. 'This place? Different. I've seen bio-warfare scenes that looked cleaner. Whatever did this – it wasn't just here to kill. It was here to say something.'

Duncan's eyes narrowed, his gaze following the shadowed hallways beyond.

'I know,' he murmured. 'I'm here to listen.'

Mr Donnelly raised an eyebrow at that. 'Then you'd best have sharp ears, lad. This place doesn't speak in whispers – it screams.'

Duncan kept his tone level. 'That's why I'm here. I need to understand what happened – how, and why.'

Donnelly gave a slow nod, folding his arms across his chest. 'You're an investigator, then?'

'Something like that.' Duncan pulled a worn notepad from his coat pocket, flipping it open. 'I'll need to ask you a few questions. Details matter – small things, too. Anything that seemed off, even before the incident.'

Donnelly gave a half-smile, dry as ash. 'Well, you've got the look of someone who's seen too much and trusts too little. Go ahead then, ask away. And call me Joseph. Only the suits call me Mr Donnelly.'

Duncan scribbled the name down with a faint nod. 'Joseph it is. And please call me Duncan.'

Joesph nodded.

Duncan then proceeded with his questions. 'Did the culprit specifically target this building?'

'Seems that way,' Joseph muttered, scratching at the edge of his beard. 'No other buildings got hit by the bees. Far as we can tell, they never even made it outside. Ghouls too – they were only spotted inside these walls.'

Duncan tilted his head slightly. 'Interesting ... Did your team find any bodies when you arrived?'

Joseph gave a short nod. 'Yeah. One of my lads – Allen – found a couple on the sixth floor. Poor bastard's still a bit shaken up.'

Duncan leant in, pen ready. 'What were the bodies like?'

Joseph grimaced. 'Docs said they were in a right state – skin pale as chalk, bone dry. Looked like they'd been drained. Covered in bite marks, and their eyes – red all through the whites. Like blood had pooled there.'

That made Duncan pause. He scratched a quick note in his pad, pencil darting over the page. 'Interesting ...' he muttered, under his breath. The symptoms didn't fit any conventional pattern. Not chemical. Not natural. Something else entirely.

He circled the words: Sixth Floor.

Joseph watched him scribble for a moment, then added, 'If you're after more details, I can take you to the general manager. Bloke's name's Charles Nicholas. He's upstairs – still got the access logs, security data, all that. Could take you now, if you like.'

Duncan clicked the pencil back into place and nodded once. 'Let's go.'

The two moved deeper into the building, stepping over broken tiles and scattered debris. As they neared a side corridor, Joseph raised his voice.

'Mr Nicholas!'

Charles Nicholas, a middle-aged man with white hair and a large white moustache. He was dressed in a navy blue suit with a blue tie featuring white stripes, a light blue shirt and a navy blue waistcoat. He held a wooden cane in his right hand.

'Who is this newly acquainted guest that you have brought to my presence?' inquired Mr Nicholas as he turned around.

'Duncan Saul, a self-employed mercenary with about three years of service. He came to investigate the place,' Joseph explained.

'Is that fine by you, Mr Nicholas?' Duncan asked.

Mr Nicholas readily allowed Duncan to enter. 'Sure, you gladly have my permission, Mr Saul.' Expressing his concern, Mr Nicholas continued. 'As the General Manager, I feel responsible for avenging the souls of our dead. The loss of my colleagues weighs heavily on me. It's almost like the death of a family member. Some of these people were close friends ... Mr Saul, I implore you to bring the heretic to justice, to prevent further casualties.'

'Don't worry, I'm on the case,' Duncan solemnly assured.

Mr Nicholas took his card from his blazer pocket and handed it to Duncan. 'Mr Saul, if you may accept this. This is my telephone number. Please call me through this line if you manage to accomplish your objective. I will gladly reward you for this.'

'Thank you, Mr Nicholas. I'll do my best not to disappoint you.'

Mr Nicholas seemed satisfied with that response. 'You are doing our business proud, Mr Saul. May God bless you.'

'You too, Mr Nicholas.'

'Gentlemen, please return to me if you manage to conjure up an answer,' Mr Nicholas instructed.

Joseph nodded towards Mr Nicholas. 'You got it.'

Joseph then turned to Duncan. 'Duncan, follow me.'

Duncan donned the hood of his bee suit, and they headed for the elevator. Upon reaching the sixth floor, they disembarked.

The corridor appeared eerie: the lights were off and the area was dim, dusty and neglected. They switched on their torches, illuminating their path as they walked and discussed the incident.

'The building has been under quarantine for a few days,' Joseph explained. 'We'll inform everyone that the business will remain closed until we completely eradicate the bees. The cleanup crew is currently working to restore this place.'

Duncan nodded in acknowledgment as they continued their investigation through the dimly lit hallway.

Joseph sighed. 'How can those little shites cause so much of a catastrophe. Bollocks, I say.'

'The news reported that the CCTV camera caught a man in a trench coat and scarf on the sixth floor, specifically in the boiler room,' Duncan said. 'Why the sixth floor, though?' he queried further.

Joseph responded. 'The sixth floor is primarily where our staff operates – CEOs, vice managers, the general manager, you name it. Some of those employees were infected, and as a result, innocent people within the building got infected, too. That guy caused a lot of damage,' he said. 'He's a coward, hiding his face to avoid being identified. I hope justice catches up with him,' Joseph added with evident anger.

'Investigators say he released the bees through the air vents,' Duncan said. 'From what I've gathered, he's not exactly experienced. Didn't even disable the CCTV before letting them loose. We need to figure out where those vents lead – it might tell us who he was really after.'

As they reached the boiler room, Joseph opened the door and announced, 'This is it, right here.'

'So, this is the room where he let those bees loose?' Duncan confirmed.

'Yes ... Ugh ... Let's locate that air vent and figure out where it leads,' Joseph replied, frustration evident in his tone.

Duncan soon located the air vent, knowing it pointed to the culprit having a degree of familiarity with the building's layout. 'So which rooms do the vents lead to?' he asked.

'Follow me.'

Duncan followed Joseph into a meeting room, though it appeared quite different from any other meeting room he had seen before. Chairs were neatly stacked, computers powered down and tables cleared of clutter.

Joseph provided some context: 'This is the meeting room where the CEO and other top employees gather.'

Duncan retrieved his notebook and pencil once more. 'Are there any other rooms with air vent grills?' he inquired.

'Another meeting room, an office room and a private room,' said Joseph.

'Got it. I'll make sure to keep track of these locations.' Duncan's pencil moved swiftly across the pages of his notebook as he recorded the crucial details. He needed to piece together the puzzle – to find the logic behind the choices made by the perpetrator.

Duncan contemplated the situation, hand on his chin, attempting to grasp the intricacies of the crime. 'The perpetrator must have been familiar with the layout, knowing that the air vents would direct the bees to the staff members' rooms. This suggests the culprit had likely been inside the building multiple times, not just on a one-off visit. This wasn't a spontaneous act; it was a calculated move – such a plan couldn't be concocted overnight ...'

Duncan stood, deep in thought. 'It's intriguing ... he didn't attack the ground floor, despite it being the most crowded area. The culprit's intention must have been to target the CEO and their co-workers on the upper floors.'

The choice of specific rooms, the avoidance of the ground floor, the deliberate focus on the CEO and top employees all hinted at a particular motive. The perpetrator wasn't aiming for chaos; they had a specific agenda. This was more than a random act of aggression – it was a targeted strike on the heart of the organisation.

'So, it's likely the person behind this is an employee of the Yellow Bull Company,' he concluded.

'That seems to connect the dots,' said Joseph, agreeing.

Duncan continued his analysis. 'The heretic might have sought revenge on his co-workers, but I won't jump to conclusions. It's possible he hired someone else to do the dirty work.' Duncan reevaluated his stance, arms folded. 'Regardless, guilt still falls on him, whether he acted alone or with an accomplice,' he said before exiting the room.

'Duncan, where are you headed?' Joseph asked.

'I'm going to speak with Mr Nicholas to request permission to access the employee records.'

'Alright, I'll come along,' said Joseph, nodding. They left the building and made their way to find Mr Nicholas.

Mr Nicholas stood as Duncan and Joseph entered his office. 'Gentlemen, have you formulated a hypothesis?' he inquired.

'Yes,' Duncan responded. 'We suspect one of the employees in the building is the culprit. The person knew the air vent led to the meeting room, likely targeting the CEO.'

'Good heavens,' Mr Nicholas replied in shock, stroking his chin. 'Indeed, someone is trying to sabotage our business. We must locate this heretic swiftly, for I sense they won't stop until all of us are harmed.'

'May I have access to any employee records? Any information that could lead me to the heretic,' Duncan inquired. 'There might be a clue to identify the culprit.'

'Yes, we store employee records in cabinets containing personnel files in the basement of this building, but my keys are needed for access,' Mr Nicholas explained. 'I'll take you there now. Follow me.'

However, Joseph intervened. 'Wait, Mr Nicholas.' He retrieved a hazmat suit and gas mask. 'You must wear these for your safety,' he insisted.

'Oh, how thoughtless of me,' Mr Nicholas responded, taking the protective gear. The three then re-entered the Yellow Bull building.

After a while, they reached the basement floor. Mr Nicholas led the way to the record room, using his key to unlock the door. He stepped inside and approached the cabinet containing the personnel files, opening it with his special key.

Duncan turned to him. 'Thank you, Mr Nicholas.'

'Don't worry, Duncan. Take all the time you need,' Joseph added.

Duncan began searching through the files, looking for the section with names starting with 'A'. He carefully pulled out a file from the cabinet and opened it, revealing the personal information and a photograph of each employee.

Duncan methodically went through the files:

Employee Record

Employee Number: 1078

- ***Last Name:*** *Brown*
- ***First Name:*** *Antonio*
- ***Age:*** *34*
- ***Phone Number:*** *555 214 683 199*
- ***Gender:*** *Male*
- ***Status:*** *Dismissed*

Employee Number: 1392

- ***Last Name:*** *Blake*
- ***First Name:*** *Alexandra*
- ***Age:*** *49*
- ***Phone Number:*** *555 497 212 436*
- ***Gender:*** *Female*
- ***Status:*** *Resigned*

Employee Number: 1643

- ***Last Name:*** *Jaeger*

- ***First Name:*** *Aaron*
- ***Age:*** *42*
- ***Phone Number:*** *555 669 241 410*
- ***Gender:*** *Male*
- ***Status:*** *Active*

Employee Number: 1923
- ***Last Name:*** *McDonald*
- ***First Name:*** *Adam*
- ***Age:*** *28*
- ***Phone Number:*** *555 328 815 441*
- ***Gender:*** *Male*
- ***Status:*** *Active*

Employee Number: 2749
- ***Last Name:*** *Kruger*
- ***First Name:*** *Allen*
- ***Age:*** *25*
- ***Phone Number:*** *555 983 548 247*
- ***Gender:*** *Male*
- ***Status:*** *Active*

Duncan stopped flicking through the pages of the files and closely peered at a name: *Antonio Brown*. 'Dismissed?' he said aloud, questioning the term.

'Ah, Antonio Brown. He worked in the marketing department for around three years,' said Mr Nicholas. 'We had to let him go recently – there was an ongoing conflict between him and the CEO. Things escalated, and unfortunately it became untenable.'

Duncan's fingers instinctively went to his chin. 'Hmm ...?' he mused aloud, considering the information at hand. The situation did raise suspicions, no doubt, but he knew the importance of caution in drawing speculation. 'We can't jump to conclusions just yet,' he said, aware that the true answer might be more complex than it initially appeared. While a disgruntled former employee could certainly be a likely suspect, there could be other motives, other players involved. The puzzle was far from complete.

Duncan's mind raced through various scenarios. He could not afford to dismiss any potential leads: the safety of these employees was at stake. It was essential to gather more information – to explore every angle before reaching any definitive conclusions. Only through careful investigation could they unravel the truth behind these troubling events.

'Here's what I'm going to do,' Duncan announced to the two men. 'I'll read more of the employees' personnel files and find those who have been dismissed. I'll send the details to my partner so that he can research them.' Duncan then continued, 'So, gentlemen, in the meantime, please bear with me.'

Mr Nicholas reassured Duncan. 'You may take your precious time, Mr Saul – as long as you are a step closer to catching this vile criminal, there is no need for me to be ungrateful.'

Duncan nodded and continued going through the files.

After some time, Duncan exited the building. He activated his smartphone and dialled Jénmar's number. 'Jénmar, I've got a list of potential suspects for the Yellow Bull attack.'

'*Great, give me their names and I'll research them on my computer*,' Jénmar replied.

'Sure.' Duncan began listing off the names. 'First, we have Antonio Brown ...'

'*An-to-nio Brown ...*'

'Next is Kylan Andersson ...'

'*Ky-lan Ander-sson ...*'

'And finally, Daniel Cross.'

'*Dan-iel Cross ...*'

'That's all,' Duncan said, concluding the list.

'*Alright, I'll send you the details via email. Check them out when you're home. My documents should include suspect photos and personal information,*' Jénmar instructed.

'Thanks, Jénmar. Your help means a lot.'

'*Focus on the task at hand, kid,*' Jénmar reminded him.

'Right,' Duncan agreed, eager to get to work.

'*Head over there and give them hell,*' Jénmar said, encouraging him.

Duncan smiled, ready to fulfil his mission. 'As you wish, Jénmar.'

'*Make me proud. Bye.*' Jénmar ended the call.

Duncan left the Yellow Bull building and set out to locate his target, determined to achieve his goal.

As Lance sat in his office preparing his video message for the House of Royals, he was interrupted by the sudden appearance of Reiman. Lance raised an eyebrow in surprise, wondering why his subordinate had come to him now. He braced himself for an argument, ready to dismiss any attempts to sway his opinion.

'Have you come to tell me to reconsider?' Lance asked. 'If so, you're wasting your time.' But to his surprise, Reiman shook his head.

'No, I have come to assist you with your message.'

Lance couldn't help but be curious about the reason behind Reiman's change of heart. He wanted to understand the shift in perspective, to grasp what had prompted this unexpected show of support. He was prepared to listen, eager to learn what had influenced his decision.

'That's surprising to hear,' Lance exclaimed, unable to hide his shock. 'I thought you said that you didn't agree with my method. Tell me, what changed your mind?'

'I have sworn my loyalty to you from the very beginning,' Reiman said firmly. 'I would go to hell and back for you. That is my choice.'

Lance was momentarily taken aback by the depth of Reiman's commitment.

'I know you have noble intentions, Lance.' Reiman continued, a small smile playing at the corners of his mouth. 'I wouldn't be much of a friend if I left you to fend for yourself.'

Lance's heart swelled with gratitude and admiration for his friend's unwavering loyalty. 'Thank you, Reiman,' he said, his voice tinged with emotion. 'I appreciate your support.'

Reiman returned a smile.

'I think about them.'

Reiman's brows furrowed in response to Lance's cryptic words.

'My allies, my comrades, my friends ... I fought long and hard for them, to recreate Flora from the ground up. All the sacrifices we made ... I certainly thought at times that death would be easier. The only thing that kept me going was my vision of Flora for the future.' Determination blazed in Lance's eyes as he stared back at Reiman. 'But all of it will be meaningless if I give up. I will ensure that Flora's future will be bright. I swear it.'

'Forgive my questioning, Lord Sainglend, but how do you think this would work? You aren't exactly on good terms with the council for obvious reasons.'

Lance acknowledged the challenges ahead, particularly his strained relationship with the council. It was not lost on him that his path was fraught with difficulties: he understood the obstacles and the complexities of the political landscape. However, he had faced challenges before and this would be no different. He was prepared to go over those hurdles to achieve his vision for Flora's future.

Lance's eyes narrowed as he replied. 'You doubt me, Reiman? Have you known I worked for them in my younger years? We share a common goal, so I know what they will say and do. This war has gone on long enough and I know the council want the best outcome for the country.'

'Very well. I trust your word, my lord.'

Lance moved to set up his video message. He reached for his laptop and turned on the recording, the camcorder trained on himself.

'Have you got your speech figured out?' Reiman asked.

'Yes. I have rehearsed and everything. Night and day,' Lance said, nodding confidently.

He hit RECORD.

'Esteemed members of the council,

I address you today not as a rebel, nor as an enemy, but as a man who has fought – bled – for the future of our nation.

I am Lance Sainglend, leader of the Night Hawks, and I am asking – sincerely – for peace.

This conflict has torn through the heart of Flora. The violence has cost us dearly – too many lives, too many futures. Now, more than ever, I believe it must end.

To prove my commitment, I offer myself into your custody. Not in defeat. Not in shame. But as a gesture of trust.

I do not ask for mercy. I do not renounce my beliefs. I surrender to protect my people.

The men and women of the Night Hawks followed me because they believed we could build something better. They still believe. I ask you to spare them – show them the mercy that can only come from strength.

They want peace, just as I do.

Thank you.'

He ended the RECORDING. The silence that followed felt heavier than before.

Reiman was watching him.

'That was powerful,' he said quietly.

Lance didn't respond. He just stared at the screen, heart thudding in his chest. He didn't know if his words would change anything.

But they had to.

They had to.

As the video message reached the council meeting in Riverdam, an old man with a bushy moustache spoke up, his voice dripping with contempt. 'Bah, preposterous! He only wishes to parley because he is on the brink of defeat.' He turned to his peers with a narrow-eyed look. 'If we buy into it even for a moment, we'll be walking right into the snake's venom.'

'I concur,' chimed in a middle-aged female council member with brown hair and glasses. 'It's challenging to place trust in the words of the Kingslayer after his act of regicide.'

But another council member spoke up in defence of Lance. 'My lords, you do mistake him. Lance is many things, but a liar isn't one of them.' The council members turned to him, their expressions wary. 'Let's say that the man does surrender. What should we do then?' he asked his colleagues.

'We'll hear whatever the man has to say,' one member said. 'If it's convincing, we will do as he asks. If it's twaddle, we shall gut him where he stands.'

'This should be interesting,' another interjected. 'However, we must remain cautious until the man acts. Agreed?'

The council members all nodded. 'Agreed!' they said in unison, their eyes fixed on Lance's video message.

Chapter XIV

FIRED AND FUELLED

Duncan arrived at Daniel Cross' house, intending to ask him some questions about the incident at the Yellow Bull building. As Duncan approached the door, he could sense the man's reluctance to have him there, but he brushed it off and focused on the investigation. Daniel was a bald man with pale blue eyes.

'Mr Cross, I understand you used to work at the Yellow Bull building. Can you tell me why you left the company?' Duncan inquired.

'I was discharged three years ago,' Daniel replied. 'We had a dispute over wages. I went on strike, demanding a raise, but those penny-pinching bastards fired me instead.'

Listening to Daniel's frustration, Duncan couldn't help but empathise with the man's plight. Corporate mistreatment was not uncommon, and he knew that sometimes employees had legitimate grievances.

'Despite the disagreements, I managed to find a much better job afterwards,' Daniel continued, a sense of relief evident in his voice. 'The new company treats me better, offering improved work hours and decent pay.'

As Daniel expressed his feelings about the previous employer, Duncan nodded in understanding. He had encountered countless cases where people harboured resentment towards their former workplaces. However, Daniel's next words struck a chord with him.

'They were arseholes but I don't believe they deserved what happened to them that night. It was too much.' Daniel sighed.

'Mr Cross, do you know anything about the bees that attacked the Yellow Bull building?' Duncan asked directly, looking for any hint of deception.

Daniel frowned in confusion. 'Bees? No, I don't know anything about that. Why the fuck would I have anything to do with those damn bees?'

Duncan assessed the man's response carefully, trying to gauge his sincerity. Something in Daniel's demeanour made Duncan believe that the man was telling the truth. Daniel had nothing to gain by lying about the bees, and his genuine bewilderment further solidified Duncan's trust in him.

'You're not lying,' Duncan said.

'Told you,' Daniel said with a grin, his satisfaction evident.

'However, I'm still going to check the house. Just part of the process, you know?'

'Go ahead, I have no secrets for you to gawp at,' Daniel retorted, keeping his nose up high.

Duncan proceeded to search the house – not because he doubted Daniel, but because it was part of his methodical investigation. To his relief, he found nothing incriminating; it seemed the man was indeed innocent of any involvement.

'You're clean,' Duncan informed him.

'So?' Daniel replied with a hint of arrogance.

'You're off the hook. My mistake,' Duncan reiterated, trying to maintain a professional demeanour despite the man's attitude.

'Good, now you can leave me alone,' Daniel said, gesturing for Duncan to leave.

'I apologise for any suspicion, Mr Cross. It's just part of my investigation. Thank you for your cooperation,' Duncan said politely.

Duncan shook his head as he left Daniel's house. Daniel had been kind of an ass, but he couldn't entirely blame him. People often reacted defensively when facing scrutiny or accusations, especially when they believed themselves to be innocent.

As he walked down the street, Duncan couldn't help but ponder the case. The bee attack at the Yellow Bull building was a puzzling one, and he had to be careful not to jump to conclusions or let emotions cloud his judgment. He knew that finding the true culprit was crucial, not just to clear innocent people like Daniel but also to ensure justice for those affected by the incident.

Taking a deep breath, Duncan reminded himself to stay focused and objective. He needed to follow every lead, explore all possibilities and gather evidence meticulously. The truth was out there somewhere, waiting to be uncovered, and he was determined to find it.

As he walked away from Daniel's house, Duncan couldn't shake the feeling that there was more to the story. He knew that the bee attack was a deliberate act and someone must be responsible for it; however, with no evidence pointing to Daniel, he had to consider other possibilities. Duncan decided to call Jénmar.

Jénmar stood outside the suspect's house, a knife in his hand, ready to intimidate for answers. As he stepped inside, he waved the blade menacingly at the man sitting there trembling in fear, clearly terrified by the sight before him.

'Please. Please stop.' The man sobbed, begging for mercy.

'Now give me an answer, or I'll—' Jénmar's phone suddenly rang, interrupting him. He quickly answered. 'Duncan, what is it?'

'*It ain't the guy,*' Duncan replied on the other end.

'Oh ... I see.' Jénmar sighed, disappointed that another of his leads had turned out to be a dead end.

'*So, what about you?*' Duncan asked, concerned.

'Well ...' Jénmar looked at the frightened man he had cornered, whimpering and crying in fear as he was strapped to a chair. 'Not well, actually,' Jénmar admitted.

'*No ... Don't tell me,*' Duncan said in shock. *'Are you torturing him!?'*

'Uhhh ...?'

'*Fuck, Jénmar!*' Duncan shouted. '*What you've done is a crime! What will happen if the public finds out!? We'll be shut down and you'll be arrested!*'

'I wanted to get the best results as fast as possible.' Jénmar pouted. 'If we take too long, the culprit could get away. And besides, I find this method more enjoyable.'

'*What if he's innocent, eh!?*' Duncan exclaimed. '*You need to control your impulses, man! What you're going to do is check the entire house, and if he isn't the one, you'll release him as soon as possible. Am I clear!?*'

'Aye, you're right.' Jénmar sighed, realising the gravity of his actions.

Jénmar decided to search through the house, going through every room and examining each corner, but to his dismay, he found nothing of significance. Then Jénmar realised he had made a mistake, which wasn't very professional of him. 'Oops, sorry pal,' he said as he returned to the victim. 'I got the wrong number. You ain't the one. So you can disappear, fly or piss off. I don't give a shit,' he added dismissively.

Jénmar used his knife to cut the ropes that bound the man, freeing him. The terrified victim wasted no time fleeing from Jénmar.

'Oh, and please leave a good review on our business page.' Jénmar called after him with a touch of dark humour. Once the man was out of sight, Jénmar returned to the call with Duncan. 'So yeah, I got the wrong guy. I searched his house and there's nothing.'

'*You idiot* ...' Duncan muttered, sighing through the phone. '*So that means our only suspect now is Antonio Brown* ...'

'Indeed.'

'*Okay, Jénmar, I'll call you back if I get anything. Make sure you don't do anything stupid*,' Duncan said, ending the call promptly.

After Jénmar's mistake, the pressure inside Duncan mounted like a kettle about to burst. Two suspects had already been ruled out – one after a long night of silence, the other shaking and swearing on his life – and now only a single name remained on their list: Antonio Brown.

Antonio Brown ...

Duncan let the name linger in his mind, tasting the bitterness of it. He stared blankly at the floor for a moment, his jaw clenched. His hands itched for action, his muscles coiled and ready – but there was a weight pressing down on his chest, a seething intensity that words couldn't reach.

He remembered the dossier: thirty-four years old, a man with a petty history of conflict – shouting matches with superiors, discipline reports, walkouts. A man with a temper and a grudge. Could that grudge have turned deadly? Could it have driven him to unleash Berserker bees, infect innocent workers, and turn them into slavering ghouls?

To Duncan, the answer wasn't just plausible. It felt inevitable.

A heretic.

Duncan's thoughts grew darker. He didn't need to see Antonio's face to know the kind of man he was. Heretics always wore the same rot behind their smiles – a hunger for power, or chaos, or some twisted ideology that gave them the excuse to hurt others and call it necessary. Duncan had seen it all before. They always thought they were smarter than the rest of the world. That their actions justified the blood they spilt.

But to Duncan, it wasn't just a crime. It was a sickness. A slow, soul-rotting infection that spread through people like Antonio.

He felt the heat in his chest swell, and his fingers curled into fists. Duncan's jaw clenched. His gaze drifted to the news reports spread across his phone – photos of the Yellow Bull massacre. Not just the dead, but the aftermath. People crying outside hospital doors. Soldiers in hazmat suits dragging out the infected like sacks of meat. The building under quarantine, cordoned off with yellow tape and guarded by policemen. Twelve employees dead. Fifteen civilians infected. Ghouls.

Antonio Brown did this. Duncan didn't care what the evidence said. The rage in his gut told him all he needed to know. Brown may not have pulled the trigger himself, but he'd loaded the gun, aimed it, and let the damn thing fire. And Duncan was going to make sure he paid for that.

His vision had narrowed. One name. One face. One target.

Antonio Brown.

The last piece on the board. The one who'd brought death into Flora's walls.

Duncan's lips curled into a thin line. His hand drifted to the pistol at his hip. Soon, he'd find the bastard. And when he did, Duncan wouldn't just be doing his job.

He'd be doing what had to be done.

The meeting room at the Yellow Bull building buzzed with low chatter as staff members prepared for the morning session. Papers rustled. Coffee cups clinked. Then the door swung open, and Antonio Brown hurried in, slightly out of breath. He was a plump man with a worn face, a ponytail of black hair, and brown eyes that looked a little too tired for the hour.

From his seat, Mr Nicholas glanced up with a sigh. 'Mr Brown ... late again.'

Antonio quickly slipped off his coat and took an empty seat at the table. 'Yes, I know. I'm sorry. My daughter missed her bus – I had to take her to school myself. It's been a morning.'

Across the table, Mr Roy, the department's senior executive, leant forwards, fingers interlaced. His tone was firm, not unkind. 'Mr Brown, this isn't just about one morning. Your attendance has been inconsistent. Your contributions, minimal.'

Antonio rubbed the back of his neck. 'I get that. But I've had a lot going on lately – back home and here. I'm doing my best, but it's not always enough.'

Roy pressed on. 'We've lost nearly a quarter of our customer base. The civil war hit everyone hard, but we're still expected to deliver. Your absence puts pressure on the rest of the team.'

Antonio exhaled sharply. 'I understand, truly. But it's not just me who's struggling. I've got family relying on me to send money home, bills stacking up, and more paperwork than I can handle. I'm not trying to slack off – I'm just overwhelmed.'

A colleague further down the table scoffed. 'We all have problems, Antonio. You can't expect us to carry your weight forever. If this company goes under, we all lose our jobs.'

Roy raised a hand. 'That's enough.' He glanced around the room. 'Let's stay on track. Mr Heyse?'

Mr Heyse stood and moved towards the whiteboard. 'Right. I've gathered some recent market data I think we should—'

The door opened again.

Everyone stood as Mr Lucas, the CEO, entered, followed by a tall man with brown hair swept into a curtain fringe and square glasses. His sharp suit and calm demeanour suggested he was someone of importance.

Roy stepped forward to greet them. 'Good morning, Mr Lucas.'

'Good morning, Mr Roy,' Lucas replied with a warm nod. 'Good morning, everyone.' He gestured for the team to sit.

As he took his seat at the head of the table, the murmurs died. Mr Lucas adjusted his cuff, then spoke, calm but serious.

'Yesterday, I had a conversation with Mr Ross,' he began. His gaze settled squarely on Antonio. 'We've come across some troubling information. Mr Brown ... there's evidence linking you to illegal activity. Specifically – counterfeiting. And drug distribution.'

The room froze.

Antonio's face went pale.

The revelation hit the room like a bombshell. Chairs creaked. Eyes darted. Antonio blinked in disbelief, his voice rising as he pushed himself halfway out of his seat.

'Drug dealing ...? Boss, what are you talking about? I'd never do something like that!' His words were rushed, shaky – more baffled than angry.

Mr Lucas remained composed, folding his hands atop the table. 'Mr Ross provided me with photographs,' he said. 'You were seen selling substances on a street corner near Westpine Station. Clear as day.'

Without a word, Mr Lucas reached into a folder beside him. He slid several printed photographs across the polished table for everyone to see.

Heads leant forwards. The room erupted in murmurs. In the photos, a man with Antonio's build and likeness stood on a grimy street corner, exchanging small bags for cash. The lighting was grainy, but the resemblance was undeniable.

Antonio's mouth opened, but no words came. He finally managed a breathless, 'This is insane. That's not me. I swear, I don't know what Ross is playing at, but I would never be involved in something like that.'

A woman in a sleek black suit leant forwards, her face stricken with disbelief. 'My God … Mr Brown, how could you? After everything this company's been through – how could you drag us into something so vile?'

Antonio looked around the room, eyes wide, pleading. 'I swear to you – this has to be some mistake. Or someone's setting me up.'

Mr Nicholas, who had been quiet until now, clenched his jaw. 'So you're not denying it outright? You expect us to believe you over photographic evidence?'

'I am denying it!' Antonio snapped, then quickly caught himself, lowering his tone. 'Sir … I've given years to this company. I've worked late, I've cut corners in my own life to show up here. Please … you've got to believe me.'

Mr Lucas shook his head slowly. 'Belief is earned, Mr Brown. And right now, all we have is a mountain of doubt.'

Antonio stood fully now, desperation lacing his every word. 'I've sacrificed so much for this place – my family, my time, my health. I believed in Yellow Bull. Why would I ever do anything to sabotage it?'

Mr Heyse, still standing by the whiteboard, spoke up coldly. 'Even if this is some misunderstanding, it's out there now. If the press gets hold of this, we're finished. Customers won't want to associate with a company that hires criminals. The damage is done.'

Antonio opened his mouth again, but nothing came. Just silence. Accusations hung thick in the air like smoke.

Then Mr Lucas stood.

'Antonio Brown,' he said firmly. 'Effective immediately, you are hereby discharged from this company. Security will escort you out.'

Antonio's face fell. He didn't move at first – just stood there, stunned.

'Please,' he whispered. 'This is my life ...'

As Mr Lucas's final words echoed through the boardroom, Antonio's world crumbled. 'Discharge you from this business.' It rang like a death knell – more than a job lost, it was the collapse of everything he'd fought to hold together.

He dropped to his knees with a thud, hands clasped tightly like a man praying for his life.

'No! No! Please, please, please! You can't do this to me!' he cried. 'If I don't deliver the money in time, they'll kick me and my daughter out of our home! I was desperate. I did it for Amy!'

The boardroom sat frozen in stunned silence. His raw plea echoed in the stillness – a father broken, his dignity scattered like glass.

'I didn't do this for me,' he went on, breath hitching. 'It was never for me. My daughter's only eight – *eight*. She's all I have. Please, boss … imagine her, out on the streets. What kind of life would that be for her?'

Mr Lucas let out a slow, burdened sigh. There was the faintest flicker of conflict in his eyes, but his voice remained cold and firm. 'Then place her in foster care while you sort yourself out.'

Antonio shook his head violently. 'But if I don't have a place to stay, they won't let me visit her! She'll be lost to the system – I'll be homeless. I'll never see her again!'

Mr Lucas said, folding his arms. 'I'm sorry, Mr Brown. But this is the consequence of your own actions. You've fallen into your own pitfall.'

Antonio's face twisted with anguish. His eyes shifted to Mr Ross, standing smugly near the corner. And in that instant, the fury exploded.

'You jealous motherfucker!' Antonio howled, lunging to his feet and jabbing a finger at Ross. 'You ratted me out! You sold me out, you snake!'

Mr Ross didn't flinch. Arms crossed, he sneered. 'You did this to yourself, Antonio. Own up to it.'

Antonio's breath quickened, rage flaring behind his eyes. 'I know why you did this … It was because of Emilia, wasn't it? She chose me over you! You couldn't fucking handle it!'

That struck a nerve. Mr Ross stepped forward, jabbing his finger in return. 'Shut your mouth, criminal! You don't get to talk anymore. You don't work here. Go back to the alleys with your junkie mates – that's where you belong!'

With a roar of fury, Antonio lunged and grabbed Ross by the collar, jerking him forward.

'I'm gonna rip your head off and stick it on the company sign, you fucking reptilian entrepreneur douchebag!'

'Mr Brown, release him at once or we'll call security!' Mr Lucas barked, rising to his feet.

Ross trembled, but forced his words through clenched teeth. 'Th-think about it, Antonio. If you lay a hand on me, security will drag you out in cuffs. Assault charges. Foster access revoked. Think.'

Mr Lucas slammed his palm on the table. 'There will be no violence in this building!'

Antonio stood there a moment longer, seething, then shoved Ross away with a growl and backed off.

He swept a furious gaze around the room.

'You're all cowards,' he spat. 'You let this weasel stay, but throw me out like garbage? Over one mistake? You're really gonna stop me seeing my daughter just to protect your fucking brand?'

He turned and stormed for the door, hurling one final curse over his shoulder.

'Fuck all of you! I'm done with this shit!'

The door flew open – then froze.

'Mr Brown, wait!' Mr Heyse called, rising quickly from his seat.

Antonio halted in the doorway, turning just enough to look over his shoulder.

Mr Heyse stepped forward, his voice quieter, more deliberate. 'I'm willing to give you a chance ... not here at the company. But as a person. I'll transfer money to your account – enough to get Amy into a safe foster home for now. Keep her stable while you get back on your feet.'

He offered Antonio a business card.

'Call me if you need help. Or advice. Or anything at all.'

Antonio's eyes flicked between the card and Mr Heyse's face. He snatched the card wordlessly, fingers trembling, then walked out.

The door slammed behind him.

Back at his house, Antonio sat on the sofa while his daughter watched television. She was a young girl with blonde pigtails adorned with black ribbons framing her heart-shaped face, her eyes a captivating shade of light blue. She wore a blue dress paired with black leggings and T-bar shoes.

As he looked at her, tears began to fall from his eyes, and he growled. 'It's not fair, it's not fair! Those bastards, I'm gonna make them pay. Ross and his evil schemes, and those spineless cowards just let him ruin *my* life! They care about their damn business more than what happens to me and my daughter. They're better off dead! You hear me ...? Dead!'

His daughter approached him, asking innocently, 'Daddy, why are you angry?'

'I'm afraid you won't be seeing me anymore, sweetie. I'm afraid this is goodbye,' he replied.

Confused, she asked, 'What does that mean?'

Antonio sighed and paused a moment, trying to find the right words. 'You have to go to a foster home and have other people take care of you. Maybe you'll make lots of friends there?'

'I don't want anyone else to take care of me! I want you to take care of me!' His daughter protested, starting to cry.

He gently rubbed her head and said, 'I know, but Daddy will visit as much as I can. Please just wait for me.'

She broke down and banged her fists on his chest, releasing her emotions. 'No! It's not fair! First, Mommy left, and now you! Why!? Why can't I stay with you!?'

Antonio's eyes filled with tears as he saw his daughter crying, hugging her tightly to console her. 'I'm sorry! I'm so sorry!'

Her whimpering continued as they hugged, and the emotional night hung between them.

A few weeks later, Antonio woke to an empty house and the dull drone of the television. The room was half-dark, littered with empty bottles that caught the weak morning light. The silence pressed down on him, thick and heavy.

A low growl rumbled from his chest – more a release than a sound. Everything inside him was burning with rage, a raw, unrelenting need to make those bastards pay. The way they'd put profits above lives – how they'd let that son of a bitch walk free while he took the fall – gnawed at him like poison. He wasn't going down without a fight.

He rubbed his face, frustration clawing at his throat until it spilled out. 'Fuck, this ain't fair,' he snapped, voice rough with anger. 'Why'm I the one paying for their mistakes? Fired like some broken tool, while that bastard's out there, laughing.'

His eyes sharpened, burning with something darker. 'I'll show 'em. Yeah, I'll show 'em all.'

Snapping upright, he grabbed his laptop and powered it on. 'There's gotta be some black-market shit on here,' he muttered, fingers flying over the keys. 'Something to turn their own game against 'em.'

A grin spread slowly as he stumbled across a shady site – Rosemary Park. Weapons. His pulse quickened.

Scrolling down, his grin twisted. 'Berserker bees, huh? Turn someone into a ghoul in seconds. Perfect.' He eyed the screen, imagining the chaos it could unleash.

The smile was cold, cruel. Revenge wasn't just a thought now – it was a plan.

Chapter XV

WHERE THE PREY LIES

The dark sky loomed over Flora. Antonio Brown was in the process of packing his possessions into his car when Duncan suddenly appeared before him.

'Are you Antonio Brown?' Duncan asked, approaching him, his pistol drawn.

'Yes, I am. Why?' a startled Antonio replied, feeling a bit bewildered by the unexpected encounter.

Duncan's voice carried an undertone of passive-aggressiveness as he spoke. 'Antonio Brown, former employee of the Yellow Bull Company. You have committed a crime by infecting those employees with Berserker bees.'

Antonio quickly retorted. 'Wait a minute! How do you know if it was me? It could have been anyone who set those things off. Why are you coming to my house and pointing a gun at me? You should be arrested for false accusation and–!'

Duncan cut him off with a cold, quiet menace. 'You were fired four weeks ago. And right after that, you decided to make them pay. Who else knew the ventilation system? Who else had access to their schedules? The bees didn't end up in the conference room by accident. That was surgical. Calculated.' He took a step forward, pistol unwavering. 'Only someone like *you* could've made it happen.'

Rage pulsed through Duncan's veins like wildfire. He fought to keep it buried beneath the surface, but his hands were itching. His mouth wanted to curl into a snarl. He wasn't just confronting a suspect – he was staring down a heretic. One of *them.*

Criminals who wrapped themselves in spells and left ruin in their wake.

Like the one who broke his father.

Like the one who vanished without consequence.

'You think I'm stupid?' Duncan continued, voice now almost a growl. 'Think I'll believe some random psycho pulled this off? I checked every name. Interviewed every one of them. You're the last one left.'

He raised the gun with deliberate calm. 'And when the last suspect standing is the one I'm pointing at, you'd better have a bloody miracle to clear your name.'

Duncan gaze sharpened, eager to hear Antonio's defence. Antonio looked at Duncan, his eyes widening, unable to come up with a convincing response. He paused for a moment and then pushed Duncan away, attempting to create some distance between them.

'Son of a bitch!' Duncan exclaimed.

Antonio's heart raced as he sprinted through the narrow alley, his breath coming in ragged gasps. Anxiety coated him in a sheen of sweat, threatening to trip him up. 'Gotta escape! Gotta shake him off! How in the hell does he know!? Damn those AMOBs!' Antonio's voice trembled with fear as he yelled out his thoughts.

He pondered his deep-seated disdain for the AMOB's laws. Law enforcement only apprehended magic users if they posed no threat to society or innocent lives. Once deemed heretics, however, they were punishable by death.

Racing forward, Antonio reached a wall, his chest heaving. He tucked himself behind the corner. 'Thank God, I managed to lose him ... Now I just need to focus on getting the hell out of here.' He muttered to himself, a shaky breath of relief escaping his lips.

Suddenly, Duncan appeared from the shadows, his pistol aimed squarely at Antonio. The gunshot shattered the air, and agony exploded as Antonio's kneecap was struck.

'Arrrggggh! Fuck!' His scream echoed off the walls, profanity punctuating his pain.

Duncan approached Antonio, his pistol trained on him. 'Antonio Brown, heretic and former worker of the Yellow Bull Company. You stand accused of heinous crimes against the people of Flora, turning twelve employees and fifteen citizens into ghouls.'

Antonio clutched his wounded knee, wincing in pain. 'How ... How do you know about that?' he managed to utter through gritted teeth.

Duncan's voice remained steady. 'The AMOB has analysed the bee samples you used to transform those people. The Silver Cross was called in to neutralise the threat, and the company's building is now under quarantine. I was assigned by somebody to eliminate you,' Duncan continued, 'but before I do that, I need answers. Where did you get those insects?' Duncan's gaze bore into Antonio's eyes. 'Tell me now, or I can assure you, your death will be far more painful.'

Antonio's head shook in fear, his voice trembling. 'I don't know ... I swear, I don't know!'

Duncan drove his heel into the gushing gunshot wound, and Antonio's screams tore through the night like a wounded animal. Blood spurted out in sickening bursts, mixing with the dirt beneath them. Antonio writhed, but Duncan felt nothing.

'Arrggghhhh!'

He deserves this. Every second of pain he's feeling is nothing compared to what he's done to those people.

Using his shoe, Duncan intensified Antonio's pain by rubbing the wound. Antonio pounded the ground and screamed. 'Stop! Stop! Stop!'

Duncan withdrew his foot. 'You'd best speak now as patience isn't my strong suit. I'm likened to a ticking bomb – any hint of bullshit will piss me off. And trust me, you won't enjoy me in that state. I might do something I'll regret later. Removing your tongue, cutting off your balls or forcing lead down your throat ... who's to say?'

Antonio's fearful response came swiftly. 'Okay, okay! I obtained it from a black marketeer named Quinto.'

Duncan leant in, his voice rising. 'Where can this black market be found? What's the store's name?'

'It's in a town called West Denwich,' Antonio replied, hastily. 'The store is called *Rosemary Park*.'

Duncan's aggression subsided. 'Look at that. You've provided the information I needed. Perhaps you've spared some lives. Nevertheless, your actions can't go unpunished.'

Antonio's head shook, his apprehension evident. 'What?'

Duncan raised his pistol with chilling calm. 'I must eliminate you ...'

Antonio's plea burst forth. 'Wait, wait, wait! Hold on a minute ... The ones I took down, they're wicked and rotten.

They canned me to protect their pockets, their image! I gave them the years out of my life, and they spat on it. My little girl's stuck in foster care, and seeing her is a distant dream. Nowhere's left for me – they booted me out. Can't you grasp their betrayal? Being knifed by those you trust, for their own selfish gains.'

Duncan's voice was cold, clipped – like a blade cutting through the thick silence.

'You chose petty vengeance instead of just letting it go.'

Antonio blinked, stunned, his voice sharp with disbelief. 'Petty? You're joking, right?'

Duncan leaned in, relentless. 'You had a way out, mate. Could've walked away clean. But no – you went off, taking shots at anyone and everyone, guilty or not. Your daughter's got nothing to hide the shit you've done.'

Antonio's face twisted, venom spilling out. 'You … you rotten son of a bitch!'

Duncan rolled his eyes, dry as ever. 'Rotten? That's rich coming from you, murderer. How many people died in that building because of you? How many families are tearing themselves apart right now, waiting on people that'll never come home? All 'cause some coward couldn't handle his own damn problems.'

Antonio took a step back, faltering, his voice cracking. 'You can't–!'

'Look, I'm not your bloody cop or detective,' Duncan cut him off, voice hard. 'Arresting scumbags isn't my job. Ending them is.'

'No! Please! Don't kill me! I'll do anything – money, my prized possessions! I've got a daughter!' Antonio begged, desperation thick in his tone.

Hearing the mention of a daughter twisted something inside Duncan, if only for a second. He knew what this meant – a father gone, a kid left behind. But Antonio was a heretic, a danger. People like him didn't get second chances. Justice came first.

As Antonio's pleas grew louder, Duncan's mentor's voice echoed sharp in his head: *Your enemies ... show them no mercy.*

With grim certainty, Duncan said aloud, 'Don't worry, Uncle Konrad. I won't.'

Antonio screamed, tears streaming, but Duncan didn't hesitate. The pistol barked in quick bursts. When the last round hit, silence swallowed the room. Duncan stared at Antonio's still form – no satisfaction, just cold finality. He holstered the gun and walked away without a word.

This kill wasn't like the others. There was a fury simmering beneath the surface – controlled, but deadly. It wasn't just duty. It was hate. Pure and raw.

Pulling his bee suit hood up, Duncan stepped inside Antonio's empty house. Outside, he moved to the boot of the car. A quick glance inside and he found the briefcase – inside, the Berserker bees.

He pulled out his anti-bee spray and popped the case open, snapping a quick photo with his phone. Then, with steady hands, he unleashed the spray. The buzzing died, one by one. Finally, a lighter's flame finished the job, turning the rest to ash.

Duncan dialled Jénmar. 'Jénmar, Antonio Brown's been dealt with.'

'Good job, Duncan,' came the familiar, proud reply. *'What did you find?'*

'Berserker bees. Same ones turning people into ghouls. Got a photo here.' He paused, voice low. 'Need you to send it to the Apollo Mage of Brotherhood. They've got to know before Silver Cross wipes the lot.'

Jénmar's voice dropped. *'Oh, God …'*

'Exactly. Send them everything I told you. Could turn the tide.'

'Understood.'

'Okay, see you later.' Duncan cut the call and slipped the phone away. Job done.

Morning light filtered weakly through the haze as Lance Sainglend stood alone before the security checkpoint at Riverdam's main gate. No comrades. No flag. No fight left to give. Just a worn man in a grey coat, arms raised, boots crunching against gravel.

A soldier's eyes caught him. They widened.

'It's the Kingslayer! The Kingslayer is here!'

The name spread like wildfire. Within moments, rifles were trained on him from every angle, red armbands marked with golden lions flashing as soldiers poured in – green camo, helmets, gas masks – all barking overlapping orders.

'Freeze!'

'Down on your knees!'

'Hands behind your head!'

Lance obeyed without a word. He knelt, calm, placing his hands behind his head. No resistance. No panic. But his stillness didn't matter. One of them cracked him hard across the back of the skull with the butt of a rifle. He grunted, head dipping, the taste of blood faint at the back of his throat.

'Back up! Back the fuck up!' the soldier shouted to the crowd nearby.

Civilians scrambled away, panic rising like smoke. A little boy clung to his mother, eyes wide with fear. Lance didn't look at them – he didn't want to see their judgement or their pity.

Then came the beating. Kicks. Blows. Rifle handles slammed down on his back, his ribs, his legs. Pain flared through his body, but he didn't cry out. He clenched his jaw, ground his teeth. He'd endured worse. Not in force, perhaps, but in meaning.

One soldier pressed his boot against Lance's spine, grinding him into the dirt. Another leaned down and hissed in his ear, voice full of smug bile.

'Not so tough now, are ya, Kingslayer?'

Lance didn't reply. What was there to say? These weren't men defending a nation – they were victors revelling in the humiliation of their enemy.

Rough hands cuffed his wrists. They frisked him for weapons or contraband.

'He's clean,' one muttered.

Langford – he assumed that was the officer in charge – spoke into a walkie-talkie.

'HQ, this is Officer Langford. We've apprehended Lance Sainglend. I repeat, Lance Sainglend is in custody. Requesting extraction vehicle.'

A crackle, then a reply:

'Roger that. Pickup truck en route. Over.'

Langford nodded, clipped and official. 'Officer Langford out.'

Another soldier, younger by the sound of his voice, chuckled as he tightened the cuffs.

'Welcome to Blackstorm, Kingslayer. Got a nice little cell with your name on it. Hope you like the company – place is crawling with psychos.'

The truck rumbled in not long after. They hauled him up – no ceremony – and tossed him into the back like cargo. The metal door slammed shut. The engine growled, and the vehicle pulled away.

Inside the dim confines of the transport, Lance leaned back against the wall, his hands aching, ribs throbbing, but his gaze fixed and steady.

They think it's over. That capturing me ends the rebellion. Fools.

He still believed in the cause. In Flora's right to choose freedom over tyranny. If this was the price, so be it. He could live with being hated. He could die being cursed. But he would not – could not – regret standing against the lie.

Lance stared ahead, calm and steady.

Let them parade me. Let them lock the doors and throw away the key. But so long as one person remembers why we fought—

He smiled faintly, just for a moment.

—then I haven't lost.

Chapter XVI

CALM BEFORE THE STORM

Duncan sat in the basement of Abraham's house, both of them engaged in conversation. Abraham was a man with neatly trimmed black hair and a subtle goatee framing his face. His eyes, a muted shade of grey, held a quiet depth as he observed the scene. Duncan's look had shifted subtly. He wore sharp blue sneakers and well-fitted jeans, an addition to his usual blue blouson jacket.

They were seated at a wooden, round table, enjoying whiskey with the clink of ice cubes. A thin haze hung in the air from Abraham's cigarette, blurring the harsh light of the desk lamp and casting murky shadows across the room.

Their talk started with Abraham asking, 'Did you do it?'

Duncan replied calmly. 'Took down the target with a .45 round. No witnesses, no bystanders, no pets … not even a sidewalk pigeon.'

'Confident, aren't we?' Abraham chuckled.

Duncan placed the photos of Antonio Brown's lifeless body on the table, spreading them out for Abraham to inspect. 'Here. Take a look for yourself.'

Abraham glanced at the photos, a satisfied grin forming. 'Excellent. May God have mercy on his soul.'

'Indeed.' Duncan nodded.

As he studied the events of the operation, Duncan couldn't help but analyse the target's mistakes. 'The man was an amateur. He didn't disable the CCTV cameras, and his methods were easy to follow.' The fact that the target hadn't done anything to cover his tracks was a glaring mistake, one that revealed a lack of thorough planning and a failure to account for potential surveillance.

Abraham nodded. 'Interesting. And what else did you do after eliminating him?'

'I had Jénmar contact the AMOB to investigate the secret black market in the basement of Rosemary Park. The Silver Cross should soon take care of the heretics there.'

'Excellent. You've made a friend happy,' Abraham said with a smile. 'Your efficiency never ceases to amaze me, Duncan. The world needs more people like you.'

'As long as there are evildoers, I'll be there to stop them.'

Abraham lit another cigarette and took a deep drag before exhaling. 'Quite the hero, you are, like those comic book characters kids read about.'

Duncan smirked. 'Well, someone has to stand up for justice in this world.'

Abraham then placed a briefcase on the table. 'Your reward, for your exceptional service to the people of Flora – twenty thousand Livres.' He opened the briefcase, revealing the cash.

Duncan was taken aback by the generosity. 'Twenty thousand? This is far more than we agreed upon.'

Abraham smiled warmly. 'Consider it a bonus for a job well done. Your efficiency and skill deserve recognition. Besides, our friendship means a lot to me and I want to maintain that mutual respect.'

Duncan felt grateful for his friend's gesture. 'Thank you, Abraham. You've always been a great friend.'

'No problem at all,' Abraham replied, grinning.

Duncan picked up the briefcase, securing the money, and bid farewell to his friend. 'Alright, I'll be on my way now. I have some other matters to attend to.'

Abraham nodded in understanding. 'Take care, and I'll see you later.'

With that, Duncan left.

Duncan returned home a few hours later, sliding his key into the lock and stepping inside. He closed the door behind him, ensuring it was securely locked.

In the cosy ambience of his living room, Duncan made his way to the refrigerator. He grabbed a chilled can of fizzy drink, then settled onto his comfortable sofa. With a deft flick of his finger, he popped open the soda can and reached for the TV remote. As he switched on the television, a lively music video burst onto the screen.

It's my life
It's now or never
I ain't gonna live forever
I just want to live while I'm alive
(It's my life)

Duncan quickly changed the channel to a dramatic soap opera, where a tearful confession of love played out.

'*Oh my gosh, of course, I'll marry you!*' the actress exclaimed.

He couldn't help but cringe at the over-the-top drama and changed the channel once more, landing on another music video.

Push it to the limit
Walk along the razor's edge
But don't look down, just keep your head
Or you'll be finished

With a slight shake of his head, Duncan switched to a gritty crime movie where two figures were locked in a tense standoff.

'Stop pointing that gun at my fucking dad!' one character shouted.

Duncan's interest waned and he changed the channel again, this time to a sports broadcast replaying a national baseball league game.

'Ah, damn. I missed it,' he muttered to himself, watching as the announcer's voice grew increasingly enthusiastic.

'Orlando managed to hit the ball! He's on the run! He's on the run!'

Just as he was getting absorbed in the game, Duncan's smartphone rang, instantly grabbing his attention. He swiftly picked it up, eager to see who was calling.

'Hello?' Duncan said.

'Heeeelloooo, Duncan.' Sara chimed in playfully.

'Mum? Why're you calling?'

'I need your help with something.'

Duncan adjusted himself in his chair, sitting up more attentively. 'And what would that be?'

'Elisa.' Sara's tone turned serious. 'S*he's applied for a course at university. But the thing is, she needs money for tuition.'*

'Okay. Which university is she attending?'

'The University of Kate.'

Duncan's face fell. 'Oh, really? The same place you attended?'

'Yep.'

'Ugh, that place ... where you had to drop out because of me.'

Sara's voice hinted annoyance. '*Duncan, don't be stupid. It was my decision to leave. I valued raising you more than finishing school.*'

Duncan sighed. 'Okay. How much do you need?'

'*Around ... twenty-five thousand Livres. Could we split that fifty-fifty between us?*'

Duncan smiled. 'Mum, who do you think you're asking? Of course, I can. No need to ask twice.'

'*Thanks, Duncan.*'

'You're welcome.'

'*So when can you send the money?*' Sara asked.

'I can come over this evening.'

Sara displayed happiness through her voice. '*That's great, thank you.*' Then she remembered something. '*Oh yeah, another thing. I heard the news about Antonio Brown's death. Was it your doing?*'

Duncan took a deep breath before speaking, his mind racing with thoughts. He knew he had to be honest with his mother, but he also feared her reaction. Antonio Brown's death was not something he felt proud of, but it was a necessary action to protect the people of Flora. He knew she deserved to know the truth, no matter how difficult it was to share.

'Yes, it was.'

'*I see ...*'

Duncan then heard a sigh from Sara through the phone, conveying a sense of discontent. His mind raced as he tried to understand his mother's reaction. He knew she had always been supportive of him, but this particular line of work seemed to be testing the limits of her understanding. He couldn't blame her entirely: after all, it wasn't a conventional job that he had chosen. However, he also felt a sense of frustration bubbling up within him. This was his passion, his calling, and he had dedicated years to honing his skills.

'Mum, not this again. I told you–' Duncan began.

'*I don't care. Just remember, no matter what you do, I'll always support you and love you.*'

Duncan was grateful to hear that. It reminded him that no matter their disagreements or worries, a mother's love for her child was unbreakable. He felt profoundly thankful for her love and understanding.

'*Alright, I'll talk to you later,*' Sara said.

'Bye, Mum.'

'*Bye,*' Sara said, and they hung up.

Duncan put his phone back in his pocket and took a moment to reflect on the conversation. While he was grateful for his mother's support, even if she didn't fully understand his work, he also felt uneasy. Why did he feel conflicted about Antonio Brown's death? Antonio Brown was a heretic, and in his mind, all heretics were scum; Antonio was no exception.

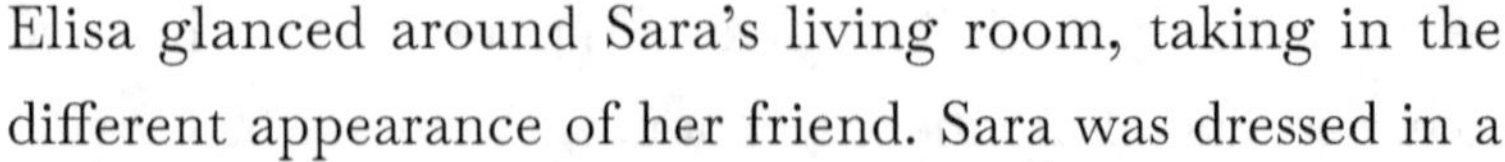

Elisa glanced around Sara's living room, taking in the different appearance of her friend. Sara was dressed in a white, vertical-striped shirt, sleeves rolled up, paired with Capri trousers and block heels. Elisa herself wore a white floral dress with small black flower patterns.

Sara was excitedly showed Elisa a red touring motorcycle featured in an auto magazine. She hit her hand on the image, pointing it out to Elisa. 'See right here, Elisa. That's what I want, right there.'

'Do you wish to purchase a motorcycle?' Elisa politely inquired.

Sara's eyes gleamed with enthusiasm as she clapped her hands together, clearly lost in a fantasy of riding the bike. 'Of course! I've always dreamt about riding one, especially when I was younger.' Pouting her lips, Sara looked at Elisa seriously. 'And I know what you're thinking – just because I'm middle-aged, a poor woman like me shouldn't ride a motorcycle.'

Elisa quickly raised her hands defensively and interjected. 'No, I assure you, such thoughts did not cross my mind at all!'

Sara folded her arms, shaking her head. 'Yeah, sure you weren't …'

'N–no, I genuinely mean it.' Elisa insisted, trying to reassure her friend. She attentively listened to Sara's excitement about the motorcycle, and upon reflection, she couldn't help but feel that riding a motorcycle with Sara would be both thrilling and worrisome. 'Forgive me, Mrs Saul, but I must admit my unfamiliarity with riding such a vehicle. I may not be the most adept passenger. However, I will not decline an offer from such a kind person.'

'Ah, thank you,' Sara said gratefully. 'But seriously, you'd be a fool if you rejected the offer of a ride. I mean, think about it, Elisa – don't you believe it'd be fun riding through the wind at high speed, feeling the breeze brush over our faces?'

Elisa nodded with a smile. 'Indeed, the prospect sounds quite enjoyable, Mrs Saul.'

Sara then playfully mimicked riding on an imaginary bike. 'Vroom! Vroom!'

Elisa couldn't help but cover her mouth and laugh delicately in response. 'Hahaha! You are truly amusing, Mrs Saul. There is never a dull moment when you are in company.'

'I love to put on a pleasant spectacle for people – I find it satisfying,' Sara remarked, sitting back in her chair.

'Oh, was that the pursuit to which you dedicated your studies? You aspired to become an actor?'

'Of course. I wanted to appear on TV, especially on those drama shows, but then Duncan came along and I had to take care of him.'

Elisa couldn't help but ponder over what Sara had said about her dreams. Could a single mistake or action truly shatter someone's chances of achieving their goals?

'Don't get the wrong idea, kid. I don't blame Duncan one bit for any of that because I chose to quit. Sometimes you must be willing to make sacrifices or you wouldn't accomplish anything. So don't let my past actions fear you.' Sara smiled brightly and lifted her thumb up. 'I'm sure you'll make your dream shine – just make the right decisions, and you'll get there.'

Elisa engaged in introspection, musing on the wisdom imparted by Sara. 'Indeed – sometimes sacrifices are necessary ... So, Mrs Saul? Have you told your son about the money?'

Sara nodded. 'Yep, he should be coming anytime soon.'

Abruptly, the doorbell rang and Sara got up excitedly. 'Oh, speak of the devil.'

Elisa watched as Sara opened the door to Duncan's polite greeting and warm smile.

'Hello, Mother. Hello, Elisa,' he said.

'Hello, Duncan,' Sara replied with a smile.

Elisa waved her hand. 'Greetings, Mr Saul.'

Duncan lifted his briefcase, showing it to his mother. 'I come with the money.'

'Yes, you do. Now come in,' Sara said.

Duncan entered the house and placed the briefcase, full of money, on the table. 'Here's twelve thousand five hundred Livres for Elisa's course – half of what we agreed.'

'Ah, thank you, Duncan. God bless you,' Sara said in appreciation.

Duncan beamed a smile. 'You should also thank Abraham for this. He's the one who provided me with a bonus to my reward.'

'Ah, how kind of him,' said Elisa.

'You can't hope to gain anything new without sacrifices. And I hope that heretic's sacrifice wasn't a waste,' said Duncan.

'Okay, let's count it,' Sara said, shifting her focus to the task at hand. She began by placing her cash on the table. 'Fifteen thousand from my savings account ...' Next, she examined the money inside the briefcase. 'Fifteen thousand from your briefcase ... Okay, when we add them both together, that makes thirty thousand. And the tuition fee for Elisa's course is about twenty-seven thousand, five hundred ...' Sara then extended her hand, offering a high five to Duncan. 'We did it! We finally did it,' she yelled with exuberance.

Duncan enthusiastically returned the high five, and they both smiled with a sense of accomplishment.

Sara hugged Duncan with gratitude and exclaimed, 'You're truly an angel, Duncan. I can't express my thanks enough!' She then released him as he chuckled.

'No need to mention it, Mother. I'm always here whenever you need help.'

Elisa observed the heartwarming scene but couldn't muster a smile. 'I can't thank you two enough. This is too much for me ... I don't deserve this ...' She held her arm, her nails digging into her flesh as if she was trying to physically torture herself. The overwhelming kindness of both Sara and Duncan made her feel a deep sense of unworthiness, as if she didn't deserve their generosity and support. Looking at them both, Elisa couldn't help but feel guilt. They had become like family to her. They had welcomed her into their lives with open arms, and she had grown to care for them deeply.

But there was something darker tormenting her mind, whispering, *You don't deserve this. You don't deserve them.* This thought cast a cloud of guilt, overshadowing any joy in the moment.

Sara then crossed her arms, seemingly irritated by Elisa's response, and said with a stern face, 'Idiot.'

Duncan crossed his arms as well and repeated after Sara. 'Idiot.'

'Huh?' Elisa said, bewildered.

Sara again chided Elisa and pointed at her. 'Fool.'

Duncan shook his head. 'Fool.'

'What are you two doing?'

'It's what my family does when somebody says something stupid,' said Duncan.

Sara frowned and nodded firmly. 'Mm-hmm.'

Duncan continued. 'Elisa, you have to know that we did this because we wanted to and you saying that makes you sort of ungrateful. As you can see, my mother and I have given you this opportunity to achieve your dream, and you should take it.'

'Thank you, Duncan. I couldn't explain it better myself,' said Sara.

Duncan then returned a smile. 'No problem, Mum. I'm just giving the word out.'

Elisa felt a deep sense of regret and remorse for her words. She had acted foolishly without considering the kindness and generosity that Sara and Duncan had shown her. Their display, while unusual, served as a powerful reminder that she should be grateful for the chance they had given her to pursue her dreams. ‘Indeed, you are correct. My judgment was hasty and unfair. I humbly ask for your forgiveness.’

‘Whatever. Just remember that we’re all in this together,’ said Duncan.

Sara rested her hands on her hips, her eyes sparkling with excitement. ‘Alright, enough of the bickering. Let’s celebrate our success in raising the money for Elisa’s course.’

Duncan settled into a chair, running a hand through his hair. ‘So, what’s the plan?’

Sara tapped her chin, deep in thought. ‘Hmm … How about we each prepare a special dish, and then we can have a little competition? We’ll taste each other’s creations, and the one who makes the best dish wins.’

‘That seems like a fine proposition, Mrs Saul.’

‘I’m not exactly a master chef, but count me in,’ Duncan replied.

Sara’s eyes lit up with enthusiasm. ‘So, are we up for a cook-off?’

‘If that’s what you want?’ Duncan confirmed. Duncan shifted his attention to Elisa. ‘And how about you, Elisa?’

Elisa responded with a smile. ‘Certainly, I will not shy away from this opportunity to showcase my culinary skills.’

Sara looked a bit puzzled. ‘Culi–what’s that now?’

Elisa simplified. ‘My cooking skills.’

‘Right–’ Sara smacked herself in the head. ‘Then allow me to start,’ she said. ‘I’m going for creamy lemon Parmesan chicken.’

'Guacamole and barbecue sauce along with chips sprinkled with seasoning and fried fish fillet,' Duncan said, calmly and reservedly.

Elisa thought briefly, trying to figure out the dish she wanted to make. 'Hmm ... I think I'm going to make vegan casserole and lasagna.'

Sara held her hips. 'Alright everyone, chop-chop, let's get a move on. But before we start, I would like to make a statement.' Sara then bowed to display her flamboyance. 'That I, Sara Saul, am going to make the finest dish in this house.'

Duncan narrowed his eyes and said solemnly, 'Yeah, right. We'll see about that.'

Elisa stepped in. 'Rest assured, I shall present a dish of such elegance and flavour that it will captivate your taste buds and earn your admiration,' she announced.

Duncan looked at Elisa out of the corner of his eye. 'Yeah, if you actually win, that is.' Then he suddenly had a realisation and voiced his concern. 'Hold on a minute, who's going to judge this competition? We have a vegetarian in the mix, so she can't taste all our dishes.'

Sara quickly stepped in. 'I'll be the judge.'

Duncan was sceptical. 'I know you, Mum, you're probably going to be biased towards your own cooking. If you're the judge, you might declare your own dish the winner no matter what.'

Sara gasped in mock outrage. 'Excuse you! I'll have you know I am a woman of impeccable taste and *flawless* objectivity.'

'Says the woman who wept over her sponge cake and called it "a gift to mankind",' Duncan muttered.

'It was *fluffy*!' she snapped, then pointed a finger at him. 'That's enough out of you. I'm the judge, and that's final.'

Duncan, slightly annoyed, rolled his eyes and mumbled under his breath. 'Whatever ...'

Sara clapped her hands to get the two ready for their cook-off. 'Now chop-chop, start getting ready.'

Chapter XVII

THE TASTE OF FAMILY

Elisa watched as they prepared for their cooking session. She tied her hair back, ensuring it wouldn't interfere with the task ahead. Sara took her place at the cooker, ready to ignite the burner.

Elisa reached for the kitchen tools, while Duncan retrieved a saucepan from the cupboard. He carefully poured vegetable oil into it, which soon began to sizzle. Duncan then took a packet of frozen chips from the freezer and dropped them into the bubbling oil.

Turning to her own dish, Elisa readied ingredients for the casserole and stirred the mixture with a wooden spoon, ensuring it blended well.

Duncan gripped the saucepan's handle firmly, giving it a gentle shake to flip the chips and cook them evenly.

Sara focused on cutting raw chicken breast with a sharp knife and deftly sliced lemons. She combined milk and Parmesan in the saucepan, infusing the mixture with flavour.

With her casserole in the oven, Elisa adjusted the temperature and set the timer, eagerly awaiting the dish's transformation.

Duncan coated a raw fish fillet in flour and egg before submerging it into the hot oil, ensuring it sizzled to perfection.

As time passed, they completed their tasks, and before long, dinner was served.

Elisa watched as Duncan skilfully plated a delicious spread. He had made guacamole and a tasty barbecue sauce for the chips, generously sprinkled with spicy seasoning. Duncan had also cooked fish fillets, fried in vegetable oil and finished with a touch of herbs.

Elisa's casserole was a mouthwatering blend of rice, cheese, potatoes, broccoli and carrots. Alongside it, she had prepared a delectable vegan lasagne, layered with vegan cheese and sliced tomatoes.

Lastly, Sara had worked her magic on chicken breasts soaked in milk and coated with melted Parmesan. She added baby spinach and slices of zesty lemon, creating a truly scrumptious creamy lemon Parmesan chicken dish.

Sara clasped her hands together in delight, clearly enamoured with the food before her. 'Ahhhhhhh! This looks delicious!' She then pointed upwards. 'This deserves to be photographed. Everyone, wait here ... I'll get the camera.'

With the two of them staying in place, Sara dashed upstairs to retrieve the camera.

Returning with the camera in hand, Sara gave them their instructions. 'Everyone, just stand right there.'

Duncan and Elisa positioned themselves, ready for the photo. Sara set the camera on a countdown and then rushed into her spot. She grabbed Duncan by the waist, a hint of annoyance in her voice. 'Come here, Duncan.'

Mildly irritated, Duncan responded, 'Ugh, you don't have to grab me like that.'

'Stop your whining and look good for the camera,' Sara retorted, beaming a bright smile. 'Everyone, say cheese!'

'We're not saying cheese,' said Duncan, shooting his mother a stern look.

'Hush!' she said with an equally stern look.

'Okay, jeez.'

Duncan and Elisa smiled, and Sara beamed even brighter as she threw her arms around them both in a warm, squishy hug. The camera clicked as it took the picture. Then Sara let them go and checked the results on the screen.

'Not bad, not bad at all. This is going to fit right into the photo album,' she said, a wide grin on her face. Sara gathered their attention. 'Okay, everyone. We have finally had this opportunity to come together as a family.'

Family? The word echoed in Elisa's mind and startled her. Hearing it in this context, among the people who had welcomed her into their lives, made her pause and reflect. For so long, Elisa had felt like an outsider, a lone soul without the safety net of a family. Her own had been tragically taken from her, and she had grown up with the understanding that she was alone.

'But I'm not family,' Elisa said.

Sara quickly reassured her. 'Yeah, but you're close to it.'

Elisa smiled at Sara.

Duncan and Elisa picked up their knives and forks, but Sara stopped everyone from eating their meals.

'Wait ... before we dig in, we must pray.'

With these words, everyone around the dinner table closed their eyes in reverence and bowed their heads.

'Heavenly Father,' Sara began, her voice earnest, 'you've brought us together today to celebrate this special occasion and provided us with this delicious meal. We've come together to support a young girl in her pursuit of her dreams, and for that, we are truly grateful. We ask for your continued guidance and assistance on our journey.'

'Amen,' they all said in unison.

Standing up, Sara lifted her wine cup and said, brightly, 'To Elisa! She has fought hard to get where she is going. And to us, for getting the money for her course.'

Duncan and Elisa both stood and lifted their wine cups, and the three of them bumped their wine vessels together. 'Here, here!'

As they returned to their seats, the room filled with laughter and Elisa couldn't help but wear a warm smile. Watching Duncan and Sara share this light-hearted moment filled her with a profound sense of contentment. It was moments like these that made her realise how much they had done for her. They had welcomed her into their lives, supported her dreams and provided her with something she hadn't experienced in a long time ... a sense of belonging. Elisa had spent much of her life alone, but being with Duncan and Sara felt like being part of a real family. They may not have been blood-related, but the bond they shared was strong and genuine.

As she watched them laugh, she couldn't help but reflect on the twists and turns life had taken to bring her there. It was a beautiful reminder that, sometimes, the family you choose can be just as meaningful as the one you're born into.

Sara raised her wine glass and took a sip. Elisa followed suit, her lips tasting the unfamiliar white grape wine. She pondered its flavour. 'I find it tastes a mix of sweet and bitter,' Elisa said.

Sara furrowed her brow. 'Is that so?'

Elisa nodded. 'Indeed, Mrs Saul. The flavour presents itself as rather distinct from my initial expectations. I had assumed it might bear a resemblance to those carbonated beverages one finds in vending machines.' Elisa then coughed as the alcohol's strength hit her. This thing was strong.

'What's wrong?' Sara asked.

Elisa, holding her head, commented, 'This beverage is rather potent. With each sip, I find myself growing increasingly lightheaded. The alcohol burns within me ... How do people partake in this without flinching?'

Sara covered her mouth and chuckled. 'Haha! That's what happens with alcohol. It's strong, and only the tough can handle it. It might taste odd at first, but you'll get used to it. Your first time trying something is a unique experience. However, I'd advise against making a habit of it, kiddo, or you might end up in a drunken stupor.'

Elisa agreed, saying, 'Yes, I harbour no intentions of taking this regularly.'

Sara took a bite of her meal, shivering with delight at the taste. 'Mmmm ... This food is so delicious.'

Duncan, curious, asked, 'Whose cooking is it?'

'*Á moi*,' Sara said, proudly boasting.

Duncan rolled his eyes. 'Of course, you'd say that.'

Sara grinned playfully. 'I'm just teasing,' she said, then flashed an A-OK hand sign. 'It's not just my dish that's delicious. Everyone's meal is *magnifique*.'

Elisa persisted. 'Indeed, Mrs Saul. I am curious to know, among this splendid array of dishes, which one do you believe merits the distinction of the finest?'

Sara rested her chin in her hand, deep in thought. 'Hmmm ...' She gave no immediate response, lost in contemplation. 'Mmmm ...'

Growing impatient, Duncan rolled his eyes and urged, 'Could you please make up your mind?'

'Perhaps ...?' Sara pondered. Then she shrugged, still unable to decide definitively. 'I don't know ...'

Duncan's frustration showed. 'Pick a winner!'

'Elisa ... no, wait ... maybe Duncan, or perhaps ... mine?' Sara replied, her indecision evident. Once again, Sara shrugged. 'I can't decide – it's too tough.'

Slightly irritated, Duncan gave his opinion. 'Well, I'll decide then. I think Elisa's meal is fantastic, but your cooking is also excellent, Mother. It's difficult to choose, so personally, I think Elisa should win.'

Elisa blushed with gratitude and responded shyly. 'Aww ... Thank you, Mr Saul.'

'But I'm the judge. I make the call. So, for me, it's a tie,' Sara retorted.

Duncan looked at his mother, annoyed. 'Ugh, really?'

Sara rubbed the back of her head. 'Enough of that – it's not important right now. What matters is that we've all come together today. Now, everyone, shut up and eat!' Sara grumbled, folding her arms.

Duncan mumbled, his mouth full of chips. 'Okay, okay, okay.' He then turned to Elisa and calmly said, 'Elisa, eat your food, or my mother will kill you.'

Elisa, flustered, stammered, 'R-right, Mr Saul!'

They continued to savour their meals.

Several hours had passed, and Elisa, in her light blue nightdress, found herself sitting on her bed. Near her bedroom door, Duncan, stood with his arms folded, seemingly lost in thought.

Elisa gazed at Duncan with a gentle blush, her gratitude evident in her eyes. 'I can't express how thankful I am, Mr Saul. You've done so much for me, and I truly appreciate it.'

Duncan opened his eyes, looking somewhat bewildered. 'Why are you thanking me? It's my mother who's been doing all the work.'

Elisa shook her head gently. 'But it was you who welcomed me into this home and made me feel like a part of your family.'

Duncan remained silent, leaning against the wall, his thoughts deepening.

Lost in her own memories, Elisa continued. 'It's been so long since I've experienced a dinner filled with laughter like this. Seeing you both smile and laugh brings back fond memories of my own family's joyous moments around the dinner table.'

'After what you've been through, you must miss those times,' he mused. 'You faced a tragic fate, but it is what it is. I wanted to prevent things like that from happening to others, but evil still persists. No matter how much good I do, it's always to a limited extent.'

Elisa moved closer to Duncan, her innocent gaze locked onto his. 'You're a good man, Mr Saul, with qualities that inspire others.'

Duncan chuckled lightly. 'Don't flatter me, kid. There's a limit to what I can do.' He then reassured Elisa. 'You, too, can achieve greatness. Just put in the time and effort, and you'll get there.'

'I will strive to do so. I promise not to disappoint you, Mr Saul,' Elisa declared.

Duncan smiled. 'I hope not.' Stepping away from the wall, Duncan turned to leave. 'Anyway, I'll be heading out.'

'Mr Saul, wait.' Elisa blushed and pinched Duncan's shirt, stopping him in his tracks. He turned to look at her. 'Mr Saul,' Elisa began hesitantly, 'would you be free again?'

Duncan responded with a warm smile. 'Yeah, just give me a call and I'll let you know when I'm available.'

Elisa beamed with joy. 'Very well. Good night, Mr Saul.'

'Good night, Elisa,' he replied, his voice soft as he stepped through the doorway and disappeared down the hall.

She stood there for a moment, listening to the silence that followed.

Silence.

It used to remind her of everything she'd lost – the laughter that no longer echoed through corridors, the voices that would never return. But tonight, it felt different. Quieter, yes, but not empty.

For the first time in what felt like years, she wasn't aching in the quiet. She was simply ... at peace.

Grief still lived in her – it always would – but here, in the soft stillness of Duncan's home, something else had taken root alongside it. A flicker of warmth. The fragile shape of belonging.

And in that fleeting moment, Elisa realised she was happy. Not because everything was fixed – it wasn't – but because, despite everything, she could still feel joy. Still feel hope.

She sat back on her bed, tucking her knees to her chest, a faint smile curving her lips. Her heart felt lighter than it had in a long time.

Duncan approached his mother's room and knocked on her door, preparing to take his leave. 'Okay, Mum. I'll be going.'

Sara closed the book she was reading and got off her bed to bid her son farewell. 'Thank you for coming over, Duncan. I'm sure Elisa will be forever grateful for what you did.'

He stuffed his hands in his pockets and concurred. 'She should be.'

Sara nodded in agreement. 'Head on downstairs, I'll close the door for you.'

Duncan nodded in appreciation.

They both descended the stairs, and as Duncan stepped outside, Sara remained by the house door, holding it open. 'You'll be coming back soon, right?' she inquired.

'Yeah, probably,' Duncan replied.

Sara couldn't help but chuckle, covering her mouth as she did so.

Duncan looked at her curiously and asked, 'What's so funny?'

She stopped laughing and smiled, saying, 'Oh ... it's just that you're coming here more often.'

'The reason why I'm attending this place more often is that Elisa needs help.'

Sara teased him with a smirk. '*Oh!* So, *Elisa's* the reason, huh? Do you have a thing for her?'

Duncan frowned at Sara. 'What? No. She's young and still needs help. If it wasn't for us, she wouldn't have entered university, and if it wasn't for me, she would've been dead or on the streets. Right now, she still needs strong support until she can stand on her own.'

Sara clasped her hands together, still grinning. 'My, my ... her hero.'

Duncan was becoming a bit irritated by her teasing, but he couldn't help but smile. 'Tch. Knock it off. Don't say it like that, especially with that grin of yours, it's annoying.'

'Well, I won't be taking any more of your time. I'll see you later.'

'If you need anything, just give me a call and I'll let you know if I'm free,' Duncan replied.

'Okay, I'll remember that,' Sara acknowledged.

Duncan smiled and waved lightly. 'Bye, Mum.'

'See ya later, Duncan,' she said as she waved her hand, closing the door behind him.

Within the Night Hawks' headquarters, Jeremy found himself among those gathered to assess their current predicament. The room was dimly lit, and a large table dominated the centre, where Lord Reiman took charge of the meeting. Jeremy sat among his comrades, and his gaze was drawn to Lord Rainer who stood resolutely beside the others.

'I've gathered you all today to convey something of utmost importance,' Reiman said. A hushed anticipation settled over the room as everyone focused on him. 'A dire circumstance has befallen us. Our leader, Lance Sainglend, is now in the custody of our enemies ...'

The people in the meeting did not react well to this news. Murmurs spread through the room, and some wore expressions of wide-eyed astonishment.

Reiman continued. 'At this moment, our primary course of action is to honour Lord Sainglend's wishes.'

This was unbearable for Jeremy who was angry at hearing this. Lance, their fearless leader, had been held captive, and they sat there talking like bureaucrats. The Night Hawks were crumbling, and these men just sat there wringing their hands. How could they be so blind to the urgency of the situation? They needed to take action, do something.

Desperately seeking a chance to speak, Jeremy attempted to interject. 'Lord Reiman, may I have a moment to speak–'

However, Lord Rainer quickly interrupted Jeremy without even glancing in his direction. 'But, Lord Reiman, our faction will gradually disintegrate without Lance's guidance. The morale of the Night Hawks has suffered, given the number of witnesses to the broadcast. If this continues, the Red Lions will undoubtedly win.'

Reiman nodded. 'I am aware of the challenges, Lord Rainer. We have limited information on Lance's whereabouts and the date of his trial. All we can do is hope that the message he sent to the House of Royals proves successful.'

Jeremy clenched his fist in anger. They ignored him like he was insignificant. But he couldn't let that stand. Lance deserved better. He raised his voice once more in an attempt to be heard. 'Forgive me, Lord Reiman, but I must speak–'

But Rainer's gaze sharpened as he turned it towards Jeremy. 'Hush, Jeremy,' he demanded. 'Do not interrupt Lord Reiman.' Rainer then shifted his attention back to Lord Reiman. 'Please, you may continue.'

'As I was saying, if we take any action that might provoke the court, we risk putting Lord Sainglend in even greater danger,' said Reiman.

Dammit. Rainer keeps cutting me off.

A heavy atmosphere of disappointment hung in the room. 'Indeed. This is a dire situation. It appears we have exhausted our options ... Perhaps the wisest course of action is to patiently await the successful completion of Lance's mission ... And if that doesn't come to pass, we might have no choice but to surrender to the enemy and negotiate a truce with the Red Lions,' said Reiman.

Murmurs of concern and disbelief swept through the meeting.

Surrender!? Jeremy thought it was madness. *Negotiate a truce? Are they joking?*

Lance hadn't sacrificed so much for the faction to throw in the towel like cowards. They should be doing everything in their power to rescue him, not surrendering! But they just sat there, discussing surrender like it was a reasonable option. Jeremy found himself unable to accept this course of action. He shook his head and rose from his seat.

'Forgive me, my lords, but I can't remain silent. We need to—'

'You've interrupted this meeting repeatedly!' Lord Rainer's voice thundered, cutting off Jeremy. 'Shut your mouth, or you'll be relieved of your duties!'

Jeremy couldn't take it anymore – especially not Reiman's foolishness. He refused to stay silent any longer. He was ready to confront them, to speak his mind, no matter the consequences: he was done holding back.

'No, I won't be reticent!'

Silence fell upon the room as everyone turned their attention to Jeremy.

'What in the world are we doing here? We should be formulating plans to free Lance, not sitting like lapdogs!' Frustration boiled within Jeremy, and he slammed his fist on the table for emphasis. 'This is *Lord Sainglend* we're talking about. He's done so much for our faction, and none of you'll lift a finger to help him! You're letting him rot like a stray dog. If it were up to me, I'd do more than sit in my chair flapping my gums – I'd be trying to break Lance out of prison! We need to take action ... now!'

Lord Reiman responded with irritation. 'Don't be a fool, Jeremy! We've already lost too many men. Do you honestly believe you can rescue Lance from the enemy stronghold?'

'I don't care! It's worth a shot. Without him, we're fucked! The Red Lions will hunt us down and wipe us out. Our entire Night Hawk army might as well have their flags torn down and be burnt to the ground!' Jeremy's gaze swept across the members of the meeting. 'Have any of you considered what might happen if Lance's plan falls apart? What if it doesn't come out as he expects? Everything we're doing will be in vain!'

Lord Rainer interjected, his frustration apparent. 'And what, Jeremy? Create more chaos? Maybe you should stop being so selfish and consider that this is what Lance wanted! You're clearly showing a lack of faith in him. If you truly want to be his friend, you should respect his wishes, not your own!'

'To hell with that! You all call yourselves Night Hawks, but you're abandoning Lance. If you won't free him, then I will!'

'Do you realise that's an act of insubordination!?' Lord Rainer rose to his feet, his tone commanding. 'Sit down, Jeremy!'

Jeremy snarled. 'Screw you, old man!'

'How dare you speak to me like that, you brute! I should strip you of your rank!'

He didn't have time for that. He was done with these people. Kissing his teeth in frustration, Jeremy left the room immediately.

'Where do you think you're going, Jeremy?' Lord Rainer demanded, but Jeremy paid him no heed. Rainer's voice grew more desperate as he called after his comrade. 'Jeremy!'

But Jeremy continued on his way, storming out of the building in a blaze of anger.

Chapter XVIII

A COLD NIGHT

The morning sun seeped through the curtains, bathing Duncan's bedroom in a warm glow. His sleep was rudely interrupted by his alarm clock. Grumbling, he reached out and turned it off, then reluctantly got out of bed. Moving on autopilot, he walked into the bathroom, grabbed his toothbrush and toothpaste and started his usual morning routine to wake up.

A few minutes later, Duncan was in the kitchen, filling a bowl with cereal and adding milk. He absentmindedly ate as the morning news played on the television. During his breakfast, Duncan's phone rang. He paused his meal to answer the call.

'Hey, Duncan,' Abraham began. *'I've got something interesting for you.'*

'Abraham?' Duncan said with a raised brow.

'Yeah, I need you to do something for me.'

'Alright, sing your song. What do you need?'

Abraham explained. *'You know that lowlife running the black market in Rosemary Park?'*

Duncan agreed, anticipating where this conversation was heading. 'Yeah, I'm following.'

'Well, I've got some information on him. Joseph Holloway. I'll send you the details. I need you to pass it along to Hendrik so he can dig deeper. Can you handle that?'

Duncan grinned. 'Abraham, you know me. They don't call me the *Heretic Hunter* for nothing. Consider it done.'

'Great, Duncan. I'm counting on you. See you later.'

Abraham hung up and Duncan returned to his breakfast, ready for the task ahead.

Duncan opened the door and spotted Jénmar standing there, dressed like he'd just stepped out of an old detective movie – a brown fedora tipped low, gold aviator sunglasses reflecting the afternoon light, and a long brown trench coat hanging from his shoulders.

Duncan welcomed Jénmar and inquired, 'Hey, Jénmar. Have you gathered the intel on our target?'

Jénmar nodded. 'Yes, I have. May I come in?'

Duncan stepped aside, granting Jénmar entry. 'Sure.'

They both made their way to Duncan's workspace. Jénmar handed over a document containing the personal information of the target, Joseph Holloway.

'This is Joseph Holloway, aged forty-seven, born on the twelfth of April. He's the head of the black-market operation in Rosemary Park. My research shows that he's currently living in a hotel in Ledwake, at forty-two Adam's Street.'

'Ledwake, that's quite a distance,' Duncan said.

'Indeed.'

'So, what's our plan, Jénmar?' Duncan inquired.

'The operation will take place at night with the target likely at his residence,' Jénmar explained.

'A suppressor should do the trick.'

'Exactly,' Jénmar agreed. Standing up, he concluded. 'So, grab your shit, Duncan. Flora needs cleaning.'

Duncan smiled. 'Consider me the caretaker.'

It was night, and wearing her yellow nightdress, Elisa made her way through the house. Her steps led her to Sara's room where Sara was sitting at her dressing table, using a hairdryer to dry her hair. Elisa entered the room, causing Sara to switch off the hairdryer and turn towards her.

'Is there something the matter, Elisa?'

Elisa hesitated for a moment before she decided to voice her concerns. 'May I ask you something?' Elisa had recently recalled a time when she had overheard Duncan muttering in his sleep. His words had struck a chord with her: *I'm sorry that I couldn't save you, Father. I regret not being able to help.* The word *regret* had lingered in her mind. It felt like a significant moment of déjà vu, and she couldn't help but empathise with Duncan. Elisa felt a pressing need to understand what had happened to his father, believing that knowing might help Duncan.

'What's on your mind, kiddo?'

Elisa broached the subject carefully. 'It's about your son.'

Sara's expression softened, drawing Elisa into a contemplative silence while Sara waited for her to continue.

Elisa decided to press on, her tone gentle yet persuasive. 'During the other night, I heard your son speaking in his sleep. He said, "I am trying, Father. I am trying. I will find them – I swear I will." Do you have any idea what that means, Mrs Saul?'

Sara averted her gaze, her expression reflecting a sense of melancholy.

Elisa, showing empathy, posed her question once more, this time with even greater tenderness. She approached Sara, reaching out to clasp her palms. 'Mrs Saul, did something happen to your husband, something that you do not wish to tell me?' Elisa drew nearer to Sara, her concern evident in her eyes as she continued. 'Look, I will confide in you, I will share a personal secret. I want to partake in your pain, and I hope you will understand.' Elisa began to reveal a piece of her past. 'I was raised in a town called Pete's Fort during my youth years.'

'Pete's Fort?' Sara replied.

Elisa nodded solemnly. 'Yes, I was one of the few survivors during that incident. I remain uncertain as to how the ghouls breached the town, or whence they came; yet there they were.' She continued. 'The experience was traumatic. One night, I was alone in my room, sleeping in my bed, and suddenly, I heard screams. When I exited my room, I saw a terrifying creature inside the building. It was someone I knew – Mother Amy.' Elisa's face showed the pain of recollection. 'She attacked the children at the orphanage, biting their necks and infecting more of them.' She sighed, her voice heavy with sorrow. Sara, shocked by the revelation, held her chest as Elisa went on. 'But it wasn't just her who was infected – others were, too. Sister Elsa, Sister Martha, Teddy, Isaac, Egbert, Allana – the children in the orphanage, all turned into ghouls.'

Sara's face softened with deep sadness, and Elisa went on, her voice trembling.

'My sister and I escaped through the window. When we got outside, the whole town was in flames. We wandered through the burning streets and saw a few men dressed in black suits.'

Sara leant forwards, eyes narrowing. 'AMOB agents.'

Elisa gave a small, firm nod. 'Yes. They … they set our town on fire. They bombed the orphanage I called home. My friends … the staff … they were all killed in the explosion.'

Sara gasped, hand flying to her mouth. 'Oh my God …'

Elisa wrapped her arms tightly around herself, as if to hold the past at bay. 'I heard people screaming. Saw ghouls gunned down. But not just ghouls – they killed anyone they thought *might* be infected. I just stood there, frozen. I thought if they saw me, they'd kill me too.'

Sara's voice dropped to a gentle murmur. 'And your sister? Did you find her?'

Elisa froze. Her heartbeat quickened, and for a moment, she felt as if she were falling. That question pierced through her like shrapnel. She had hoped Sara wouldn't ask.

'No …' she whispered. Her throat tightened. 'She … she became one of them. Her eyes … her fangs …'

Her breath caught. 'She was in pain and I … I …'

The rest of the sentence stuck in her throat. The room faded around her – too quiet, too bright. Her vision blurred at the edges.

Smoke. Screaming. Blood. The smell of ash filled her nose – though it wasn't really there. *Pete's Fort.* The memories slammed into her with no warning.

Elisa gasped. Her breath turned shallow, sharp. Her chest burnt, each inhale jagged like broken glass. She curled in slightly, arms drawn tight, trembling.

You couldn't save her.

She didn't want to cry in front of Sara, but she couldn't stop it. Her heart pounded against her ribs. It felt like drowning – no air, no space, no escape.

'Hey! Hey, are you alright!?'

Sara was suddenly by her side, her voice urgent, her hands cupping Elisa's tear-streaked face. She wiped her cheeks with her thumb, grounding her.

Gradually, the haze lifted. Elisa met Sara's gaze, eyes raw and wet. Her voice was hoarse. 'I'm so sorry for tearing up, Mrs Saul. I just ... I just wanted to feel like someone understood.'

Sara shook her head. 'Don't be daft. What've you got to be sorry for?' She let out a shaky breath. 'If anyone should apologise, it's me – I should've told you what happened to my husband, Jon.'

Her expression turned grave. 'He was attacked by a heretic.'

Elisa said nothing – her eyes, still glassy, never leaving Sara's.

'One night, when Jon came home, he had been completely transformed,' Sara continued. 'It was as if he had aged thirty years overnight. His hair had turned grey, one of his eyes had gone pale, his skin looked withered and his body had become so emaciated that you could see his bones. The police mentioned that the heretic used something they called *energy leeches*. These leeches drained their victims' energy and channelled it within themselves. These are what caused Jon to become so terribly ill,' Sara added, her voice heavy with emotion. 'Duncan was just thirteen years old when Jon left.'

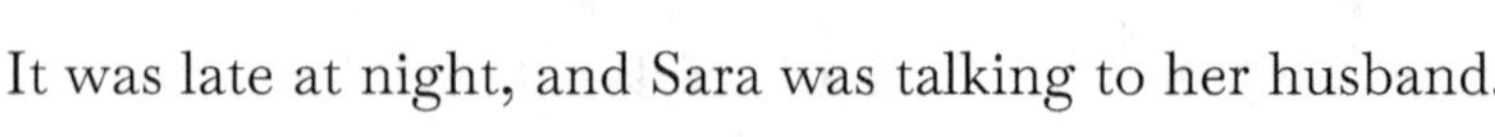

It was late at night, and Sara was talking to her husband. 'Duncan is your son, Jon. You can't just leave him behind.'

Jon looked extremely unwell. His face was discoloured, with purple thread veins visible. His eyes had turned yellow, his skin had become wrinkled and he had a gaunt physique. He clutched his left arm, and his hair had gone grey as if he were ageing rapidly. 'I know, but the leeches inside me are draining me, and the effects are still lingering,' Jon replied, weakly. He narrowed his eyes and continued. 'It's going to kill me sooner or later if I don't do something about it. My best option is to try to find a way to get rid of these things.'

Sara grabbed Jon's arm to stop him from leaving. 'We can just call the hospital to help you. We could also contact the police to investigate what has happened and track down the heretic.'

'No! You can't do that!' Jon yelled, coughing weakly.

Perplexed, Sara asked, 'Why not?'

'The hospital would hand me over to the Apollo Mage of Brotherhood who'd use me as a guinea pig. Even worse, the Silver Cross might try to kill me because they might consider me a threat,' Jon explained. 'And what if, Sara, the heretic targets this family because you reported it? What if he kills you both to tie up loose ends? So please, allow me to go off by myself.' Jon frowned, a dejected look on his face.

Sara pleaded with him. 'I don't want Duncan to be raised by a widow. I can't do this without you. I can't raise a thirteen-year-old boy on my own. It's too much for me.'

Jon looked away and returned with a sad expression. 'I'm sorry, but I can't.' Sara sighed with frustration, but Jon tried to comfort her, saying, 'Don't worry, I'll try my best to sort this thing out. I'll come back to you, and when I do, you'll have tears of joy.'

Sara covered her mouth and whimpered, her tears flowing.

'Listen, don't cry,' Jon said gently as he approached her.

Sara became extremely infuriated and pushed Jon. 'Just go, get out! Leave! If you don't want us to help you, then fine! Be a selfish father!'

Jon frowned with guilt and lifted his hand to reach out to her, but he lowered it with a sigh. 'Sara ... I ...'

'What's going to happen to my son, huh?' Sara yelled. 'How's he going to feel being raised without a father?' Jon remained silent and withdrew his hand. 'So ... fine. If you must go, I won't stop you ...'

Duncan woke: the heated voices of his parents arguing downstairs had roused him from his slumber. Concern etched across his face, he made his way to the living room. 'Mum, Dad, what's going on?' His voice was tinged with sleep as he rubbed his eyes.

Duncan's parents exchanged a fleeting glance, then his mother diverted her gaze, remaining silent.

His father sighed heavily. 'I have to go.'

Duncan's heart raced as panic set in. 'Wh–why?'

'I need to go away from here,' Jon replied.

His cryptic response and that faint smile sent shivers down Duncan's spine.

Is he trying to protect me? Duncan wondered, frustration bubbling to the surface.

Duncan's anxiety intensified. 'I don't understand. What's going on? Why has this happened? Who did this to you? Can you please tell me why?'

'I can't explain everything because I'm running out of time,' Jon explained, placing his hand on his son's shoulder and offering a faint smile. 'Remember the times we had together? Remember when we played table football and air hockey?'

No, he couldn't lose him. He couldn't lose his father.

Duncan's heart raced, panic intensifying. He snapped, 'Don't speak like that! Don't speak to me as if you're going to die!' This wasn't happening. Duncan was too young to experience this. Why him? Why did they have to target his dad? 'I don't understand!' he yelled, emotions overwhelming him. 'I don't know why this is happening! Why must it be you!? This is a nightmare! This is so unfair!'

He couldn't bear the thought of losing his father and refused to accept it. Overwhelmed, Duncan began to break down, tears streaming down his face.

Jon gently rubbed Duncan's head with his palm, trying to offer some comfort. 'Look, cheer up ... Who says that I'm going to die? I'll come back. When I do, we're going to go on a vacation as a family – remember that amusement park you saw on TV, Rush Peak Amusement Park? I heard you wanted to ride the T-Rex Chaser. So make sure you have a welcome-home card waiting for me, okay?'

Duncan nodded and clung tightly to his father. Jon managed a brief smile and continued to soothe his son with gentle strokes.

'I'm sorry for this, kiddo. I know life's going to be tough without me. Don't hate me for this ...'

Jon's departure was imminent, and it struck Duncan like a devastating blow. The reality that his father was leaving and might never return gnawed at him, filling his heart with a paralysing fear. Duncan buried his face in his shirt, muffling his sobs. 'I don't ... I just don't want you to leave. It's scary out there ... I can't do it alone ...'

'I know, kiddo ... Life is scary, but you just need to throw your fears aside ...' Jon rose to his feet, turning away. 'I have to go now ... If this is truly the end of the road for me, kiddo, just remember I love you, no matter what ...'

Jon's gaze briefly met Sara's, and her unhappiness was clear. She remained silent, her arms folded. Duncan turned to his mother with a quizzical look.

Why's Mum just standing there? Why isn't she stopping him? Doesn't she care? Why's she letting him leave like it's no big deal? It's like she doesn't even want to try.

So many questions raced through his mind, and none of them made any damn sense.

Jon limped away from their home and, suddenly, he collapsed to the ground. Gasping for air, blood trickled from his nostrils and eyes. He clamped his hand over his mouth and then vomited onto the ground, expelling not only blood but also strange, leech-like creatures. He examined his bloody palm in shock.

Duncan watched in helpless shock as his father's health rapidly deteriorated, blood and bizarre creatures emerging from his body.

'I–I can't stay here ... Must keep going,' Jon said, panting weakly, determination pushing him forward.

Duncan's panic reached its zenith when he saw his father collapse to the ground. His instinct to rush to his father's side was overwhelming, but Sara's grip held him back. 'Dad, no! You can't leave!'

Sara struggled to hold back Duncan as he pounded his mother's hand and wriggled about. 'Duncan, stop!' she yelled.

Tears streaming down his face, Duncan cried out. 'Let go of me! This isn't fair. This isn't fair! Why did they do this to him? He didn't do anything wrong!'

Sara, her voice strained, grabbed Duncan around the waist and implored, saying, 'Duncan, please stop!'

Jon looked at Duncan with tears in his eyes and whispered, 'I'm sorry, kiddo. I'm so sorry, kiddo.'

'Dad, *please*! Dad, please don't go! Don't leave me!'

With all his strength, Jon limped away from the house, quickening his pace. 'I'm sorry, I'm so sorry!'

Duncan turned to his father and screamed, 'No, Father! Please come back. Please come back!'

Jon departed that night, and he never returned, leaving Duncan and Sara behind, their world forever altered.

Sara let out a heavy sigh, her voice soft with weariness. 'Ever since that day ... my son's only goal has been to bring his father home. But it never happened. Now, all he wants is to kill the heretic who attacked Jon. Duncan hasn't rested since – and he won't, not until the heretic is dead.'

Elisa studied her for a long moment, then spoke with quiet gravity. 'May I ask ... do you truly believe the heretic deserves death? Do you believe your son is right to seek such an end?'

Sara met her gaze, her expression firm – yet conflicted. 'Deserve to die? Maybe. That man ... he took someone irreplaceable from Duncan. A father, yes – but more than that. Jon gave him joy. Encouragement. He made him feel like he mattered.'

She folded her arms, shoulders drawing in under the weight of her thoughts. 'I don't think someone like that should walk free. Especially not if he's still out there, hurting people. And yes ... I want Duncan to do something about it. But I'm scared, too.'

She paused, her voice faltering. 'I don't want this to change him. I don't want his sense of justice to twist into something else. I don't want my son to become a killer in the name of someone he loved.'

Her hands clenched at her sides. For a moment, she said nothing. Then, in a sudden burst, she pressed her palms to her forehead and groaned. 'God, I'm such an idiot. Why did I keep this from you? For his sake? What was I thinking?'

She began to pace, her voice tight with guilt. 'He begged me not to say anything – said he could handle it. But he's wrong. That kind of pain, that kind of loss ... it festers. And I let him bury it. Let him lock it away like a cage inside his chest.'

She turned back to Elisa, anguish plain across her face. 'You deserved to know. You came into our lives with your own grief, your own problems. I should've trusted you.'

Elisa's expression softened, her eyes warm with empathy, but she said nothing – letting Sara continue.

'You've already suffered so much,' Sara went on gently. 'Your home, your name, the people who raised you ... all gone. I should never have made you feel like an outsider. I'm sorry.'

She stood slowly, smoothing her skirt as if steadying herself. 'It felt right to tell you this now – because you'd understand. You've always had that kind of heart.'

A pause. Then a faint smile touched her lips. 'And ... I think you should speak to Duncan. About everything. Even what happened at Pete's Fort. I truly believe he would listen.'

Elisa hesitated. 'You do not think he would be … upset with me?'

Sara gave a soft snort and waved the thought away. 'If he is, I'll deal with him myself. He's not allowed to sulk about something this important.'

She turned towards the mirror, brushing the last loose strands of her hair into place.

'Now, get ready for bed. I've got work in the morning, and I don't want to catch you up reading by candlelight again.'

Elisa gave a small nod, smiling faintly. 'Yes, Mrs Saul.'

But as she reached the doorway, Sara called out, stopping her. 'Elisa … don't let your sister's death be in vain. Make her proud. Be the woman you wish to become. Not for anyone else – but for her. And for you.'

Elisa paused. Her expression clouded for a moment. Then she looked back at Sara, her voice quiet but steady. 'I shall try. Truly. I only pray I am not too far gone to become her.'

Sara's smile deepened with quiet pride. 'Good. That's all I ask.'

Jeremy stormed into the bar, his mood dark as a thundercloud. He needed something strong – something sharp enough to cut through the endless noise in his head. Without a second thought, he unleashed his frustration like a volcano ready to erupt.

'Bartender! Get me a vodka. Strong. And make it quick!'

The bartender blinked, clearly caught off guard by the sudden outburst. Jeremy's eyes narrowed. *Are you seriously going to make me wait?*

Impatience snapped like a wire inside him. He shot up from his stool, voice low and dangerous.

'Are you fucking deaf? I said now.'

The bartender swallowed hard, hands trembling as he hurried to comply. Jeremy barely noticed – his anger was a beast consuming every corner of his mind.

The bottle rattled as the bartender poured. Jeremy grabbed it, the man retreating as if expecting a storm to break loose. He returned to his seat, his hand heavy against his cheek, jaw clenched tight.

'If that bloody idiot Norman hadn't fucked us over, Lance would still be standing. Still fighting.' He spat the words out like venom. 'All of this – gone. Because of him. And that—' He paused, bitterness thick in his voice. 'That bitch showing him that damn letter. If she hadn't, he'd still be with us.'

The bartender cautiously set the shot glass down. Jeremy seized it instantly, the fiery burn of vodka stinging his throat as he swallowed it whole. A shudder ran through him – rage flaring hotter than the liquor.

'Fuck!' He slammed his fist against the table, the sound sharp and angry. 'We fought for every inch. Sacrificed everything. And now ... just like that, it's all gone. Complete fucking bullshit.'

He drained another shot, letting the liquid drown the bitterness – but the fire in his chest only grew fiercer.

Drunk and stumbling, Jeremy staggered down the empty streets, the night pressing in around him like a heavy shroud. The only sound slicing the silence was the distant bark of a dog, sharp and solitary. He fumbled through his pockets, panic prickling beneath the haze.

'W–where the bloody hell's that key?' he slurred, voice rough and thick with frustration.

Eventually, he found it and forced the lock open, collapsing inside with a grunt. His grey trench coat clung to him like a second skin, and he didn't bother peeling it off – too drained, too weighed down.

Hours passed. Slowly, clarity edged back into his mind, though his hair was a mess and his clothes smelled of stale alcohol and sweat. He pushed himself up and shuffled towards the bathroom.

In the harsh light of the mirror, he caught sight of himself – dishevelled, furious, broken. Rage boiled over and, with a violent sweep, he sent everything on the sink crashing to the floor.

'This can't be happening!' he shouted, voice cracking. 'What was it all for? The lives I've taken, the ones I've saved ... The allies we've lost ...' His fury shattered into despair. 'None of it means a damn thing anymore.'

This isn't fair.

They'd bled for this cause. Every sacrifice carved deep scars. And Lance ... Lance was the glue holding it all together. Now, he was gone – locked away, ripped from their grasp.

Tears burned down Jeremy's face as his voice dropped to a broken whisper. 'It's not fair ... not fucking fair.' He spat the words out bitterly. 'All because of that stupid woman ... and Norman, that useless parasite ...'

He drew in a ragged breath, gathering what little strength remained. Shaking his head, he hissed, 'No. I'll get Lance back. I'll win this war – even if I have to tear the whole damn city apart.'

His eyes narrowed, burning with fierce determination as he stared at his reflection. 'What I need is an army. A fucking army.'

His voice was low, a growl behind clenched teeth. 'I'll launch an assault on Riverdam. I don't care about the military or the officials. Their lives mean nothing to me. Only Lance matters.'

Lance was the last thing tethering Jeremy to this brutal war. The endless combat, the gnawing fear, the strain on his mind and soul – they'd all taken their toll. But for Lance, Jeremy would endure whatever hell came next.

Chapter XIX

JUSTICE IS SERVED

Duncan and his mother were inside the inspector's office of a police station. They were accompanied by a man sitting at a desk. He had brown hair that was greying at the side and he had a moustache. He wore a blue suit and a red-striped tie. He stood up to introduce himself. 'I am Chief Inspector Joseph Charlie of the FPA Investigation Team – how may I be of assistance?'

Sara extended a friendly introduction, saying, 'My name is Sara Saul and this is my son, Duncan.'

Chief Inspector Charlie cordially shook hands with Sara and offered a polite greeting. 'It's an honour to meet you both. Please, have a seat.'

Following the chief inspector's lead, everyone settled into their seats.

Curious about their visit, Chief Inspector Charlie inquired, 'So what brings you here, Mrs Saul?'

Sara, looking a bit concerned, replied, 'It's my husband. He was attacked by a criminal last week.'

The chief inspector leant in, intrigued. 'Is that so? Do you have any evidence to support what happened?'

Sara nodded and proceeded to present several photographs onto the desk along with a jar containing strange, glowing leech-like creatures. 'This is what my son found outside of our house. These are what came out of my husband, Jon.'

Chief Inspector Charlie took the jar and examined the creatures closely with his right eye, musing. 'Hmm ... Interesting ... interesting. These are energy leeches. They're imbued with magical energy. They consume and channel the energy of their victim, even when their victim is no longer alive. They slowly sap the victim's life, causing them to have a slow death.' Setting the jar back on the desk, the chief inspector ventured a hypothesis. 'This is no doubt the work of a heretic.'

Now understanding the gravity of the situation, Sara responded. 'A heretic ... I thought so ...'

'It seems you have some knowledge about them.'

'Yes, I've heard they're dangerous criminals involved in magical activities.'

'Indeed, you are correct.'

Heretics …

Sara recalled an ancient story about Arneis, a powerful magic user who sought to dominate the world. Driven by ambition, he experimented with forbidden magic, tapping into cosmic forces to amplify his power beyond all limits. His creation was an immensely destructive spell intended to subjugate rival kingdoms – but it was unstable and beyond his control. When unleashed, it backfired, causing a catastrophic event known as *The Cataclysm.*

The Cataclysm wrought massive earthquakes, fires and deadly storms that ravaged the continent. Entire cities were destroyed, millions perished, and the environment was devastated. Survivors faced a broken world.

The non-magical population, bearing the brunt of the disaster, grew fearful and distrustful of magic users. In response, surviving magicians formed the AMOB to regulate magic's use, enforcing strict laws. Among the first was the Death Penalty for Misuse of Magic: any magic user who posed a threat to society or committed murder by magical means would be executed. The aim was to prevent another *Cataclysm* and restore trust.

Over centuries, the AMOB's law became a cornerstone of the legal system. Though seen by some as draconian, most accepted it as necessary for society's safety. The AMOB's strict oversight made severe misuse of magic rare.

'I don't know much about magic. Could you tell me more?' Sara asked.

Chief Inspector Charlie nodded. 'Magic's everywhere – like energy flowing through all living things. Everyone has the potential, but only a few can actually use it.'

'And how do you detect it? I mean, how do you know when someone's using magic or not?'

'Body temperature spikes when magic is in use. We use thermal scanners and other tech to pick it up,' he explained. 'These days, it's harder for magic users to stay hidden. We also use silver – it can suppress magic temporarily.'

Humans had outpaced other races with their tech and sheer numbers, their fast reproduction and innovation giving them the upper hand.

Charlie brought the conversation back. 'Right. Let's talk about that day. What was the first thing you noticed?'

Sara paused, thinking. 'It was an ordinary day. Duncan went to school, Jon and I went to work. But that evening, Jon came home ... different. He looked awful – pale skin, dull eyes, visible veins. He collapsed as soon as he stepped inside. We had no idea what was wrong.'

Charlie nodded, taking mental notes.

'We wanted to call the hospital. Even the police,' Sara went on, voice quieter. 'But he wouldn't let us.'

Charlie leaned forward slightly. 'Any idea why?'

Sara looked away. The words caught in her throat. Jon had warned her – about AMOB, about Silver Cross. She didn't want to betray him. But keeping silent made her stomach knot.

'I'm sorry ... I can't say,' she murmured.

Charlie studied her for a moment, then gave a soft nod. 'Fair enough. Sounds like a private matter, and I won't press you.' He paused. 'Can you at least tell me when this happened? Roughly the month and time?'

Sara reached into her bag and pulled out a camera. 'We managed to take a photo of Jon – in secret,' she said, handing it over.

Chief Inspector Charlie studied the image. The timestamp read: *17 November, 4.06 a.m.*

'How long after the incident was this taken?' he asked.

'About two days,' Sara replied.

'Two days ... I see.' He looked up. 'What happened after that? Can you walk me through it?'

Duncan shifted in his seat, his hands balled into fists. Rage flickered across his face before it finally burst free.

'He left!' Duncan shouted, voice cracking. 'He left and never came back!'

Charlie blinked. Sara stared, stunned. 'Duncan!' she said sharply. *What's gotten into him?* She knew he was struggling, but now wasn't the time to lose control.

Charlie remained composed, though a faint crease formed between his brows. 'Is that so? Did he say where he was going?'

Duncan shook his head, eyes filling with tears. 'Not a word ... Just said he was gonna fix everything. Promised he'd come back.' He clenched his jaw, then screamed, voice raw. 'But he didn't! You have to find him – *please*!'

Charlie raised both hands in a calming gesture. 'Alright, alright – just breathe. We'll do what we can. Sit down, son.'

Duncan slumped back, wiping at his face. Charlie turned back to Sara.

'If your husband were here, we'd question him directly. Since we can't, it would help if you could bring us any of his personal documents – passport, marriage certificate, anything relevant.'

'I can get his passport, if that's what you need,' Sara replied.

'That'll do,' he said with a nod. His tone softened. 'Mrs Saul, don't worry. We'll start the investigation immediately and let you know if anything turns up.'

Sara gave a quiet nod, placing her faith – however fragile – in the process. 'Okay.'

Charlie glanced at the camera. 'I'll pass this on to forensics for further analysis.' He handed Sara a card. 'If you remember anything else – anything at all – contact me directly.'

She took the card and gave a firm nod. For now, all she could do was wait.

Duncan stormed out of the station, fists clenched, his breath sharp and ragged. Every step pounded with fury and grief. He barely noticed his mother hurrying after him.

'Duncan, please wait!' Sara called, catching up. 'Stop and talk to me!'

He didn't respond.

She grabbed his shoulder, forcing him to turn. 'What's bothering you?'

He spun on her, eyes blazing. 'That criminal doesn't deserve to live!' he snapped, voice cracking. 'He had no right – *no right* – to take Dad away from us!'

The rage boiled inside him, choking. It wasn't just grief. It was hate. Burning, relentless hate for the person who'd hurt his father – who'd ruined everything. How could anyone do something so vile?

His breathing quickened. He clutched his head, shaking. 'This can't be happening ...' His voice broke. 'Why *him*? Out of everyone ... why did it have to be *him*?'

The tears came fast. He stumbled forward, grabbing at his mother's shirt and pounding weakly against her chest. 'Why didn't you stop him, Mum? Why didn't you do something? You *should've* stopped him!'

Sara froze, stunned. Her mouth opened, but only broken words came. 'I ... I ...'

Duncan collapsed to his knees, letting out a raw, wordless scream – the kind that tore from somewhere deep, too deep to reach. The pain, the anger, the confusion – it all bled out of him in that cry. And when it passed, he was left hollow, trembling.

He whimpered softly, barely able to breathe.

Sara knelt beside him, arms wrapping around his shoulders. Her voice was a whisper in his ear. 'I'm sorry, Duncan … I'm so sorry …'

'Shh … Shh …' she murmured, rocking him gently.

And there they stayed – a boy shattered, held by the only person he had left. His father was gone. Their home would never feel the same again. No voice waiting in the hall. No steady hand to guide him. Just silence – and the crushing ache of loss.

During the night, Duncan and Jénmar hailed a taxi, their destination set for the bustling city of Ledwake. The city's vibrant pulse unfolded before them as they arrived, its roads alive with the glow of streetlights and the dance of traffic signals.

Pulling up to the Pennysilver Hotel, the two men stepped out and made their way to the front entrance. Inside, a poised female concierge greeted them with a polite smile. 'How may I assist you, gentlemen?'

'I'm Hendrik Jénmar and this is Duncan Saul. We're freelancers working for a local outfit called Centurion Arms.' Jénmar introduced them while Duncan subtly displayed his Wings of Authority badge. 'We're here regarding a man named Joseph Holloway who we believe may be staying in this establishment,' Jénmar explained.

'And what business do you have with him?'

In response, Jénmar presented a dossier containing information and a photograph of their target. 'We have reason to believe he's been operating a black market in Rosemary.'

'I'm sorry, but we can't disclose guest information without proper authorisation from my manager.'

Jénmar remained firm, stating, 'I see ... We'll have to inform the AMOB that you've been uncooperative.'

'The AMOB?'

Jénmar also flashed his Wings of Authority badge, causing a flicker of panic to cross the concierge's face.

'No, please!'

Duncan interjected, seeking to reassure her. 'Don't worry, ma'am. We'll simply brief your supervisor on the situation. Here's our business card. Do reach out if anything happens.'

'Very well. He's in room two hundred and one.' The concierge retrieved the key from its holder with a hint of concern. 'I hope I won't get fired for this ...' she said, grumbling under her breath.

Jénmar accepted the key and they proceeded to find Holloway.

Duncan pressed his back against the peeling wallpaper of the hotel hallway, ears straining. Behind the thin door, fabric rustled, feet shuffled, and something heavy scraped across the floor.

Someone was packing. *Panicked.*

Joseph Holloway.

Duncan's gut twisted. He couldn't be sure – not yet – but he'd heard this rhythm of desperation before. Quick. Erratic. Like prey trying to outrun a bullet already in the chamber.

Jénmar stood beside him, practically vibrating with anticipation. The heretic was close – Duncan could feel it – but it was Jénmar's expression that caught his attention first.

It wasn't the usual look of sharp focus or the quiet intensity Duncan had grown accustomed to when they hunted. No, this was something else. A flash of something feral. Hungry.

The way his lips barely twitched into a grin, the gleam in his eyes burning brighter with each step closer to their prey.

Duncan wasn't unfamiliar with that look. He'd seen it before. Too many times.

It was the kind of expression that came just before Jénmar killed. Before he could taste the blood in the air, feel the rush of chaos as the life drained out of someone. It wasn't just about survival anymore. It was the thrill of it – the satisfaction of suffering.

Duncan didn't look away. He knew better by now. He was used to it.

'You ready?' he asked, voice sharp and hungry.

'Yeah.' Duncan's grip tightened on the handle. Every nerve braced.

'This is gonna be fun.' Jénmar grinned.

Then – *silence.*

The kind that feels wrong.

The kind that tells you the storm's already inside the room.

The door slammed open.

A wave of pressure burst out, magic cracking the air, warping the space with violent force. A cupboard – massive, damp, and stinking of rot – hurtled towards them like a battering ram.

Duncan ducked left. The cupboard exploded against the wall with a deafening crack. Splinters rained across the hallway.

Jénmar stayed low on the floor, narrowly avoiding the flying cupboard as he struggled to regain his footing.

Duncan rose fast, eyes locking on Holloway. The man stood wild-eyed, sweat gleaming on his brow, hand reaching for a pistol.

No time to think.

Duncan snatched the lamp from the nightstand – a cheap, dusty thing – and hurled it. It smashed into Holloway's wrist with a sickening crunch, sending the gun skidding across the floor.

Duncan surged forward, boots hammering over threadbare carpet. A vicious kick drove Holloway to the ground.

But he wasn't finished.

Snarling, Holloway raised his hands. The air snapped, the scent of scorched copper filling the room. His magic surged – splintered furniture, bed linen, shards of debris lifted like shrapnel and tore through the air.

Duncan dropped flat. A desk leg scraped past his shoulder as he hit the ground hard, the breath punching from his lungs.

Across the room, Holloway scrambled for the fallen pistol.

Duncan stood up, his fingers closed around his own.

He fired.

The shot cracked the air. Holloway jerked sideways, blood blooming across his ribs – but he didn't fall. Staggering back, he dragged himself towards the door, breathing ragged.

Duncan moved to finish it – but a voice cut through the noise behind him.

'Hey, cunt!'

Jénmar's shout snapped the air in two. Duncan turned just as Jénmar smashed the broken lamp across Holloway's face. The heretic reeled, blood spraying from his nose – but his finger spasmed on the trigger.

Then – *bang*.

Jénmar grunted, stumbling back, clutching his shoulder. Blood soaked into his shirt. The pistol finally slipped from Holloway's grip and clattered to the floor.

'Jénmar!' Duncan's heart jumped. 'You alright!?'

'*Fine*,' Jénmar hissed. 'Don't worry about me. Just *go!*'

Duncan didn't hesitate. He pivoted towards the hallway, adrenaline surging. Holloway was already limping down the stairs, one hand pressed to his side, the other dragging along the wall.

Duncan followed.

But as he passed Jénmar, who sagged against the doorframe, he threw him a quick glance.

'Stay down. I'll finish this.'

And then he was gone – boots pounding, breath hot in his chest – chasing the man who had no idea what was coming for him.

Duncan understood they couldn't let the bastard escape. He barged into the adjacent room, the flimsy hotel door shattering off its hinges. Inside, Holloway was halfway out the window, the frame creaking under his weight.

Time slowed.

Duncan fired twice.

The shots cracked like thunder, but Holloway twisted his body with inhuman speed – dodging both bullets. He vanished through the window in a blink, leaving only the fluttering curtains behind him.

'Shit–'

Duncan didn't waste another second. He tore through the hallway, boots pounding as he stormed up the stairwell two at a time. Bursting through the rooftop door, cold night air hit him full in the face.

There – across the rooftops.

Holloway, a blur of motion, was already leaping the gap between buildings like a man possessed.

'Son of a bitch,' Duncan hissed.

He gave chase without hesitation.

Boots slammed against wet gravel and concrete as Duncan sprinted after him, leaping the first rooftop gap. He landed hard, rolled with the impact, and kept moving. The city skyline stretched around them – neon lights bleeding through the misty dark.

Ahead, Holloway turned, desperate. He fired back wildly as he ran.

'Get away from me!' the heretic howled.

Bullets whipped past Duncan, forcing him to dive behind a large ventilation unit. Metal pinged and sparked as rounds struck the side. Duncan gritted his teeth and peeked out, retaliating with two quick shots. Both missed – the bastard kept running, limping slightly now.

'Fuck,' Duncan muttered under his breath.

He couldn't lose him. Not now.

He sprinted once more, refusing to slow, lungs burning. Holloway located a rooftop ladder and began clambering down in frantic haste, disappearing into the alley below. Duncan followed without pause, gripping the cold rungs and sliding down. The soles of his boots hit wet pavement with a slap.

The alley was filthy and narrow, littered with bins, broken glass, and puddles that stank of rot. Neon graffiti flickered across the walls in the darkness like warped sigils.

Duncan's eyes locked on Holloway ahead, just as the heretic scaled a metal fence and dropped down the other side.

Duncan didn't hesitate. He sprinted forwards, grabbed the rusted bars, and launched himself over. His boots splashed into a filthy puddle as he landed. His pistol came up.

BANG!

The shot struck Holloway in the thigh.

The heretic screamed, stumbling into the water with a wet crash, mud and grime flying around him.

Duncan closed the gap, tackled him hard, and drove the man into the ground with a triumphant grunt.

'Got you, arsehole!'

But Holloway wasn't done yet.

With a strained growl, he raised a hand – and a glass bottle from the ground flew up, guided by a sudden pulse of telekinetic energy. It shattered across Duncan's face, slicing a deep cut into his cheek.

'Ah—fuck!'

Duncan recoiled, blood trailing from the wound as he fell sideways into the filth.

Holloway scrambled to his feet, limping heavily. He hissed in pain, but used the opening. He ran.

Duncan groaned, one hand pressed to his face, his fingers sticky with his own blood. 'Telekinesis?' he muttered, wincing.

No time to dwell. He forced himself up, shook off the dizziness, and bolted forwards once more.

Out of the alley and into the chaotic pulse of the city.

Streetlights cast long shadows across the road. Cars raced by, horns blaring. Then – he saw him. Holloway, bloodied and limping, pushing through the traffic.

Duncan surged forward.

He darted onto the street, weaving through moving vehicles. Tyres screeched as angry drivers swerved to avoid him.

'What the hell are you doing, you idiot!? Are you out of your fucking mind?!' a driver screamed from his window.

Duncan ignored him. All he saw was the heretic.

Holloway staggered mid-turn, pistol still in hand, blood darkening his sleeve as he tried to lift the weapon.

He fired – shots sparking off metal and glass, causing drivers to panic. One bullet hit a tyre. The car swerved wildly.

Duncan reacted instantly, diving to the side. A wall of steel missed him by inches, crashing into a lamppost with a deafening crunch. The pole collapsed in a shower of sparks and groaning metal.

Still, Holloway limped.

He fired again and again, forcing more cars to spin and collide. Screams echoed in the street. One vehicle skidded towards Duncan. He leapt over it, landing in a sprint without breaking stride.

'You're done,' Duncan muttered.

His legs pushed harder. The pain in his cheek throbbed, but he could see the fear now – etched across Holloway's face.

The heretic's pistol clicked empty.

Click click click.

With a curse, Holloway hurled the empty weapon aside and veered towards a nearby school building. He shoved through the rusted gate, limping towards the rear doors.

Duncan was right behind him, breath ragged, fury burning in his chest like fire.

And he wasn't stopping.

Duncan's hand was steady as he fired again, the bullet slamming into Holloway's shoulder with a sickening thud. The impact sent the heretic flying through the school window, the glass exploding in a shower of shards. Duncan didn't flinch as the glittering fragments rained around him. His focus never wavered from Holloway, now sprawled on the ground amidst the broken glass.

No time to waste.

With a growl, Duncan moved quickly through the jagged window frame, every step calculated to avoid cutting himself. The school was dark, the oppressive silence thick in the air. Duncan's eyes adjusted, but the shadows seemed to devour everything. He drew his double-action revolver, the cold steel familiar in his grip, and flicked on the torch. He loaded it with six silver bullets.

The silence stretched.

Duncan's breath was shallow, his senses on high alert. Every sound felt amplified. A faint scrape, a shuffle – his head snapped towards the noise, instinctively raising his weapon.

A trail of blood.

It led down a narrow hallway, streaking against the floor. Duncan's pulse quickened. He followed it, his feet light, moving with the utmost caution, the beam of his torch tracing the crimson path.

The blood led him to a classroom. Duncan paused at the door, his finger tight on the trigger. With a slow, deliberate movement, he stepped into the threshold, his torch's beam cutting through the gloom.

Then, in the blink of an eye, Holloway's gaze snapped up.

Duncan barely had time to react.

With a burst of energy, Holloway's telekinetic powers flared. A dozen chairs flew at Duncan, faster than he could process. The sudden onslaught caught him off guard, and he threw his arms up instinctively to shield his face. The chairs collided with him, their weight and force throwing him to the ground. Pain exploded in his chest as they piled on top of him, but Duncan gritted his teeth, fighting against the crushing weight.

His chest heaved with exertion. He struggled to breathe, pushing the chairs off one by one. His revolver had fallen to the side, but it was still within reach. His hands trembled as he grabbed it and swung it up, aiming down the sights with a steady, practiced hand.

Holloway, dazed and disoriented, struggled to his feet. Duncan didn't hesitate. He squeezed the trigger.

The shot rang out, sharp and clear.

The bullet tore into Holloway's arm, sending shockwaves of agony through his body. Holloway's form jerked violently, his face twisting in a howl of pain as blood poured from the wound.

Duncan didn't give him a moment to recover. He rose swiftly, his knees protesting the effort, but he was relentless. He stepped towards the heretic, the room spinning with tension. Holloway staggered back, his telekinetic powers now wild, unstable, as if struggling to focus.

Fear bled into Holloway's voice, raw and desperate.

'What the hell is happening?!'

Duncan's jaw tightened. Holloway's powers were faltering. The silver bullet had done its job. Duncan could feel the triumph creeping into his chest, but he knew better than to let it cloud his focus.

Duncan scowled, his eyes narrowing as he closed in on his prey.

'Wait, stay away from me! Get away!' Holloway's voice was frantic, desperation lacing every word.

Ignoring the heretic's pleas, Duncan slammed a powerful right hook into Holloway's jaw. The blow sent him sprawling to the floor, blood splattering from his mouth. Holloway groaned, clutching his leg, but Duncan's revolver was already aimed at him. He fired.

The gunshot echoed in the room as Holloway screamed in agony.

'Please don't kill me! I didn't do anything wrong!' Holloway cried, his voice breaking.

Duncan kept the gun trained on him, his expression cold. 'You shot my partner.'

'Wha ... What?' Holloway stammered, disbelief flickering in his eyes.

Duncan pulled the trigger slowly, deliberately.

'Wait, please, wait!' Holloway's voice cracked, desperation rising.

But Duncan didn't relent. He fired again, and again, each shot punctuating the air with sickening finality. The room fell silent, the acrid scent of gun smoke hanging heavy in the air. Duncan holstered his pistol, his face an impassive mask, and walked away from the lifeless corpse, leaving it behind in a pool of fresh blood.

Duncan returned to the hotel and noticed the arrival of the police and ambulance crews. His gaze fell upon Jénmar who was being attended to by a paramedic. With steady hands, the paramedic skilfully used a needle to stitch Jénmar's wound together.

Approaching Jénmar and the medic, Duncan enquired, 'Doctor, how's he doing?'

Wiping sweat from his forehead, the paramedic responded, 'We've managed to stop the bleeding and stabilise him. The bullet went through his shoulder – he's lucky it missed any major arteries. He's showing some weakness in that arm, which could indicate nerve involvement, but we won't know for certain until he's properly examined at the hospital.'

Wincing as he tried to move, Jénmar groaned. 'Ah, shite! I rely on this arm for everything. Work's going to be a nightmare without it.'

The medic, maintaining a calm tone, reassured him, 'It'll take some time, but injuries like this often improve with the right care. You'll need a full check-up at the hospital, and they may bring in a neurologist to assess whether there's any nerve damage. It's too early to say for certain, but with physiotherapy, you should regain good function.'

Jénmar let out a frustrated sigh. 'I'm going to miss all the action for a while, aren't I?'

'Focus on healing first,' the medic replied. 'We'll get you transported soon. With some rehab and time, you'll be back in shape. Just don't push yourself too soon.'

'Alright, thanks, doc. I appreciate it,' Jénmar said, exhaling.

'Just doing my job.' The medic nodded before stepping aside.

Duncan moved closer, giving Jénmar a reassuring glance. 'You've been through worse. You'll manage.'

Jénmar chuckled weakly. 'Yeah, but hospitals, mate. Needles in the arm? I'd rather eat glass.'

Duncan smirked and teased, 'Come on, they'll probably give you a lollipop for being a good boy.'

'Shut it,' Jénmar replied, grinning. 'At least I'm not getting jabbed in the arse, though. High school would've been rough if that made it into the yearbook.'

Duncan clapped his hand on Jénmar's good shoulder, chuckling. 'You'll be fine. We'll get through this.'

'Thanks, mate,' Jénmar replied with a small, grateful smile.

Chapter XX

THE PRICE OF PRINCIPLES

Elisa was sitting in her room at her study desk, wearing a cherry-coloured jumper and round glasses. Her room had undergone a significant transformation from a plain, empty space to one that reflected her style. It featured a bed with a pink pillow and white duvet, a pink bedside lamp with white spots, a small alarm clock and a collection of flowers by the window, including roses, peonies and anemones. Her study desk held a laptop, a desk lamp, a pen holder and stacks of books. She also had a black swivel chair and a poster of her favourite Floran politician on the wall.

Elisa sat hunched over her laptop, earphones snug in place, shutting out the rest of the world. On-screen, Lance stood at a podium, his voice rich with conviction as he addressed the crowd. His hands moved with precise confidence – not too stiff, not too loose. Elisa narrowed her eyes, tracking every motion. That subtle hand gesture – was it rehearsed or instinctive? She paused the video and jotted a note in her notebook, her handwriting tight and careful. *Projecting control without arrogance – effective.*

She rewound a few seconds, watching the shift in his tone. Was that deliberate emphasis or genuine emotion? Hard to tell. She pressed play again, brow furrowed, entirely absorbed in dissecting the man behind the speech.

'Ladies and gentlemen, let me share with you the essence of leadership! It's not about commanding from above but about inspiring from within. It's about connecting with people on a fundamental level, understanding their fears, their dreams, their aspirations!

'Leadership isn't a title or a position – it's a responsibility. A responsibility to guide, uplift, and empower those around you. You don't lead by barking orders from behind a desk – you lead by standing with your people, shoulder to shoulder, through the mud. If they're cold, you freeze with them; if they're starving, you starve with them. That's where trust is built – not in words, but in the burden you carry beside them.'

Beside her laptop, a stack of books on leadership strategies awaited her attention. Elisa reached for one, flipping through its pages eagerly as she cross-referenced Lance's techniques.

'As leaders, we must govern by example, embodying the values we set and inspiring others to do the same. It's in the fire that resolve is tested – and ours does not break.

'This is what King Ivar failed to grasp. Instead of ruling Flora with an open heart, he wielded power through fear and governed with paranoia. He saw his subjects not as partners in progress but as pawns in a game.

'But above all, true leadership begins with humility – knowing you walk beside your people, not above them.

'Leadership is not an easy path – but if we walk it with honour, with humility, and with open minds, we may become the leaders our world truly needs. Not rulers, but torchbearers. Not tyrants, but examples. Let us rise – not alone, but together – towards a future forged in unity and hope!'

As the video concluded, Elisa leant back in her seat, her mind swirling with thoughts. Perhaps she could lend her support to Lance and assist in persuading the council to cease the civil war. If only she had more confidence – if she weren't so reliant on Sara and Duncan – she could excel in her endeavours.

Deep down, she recognised her potential to emerge as a leader and enact change, lending her voice to important matters. Yet, as she pondered the daunting task ahead, a familiar sense of hesitation enveloped her. The weight of her insecurities, her dependence on others for validation and support, loomed large, threatening to hinder her from fully embracing her own power. Elisa then returned to work on her thesis, reopening the page of the notebook where she had left off.

Sara entered the room with a warm greeting. 'Hey, kid. I just got back from work. How're ya doing?'

Elisa turned her chair around and removed her earphones. 'Hello, Mrs Saul.'

Sara approached Elisa's desk. 'Whatcha working on?' she inquired.

Elisa adjusted her glasses and replied, 'I'm working on my thesis. It's about the principles I believe a political leader should adhere to.'

'Interesting.'

'Mrs Saul, may I ask you something?'

'Of course, kid. Go ahead.'

'Do you believe that all life is equal?'

'Yes, I do – just like God does.'

'Yes, but some would disagree.'

Sara raised an eyebrow, prompting Elisa to continue.

'Mrs Saul, you are aware of the non-human species living in our world, correct?'

Sara nodded. 'Yes, I am. What about them?'

'I once knew a Dökkálfar named Ryonil – a half-breed, part human and part Dökkálfar. He lived in Gothenburg, a city ruled by the Night Hawks. His mother had been exiled, leaving him with only his human father, who fought bravely to protect their home despite the abuse they suffered. Tragically, his father was murdered – they believed he would betray his own kind for Ryonil. After that, Ryonil was left utterly alone.'

Sara's face softened with sympathy as she listened.

Elisa continued, 'It became even harder for him to remain there. He endured abuse daily, both from citizens and the police alike.'

A pang of empathy swelled in Elisa's heart – for Ryonil, for anyone cast out for their heritage. Yet beneath it lay frustration – frustration at the ignorance that still thrived despite her belief in the equality of all life. She longed for a world where individuals like Ryonil could be celebrated, not persecuted.

'Oh, that sounds absolutely dreadful,' Sara murmured, clutching her chest.

'Indeed,' Elisa replied firmly. 'Ryonil has been alone since his father's death. I sympathise, though I have never known such profound loneliness. I had May, Archer, and all of you to care for me.' She leaned back, folding her arms. 'He is far stronger than I am. Like a knight, he endured the loneliness and cruelty of that city alone, unwavering despite the danger.' She paused, then mused quietly, 'I do not truly know what it means to be utterly alone. What would I have become if Mr Saul had not been there for me?' She gave a sad chuckle. 'Loneliness is a dreadful thing, is it not?'

'Yes, it is,' Sara agreed softly. 'After my husband died, I felt lonely too. But I had friends at work, and Duncan was still there.'

'I see ...'

'So, what happened to Ryonil? Is he alright?' Sara asked.

Elisa hesitated. 'I do not know. Most likely, the municipal police have taken him into custody. If so, I fear he will not receive a fair trial. It is unlikely he will survive.'

Frustration tightened Elisa's fists – anger mixed with helplessness. The idea that someone could suffer for simply existing was infuriating.

'It's just not fair,' she muttered. 'Why should someone be punished for what they cannot control?'

Sara shrugged. 'Well, Elisa, things were different back then.'

Elisa's thoughts churned as Sara's words echoed. The world had changed, yes – but prejudice and hatred still clung stubbornly, shadowing those deemed 'other.'

'May I ask you something?' Elisa said.

Sara smiled warmly. 'What's on your mind, kiddo?'

'Do you hate them as well, Mrs Saul?'

Sara shook her head firmly. 'No, not really. I couldn't care less about the history between them and us. There's no point dwelling on it now.'

Elisa nodded thoughtfully, cupping her chin. 'How am I to create harmony between humans and non-humans? I know they are near extinction, yet we must preserve them. People label them as horrific monsters, but surely they cannot be all that dreadful? How can I change their minds – show them they are not as fearsome as they seem? I wish to make the world better, but how can I do that when there is so much hatred?'

Sara shrugged, offering a warm smile. 'That's for you to decide, Elisa. You must speak your truth and fight for what's right. Be a compelling speaker – make your message loud and clear so people can't ignore it. But remember, folks don't want someone who just talks; they want someone who can make things happen.' She sighed. 'Though who am I to say? I'm just a middle-aged mum with a twenty-three-year-old son to worry about.'

Her words struck a chord with Elisa. It was not enough to hold beliefs silently; she had to act, to make her message both heard and understood – the importance of unity and preservation.

Sara moved towards the door, turning back with a final piece of advice. 'Just don't lose yourself, kid. Always stay self-aware ... and mindful of the consequences.'

She left, and Elisa remained seated, the weight of her thoughts heavy. Slowly, she returned to her essay, pen poised, determined.

Jeremy spoke quietly with another Night Hawk – short, neat brown hair, sharp brown eyes and a goatee.

They were gathered in a modest living room. The space was neat and orderly, with a few personal touches – family photos on the shelves and a worn leather armchair by the window. Outside, the city carried on its restless rhythm, but inside, the air was heavy.

'Do you realise what you're suggesting? It's nothing short of suicide,' the man said.

Jeremy met his gaze steadily. *Suicide or salvation?* The question gnawed at him. *Lance is more than a leader – he's the last hope. If we fail, it's not just strategy lost, it's a brother dead.* But hesitation would kill them all.

'The Night Hawks are dragging their feet,' Jeremy said. 'Lord Reiman seems lost on how serious this is. Our only chance is to raise an army and try to free Lance.'

The man frowned, concern clear. 'Jeremy, do you understand the consequences? We'd be defying the Night Hawks. You know what that means.'

Jeremy closed his eyes briefly, then answered, 'I'm aware of the risks.'

'Are you now?' The man shook his head. 'An assault on Riverdam could be catastrophic. If we fail, Lance will be executed, and our reputation ruined. We'll lose men.'

'I understand,' Jeremy said calmly. 'But ask yourself – would you rather be hunted like prey by the Red Lions, or risk everything for a chance to save Lance?'

'But this goes against Lance's plan. He intended to sacrifice himself to save lives. If we ignore that, we carry the weight of our brothers' and sisters' blood. And if we fail? Their sacrifice is wasted.'

Giovani's words hit hard. Lance's plan was born of sacrifice – a noble attempt to limit casualties. Defying it was reckless. Still, Jeremy knew they couldn't wait.

'I hear you,' Jeremy said. 'But Lance is the Kingslayer to the Red Lions. His words won't stop them. We must take this risk.'

Giovani's brow furrowed deeper. 'How can you be certain your plan will work? We might put everyone in even greater danger.'

Jeremy's voice was steady, though uncertain. 'I can't promise success. But if we keep playing it safe, we'll never win. We have few options left – it's time to act.'

Giovani was silent for a long moment. Then he sighed. 'Jeremy ... I share your worries. But fine.'

Relief flooded Jeremy. 'Thank you. We meet at the bar tomorrow night. I'll lay out the plan.'

Giovani's gaze sharpened. 'Don't thank me yet. I want results, not words. Don't fail us.'

Jeremy met that gaze, resolve hardening. 'I won't fail you. I'll do everything I can to make this work.'

As Giovani left, Jeremy's thoughts turned to Lance. *Hang on, Lance. We're coming.*

Chapter XXI

RESONANCE

Duncan sat hunched on the park bench, elbows on knees, chin resting in his palm. The sky above was painfully bright, too blue for the way he felt inside. Laughter echoed from the nearby field where children chased after a football, their voices light and unburdened.

'Pass it to me! Pass it to me!' one boy shouted, giggling as he ran barefoot across the grass.

Duncan didn't move. He watched them like he was staring through glass – separated, distant. Like joy belonged in some other world now. A world where his dad still existed.

He could've been out there with them, running wild, letting the sun warm his face. But the idea made his stomach twist. *How could they laugh? How could anyone?*

He didn't blame himself for sitting out. What was the point? Chasing a ball wouldn't fill the hole inside him. It wouldn't bring his father back.

The bench creaked slightly as someone took the seat beside him.

Duncan didn't need to look. He already knew who it was by the sound of those polished shoes and the faint scent of cologne that always lingered like smoke – Uncle Konrad.

'Why aren't you joining the other kids in play?' Konrad asked.

Duncan didn't answer. He shifted his gaze towards the ground, brow furrowed. *What kind of question was that?* Like kicking a football could fix everything. Like he could just laugh again and pretend nothing was broken.

Did Konrad not get it? Or did he just not care?

'Listen, kid, sitting here sulking won't improve the situation. In fact, it'll only make things worse.'

Duncan's jaw tensed. He didn't look up. The words slid off him like rain on glass. *You think I don't know that?* He didn't need a lecture. He needed his dad.

He said nothing, eyes locked on a dandelion swaying in the breeze.

'Tell me what's up, kid,' Konrad said again, his tone firmer now. 'Your grades are dropping, you don't talk to anyone at school. You won't speak to your mother or me, even when we try to reach out. It's beginning to worry us.'

Still nothing.

Let them worry. Worry wouldn't bring back the sound of his father's voice. It wouldn't erase the image of his mother crying behind closed doors when she thought he wasn't listening. All of it felt hollow. Fake. Like he was stuck in a life someone else had designed.

He folded deeper into himself, eyes blank. The football game in the distance blurred into colours and noise.

Konrad let out a sigh and shifted beside him. Then his voice softened. 'Alright, kid. Talk to your uncle. Tell me how you're feeling. I'm here to listen.'

Duncan's hands trembled at his sides. He didn't notice how tightly they were balled into fists until his nails bit into skin. His chest burned, and the pressure behind his eyes swelled like a dam ready to split.

Then it snapped.

'How I'm feeling!?' he spat, voice cracking under the weight of everything he'd held back. 'I'm furious! He had no right to do this to us. No right at all!'

The words tore out of him. Like ripping open a wound that had barely begun to scar.

'I miss Dad! I miss him so bloody much!' His throat strained, each word like fire. 'I wish this had never happened.

Why did that heretic go after him? Why couldn't he have gone after anyone else!?'

He hated how small he sounded, how useless. Like all the anger in him still wasn't enough to fix anything.

He didn't look at Konrad, didn't want to see pity on his face. Didn't want sympathy. Didn't want comfort. He wanted his father back.

'Duncan, please, try to calm down,' Konrad said, voice low, careful. Like Duncan was some animal on edge, liable to lash out or break down.

Duncan's breathing came fast, uneven, chest rising and falling as he stood shaking. His eyes stung. He rubbed at them angrily and dropped back onto the bench, shoving his face into his hands. He didn't want to cry. Heroes didn't cry helplessly, did they?

Konrad's voice drifted beside him, softer this time. 'I'm so sorry this happened to you, truly, I am. It's all so unfair. You didn't deserve any of this.'

Yeah, Duncan thought bitterly. *I didn't. But that didn't stop it from happening, did it?*

A silence fell between them, heavy and suffocating. Then Konrad spoke again.

'But, kid, I wanna ask you something. What're you gonna do about it? What do you wanna achieve? What do you want?'

Duncan blinked behind his hands. The question lingered, echoing in the hollow spaces grief had carved out inside him. What did he want?

He sat up slowly, eyes red. He looked at his palm, still curled into a fist, skin marked red from pressure.

'What I want …' he murmured. His voice was steadier now, but low, hard. 'I wanna become a hero. I wanna find my father. Bring him back home. I wanna hunt that heretic down and make him pay. Not just for me – for everyone. I don't want anyone else to go through what I'm feeling right now.'

He meant it. Every word. His pain needed to mean something. If he couldn't stop it for himself, maybe he could stop it for someone else.

Konrad tilted his head, a small smirk playing at the corner of his lips. 'Interesting … So, you wanna be like those heroes in comic books and on TV, don't you?'

Duncan met his gaze and nodded without hesitation. 'Yeah. I do. A hero who fights for good and stands against evil. A real one.'

Konrad's smile grew warmer. 'I see … I hope you become an outstanding hero, kid. Make sure your dream shines.' He reached over and ruffled Duncan's hair. 'Dreams don't come true by sulking around. You've got to act. Think of The Human Spider. He became a hero after someone he loved was killed by a criminal.'

Duncan looked up, listening.

'He didn't sit in a corner crying about it. He got up. He went after the one who did it.'

Duncan frowned thoughtfully. 'Oh … I see.'

'He took all that pain and did something with it. You could too.'

He stared ahead at nothing in particular, jaw tense. Could he really? Could he become someone like that?

'Really?' he asked, the hope in his voice so faint it almost embarrassed him.

Konrad nodded. 'Of course. But it's not easy. Being a hero takes more than anger. It takes strength, responsibility. A willingness to get hurt, to suffer for the sake of others. That's what it means to be selfless.'

Duncan swallowed, caught off guard by how heavy the word 'selfless' felt.

He thought of his father then. Not just the good times, but the way he carried himself. The way he'd smile when things were falling apart. The way he'd encourage Duncan to keep going, even when he didn't feel like he could.

'My dad used to say something like that ...' Duncan whispered. 'He inspired me. He was always doing good – helping us, helping others. He told me I should aim to be better than him. That's what I'm trying to do.'

Konrad nodded. 'Be a hero for the people. One day, I hope they cheer your name. Maybe you'll stand on a grand stage, getting a medal from the emperor himself ... or even be knighted by the king.'

Duncan let out a quiet laugh – half disbelief, half longing. A future like that felt so far away ... but not impossible. Not with Konrad beside him.

Something warm stirred in his chest. He leant forwards, throwing his arms around Konrad's middle in a clumsy but heartfelt hug.

'Thank you, Uncle Konrad. I don't know what I'd do without you.'

He felt Konrad's hand pat his back. 'There are many ways to be a hero. Police officer. Detective. Even a mercenary. What matters is your heart's in the right place.'

Duncan nodded. He wasn't sure yet what path he'd take – but for the first time in a long while, he had direction. The shadows inside him hadn't gone – but at least now, he had a light to follow.

A goal. A purpose. A dream worth chasing.

Konrad's arm wrapped around his shoulders. 'Come here, kid.'

Duncan rested his head there, letting the moment hold him.

And for just a little while ... the world didn't feel so cruel.

Duncan stood in the basement, sweat clinging to his brow, apron already stained from earlier attempts. The old workbench was cluttered with notes and scorch marks. He tossed a blanket over it, placed a plain rock in the centre, and rolled back his sleeves.

'Focus ...' he muttered, closing his eyes. Energy gathered in his palms, a soft blue light flickering to life. 'Analyse the material ...'

The magic of *Material Alteration* pulsed from his hands, and the rock began to change – dull stone giving way to the shimmer of metal. But the process fought him. His fingers trembled. The light flickered.

'C'mon ... C'mon ...'

It was nearly there. Nearly perfect. Then—

Crack!

The rock shattered, sharp shards slicing across his hand. He cursed, recoiling with a grimace. Blood welled in shallow cuts across his palm.

'Dammit!' he hissed. He grabbed a towel, pressing it to the wound as he slumped into the nearest chair. 'Magic's a bloody nightmare. If I could just get this right, I'd stop wasting money on silver rounds ...'

He picked up a book on magical energy, flipping it open absently. Pages rustled as he skimmed. Nothing new. Nothing useful. He knew what he was missing: control. Consistency. But he didn't know how to fix that yet.

Duncan climbed the stairs, rubbing his aching hand. His head was pounding from magical strain. He wiped the sweat from his face and flopped into his living room chair.

Then his phone buzzed.

He groaned softly, pulled it from his pocket. 'Hello?'

'Hello, Mr Saul, it's Elisa.'

He blinked. 'Oh. Hey, Elisa. What's up?'

Her voice was a little hesitant, but polite as ever. *'Today is Saturday, and if you recall, I previously expressed my desire for us to spend time together as friends.'*

Right. That conversation. He remembered it now – vague plans, lightly suggested. 'I do recall.'

'I had hoped that would come to fruition today. Do you have some free time?'

Duncan glanced at his bandaged hand, then at the notes on his desk. Magic could wait. He needed a break anyway.

Still, something tightened in his chest. *Is this a date? Does she think it is?*

He'd never really been on one. Not properly. Girls in the past had flirted with him, but nothing ever stuck. He didn't know what he was supposed to *do* – how to act, what to say. Elisa was different too. She asked questions that got under his skin, didn't always respect his space. And yet ... she was kind. Honest. Soft in a way that didn't feel fake.

Maybe this was a mistake. Maybe it wasn't. But part of him – a part tired of blood and death and failure – wanted to know what it was like to just ... be around someone like her. Just for a day.

He leant back in his chair, eyes drifting to the ceiling. 'Well ... I guess I'm free. I don't have anything up right now, so I can swing by.'

Elisa's voice brightened immediately. *'Truly? That is splendid news! May I inquire about your anticipated arrival time?'*

'Hmm ... Let's say about two?'

'Ah, I see. That arrangement suits me perfectly well.'

The call ended, and Duncan exhaled through his nose, staring at the phone in his hand.

This girl was definitely not going to give him a break.

Elisa turned off her smartphone, her heart thudding like a drum in her chest.

'So, what did he say?' Sara asked, leaning in with the kind of enthusiasm only a doting mother could muster.

Elisa clasped her hands and squealed, practically bouncing on her heels. 'He said yes! He said yes!'

Sara grinned from ear to ear. 'Ah! Congratulations, Elisa! You're going on a date with my son. You two make a cute pair.'

Elisa could hardly believe it. Duncan – *Duncan* – had agreed. He was actually taking her on a date. Her stomach swirled with excitement and dread in equal measure. She'd never done this before. What if it was awkward? What if they had nothing to talk about? What if she said something ridiculous and he looked at her like she'd sprouted a second head?

But still, there was a giddy, fragile hope blooming inside her. Maybe this could be something wonderful.

Then Sara folded her arms, that mischievous glint back in her eye. 'Now, tell me – do you have a little crush on him, hm?'

Elisa blinked. *A little*?

She laughed, caught off guard. 'Well, I do hold him in high regard. He's brave, courageous ... incredibly selfless.'

It wasn't a lie. Just ... strategically worded.

Sara raised an eyebrow. 'Oh really? That's all? Nothing more ... fluttery? Romantic? Something that might make a girl squeal into her pillow at night?'

'N–no, Mrs Saul!' Elisa blurted, her cheeks heating. 'He's just ... a good friend, I assure you.'

Sara didn't look remotely convinced. 'Mm-hmm. Right.' She pointed dramatically. 'Anyway! If you want to really knock his socks off today, I've got just the plan. Hair, outfit, earrings – I'm bringing out the full arsenal.'

'Oh, that's not necessary—'

'Oh, it *absolutely* is,' Sara said, already marching towards the dressing table. 'I want my son to be floored. Gobsmacked. Utterly thunderstruck. And, frankly, I want some credit.'

Elisa laughed, despite herself. 'You do sound very confident, Mrs Saul.'

Sara grinned. 'Darling, I didn't almost become famous for nothing. I may not have won an award, but I had *range*. Now – sit!'

Elisa obeyed, sliding into the seat as Sara hovered behind her like a general preparing for battle.

'You're really pretty, you know – especially with that red hair,' Sara said, her tone softening as she brushed through Elisa's hair with surprising tenderness.

Elisa found herself relaxing into the moment. There was something oddly comforting about letting someone else take over for a bit. She didn't have to overthink or prepare a speech or measure her every word like she did in school. She could just ... be.

Sara worked with fast fingers, braiding and twisting until Elisa's hair was swept into a beautiful half-up, half-down style. Then came the make-up – subtle touches, not too much, but enough to make her feel like someone different. Or perhaps just someone braver.

When Sara stepped back with a proud little flourish and a 'Voilà!', Elisa stared at the mirror.

Her lips carried a delicate rose-pink sheen, her complexion softly radiant, her eyes framed with subtle artistry that lent her an air of effortless grace. The braids – intricate yet elegant – crowned her like woven sunlight, while her auburn hair spilled in soft, lustrous waves.

She blinked, taking in the sight. Was this really Sara's handiwork? Elisa had never imagined the woman could pull off such a sophisticated look. She turned her head, admiring the braids. 'It looks amazing,' she said sincerely. 'Thank you. I believe Mr Saul will be most ... flattered.'

Sara clapped her hands like a child offered sweets. 'Now! Let's pick your outfit. Come along, kiddo.'

Elisa stood, her legs wobbling slightly beneath her. She followed Sara up the stairs, heart fluttering all over again – excitement mingling with nerves, like butterflies staging a coup in her chest.

As Elisa admired her finished makeover, Duncan seized the opportunity to shower. The cool water hit his skin, and he closed his eyes, letting it wash away the weight of the day. His fingers traced over his face, scrubbing at the grime.

He stepped out, towel around his waist, and caught his reflection in the bathroom mirror – the face of a man shaped by battle and survival. A man who didn't make room for softness. As he combed his hair, a flicker of something tugged at his chest. He shoved it aside.

With quick, automatic movements, he applied his black eye make-up. The routine was familiar, grounding.

At his wardrobe, Duncan stared like it had just insulted him. Shirts. Jumpers. T-shirts. Blazers. All neat, folded, colour-coded – and utterly useless. What the hell did someone wear to a midday hangout that wasn't quite a date but sort of was?

He scratched the back of his neck. This wasn't battlefield prep, and yet somehow, it felt more nerve-wracking.

Eventually, he reached for an olive-green turtleneck jumper – clean, fitted, not too flashy – and paired it with a black blazer and his best pair of Damien jeans. White sneakers completed the look. It was fine. Nice, even. But it felt ... off. Like trying to smile with someone else's mouth.

He stepped back, frowning at the mirror. Did it look like he was trying too hard? Or not trying enough? Should he have shaved?

He sprayed some cologne, then immediately winced. Two spritzes? Was that too much? Should he air it out a bit?

He'd never been good at this sort of thing – whatever *this* was. His hand hovered near the bottle, then fell away with a sigh.

He stepped out of the house with the knot in his stomach tightening. Pretended not to notice it.

The drive to Sara's blurred past in silence. Buildings, roads, people – all background noise to the noise inside his head. Every thought curved back to Elisa.

She wasn't just Elisa anymore – not the odd girl with the formal voice and too many questions. Lately, she'd begun to occupy a space in his thoughts that made him uneasy.

It wasn't just her looks – he'd met plenty of beautiful women. It was the way she looked at him, like he was more than what the world had turned him into. The way she spoke to him like he still mattered.

It was just a date. A friendly hangout. But his chest felt tight. He didn't know what this feeling was – hope, maybe. Or fear. Maybe both. And it annoyed him how much he cared.

He parked his red muscle car outside and made his way in, forcing his usual cool confidence to the surface.

'Hello, Mum. Is Elisa ready?' he asked, his tone polite.

'She's just getting ready,' Sara replied, but the grin she wore – the gleam in her eyes – told him everything. She was up to something.

'What's with that grin?' Duncan asked, trying to keep his unease in check.

Sara quickly looked away, her smile turning into a knowing smirk. 'Nothing.'

Before Duncan could say more, he heard the click of heels. Elisa appeared, and everything inside him stilled. His breath caught. The sight of her – transformed – was overwhelming. Her white floral dress, the Panama straw hat perched atop her head, and those shimmering gold earrings – she looked impossibly beautiful.

His gaze followed her as she moved. Every detail about her, from the delicate elegance of her dress to the way the light from the window caught her accessories, hit him harder than he'd expected. He couldn't look away.

'Wow ...' The word slipped from his lips, softer than he intended. He felt almost caught off guard, unsure of what to do with the feelings swirling inside him.

Sara snickered, but Duncan barely heard her. He was too distracted by Elisa's transformed appearance. There was something about her that made it hard to breathe, like he was seeing her in a completely new light. He wanted to draw her close, to whisper into her ear how stunning she looked, to trace his fingers along her delicate jawline and feel her warmth against him.

Elisa's bright smile lit up the room as she hurried towards him, excitement evident in every step. But then, in an instant, her heel caught the edge of the stairs, and she stumbled forwards.

'Oh, gosh!' she gasped.

Before his mind could catch up, Duncan's body reacted. His arms shot out, catching her mid-fall and lifting her effortlessly into his embrace. Her warmth jolted through him – electric, undeniable. She felt softer than he expected, more delicate than anyone he'd ever held.

'Hey!' His voice came out strained, but his grip was steady.

'Be careful!' Sara's voice floated from behind them, but Duncan barely heard her. All he could focus on was Elisa's breath, soft and steady against his chest. She was too close. And for a moment, his heart skipped – hammering in a rhythm he didn't recognise.

Her scent – soft, floral – wrapped around him, mixing with the air between them, making everything feel more intimate. It was a sweet contrast to the sharp edges of his world, a world that suddenly seemed far away.

He felt the heat radiating from her, the rise and fall of her breath syncing with his. Time slowed, leaving only the two of them in this fragile, charged space. The moment stretched, and for the first time in ages, Duncan didn't feel the weight of everything else. Just her.

How embarrassing ...

Elisa's heart slammed against her ribs as she found herself flush against Duncan's chest. Her body fit perfectly against his, and his arms held her securely, warm and steady. For one absurd, terrifying moment, she couldn't move.

Okay. This is fine. Perfectly fine. You have simply thrown yourself into his arms like a swooning heroine. How very dignified.

She swallowed, forcing her limbs to work, but they felt like jelly. Her gaze inched up – slow, cautious – until it met his. Their faces were far too close. A single heartbeat, and their lips could meet.

Sweet heavens, he is exceedingly handsome. And he smells – God, why does he smell so good? It is most unfair.

She blinked. Once. Twice. She could feel the heat rising in her cheeks, and no matter how many breathing exercises she'd practised, they weren't helping now.

Her gaze lifted, locking onto his. She longed to pull away, but of course, she couldn't. Held so securely in his arms, all she could do was stare like a daft schoolgirl.

However, his eyes didn't mock her. They were ... kind. Confused, maybe. Curious.

'Ah! Th–thank you, Mr Saul ... Oh my gosh, this is so embarrassing ... I must've looked really silly, did I not?' Duncan let go of Elisa, and she rubbed the back of her head, offering an apology. 'S–sorry, everyone.'

Duncan sighed, and he then looked at Elisa, head to toe. He hummed, impressed. 'I'm not one to usually dish out compliments to girls, but ... you look ... cute and ... hmm ... *attractive*, yeah.'

Sara shook her head in disappointment and said, 'Ah jeez ...'

Despite Duncan's awkward reply, Elisa looked away shyly, twirling a lock of hair between her fingers. 'Aww ... thank you, Mr Saul. I wanted to look nice – *especially* for you.' She was pleasantly surprised he'd noticed her effort. His compliment warmed her heart, making her glad she'd taken the trouble to dress up. For a moment, she allowed herself to believe he genuinely enjoyed spending time with her. When he admitted he wasn't one to 'usually dish out compliments,' her heart skipped a beat.

Sara chimed in. 'Uh, hello. I did most of the work.'

Elisa turned to Sara and apologised. 'Oh, forgive my impudence, Mrs Saul.' Elisa redirected her attention to Duncan, explaining, 'I forgot to mention that your mother deserves the credit for my stunning look. She's the artist behind it all. Her fashion sense is remarkable.'

Duncan glanced at his mother, a smile forming. 'You did an amazing job, Mum. Maybe you should become a make-up artist.'

Sara blushed and brushed off the praise. 'Oh, come on now.'

Elisa's cheeks also flushed, a nervous smile tugging at her lips. 'So, Mr Saul ... are we all set to head out?'

'Absolutely,' Duncan said, responding with a smile.

Elisa was about to go on a date. Her first date! This experience was going to be unforgettable – one way or another.

Elisa excused herself for a moment to collect a forgotten lipstick from her bedroom, a small fib to give herself pause to steady her nerves.

Sara smirked and nudged Duncan with her elbow. 'Well, well, well. My boy finally became a man.'

Ugh ... Does she have to put it that way? Duncan thought, rolling his eyes in response to his mother's teasing. 'Ugh ... Yes, yes. Elisa was the one who arranged this.'

'I mean the way Elisa speaks and looks at you, she has a total crush on you.'

Duncan was starting to get annoyed by his mother. 'Yeah, I know. You don't have to keep saying it.'

'It's unsurprising.' Sara smiled, her gaze travelling up and down Duncan's form. 'I mean, you look so handsome. You should be irresistible to girls. But then again, maybe it's because you don't chat them up that often.'

Sara's gaze left Duncan feeling exposed, as if under a spotlight. Her straightforward compliments caught him off guard, momentarily stroking his ego. The idea of being attractive to girls was something he hadn't given much thought to. His attention was reserved for more pressing matters.

'I usually have a lot of work to do,' Duncan replied, 'so I don't spend much time developing my social skills or hanging out with other people.'

'Yeah, because all you ever do is work. You never really hang out all that much – you should try enjoying yourself more and relax.'

Duncan shook his head. 'As the world is right now, relaxing should come later. For as long as Flora needs saving, I won't stop doing my duty.' Duncan's reply was direct, his words emphasising his dedication to his responsibilities. His work had consistently shaped his routines and habits. He was a man of action, focused on tasks aligned with his goals.

'You sound like a workaholic ... A slave to your duty.'

Sara's words carried a hint of disappointment that Duncan couldn't overlook. Her gaze held concern for his well-being, and her judgment was evident. The term 'workaholic' stung slightly, its accuracy undeniable. It served as a reminder that his dedication might be causing him to overlook other aspects of life.

Duncan's eyes narrowed. 'Mum, leisure isn't on my radar. It doesn't align with my work or goals – it's just a waste of time.'

'Then why agree to this date with Elisa?' Sara asked.

His mother's question about going on a date with Elisa was like throwing a curveball at Duncan. He paused briefly, then answered, 'Well ... She's an exception and I didn't wanna let her down.'

'I see ...' Sara smirked. 'She enjoys your company, so keep it going. She's cute, smart, kind, outgoing ... and a fantastic cook. What more could you ask from a girl?'

Duncan remained silent.

Sara grinned cheekily. 'I mean, don't be like me ... a single mum ... waiting to be fucked by a guy.'

Duncan was bemused. 'Mum, what the hell?' he said, perplexed.

Sara crouched down and burst into laughter. She flicked the left side of her hair away to keep it out of her face. 'Hahahaha! I'm just messing with you! Lighten up.' Her expression softened. 'I really care about you, you know. It's just ... what you're doing, it doesn't seem healthy. Constantly going around taking lives and working non-stop. I just want you to enjoy life, have some normality. I want you to be happy.'

Sara's observation lingered in his mind, a gentle but pointed critique. Duncan considered the truth in her words. The reality of his existence, as seen through her eyes, revealed a pattern of relentless pursuit.

Sara turned her gaze to Elisa who was descending the stairs. Sara watched as Elisa pulled out a small mirror to check her appearance and smooth her hair. 'Elisa has been through so much, and both of you have faced your fair share of challenges. You really only have each other. So, please, be there for one another,' she said quietly, her concern evident.

Duncan smiled warmly, reassuring Sara. 'Don't worry, Mum. I'll make sure we make the most of our time together,' he whispered.

'That's good to hear.'

Duncan turned to Elisa and beckoned. 'Alright, let's go, Elisa.'

Elisa's smile brightened and she followed Duncan's lead. 'Okay, Mr Saul.' The two waved goodbye to Sara.

As they stepped outside, Sara waved back. 'See ya around, kiddos!' She closed the door, and the two began their journey.

Chapter XXII

A DAY OUT

Clouds drifted lazily above, casting shifting shadows over the street. The sunlight broke through in fleeting bursts, warming Duncan's shoulders as he walked alongside Elisa. She looked ... oddly at ease today. Perhaps it was the way the wind teased her hair, or how she didn't seem so guarded for once.

'So,' Duncan began, shoving his hands into his blazer pockets, 'where d'you wanna go?'

Elisa turned to him with a smile. 'Wherever you wish, Mr Saul. I shall be delighted to follow your lead.'

Duncan raised a brow. 'You know, you don't have to be polite about everything. Just pick something. I really don't mind.'

She brought a finger to her chin, tilting her head ever so slightly as she pondered. 'Hmm ... perhaps a sightseeing stroll through the park, followed by a visit to the library? That would be quite charming, don't you think?'

He chuckled. Trust her to suggest a library. 'Or we could grab some sandwiches, find a patch of grass – maybe get some ice cream? Actually enjoy the sun while it's out?'

That made her smile – soft, genuine. 'That does sound rather delightful.'

The two of them crossed the busy bridge, surrounded by the flow of city life – businessmen checking their watches, children weaving through the crowd, teenagers laughing too loudly. A boy sped by on a squeaky bicycle, and just behind him, a pair of soldiers lingered near the railing, eyes scanning the passing vehicles: regular cars intermingled with matte grey military vans. Duncan noted the tension in Elisa's posture – how her hands settled behind her back, as though trying not to be in the way.

'Mr Saul,' she began, her voice light but curious, 'I believe you mentioned once that you were with the military – is that correct?'

He glanced at her. 'Reservist, yeah. Why?'

'Forgive my curiosity, but ... did you ever see battle?'

Duncan scratched at his chin. The question hit a little harder than expected – not because of the memories, but because of how little there was to remember.

'Not really,' he said. 'Wasn't much going on when I served. No war, no real deployment. Mostly just running drills, doing inspections, getting screamed at by some mad drill instructor who thought he was the bloody Emperor. I swear, he wrecked my right ear. Still rings sometimes.' He rubbed at it absent-mindedly. 'Truth is, I realised pretty quick it wasn't for me. All that structure, all the rules ... I wanted to help people, yeah, but not like that.'

Elisa listened quietly, her gaze fixed on him like she was trying to piece him together.

'I thought about joining the police,' Duncan went on, his voice growing quieter. 'Figured it'd be better – solving crimes, stopping the bad guys. But even that didn't work out. You're stuck under someone else's boot. Can't do what needs to be done half the time. And then there were ... disagreements. Some criminals kept slipping through the cracks. Some got out and hurt people again. Wasn't something I could sit with.'

He shrugged, eyes on the pavement ahead.

'Then Jénmar came along. He ran Centurion Arms – one of the bigger outfits. I'd been freelancing for a while, but working with him opened doors. We kept it simple: he handled the clients, I handled the jobs.'

There was a pause. Elisa's steps slowed just a little, as though giving him space.

'And what, if I may inquire, led you to pursue the life of a mercenary?' she asked softly. 'What drove you to make such a … personal decision?'

Duncan didn't answer straight away. The sounds around them – traffic, footsteps, laughter – seemed to fade, and all he could hear was the thudding echo of something older. Something heavier.

He exhaled through his nose.

'There was someone important to me. Someone I looked up to.' His voice dropped low. 'My dad. He made a lot of mistakes. Knew he was a bit of a shit person, but … he wanted better for me. Always said I shouldn't turn out like him. Wanted me to go further – be stronger, smarter. Said it was a kid's job to surpass their parent.'

Duncan stared out over the water, watching how the current caught the light. He didn't say the rest – that his father's love, though real, was imperfect. Flawed in quiet ways Duncan still didn't fully understand. But he'd tried.

Duncan didn't quite know why he'd brought up his father.

Maybe he just wanted to be honest. Or maybe he was tired of acting like the past didn't still gnaw at the edges.

But when Elisa tilted her head slightly, that ever-curious look in her eyes, he felt it coming – the question.

'Why does your father regard himself in such a way … as a terrible person?'

And there it was.

Duncan exhaled, folding his arms. He stared at the ground for a beat before answering.

'Look ... I like you, Elisa. I do. But you're askin' a lot of questions, and there are some things I'd rather keep to myself, yeah?'

Her expression softened immediately. 'Forgive me. I did not intend to pry.'

He shrugged, letting the tension ease from his shoulders. 'Nah, it's alright. Just not ready to crack open that box yet.'

The silence between them was comfortable now, not heavy. The kind that said, *We're alright – let's just move on.*

Duncan gave her a sideways glance. 'Anyway, enough about me. Let's talk about you, posh girl. What was it like growing up in a mansion surrounded by butlers, gold spoons and, I dunno, opera music?'

She let out a delicate laugh. 'You jest, but you are not entirely wrong. My childhood was marked by a rather strict and refined upbringing – afternoon teas, porcelain napkins, and the constant presence of distinguished guests. Education was paramount. We had a rotating cast of private tutors for every conceivable subject.'

Duncan whistled under his breath. 'Sounds dead posh.'

'I suppose it was,' she replied with a nostalgic smile. 'My parents corrected the slightest imperfection in our speech. We were trained in etiquette, diction, posture ... My mother was particularly relentless about not speaking with food in one's mouth. Her scoldings were fierce.' She giggled softly. 'But I did learn proper table manners, I must admit.'

Duncan smirked. 'I bet you were the kind of kid who sat upright like a ruler and never burped once.'

Elisa raised a brow, clearly amused. 'Of course not. Burping at the dinner table would've been social suicide.'

He chuckled. 'Yeah, can't imagine you scrappin' over the last biscuit like the rest of us.'

Her smile lingered, but there was something quieter behind it now. 'In truth, that world shielded me from understanding the realities most people face. It wasn't until I met Archer that I truly began to see beyond it.'

Duncan's smirk faded slightly at the name, but he nodded. 'He meant a lot to you, didn't he?'

'Yes,' she said gently. 'More than I can ever fully explain.'

He kicked a pebble along the path. 'What about your parents? What did they do?'

'My father was an entrepreneur, the proprietor of a company named Clint, while my mother was a psychiatrist.'

'Smart and rich,' Duncan muttered. 'No wonder you talk like a poem.'

Elisa gave a soft laugh at that.

He scratched the back of his neck, gaze drifting. 'And after they died ... you ended up in the orphanage, right? Was it awful? Or did you make it through alright?'

She grew a little more reserved then, her hands clasping behind her back. 'My sister and I concealed our family name to avoid attracting attention. Despite this, we managed to make a few close friends. Mother Amy – she was the caretaker – treated us with such warmth. We were, I suppose, her best-behaved children, and she doted on us.'

'That's rare,' Duncan said. 'Most places like that … ain't exactly gentle.'

Elisa nodded slowly. 'We were fortunate. But everything changed once our parents' killers were apprehended.'

Duncan looked at her properly then. 'Did life get easier?'

'For a time, yes. There was a sense of relief. We were meant to be adopted by the Olsen family … but unforeseen events prevented that.'

'What happened to the ones who did it?' he asked. 'Why'd they do it?'

She inhaled. 'The police claimed it was business rivalry. My father's competitors hired a man – Benedict Blue. He was arrested, tried and convicted. Lifetime sentence. Justice was served, in a sense.'

Duncan shook his head. 'Bloody hell. All that … just for business? Bastard got what he deserved.'

Elisa smiled faintly. 'Indeed. Justice, though slow, does find its way.'

Their eyes met, and for a fleeting moment, they shared a quiet laugh – one that didn't come from humour, but from something simpler. Understanding.

The library smelled faintly of dust and polished wood – quiet, still, the kind of silence Duncan didn't mind. He leaned back in the chair, earphones in, letting the hum of a ballad drown out the world while Elisa wandered the aisles like she was gathering treasure. When she returned, her arms stacked with books nearly to her chin, he tugged one earphone out.

'Elisa, are you planning to read the whole damn library?'

She set the books down with care, brushing off her skirt. 'I've acquired a modest selection on political science, civil rights, legal theory, sociology, philosophy, and democratic governance.'

Duncan folded his arms, raising a brow. 'That's not a selection – that's a syllabus. You sure you're not takin' on too much?'

Elisa gave a small shake of her head, firm but graceful. 'Not in the slightest, Mr Saul. It simply reflects my dedication. If I am to reach my aspirations, I must begin by immersing myself in knowledge.'

He smirked. 'Right. But maybe tone it down a bit, yeah? You sound like a walking textbook. Try speakin' like a person, not a speechwriter.'

That earned a light laugh. 'My apologies. I shall attempt to keep things ... simple – though I do hope our mutual understanding shall remain intact.'

Duncan snorted, half amused, half worn out. She had a way of talking that wrapped around itself like ribbon – posh, rehearsed, almost too polished. Still, she meant every word. He could see that. Eyes bright, back straight, completely serious about whatever dream she was chasing. Even if he couldn't quite keep up with half her vocabulary, he couldn't deny the effort.

He nodded slowly. 'Fair enough. Every journey starts somewhere. Gotta respect the grind – you've got fire in you.'

Elisa smiled at that, just a little. 'Your encouragement means a great deal. I intend to make full use of this opportunity.'

Duncan crossed his arms again, studying her face. 'Good. Be a shame to waste all that effort.'

Her eyes flicked down to her stack of books, something proud in her posture. 'These shall greatly assist me in refining my thesis.'

That caught him off guard. 'You're writin' a thesis already?'

'Indeed,' she said, chin held high. 'I have begun compiling thoughts and arguments. Once complete, I was hoping to present it – to both you and Mrs Saul, perhaps.'

Duncan tilted his head. 'Bit early for that, innit? Don't most people wait till the end of the course to worry about all that?'

'Quite right,' she said, not missing a beat. 'But I thought I might get a head start. If I tackle it now, I shall have fewer burdens later.'

He slipped his hands into his pockets. 'Makes sense. Less panic when deadlines hit.'

Elisa gave a polite nod. 'Precisely.'

'Remind me,' he said, 'when's uni start for you?'

'Induction begins at the end of summer.'

'And your major's what – Politics and Law, right?'

'Correct.'

He gave a low whistle. 'Big brain stuff. That's good to know.'

Leaving the library behind, the two found themselves in a park, sharing a bench and enjoying ice cream. As she gazed at her cone, Elisa's thoughts wandered. Eventually, she gathered the courage to speak.

'I have been curious, Mr Saul. With so many people in need, why did you choose to help me? Why invite me into your home? There were likely others in worse situations.'

Duncan, slightly annoyed, crossed his arms. 'You're still on about that?' he muttered. But his tone softened as he went on. 'I helped because I wanted to. I don't need a specific reason to help someone. Helping is what I believe a hero would do – and I've always wanted to be one. So, please, let go of any notion that you're unworthy of this support. You should just be grateful.'

The idea of helping simply because it was right struck a chord with Elisa. She found herself drawn to his notion of heroism – of doing good not for reward, but because it mattered. Yet, as he concluded, the word *grateful* lingered. His words reminded her that, sometimes, help arrives without explanation – and deserving it isn't about comparing one's pain to another's.

Elisa paused, taking in what he had said. Then she offered him a warm smile and murmured, 'I see ... These are the traits I find most endearing in you.'

'What?'

Elisa immediately blushed, suddenly aware of what she'd said. 'Huh!? I mean – I think you're a great person! I find you admirable!'

Why had the conversation turned so awkward? She'd never dated before, and now she was stumbling over her words like a fool. She had thought she could manage this, but clearly her lack of experience was showing. Internally, she scolded herself for not being able to string together a coherent thought.

Her mind raced. Elisa thought of all the romantic films she'd watched, the advice from friends – but none of it applied in this moment. She wished she could relax and simply be herself, but that seemed impossible with her heart pounding like a drum and her thoughts in disarray.

Her cheeks burned with embarrassment as she fumbled through her response. She wished she could rewind time and come up with something smoother. But she also realised, perhaps, that these awkward moments were part of the process. Maybe, in time, she would get better at this whole *romantic connection* business.

Duncan grinned and delivered a teasing remark. 'Thanks for the compliments, Elisa ... maybe you should start writin' love poems to me, too.'

Elisa raised her hands defensively, her face now as red as a tomato. 'Wh–what!?'

Why on earth would he bring up writing love poems? Elisa's mind raced to catch up with the unexpected turn in the conversation. True, Duncan had a teasing smile on his face – but the idea of writing love poems felt like a huge leap from where they stood. They were just friends, weren't they? The thought of romantic gestures like that seemed far too advanced for their relationship.

Duncan's smile faded. 'I'm just kidding ... I wasn't being serious.'

Idiot. It was just a playful jab, not a serious proposal. Elisa's cheeks warmed as she realised how awkward it must have sounded. Amusement tugged at her lips, though the embarrassment lingered like an unwanted guest. *And Duncan – being this handsome – definitely wasn't helping!*

'By the way, is it okay if I call you Kid? As a nickname ...' Duncan asked.

'Why?' Elisa frowned, perplexed.

Caught off guard by Elisa's inquiry, Duncan searched for the right words. 'Because ... it's just a term I use to express fondness. I see you as a young woman with a lot of potential. You know, like a mentor addressing their protégé.'

Elisa didn't know how to feel about that. On one hand, it was nice that he saw potential in her – but on the other, the nickname made it seem as though she were being treated as younger than her actual age. While Duncan was indeed older, the age gap wasn't significant. She pondered the possibility that he saw himself as a mentor. She narrowed her eyes and stared at Duncan in silence.

'What?' Duncan asked.

In the end, she chose to interpret the nickname as a compliment. 'Ugh. Very well, but you shall only use it sparingly.'

'Awesome,' Duncan said cheerfully, pumping his fist. 'So yeah ...'

He had best refrain from uttering it now ... A palpable awkwardness settled between them, leaving a lingering silence.

Duncan then asked, 'Oh, by the way, there's something I've been curious about. The first time we met, you had a gun pointed at me.' He fixed her with a serious gaze. 'Would you have shot me? If I hadn't calmed you down?'

'What? Why would you ask me that?' Elisa frowned. 'No, absolutely not. I cannot bring myself to take a life, as I believe it is wrong and I lack the courage to do so.'

Duncan raised a brow. 'You believe killing is wrong?'

'Well, up to a degree ... In your case, you kill people to prevent them from hurting others, correct?' Duncan remained silent, and Elisa continued. 'I understand your noble intentions, Mr Saul, and I do agree with them to an extent. However, I don't believe killing, intimidation, and violence are always the solution. Often, they merely lead to more of the same. Let's consider a scenario – one person takes another's life as retribution for a crime, and then someone else seeks revenge on the first person. It becomes a never-ending cycle of violence ...'

Duncan folded his arms, took a moment to ponder, and then spoke. 'You bring up a valid point, Kid. But let me pose a question to you. Do you believe that negotiation and civil discussions can always resolve violence and hatred?'

Elisa ran her fingers through her hair, contemplating for a moment before responding. 'Well ...'

Duncan pressed on. 'Think about war criminals. Terrorists. Murderers. The kind who won't listen to reason – the worst bastards you can imagine. You reckon the public just walks up and politely asks them to stop? No – they take drastic measures to put them down before more people get hurt.' Duncan adjusted his stance and continued. 'Consider this. Even some of the most celebrated figures in history have committed acts similar to what I have done. Call it justifiable homicide.'

Elisa looked down, lost in thought. *He is not wrong.* Even though violence wasn't always the solution, neither were negotiations.

'Now, you know words aren't always gonna cut it. Sometimes, action is necessary to grab people's attention. However, I get where you're coming from, Elisa. But someone has to bear the burden and responsibility to ensure the happiness and safety of others.'

'I see,' Elisa said, her gaze fixed on the ground.

Duncan folded his arms and said, 'If you wanna change the world, Elisa, you'll have to go through a lot of pain, suffering and sacrifice. Take a page from the civil war as an example. See what Lance has to go through, see what I have to go through.'

Elisa remained silent. She knew he was right. Words alone had limits. Duncan had a valid point about the necessity of taking action. As he spoke, the path to making the world better seemed to become clearer. Lance's sacrifices and Duncan's struggles were proof of the hardships that came with it.

Duncan stood up from the bench. 'Well, that's enough for one day ... We should head back because the sun is starting to set.'

'Wait, Mr Saul. Can we gaze at the sun from the bridge before we go?'

Duncan smiled. 'Sure, but not too long.'

Chapter XXIII

EXPLOSIVE ANGER

The sea shimmered beneath the bridge, the setting sun casting amber hues across the gentle tides. Seagulls circled above, their cries soft against the breeze. Boats drifted across the water – catamarans, trawlers, small fishing decks – all part of a tranquil scene that reminded Elisa, fleetingly, of simpler days.

'The sun is rather delightful this evening,' she remarked, her voice light, though thoughtful.

'Yeah ...' Duncan nodded beside her, arms resting on the rail. 'Got lucky with the weather, I guess.'

A quiet moment passed between them – the kind that hung too long on her chest, urging her to speak.

'Mr Saul,' Elisa began gently, folding her hands in front of her, 'before we conclude the day, I feel I must tell you something.'

His posture straightened slightly. 'What's on your mind?'

She took a breath. 'Regarding your work as a mercenary ... it appears your motivations run deeper than merely upholding justice or preserving social order.'

Duncan blinked, visibly thrown. 'What? What're you talking about?'

Elisa kept her composure, though she could feel her pulse quicken. 'You became a mercenary after the death of your father, did you not? At the hands of a heretic. The incident occurred ten years ago, if I recall correctly.'

His eyes widened, and the shift in his demeanour was immediate.

'No ... Don't – don't talk about that,' he muttered, shaking his head. 'Just leave it.'

The way he recoiled – his voice tight with panic, his shoulders tense – unsettled her more than she had anticipated. She had not expected this reaction, not from him.

'I ... I meant no offence,' she said softly, stepping towards him. 'Have I ... have I said something that upset you? I only wished to understand you better. If this is difficult to speak of, I shall not push. But I—'

'Just stop!'

His voice rang out across the bridge, sharp and sudden.

Elisa stood frozen, her breath caught in her throat. *What have I done?*

She hadn't meant to pry – not truly. And yet, some part of her had needed to understand the man beside her. The one who carried pain in his silences.

Duncan clutched his head in both hands, teeth gritted. 'Bloody hell, you're so annoying! Why d'you keep diggin' at things that ain't yours to touch? Just 'cause I gave you a roof doesn't mean you get to rifle through every part of my life!'

His anger startled her, the bitterness behind it even more so. She took a step back, words catching.

'I ... I did not mean to upset you. It was your mother – she mentioned the matter. Not with malice, but ... concern. She only spoke of how deeply it affected you.'

He snapped his gaze towards her, stunned. 'She told you!?'

His voice cracked with disbelief. 'She fucking told you what happened? After I *explicitly* asked her not to!?'

The shout that followed was raw. 'Why's she always gotta do this?! Why can't she just – just keep things to herself for once?!'

Each word landed like a blow. Elisa flinched, heart sinking. She had never seen Duncan like this. So unguarded. So furious.

Then, without warning, he turned and stormed off.

'Mr Saul!' she called out, hurrying after him. 'Wait!'

Her boots clicked rapidly along the path as she tried to keep up. 'Why are you so angry? Why won't you talk about it? Why does this trouble you so deeply?'

He didn't turn around. His voice came sharp, clipped, loud. 'Stop talking, Elisa! I need to have a word with my mother.'

And with that, he marched ahead – leaving her with only the echo of his fury and the sting of her own misstep.

Sara was typing on her laptop when Duncan stormed into the house, forcefully swinging the door open in a fit of anger.

'Did you tell her?' Duncan yelled, marching towards his mother. He was angry, so angry that he couldn't think straight.

Why the hell would she betray me like this?

Why didn't she consider how I'd feel?

She just lied to me. Straight to my face.

'Wait, Duncan, let me explain,' Sara said, raising her hands.

Duncan advanced towards her with anger in his voice, shouting, 'Haven't you noticed that she's not part of the family yet!? You can't be sharing secrets so casually. I explicitly told you not to tell her, and you lied to my face!'

Sara retorted. 'Well, I can't keep quiet, either, you know! I can't always do what you want. Just because you couldn't find the culprit and save your father doesn't mean I should hide my feelings for your sake. You need to stop being so selfish and consider my feelings, too!'

But Sara's retort, her refusal to bow to his demands, only fuelled his anger further.

She couldn't keep her mouth shut? My selfishness?

All of it was like a slap to the face. And when she mentioned his father's attack, his failure to protect him, it was as if an old wound had been torn open.

How dare she speak to me like this!

Duncan slammed his hand against the table. The sharp thud echoed through the room, making Sara flinch. Her eyes widened as she raised her hands instinctively in defence.

'How bloody *dare* you!?' he snapped, voice tight with fury. '*Me*, selfish? That's rich –coming from the one who lied straight to my face yesterday!'

'Don't you dare speak to me like that! Do you forget that I am your mother!?'

'Argh!' Duncan growled and turned away dismissively.

Sara, not allowing him to leave the conversation, shouted after him. 'Hey, I'm not finished talking to you, mister! Don't walk away when I'm trying to speak with you!'

Duncan turned around, his voice filled with rage, and yelled back. 'You had no right, Mum! You had no fucking right!'

Sara stood up, infuriated, and screamed. 'You've got some nerve using those words against me, you idiot! Right now, you're acting like a selfish brat!'

Duncan paused, his eyes narrowing as he snarled. 'Selfish ... Look who's talking, fucking hypocrite.'

Sara stood there, visibly shocked and hurt.

Duncan then headed for the house door and let out a frustrated growl before opening and slamming it as he stormed outside.

Sara grabbed her hair, letting out a scream of frustration. 'Argh! That boy drives me crazy!' She settled back into her chair, crossing her arms. 'I swear, if he were still a child, I'd have given him a good smack across the face. Ridiculous!'

Elisa placed her hand on Sara's shoulder. 'Mrs Saul, allow me to speak with him. Perhaps I can reach him.'

Sara managed a faint smile and gave her consent, saying, 'Well, you've been studying negotiation techniques. You might be able to talk some sense into him.'

Elisa nodded. 'I shall give it a try.' Elisa turned to leave.

Sara, wearing a troubled expression, whispered to herself. 'Did I mess up here?'

As Elisa reached the door, she paused and glanced back at Sara, her eyes filled with uncertainty. Had they made the right choices?

Duncan crouched outside by the cold brick wall, head bowed, fists clenched. Stress and frustration churned inside him like a storm with no end. He muttered under his breath, voice thick with bitterness.

'No matter what I do, I end up in the same place,' he growled. 'I've busted my arse for years, and I've still got nothing to show for it. It's a bloody joke.'

All the sleepless nights, all the plans – every sacrifice – flashed through his mind. But the results never matched the effort. The gap between what he wanted and what he got felt like a canyon.

With a grunt of anger, Duncan struck the wall. The dull thud of his knuckles against stone stung, but the pain grounded him – however briefly. He hit it again. And again. Not because the wall deserved it, but because he did.

Footsteps approached.

'Mr Saul,' Elisa's voice came, soft and careful. 'Might we speak, just for a moment?'

Duncan lifted his head, shooting Elisa a glare. '*You* ... you've got no right to talk to me after what you did. Boundaries mean nothing to you – do they?'

Elisa hesitated, visibly troubled. 'I ... I merely wished to say – I believe I understand what you are feeling.'

But as Elisa's words emerged, Duncan's initial reaction was one of disbelief. Her claim to understand seemed impossible, an assertion clashing against his raw emotions.

Duncan laughed, short and bitter. It wasn't amusement – it was disbelief. 'Understand? You?' His tone turned cold. 'Don't insult me, Elisa. You've no clue what it's like. You've never felt powerless. You've never lived with the weight of knowing you *failed* someone you loved.'

His voice rose, words tumbling out, thick with emotion. 'It was my fault. I spent ten years chasing, hoping to find the bastard who did it. I thought – if I could just bring Dad home, maybe I'd make it right. But I couldn't. I never did. So don't stand there and pretend—'

'Shut up!' Elisa shouted, sudden and sharp.

Duncan blinked, taken aback by her outburst. The fury in her voice stopped him cold. He stared at her, frowning in shock.

'I beg your pardon for being so direct, Mr Saul,' she said, her voice shaking, 'but *listen*. I *do* understand. I was at Pete's Fort.'

The words hit him like a slap. 'You were at Pete's Fort?'

Tears welled in her eyes, and her voice cracked. 'Yes. I was the sole survivor. Everyone else – my friends, my caregivers ... my sister, May – they all died. They turned. And I ... I couldn't save a single one of them.'

Duncan's breath caught. He hadn't known. Not this. Guilt twisted in his chest as he turned his gaze away, his earlier anger hollow now.

Elisa clenched her fists tightly. 'So do not tell me that I know not what it feels like to be powerless. Don't you *dare*.'

Duncan's voice cracked, as if on the verge of tears. 'Just shut up! What do *you* know, eh? You can't possibly understand my life. You haven't walked in my shoes. You can't act like you know everything about me!'

'You are right, I am not you after all ... But I could say the same thing about you – you do not know what I've been going through in my life, either. But what we *do* know – what we share – is pain. Loss. Regret. So what now? Drown in it? Let it rot us from the inside? Suppressing it will not save you, Mr Saul. It will only destroy you.'

Duncan retorted with intensity. 'Elisa, d'you think it's bloody easy, eh? Losing someone? When I was a kid, all I wanted was to bring him back – save him – but I couldn't. I failed. That's why I don't talk about it. It just reminds me of how badly I've fucked up. If I shove it down, I can focus on the job. If I let it swallow me, I won't get anything done.'

'I never said it was easy,' Elisa replied, her voice softening. 'There was a time I nearly gave up completely. I was lost. But then I met *you*.'

Duncan looked at her, unsure.

'You offered me help when no one else would. You gave me direction, a reason to hope again. You didn't even realise it – but you changed the way I saw the world. You reminded me that I mattered.'

Her words landed like a quiet punch to the chest. Duncan stood still, stunned. He hadn't known. Not really. He never thought he'd made such a difference. It wasn't about saving her – it was about *being there* when she needed someone. He extended a hand, and she'd taken it.

He sighed, eyes heavy. 'Elisa ...'

She lifted her hand, palm up. 'Please – say no more. I shall return home.'

Duncan silently watched as Elisa left.

Duncan lay in his darkened room, staring at the ceiling. Sleep wouldn't come. His mind churned with restless thoughts, replaying the events of the day over and over. He felt overwhelmed – not just by what had happened, but by what he hadn't done.

Elisa was the only survivor of the incident at Pete's fort. The thought gnawed at him. Her friends and sister had turned into ghouls, and she had been forced to witness it all. He had been so caught up in his own turmoil that he hadn't seen her pain, hadn't truly understood what she was going through. That *realisation* stung more than he expected.

She suffered the same way I did. The irony of it all was suffocating. He had sworn to protect people, to stop tragedies like this from happening – yet he'd been blind to the suffering of someone right in front of him.

His fingers curled into the duvet. Guilt clawed at him, a weight pressing deep into his chest. He had been so focused on his own burdens that he had failed to notice hers. How could he call himself a hero when he couldn't even see the pain of someone he cared about?

Frustration surged through him. He clenched his fist and slammed it against the mattress. 'Dammit!' he muttered bitterly. 'Some hero I am ...'

The title he had sought, the mantle of heroism he had hoped to wear with pride, now felt like an ill-fitting mask, revealing his true inadequacies.

In the midst of his turmoil, Duncan couldn't help but seek solace in the memory of his father, the one person he had always looked up to for guidance.

'Father, what should I do ...?' he whispered.

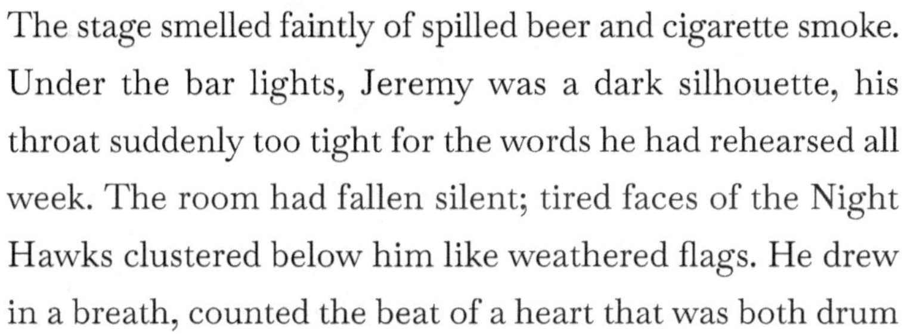

The stage smelled faintly of spilled beer and cigarette smoke. Under the bar lights, Jeremy was a dark silhouette, his throat suddenly too tight for the words he had rehearsed all week. The room had fallen silent; tired faces of the Night Hawks clustered below him like weathered flags. He drew in a breath, counted the beat of a heart that was both drum and metronome, and let his voice find its shape.

'Brothers and sisters,' Jeremy began. 'Lance Sainglend, our leader, the man who has risked everything for us, is in captivity. He gave his freedom, his safety – everything – for our cause. Now it's our turn to stand for him. We must act, and we must act together, before it's too late.'

He scanned the crowd for the flinch of belief. He had learned to read faces as others read maps – every line a contour of loyalty or doubt.

Some would call negotiation cowardice. Some would call his plan madness. He knew that; he had accounted for both. Yet the truth he tasted was simpler, more brutal: do nothing, and they would be hunted, their names spat out by those who had teeth. He let that truth press against the edges of his speech until it could no longer be ignored.

'I understand that some of you may harbour reservations. Lance has voiced his intention to negotiate with the enemy, and we're all too aware of the risks involved. But if we do nothing, if we remain idle, we condemn ourselves to a fate of being hunted down and mercilessly executed. We can't let that happen.'

No one was saying anything. Was he really going to convince these people? His eyes locked with each person in the crowd.

'I implore you. Stand with me in this mission. Together, we can ensure that Lance is liberated and secure the future of the Night Hawks.'

A lot of them were not paying any attention. They were defeated at that point. They had lost Lance; they had lost many men. Most importantly, they had lost their hope. Deep down, Jeremy knew that persuading his comrades to rally behind him wouldn't be easy, especially after all they had endured.

Suddenly, a Night Hawk stepped forward. 'I follow in your steps, Jeremy. My own brother fell victim to the Red Lions, shot down like a defenceless animal. He did nothing wrong. So, I stand beside you.'

Jeremy nodded, his eyes meeting the Night Hawk's with understanding and gratitude. 'Thank you for your courage. Anyone else?'

More – but very few – Night Hawks stepped forward. 'We stand beside you, Jeremy!'

Although the numbers were not as high as he had hoped, Jeremy understood that the Night Hawks who had chosen to stay were the ones who believed in the cause. His gaze swept across those who remained, his expression firm but respectful.

'For those who choose not to join us, you're free to leave.'

Regrettably, most of the remaining Night Hawks decided to walk away, their faces filled with doubt and uncertainty. 'This man is mad ...' one of them said.

As Jeremy heard the dismissive comment from the departing Night Hawk, he couldn't help but feel disappointment. It was disheartening to witness the scepticism and doubt that had taken hold of some within their ranks. He had hoped that his impassioned plea would have swayed more of them to join the cause, but it seemed that not everyone was willing to take the risk.

With that, Jeremy turned his attention back to those who had joined him. 'For those who stand with me, let's move forward. Our mission is to shape our own destiny ... together!'

Chapter XXIV

RECONCILIATION

In a small house in Lancefield, Duncan sat on his bed, gazing out the window. His eyes were focused on the horizon as the fading sunlight painted shadows on his face.

Since the day the heretic attacked his father, Duncan's life had completely changed. The event had hurt him deeply, leaving him with a strong desire for revenge. The pain and frustration overwhelmed him, feeding a relentless anger that would take over his every thought and action.

Duncan's attention snapped to the doorway as Konrad entered his room. He sat up in bed, his gaze fixed on his uncle.

'Duncan, I need you to join me in the basement,' Konrad stated.

'Why?'

A mysterious glint sparkled in Konrad's eyes as he replied. 'I'll show you.'

They entered the basement of the house. The air was slightly cooler than upstairs, carrying a faint scent of earthiness. Fluorescent lights flickered overhead, casting a gentle glow over the space. Along one wall stood shelves stacked with assorted boxes and bins labelled in faded marker pen with contents like 'holiday decorations', 'old books' and 'household supplies'. A washer and dryer hummed softly in one corner, their dull white exteriors blending into the neutral palette of the room.

The concrete floor, speckled with dust and occasional stains, stretched out beneath their feet. A water heater whirred quietly in another corner, its low drone providing a steady background noise. Overall, the basement appeared to be a functional if somewhat unremarkable space, serving its purpose as storage and utility area for the household above.

'Kid, come sit,' Konrad said, gesturing to a wooden stool beside a small training mat.

Duncan obliged, his eyes still heavy with unresolved fury. 'Why are we here?' he asked with bitterness.

Konrad placed his hands on Duncan's shoulders, his touch firm yet gentle. 'We're here because I wanna teach you something. Something that goes beyond fighting. I wanna teach you how to control your anger.'

Duncan couldn't help but feel a surge of resistance. Why should he control it? Why should he let go of the very thing that fuelled his determination to find the person responsible? To him, anger was a driving force, a relentless fire that pushed him to keep searching, to keep fighting.

Duncan's brows furrowed in confusion. 'Control my anger? But why? I have every right to be angry, don't I?'

Konrad nodded. 'Yes, kid, you do. Your anger is justified. But if you let it consume you, it'll cloud your judgment. It will blind you to the truth and turn you into something you're not.'

Duncan clenched his fists, his fury rising. 'I don't care! All I care about is catching that criminal. He ruined our lives. He took my father away!'

'And that's why we're here, Duncan. I wanna teach you how to channel that rage, how to use it as a tool rather than a weapon that will harm you as much as your enemy.'

Konrad's words seemed to strike a chord. The mention of his anger becoming a weapon against himself gave Duncan pause. He realised that, in his pursuit of vengeance, he might lose sight of what truly mattered. His anger could turn him into a person he didn't want to be, someone consumed by hatred and blinded to the world around him.

He glanced down at his fists, breath uneven. *Would Dad even recognise me like this?*

'Can you really teach me that, Uncle?'

Konrad smiled. 'I can, kid. But you must be willing to learn to let go of the anger that shackles you.'

Duncan took a deep breath, his knuckles gradually unclenching. 'Fine, if it would help me.'

'I want you to hit me.'

Duncan's gaze hardened with scepticism. 'Hit you? But, Uncle Konrad, you're an experienced fighter. You might hurt me in the process.'

Konrad's steady gaze met Duncan's. 'Don't worry about me, kid. I won't retaliate. This exercise isn't about harming me physically. It's about learning control.'

Duncan hesitated, then gave a small nod. He trusted Konrad. He had to. If there was any way to turn this rage into something useful, it was now.

Konrad assumed a defensive stance. 'Remember, it's not about punching harder. It's about knowing yourself. Knowing when to strike – and when not to.'

Duncan lunged.

His fists flew, wild and fast, every blow driven by frustration and instinct. But Konrad moved like water, slipping past each strike with practiced ease. He didn't counter—just dodged, redirected. Precise. Calm.

Every miss made Duncan angrier. Every slip, every stumble, just another reminder of how powerless he still felt.

Why can't I hit him? Why can't I land a single damn blow?

And beneath it all, a bitter truth whispered—

Anger wasn't enough.

As the minutes passed, fatigue began to creep into Duncan's muscles, his swings becoming less controlled, more erratic. He then lunged forwards, his fist aimed at Konrad, fuelled by frustration. But Konrad, displaying nimble agility, evaded the blow with a sidestep. Duncan's punch sailed through empty air, leaving him off balance and crashing to the ground. Duncan growled at Konrad with frustration.

Seizing the opportunity, Konrad descended to Duncan's level, their eyes locked in an intense gaze. He spoke with a firm tone. 'You're like a fierce wolf – wild and relentless. But if you don't master your rage, it'll turn feral and devour you from within. Harness it, or be ruled by it.'

Duncan halted for a moment, his panting breaths filling the silence. His uncle's words resonated within him.

Konrad continued. 'Remember, Duncan, don't let your anger dictate your movements. Focus. Breathe. Channel your emotions into purposeful strikes.'

Duncan resumed his attack, but this time his fists moved with intention, each blow infused with controlled anger rather than blind rage. Slowly, he started to find openings in Konrad's defences, landing calculated strikes that echoed with a satisfying thud. With each connection, Duncan's anger began to transform into something else: a determination to strike rather than merely lash out.

Konrad nodded approvingly as he parried another of Duncan's blows. 'That's it, kid! You're finding your rhythm.'

After some time, Duncan lay sprawled on the mat, his breathing heavy and his body aching. As his breath steadied, a sense of accomplishment washed over him, his gaze fixed on Konrad.

'I ... I think I'm starting to understand, Uncle Konrad. It's not just about hitting but knowing why I'm hitting, where I'm directing my anger.'

Konrad nodded, crouching beside him. 'Good. You're not here to flail – you're here to fight. And that means knowing why you throw every punch.'

A few days later, Duncan walked towards his mother's house, clutching a box of chocolates and a stuffed lion. The toy's stitched eyes stared up at him like it had something to say – a quiet judgement, perhaps, about how long it had taken him to come back.

He hated this. Apologies. Emotions. All of it. But the guilt wouldn't leave him alone. He'd snapped – at Elisa, at his mum – and he knew it. Still, part of him wasn't ready to let go of the anger. They'd crossed a line. Even if they meant well, they'd dug into wounds that weren't theirs to touch. That wasn't kindness. That was intrusion.

He stopped at the doorstep. His fingers tightened slightly around the stuffed lion. The thing suddenly felt heavier than it should have, like it knew it was part peace offering, part emotional bribe.

'Here we go,' he muttered under his breath, then knocked.

The door creaked open.

'Oh ... it's you, Duncan,' Sara said softly.

Her voice wasn't angry. Just tired. There was sadness in her eyes – real sadness – and something else too. Guilt, maybe.

'Yeah, it's me,' he said, rubbing the back of his neck. The words came slowly, like hauling stones from his chest. 'Listen ... about the other day. I'm sorry. I went too far. The way I spoke to you – it wasn't fair. It was disrespectful.'

Sara folded her arms. She didn't say anything straight away. Just stood there, unreadable. It made him nervous, but he pressed on.

'That said ...' he shifted awkwardly, the lion tucked under one arm, 'I need you to understand that my anger wasn't without reason. You shared something that wasn't yours to share.'

Her eyes dropped to the floor, and he could see her shoulders rise and fall with a quiet breath. She looked smaller than usual. Softer.

'I know,' she said, barely audible.

'I need to hear it from you,' Duncan said. He didn't want to be harsh – but he had to say it. 'An apology. Properly.'

Sara finally met his gaze, and he noticed the gloss in her eyes.

'I'm sorry, Duncan. I should've respected your privacy. I shouldn't have said anything.' She hesitated, her throat tightening. 'I just ... I saw how much pain Elisa was in. And maybe – maybe I wanted to help her. Or maybe I was trying to help myself too.'

He frowned, caught off guard by that.

'What do you mean?'

She let out a small, trembling laugh – one of those half-sob, half-chuckle sounds that always unsettled him. 'Sometimes I tell people about your father ... to make it easier. I'll joke about it, or talk like I've made peace with it. Like it's just another old scar.'

She paused, then smiled weakly. It wasn't convincing.

'But no matter how many times I talk about it, or try to laugh it off – it still hurts. Every bloody time.'

Duncan's heart squeezed, the anger bleeding out of him like air from a punctured tyre. He hated seeing her like this. Vulnerable. Honest.

'I didn't mean to hurt you,' she whispered. 'Or betray you. I just ... I wanted it to mean something. If I said it out loud to someone like Elisa, maybe it wouldn't feel so empty. Maybe the pain would count for something.'

Duncan stared down at the lion again. Its little sewn smile suddenly felt cruel.

He sighed.

'Do you think I'm a terrible mother?' she asked, her voice small.

He looked at her. Really looked at her.

'Sometimes,' he said.

The word landed heavy in the air.

Sara flinched. Her lips trembled, and she blinked a little too fast.

But then Duncan's tone softened. The edge dulled.

'But ... I appreciate you apologising,' he added. He stepped forward, extending his arms. 'Come here.'

She didn't even hesitate. She wrapped her arms around him like she was afraid he'd vanish. He held her tight, letting himself breathe in her warmth – the scent of old perfume and tea and stubborn love.

Tears wet his shoulder. Hers, not his. But maybe if she cried enough for the both of them, that was okay.

'I love you, you grumpy sod,' she whispered, voice thick with emotion.

'Love you too, Mum,' he murmured.

And for a moment, everything else – his guilt, her guilt, Elisa, the war, the pain – faded into something that almost felt like peace.

After their hug, Duncan inquired, 'Where's Elisa?'

'She's studying.'

'Can I speak to her?'

'It depends. If she's still hurt, that is.'

Duncan felt a pang of anticipation at Sara's response. He wasn't sure what to expect from their conversation and braced himself for the unknown, knowing that the outcome was beyond his control.

Sara sighed and then headed towards the staircase. 'I'll call her. Elisa, come down here!'

'Coming!' Elisa's voice echoed as she hurried down. As she reached the living room, her eyes widened in surprise at Duncan's unexpected presence. 'Mr Saul ...?'

Duncan met her gaze nervously and offered a hesitant greeting. 'Yeah … hi, Elisa …'

His gaze drifted to her, and something in his chest snagged.

She looked different today. The cherry-coloured jumper hugged her frame in a way that made the room feel a little warmer. Her glasses – new, maybe – caught the light, giving her a thoughtful, bookish look, like she'd stepped out of a different world entirely. And her hair, pulled back in a simple ponytail, exposed the soft lines of her face. She looked … cute.

Elisa listened as Duncan began his atonement. 'I wanted to apologise—'

'I wanted to apologise as well. You had every right to be upset with me. I'm not part of this family. I never have been. Forgive me for being so invasive. I only wanted to—'

Duncan immediately gave the chocolate and stuffed animal to Elisa. 'Alright … here! Take it, but you owe me.'

'But I—'

'You were more than sorry. Maybe *too* sorry …'

'Why are you giving this to me? You haven't done anything wrong.'

She was wrong about that. Duncan did end up ruining their date, and his interactions with Sara and Elisa were marked by rudeness, though not completely unjustified.

He turned slightly, his face flushing. 'It's because I want us to spend time together and make up for the date I ruined the other evening.'

The blush of his cheeks as he presented the gifts revealed another side of Duncan. He, the hardened mercenary, wasn't accustomed to such gestures, and it made him slightly uncomfortable.

Elisa accepted the gift, her cheeks also tinged with red. 'Aww … How sweet … You really went out of your way to get these for me, even though I don't deserve them.' She examined the stuffed animal, bringing it closer to her face as she beamed a bright smile. 'Although I may have outgrown the age for playing with stuffed animals, I shall keep this as a souvenir.'

Duncan looked away, his cheeks reddening further. 'I also wanna treat you to dinner,' he mumbled.

'I'm sorry?'

Duncan raised his voice. 'I wanna treat you to dinner.'

Duncan clenched his jaw, swallowing the sting of his own pride. It tasted bitter – like rust and regret. He knew this wasn't about being right anymore. His ego, his bloody stubbornness – none of it mattered now. Not if he wanted to fix things.

It felt like chewing glass, putting himself out there like this. Vulnerability wasn't something he was built for. But he forced himself to do it anyway, hoping – no, needing – Elisa to see it for what it was. Not weakness. Not performance. Just him, stripped back, trying to make it right. He didn't have the words for it, not properly. But he hoped the gesture spoke loud enough.

'Hmm, very well then ... However, you must fulfil a request of mine ...'

Duncan's brow furrowed slightly as he anticipated Elisa's favour. 'Alright, what's the deal?'

'I will decide the venue for our meal ...'

Duncan's face lit up with relief as he agreed. 'Just don't go over fifty Livres and we'll consider it even.' His gaze shifted as he scrutinised Elisa's appearance. 'Oh, by the way – didn't know you wore glasses.'

Elisa's brow furrowed, and she pursed her lips slightly. 'Is there a particular issue with that?'

Duncan quickly shook his head, a reassuring grin forming on his face. 'No, not at all. I mean, you actually look ... pretty cute with them on. You've got this teacher vibe.'

Elisa's hand instinctively touched her cheek, and another blush graced her face, accompanied by a contented grin. 'Oh, my, you truly think so?'

Duncan nodded. 'Yeah.'

Sara swooped in with a grin, hooking an arm around both their waists and tugging them close. 'Aww ... You two lovebirds finally made up.'

'Huh? Mrs Saul!' Elisa protested, embarrassed.

Duncan was equally mortified. 'What!? Mother, we're just friends! And please, *don't* do that – it's weird.'

After their banter, Elisa quickly excused herself, saying, 'Well, I shall go and get ready,' before rushing upstairs.

Sara flicked Duncan on the forehead, making him wince.

'Ow ... What the hell was that for?' he said, rubbing his forehead.

Sara rested her hands on her hips. 'Getting a girl gifts. That's the first time I've seen you do that.'

'Don't get used to it.'

Duncan's thoughts drifted inward. He couldn't deny the truth in his mother's words, and it made him pause. He wasn't the type to give gifts – not in that tender, thoughtful sort of way. It felt foreign, almost too sentimental for someone like him. A part of him knew it was out of character, a break from his usual blunt, no-nonsense self.

Sara offered reassurance, her tone gentle. 'Well, at least we all recognised our mistakes.' She then rushed to the sofa, grabbing the TV remote to switch it on. 'Let's see what's happening in the news!'

Duncan frowned as he watched his mother collapse on the sofa.

The television flickered to life, revealing a female presenter with chin-length black hair, glasses, and a sharp black blazer over a dark pink blouse.

'As news of Lance Sainglend's arrest broke, violence erupted in various parts of Flora,' she announced in a calm but urgent tone. *'Protesters are demanding Lance's freedom, and riot police have been deployed to maintain order.'*

The TV cut to a chaotic street in Flora, where protesters clashed violently with the police. The officers, clad in Kevlar armour, bulletproof helmets, and visor guards, stood firm behind their shields. They carried batons, ready to subdue with non-lethal force. The protesters, undeterred, charged forward, using their bodies to slam against the shields.

One protester hurled a Molotov cocktail at the police, shouting, *'Take this, bastards!'*

The police responded quickly, raising their shields for protection, and unleashed a cloud of tear gas. The thick smoke filled the air, forcing the protesters to cry and cough as they scrambled to shield their eyes from the burning sting.

The screen shifted back to the female presenter, who spoke again, her voice steady amidst the chaos. *'As you can see, the military is escorting Lance through a hostile crowd.'*

Lance appeared, flanked by soldiers, walking through barricades with bruises and cuts visible on his face. The crowd jeered, their anger palpable.

'Murderer! Murderer!'

'Bring the Kingslayer to justice! He killed our king!'

'He deserves to die!'

'He's ruined our country!'

A can of fizzy drink flew from the crowd, striking Lance on the head. He grunted in pain but continued walking, unfazed, as more litter was thrown in his direction.

Duncan, sitting nearby, glanced at the screen with little more than a flicker of indifference. Why should he care? It was Lance's mess to clean up. The only reason he'd even got involved was to help Elisa deliver her letter to him.

The TV returned to the female presenter. *'Lance will be tried at the Royal High Court in Riverdam, City of Rayguard, on the twenty-second of July. The presiding judge will be Lord Reginald.'*

Sara responded to the news with a casual shrug. 'Well, it was bound to happen sooner or later. The battle couldn't go on forever. Who knows? Maybe this is a good thing.'

Elisa, however, firmly disagreed. 'It is *not* a good thing.'

Both Duncan and Sara turned their attention to Elisa. They noticed the seriousness in her expression.

'Lance mustn't fail,' Elisa continued. 'He needs to succeed, otherwise, Archer's death would have been in vain.'

A heavy silence settled between Duncan and Sara.

'I support Lance. He is honourable, and he genuinely cares for the people. In fact, I would have been grateful if he had won the war,' Elisa said.

As he listened to Elisa's passionate words, Duncan found himself reflecting on his own feelings about the war and Lance's mission. He had always been somewhat detached from the larger conflict. But Elisa's conviction was making him rethink his stance. It was clear that she wholeheartedly believed in Lance's cause.

Sara paused for a moment, then walked over to Elisa and placed her hands on her shoulders. 'You know what? I take back what I said earlier. I can see you're taking this very seriously,' she said with a reassuring smile and a wink. 'Don't worry, kiddo. I'm pretty sure Lance has this all planned out. I mean, do you really think he'd just stroll into enemy territory without knowing what he's doing? Come on, he commanded the entire Night Hawks, for Pete's sake.'

Duncan chimed in. 'Yeah, Mum's right. Lance isn't a moron. He knows what he's doing. Like Mum said, he's leading an entire fucking army. You don't get to that position by being careless. The most important quality a leader should have is the ability to make smart plans for the whole team.'

Sara folded her arms and tutted. 'What did I say about swearing?'

'Oh! So, it's okay when *you* say it.' Duncan shook his head and returned to the subject. 'Anyway, Elisa, don't get your knickers in a twist. Lance should have this all figured out.'

Elisa nodded, striving to alleviate her concerns. 'Very well, Mr Saul. I shall place my trust in your words.'

Sara then reminded her, 'Well, dear, you should start heading out now.'

'Yes, you are absolutely right.' Elisa followed closely behind Duncan.

Duncan waved towards his mother, saying, 'Goodbye, Mum.'

'Goodbye, Mrs Saul,' Elisa said, waving to Sara.

Sara waved back and called out, 'Have a great time, kiddos. Just don't stay out too late.'

Chapter XXV

A NIGHT OUT

Duncan and Elisa sat at a table in the Tropical Island restaurant, waiting for a waitress to take their order. Soon, a young waitress with a brown ponytail approached them and greeted them politely.

'Hello, sir and ma'am, what would you like today?'

Resting his cheek on his knuckles, Duncan gave his order. 'Could you give me an apple pie with potato slices?'

Elisa pointed at the menu and made her order. 'I would like to have the spicy vegetable egg fried rice, a veggie spaghetti, tomato and cheese pizza, sweet potato cakes with poached eggs, roasted aubergine and tomato curry, bread rolls, along with apple crumble and a couple of orange sodas.'

Duncan and the waitress both displayed shocked expressions in response to Elisa's extensive order.

The waitress nervously asked, 'Uhhh ... So that's it, then?'

'Yes.'

The waitress nodded and then went to fulfil the order.

What the hell? Is this girl, okay? Duncan couldn't help but be taken aback by the sheer amount of food Elisa had ordered. How much were they going to spend? He needed to check his bank account after this.

Duncan leant closer to Elisa and whispered, 'How much did you order?'

'I tried ordering as much as I could,' Elisa responded.

'Yeah, but how are you gonna finish all of this?'

Elisa shrugged her shoulders. 'We just have to wait and see.'

Duncan leant back in his chair, sighing, arms crossed, and waited patiently for the meals to be delivered. After a while, a group of waiters and waitresses arrived at their table and placed their meals one by one.

The female waitress from earlier smiled and said kindly, 'Here you go ... enjoy.'

On the table, there were many dishes. Duncan couldn't help but be astounded by the sheer quantity of food that had been brought to their table. He had opted for a simpler meal, not expecting Elisa to order such an extravagant feast. As he surveyed the multitude of dishes, he couldn't fathom how one person could possibly eat all of it.

Duncan's eyes widened. 'How the ...? How the hell are you gonna eat of all this!?'

Elisa deftly moved her fork, quickly delivering a big helping of spaghetti into her mouth. She swallowed it down eagerly, making a noticeable slurping sound. Duncan couldn't help but grimace as she ate.

With her cheeks now slightly bloated from the mouthful of spaghetti, Elisa attempted to speak, though her words came out muffled. 'Uhh ... I dewna.'

Duncan sat with folded arms, demanding, 'Finish chewing your food, Elisa.'

Elisa delicately finished her spaghetti, then looked at Duncan with a chuckle. Duncan observed Elisa's eating style and couldn't help but grimace at the lack of refinement he perceived.

'Uh ... You seem to have quite the appetite ...'

Elisa, with a slight giggle, grabbed a napkin and wiped her mouth. 'Oh, my apologies, I should have been more mindful of my manners. When I encounter delectable dishes, I tend to get carried away.'

'Yeah, no kidding ...' Duncan glanced aside and muttered under his breath. 'Why did you order so much?' Duncan inquired.

Elisa shrugged, explaining, 'I managed to stay well within the fifty Livres limit, as you requested. I viewed this as an opportunity to savour several meals while adhering to the budget.'

Duncan rubbed the back of his head and responded. 'I suppose ... but you still haven't answered my earlier question. How do you plan to finish all of this?'

Elisa shrugged. 'I haven't entirely decided ... Perhaps I'll consume as much as I can and see how far I get.'

'Okay then ...'

Elisa concluded her first dish and then transitioned to her second: a portion of fried rice. She took hold of a spoon and deftly consumed bites of rice, murmuring appreciatively to herself.

Duncan wore a slightly concerned expression, mingled with a nervous grin. 'Wow, this girl has quite the appetite ...'

'No need to worry, Mr Saul. I'm not the sole consumer here. We are sharing this meal, after all. Are not you trying some of what I'm enjoying? We shall make swift work of this together.' Elisa gestured encouragingly. 'Now, don't just sit there, have some.'

'If you say so.' Duncan grabbed a fork and took a bite of his apple pie. He couldn't help but notice how Elisa's appetite was both unusual and endearing. This girl was many things.

Elisa delicately set down her fork, allowing a gentle wave of nostalgia to wash over her.

'Ah, that does bring back a memory ... I must confess, I used to be quite the spoilt little girl,' she admitted. 'Whenever my parents and I visited a restaurant, I would often find myself overwhelmed by the endless options on the menu. My solution was to order an array of dishes. In my youthful mind, I believed that, given our family's wealth, why shouldn't I indulge in everything that caught my fancy? Oh, how my dear mother and sister would gently chastise me for my lavish appetite.'

She laughed. 'I sometimes wonder if my bottomless hunger cost them a small fortune.'

Duncan let out a quiet chuckle, though part of him was still trying to recover from how good she looked tonight. That ponytail, those glasses – it did something strange to him. She had this way of being impossibly elegant and endearingly awkward all at once.

'You sound like you were a real financial handful,' he said dryly.

Elisa's smile softened. 'If my family hadn't tragically passed away,' she mused quietly, 'my life would have taken a vastly different path. I would probably still be that spoilt, privileged girl. It is funny how fragile life is – how it holds within it countless mysteries and surprises.'

She glanced at him, her voice turning thoughtful. 'If the tragedy had never occurred, do you think our paths still would have crossed?'

That question hit deeper than she probably realised.

Duncan hesitated, blinking slowly as her words settled in. He tried to picture a world where Elisa was still a noble's daughter, surrounded by wealth and comfort, untouched by grief. A world where he was still a mercenary, with no reason to meet someone like her.

'Who can say for certain?' he said at last, his voice quieter. 'Maybe we would've crossed paths somehow, but things between us would've been ... different.'

He paused. 'You're a very lucky girl.'

She tilted her head, pausing mid-chew. 'What do you mean?'

Duncan cleared his throat and leant back, glancing briefly at the ceiling before replying.

'You're actually moving forward with your life,' he said. 'You were on your own back then, with no one by your side ... then you stumbled across me. My mum and I gave you the chance to study at university. What was it again – what are you studying?'

'Politics and Law,' Elisa replied.

'Right,' Duncan nodded. 'You've got a dream, a goal, and you're a step closer to reaching it.'

He stared up at the light above them, its glow blurring slightly as his thoughts turned inwards.

'But me ... I've been stuck for far too long.'

The words surprised even him. He wasn't usually this open.

But here, with her – he didn't feel like a weapon, or a mission. He just felt ... human.

'Most of my life, I've been grappling with the same problems,' he murmured. 'Haunted by the same nightmares. Burdened by the same bloody issues. It's like I'm trapped in an endless cycle, unable to move an inch. Everything I do just circles back to the same damn place.'

He wasn't sure why he'd said all that out loud.

Maybe because it felt good to be heard.

Elisa leant forwards, resting her elbow gently on the table. 'I see ... Mr Saul, may I ask you something?'

His gaze flicked down to meet hers. 'Go ahead.'

She took another bite of her sweet potato cakes. 'What do you plan on doing after you achieve your goal?' she asked softly. 'What else do you desire in life?'

He exhaled through his nose, leaning his forearms on the table. 'I dunno,' he said, 'for the longest time, I believed my only purpose was to find the heretic who attacked my dad. It's consumed my thoughts since I was a kid – to the point where I've forgotten what I even want from life.'

There was a pause.

A flicker of something – something old and innocent – stirred in him.

'However,' Duncan continued, a faint smile curling at his lips, 'I do remember that when I was young, I had dreams of being a hero. Like the superheroes in the comics I used to read. I wanted to be someone people could look up to. I imagined myself in some hall of fame, making my family proud.'

He chuckled under his breath and took a sip of his soft drink, the carbonation catching slightly in his throat. 'Me being a hero ... that sounds daft, doesn't it?'

Elisa chuckled lightly. 'No, I think it's very ... What do young people often say – *cool*?'

That smile. Dammit.

It disarmed him.

His cheeks flushed before he could stop it, heat prickling up his neck. He turned his head slightly, pretending to inspect something on the wall beside them, but his heart thudded faster than he liked. Why did her approval mean so much?

He rubbed the back of his neck, the words she'd said looping in his mind.

Cool. She thought it was cool.

He wasn't used to compliments that weren't laced with sarcasm or ulterior motives.

Especially not from someone who saw the man behind the gun.

She really was something else. 'If your father had never been attacked by the heretic, how would your life be right now?'

'I don't know. It's possible I wouldn't have become a mercenary. Maybe my life would have been very different.'

Elisa inquired further. 'Do you think that solving your father's case will bring you happiness?'

'Of course, it will. All of my hard work wouldn't have been in vain. It's the goal I've lived my entire life for, and I won't let it go to waste. If I back down now, I'll be betraying my father and abandoning his wishes.'

'What do you know so far about the attack on your father?'

'I know that it happened in November,' Duncan replied. 'The heretic used something called energy leeches to attack my father. These leeches are used to channel energy, either to power up a device or for powerful magic that requires a large amount of magical energy.' Duncan sighed. 'If my father hadn't run away, this case might have been easier to solve. There were several kidnappings in Flora during that time, but they gradually stopped. So, either the heretic stopped or he fled to another location. I'm dealing with someone dangerous, and even Jénmar, with his hawk-like tracking skills, couldn't find him.' Duncan leant back in his chair, folded his arms and continued, 'However, you still have time, Kid. You have options. I've already made my choice to become a mercenary. Think about it – imagine Miss Evergreen running for prime minister of Flora. You'd have the political power to change the current state of Flora.'

Elisa nodded as she understood his words.

'Well, I've rambled enough for now. Let's focus on eating our meals. Elisa, you probably won't be interested, but do you know about the arcade? Would you like to go there after this?'

Elisa pondered for a moment. 'The arcade ... Well, I did play games with Archer occasionally. I found them enjoyable because of the dopamine rush when I won. Would you be kind enough to accompany me?'

'Sure,' Duncan said, smiling warmly.

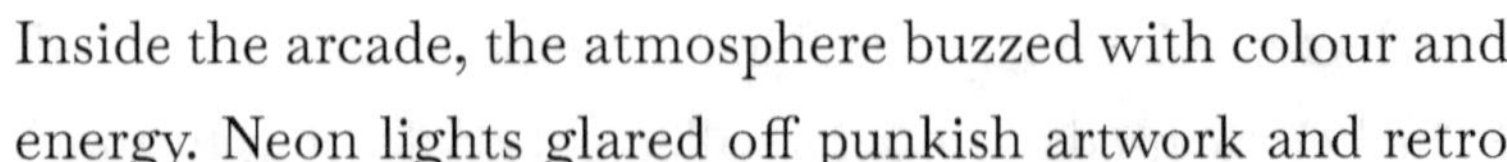

Inside the arcade, the atmosphere buzzed with colour and energy. Neon lights glared off punkish artwork and retro posters plastered across the walls, while bass-heavy hip-hop thumped lazily from scattered speakers. It was late, so the place wasn't packed – just a few groups chatting over drinks by the window, slouched on barstools.

Duncan and Elisa stood at the air hockey table, paddles in hand. The game was quick and sharp, each move met with swift counters. She was keeping up with him – and then some.

'Bloody hell,' Duncan muttered with a grin. 'You've got fast hands, girl. Didn't see that coming.'

Elisa narrowed her eyes in mock challenge. 'And you, Mr Saul, are surprisingly agile for someone so ... rugged.'

He barked a laugh – right before sinking a shot past her guard. The puck clacked in, and he straightened with a curious look.

'So, real question – how old are you? I know you're somewhere in your teens, but ... what, eighteen? Nineteen?'

Before she even replied, she smacked the puck straight into his goal with unnerving precision.

'Oi—' Duncan blinked. 'Alright, alright! Damn good shot, that.'

Elisa giggled, clearly pleased with herself. 'I'm nineteen.'

Nineteen. That gave him pause. Four years between them. Not much in the grand scheme of things, but still – she felt younger than that sometimes. And older, in strange ways.

'Huh. Makes me four years your senior,' he said, placing the puck back in the centre as they reset.

She scored again.

'Ah, crap.' Duncan shook his head, smirking. 'You're on fire. I've got to stop messing about.'

Determined now, he slammed the puck across the table – clean shot, straight in.

Elisa gasped. 'Goodness! That had real force behind it.'

She stepped back, thoughtful, then pointed to the corner. 'Shall we try snooker next?'

'You know how to play?' Duncan raised an eyebrow.

Elisa's smile widened, ever so proud. 'Naturally.'

There was a mischievous glint in her eyes as she added, 'Care for a match? If I win, I would quite like a brief test drive of your car.'

Duncan snorted. 'Yeah? You're on.'

They made their way over to the snooker table. Chalk dust in the air, clack of balls being racked – and the unspoken tension of competition building between them.

They walked along the nearly deserted streets illuminated by streetlights, with many of the shops closed. Duncan put his hands in his jacket pockets and glanced at the darkening sky, remarking, 'It's getting late.'

Elisa walked beside him, her arms wrapped around herself, more out of habit than cold. The quiet of the streets was oddly peaceful, the occasional hum of a passing car filling the silence between them.

'You didn't have to walk me home,' Elisa said after a moment, sneaking a glance at him.

Duncan shrugged. 'Didn't feel right letting you go alone.'

She gave him a small, appreciative smile. 'Well ... thank you.' Elisa blushed and pulled a digital camera from her coat pocket. Shyly, she asked, 'Mr Saul, would you take a picture with me?'

Duncan casually shrugged. 'Sure, why not?'

They positioned themselves next to each other, and Elisa, still blushing, turned the camera towards them both, holding it above their heads. She counted down. 'Three ... two ... one ...'

The camera flashed, capturing the moment with a satisfying snap. Elisa's smile remained as she reviewed the photo and commenting. 'It looks splendid.'

Duncan smiled, too, folding his arms. While browsing the camera's collection of photos, he noticed a picture of a younger Elisa and a man on a sunny bridge. He pointed at it and inquired, 'Wait ... Who's that?'

Elisa enlarged the photo and answered. 'Oh, that's Archer.'

Duncan scrutinised Archer's appearance, saying, 'So that's what he looked like.'

Elisa nodded. 'Yep ... that was taken on Kinsmurd bridge.' She then displayed another image of her and Archer happily riding a Ferris wheel in Marian Park. She moved on to a recorded video, saying, 'And this is us by the seaside at Lake Longwalk.'

Playing the video, they watched a sunny day recorded on 19 June. Elisa was holding onto her straw hat against the strong winds as Archer filmed the scene.

Her image exclaimed with joy, '*The waves look beautiful, don't they!?*'

Archer's voice warned her, saying, '*You better not lose your hat, Elisa!*'

Elisa held her straw hat more tightly and continued. '*It's so windy here! But that's not all bad – it just makes the waves nicer to look at. I mean, look at how big that wave is!*'

The video ended, and Duncan smiled warmly, suggesting, 'You should keep that camera safe if you want to remember Archer. Take it to the nearest print shop, frame one of the photos, and display it in your room.'

Elisa glanced at the camera in her hands, a soft smile forming on her lips. 'Would that be all right in your old room?' she asked hesitantly.

Duncan shrugged. 'I don't mind where. It's your closest friend, after all.'

They continued walking, the sound of their footsteps mingling with the cool night air. As they neared Sara's house, Elisa grew quiet, the weight of the moment sinking in. When they reached her doorstep, she hesitated before turning to face him.

'Mr Saul, wait,' she called softly, prompting Duncan to stop and turn back towards her.

She looked up at him, her face slightly flushed, her voice laced with genuine gratitude. 'I just wanted to thank you for everything today. I know it wasn't easy.'

Duncan shook his head, his gaze softening. 'No need for thanks. I wanted to make up for being a bit of a jerk recently.'

Elisa shook her head in turn. 'You're wrong. You weren't a jerk. You had every right to be upset with me. I was so desperate to know your secrets because I wanted to connect with you. It's been really tough and lonely without Archer.'

'Hmm ... You're quite right. I was pretty pissed off at you for prying and not respecting my boundaries, but I get it – you just wanted some connection. However, you've been going about it the wrong way. Just give people time to open up, and they will.'

Duncan's understanding response struck a chord with her. She saw that he had a point: her approach had been misguided. The longing for connection didn't excuse her invasive behaviour. She understood that people needed their space and forcing them to open up was counterproductive.

'I understand, Mr Saul. Just know that I empathise with your pain. When my sister turned into one of those monsters, I could not save her. She was the only family I had left during that time ... As much as I want to undo the things that happened in that place, I have to live with it. The least I can do is make a better place for Flora.'

'Let me ask you something ... Are you ready to own up to the mistakes you've made? To stand up for those who can't defend themselves when the strong push them around? What are you gonna do if one of those mistakes ends up costing someone their life? It's not about how many punches you can throw, Elisa. It's about how many you can take and keep going.'

That was a good question. It made her reflect on the many hardships Duncan had endured. Perhaps becoming a politician wasn't as straightforward as she'd initially believed. Dreaming big was one thing, but taking meaningful action was an entirely different challenge.

Elisa shook her head. 'I do not know ...'

Duncan looked at the sky and said, 'When I was a kid, I wanted to be a hero. As I grew up, I now know the burden is so much to bear. It's difficult, especially with the amount of blood I have on my hands. But as long as I am helping the world, it's totally worth it.'

'Mr Saul, my life has been marked by hardships many would scarcely comprehend. Yet, I am fully aware that greater responsibilities await me, and I shall not shirk from them.'

She stepped forward, her voice steady despite the weight behind it.

'Know this – I will strive with every ounce of my being. I promise you, I shall see my dream fulfilled.'

Duncan smiled warmly and remarked, 'Those were the very words I used to say. Maybe, we aren't all that different after all. One more thing ...' he added, 'spending time with you makes me feel normal, at least for a while. It's a welcome break from my usual routine of work and violence. I really enjoy our time together, just being like a regular person.'

Normal?

Elisa couldn't help but smile at Duncan's words. As she looked at him, she felt a sense of appreciation for being able to offer him this respite from his demanding life as a mercenary. She realised that their time together – as ordinary as it might seem – held a special place in Duncan's heart and that made her cherish their friendship even more.

Duncan then offered a casual wave. 'See ya around, Kid.'

Left alone, Elisa smiled, albeit a small one, as she watched him walk away.

Chapter XXVI

A FRIENDLY VISIT

The sun was shining and fluffy clouds decorated the sky as Duncan and Konrad played a game of catch with a baseball on the lush green fields of the park.

'How many people do you want to save?' Konrad asked. He threw the ball towards Duncan who skilfully caught it with his baseball glove.

'I want to save as many as I can,' Duncan replied.

'You do realise you can't save everyone.'

'Yeah, I know. Heroes can't save everyone. I've seen people say that all the time in comics and TV shows.'

Konrad sighed. 'I'm not gonna sugarcoat things, kid, but you need to know the truth. When you want to deal with injustice, you sometimes need to do things that you normally wouldn't. People who get in your way won't hold back, and neither should you. You must be prepared for the challenges that await you. Got it?'

Duncan nodded firmly and threw the ball back at him. 'Yeah, of course, I do.'

Konrad caught the ball. 'Good,' he said, satisfied with Duncan's response. He threw the ball back at Duncan who caught it and contemplated it for a moment.

Duncan was no stranger to the harsh truths of the world, even in his youth. He knew that not every situation had a happy ending and not every problem could be solved. But that didn't deter him. 'I know this ain't gonna be easy ...'

'Of course not,' Konrad said, strongly agreeing. 'Things are never easy, but that's what makes life worth it. If things were simple, it would be boring. It would make us humans weak and give us nothing much to fight for.'

Duncan tossed the ball back. 'Uncle Konrad, I wanted to ask you something.'

'Go ahead.'

Duncan hesitated, then asked the question that had been tugging at him for days.

'What were you like before ... and I mean before you met Dad?'

Konrad's gaze drifted to the ball resting by his feet. His face shifted – tightening, like the question had scraped something raw.

'Before was a nightmare,' he said, voice quieter now. 'I didn't have a family like you. I was alone. No one to lean on. Had to fight for everything.'

Duncan watched him closely. Konrad rarely talked about himself – at least not like this. Something about it made Duncan uneasy ... and curious.

Then Konrad's expression softened, the edge fading as he looked back at Duncan.

'But then I met your dad. And things changed. Back then I was just drifting. Existing. Life felt ... hollow. But he made it better. For the first time, I had someone real. It was ... nice.'

Duncan felt something stir in his chest – a strange warmth he hadn't expected. Hearing that his father had made such a difference, even to someone like Konrad ... it made the ache in his chest lighten, just a little.

His father wasn't just *his* hero.

He mattered to other people too.

Konrad went on, voice softer. 'And when you came along ... that's when I really felt it. What family could be. I didn't just find a friend in your father – I found a reason to live. You and him ... you gave me purpose.'

Duncan blinked, caught off guard by the weight of those words. He didn't know what to say. He just stared at Konrad, and for a moment, that old heaviness – the grief, the guilt – loosened its grip.

Maybe his father hadn't vanished without leaving something behind. Maybe Duncan wasn't as alone as he thought.

Felt like he had a child?

The mention of this was unexpected: his uncle had never opened up to him like this before. It deepened Duncan's understanding of the relationship he shared with Konrad. While they had always been close, this conversation revealed a new layer to their friendship.

'Oh, thank you, Uncle Konrad. I'm happy that you're part of the family now, too,' Duncan said with surprise.

'And maybe I took too long to say it.' Konrad tossed the ball at Duncan. 'Listen, you can do it, kid. You can be a hero for your father and Flora. I believe in you.'

'You really think so?'

'Of course.' Konrad nodded. 'Just remember ... wherever you are, I'll be rooting for you.'

Sporting a black hoodie and a pair of blue jeans, Duncan made his way to the hospital to visit Jénmar. When he arrived at Jénmar's room, he found the doctor there, attending to him.

'Mr Jénmar, you have a visitor,' said the doctor, a dark-skinned man.

Duncan extended his hand. 'Hello, my name is Duncan.'

The doctor reciprocated the handshake. 'I'm Doctor Salaza.'

Duncan inquired about Jénmar's condition, asking, 'Doctor, how is he?'

Dr Salaza began to explain. 'I conducted a thorough examination of the patient. The bullet caused a fracture in his clavicle, making it challenging for him to move his arm. Additionally, it punctured his left subclavian artery which we managed to repair through surgery, preventing a life-threatening haemorrhage. Fortunately, there's been some improvement in the bone since his last check-up.'

Duncan sought more assurance, asking, 'So, will he recover fully?'

The doctor nodded. 'Absolutely. Bones have the remarkable ability to heal themselves. It should take a minimum of two months for a full recovery and for his arm to regain its full functionality.'

In discomfort, Jénmar let out a groan, voicing his frustration. 'Ugh ...'

Dr Salaza glanced at Jénmar and continued. 'My advice for now is to rest and allow your arm to heal. You wouldn't want to risk any dislocation.'

'Ah, dammit! Seriously? I can barely hold a lousy pistol with my left arm. It's even a struggle to, you know, take care of basic stuff! My partner and I need to be out there on operations together – two heads are always better than one, you know.'

'Don't worry, Jénmar. The doctor said it's not permanent. You'll be back in action before you know it.'

The doctor’s assurance of his eventual recovery did bring some comfort, yet Duncan couldn’t shake his concerns. How long would he have to do things solo? What if he was on a dangerous mission that required more than one person? Who else could he rely on?

The doctor empathised with Jénmar, stating, ‘I understand your frustration, but given the circumstances, it’s the best course of action right now. You can take your leave and rest at home now.‘

Jénmar put on his brown jacket. ‘Yeah, whatever …’ he responded, resignedly.

Dr Salaza bid them farewell, saying, ‘It was nice meeting with you, Mr Jénmar.’

Jénmar nodded. ‘You too, doc.’

Exiting the hospital together, Jénmar turned to Duncan, remarking, ‘Well, I’ll be at home if you need me.’

‘Yeah, I hope you recover soon, Jénmar. Just give me a call and I’ll be there.’

Jénmar smiled and said, ‘See ya later, mate.’

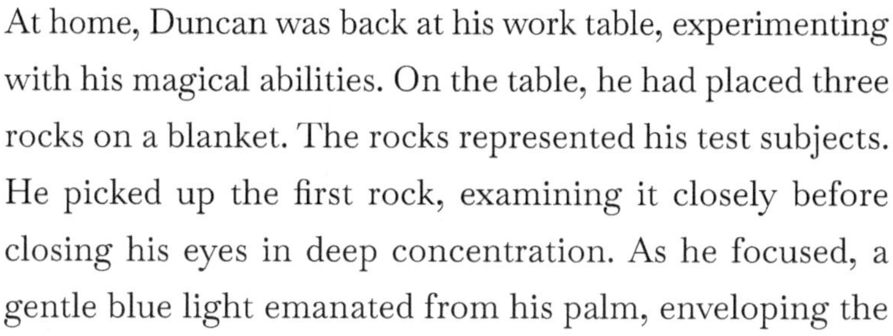

At home, Duncan was back at his work table, experimenting with his magical abilities. On the table, he had placed three rocks on a blanket. The rocks represented his test subjects. He picked up the first rock, examining it closely before closing his eyes in deep concentration. As he focused, a gentle blue light emanated from his palm, enveloping the rock. Gradually, the rock transformed into a glass ball, a successful alteration.

Duncan held the glass ball up and marvelled, saying to himself, 'This was much easier than I thought ... Now to move on to the next one.'

After stretching his fingers, Duncan proceeded to the next experiment. This time, he aimed to change the rock into metal. This proved to be a more challenging task. With a determined look, Duncan successfully turned the rock into iron, albeit taking a bit longer than the previous transformation.

He examined the metal result and sighed with relief. 'I finally did it ...' He readied himself for the final rock, saying, 'Okay, the next one ...'

He concentrated his magic once again, attempting to transform the rock into wood, which was considerably tougher. Duncan found it difficult to maintain his focus. His face twitched and he gritted his teeth, but the rock eventually shattered into pieces. In the process, Duncan injured his hand, and he winced in pain. Clutching his hand, Duncan examined the shattered rock with a sigh of disappointment. He grabbed a notebook and pen, jotting down his observations.

'It appears that the material's strength plays a crucial role,' he said aloud as he wrote. 'The weaker the material, the easier it is to perform this magic. Glass is weaker than metal, and metal is weaker than wood.'

Standing up, he grabbed a towel to wipe the sweat from his face.

As Duncan watched an action-packed movie programme, the familiar ring of his phone disrupted the scene on the screen. He fished his phone out of his pocket and answered.

'Hello, Duncan Saul speaking ...'

'Hello, Mr Saul. This is Dan Duke from the Floran Military HQ Army Reception. Colonel Callen from the Seventh Brigade wishes to speak with you.'

'Sure, put him through,' said Duncan.

'Hello, is this the mercenary, Duncan Saul?' asked Colonel Callen, the commanding officer of the Red Lions.

'Yes, Colonel. What can I do for you?' Duncan replied.

The Colonel then briefed him. *'A few days ago, our forces engaged in a battle with the Night Hawks in the Ballylawn region. After the battle, I sent a patrol squad to search for survivors, but they haven't reported back. I fear something serious may have happened. We need someone to locate them and find out what transpired.'*

Duncan contemplated the task, saying, 'I see.'

The Colonel continued. *'We believe you're the right person for this job, Mr Saul.'*

'I understand, Colonel. Where should I meet you?' Duncan asked.

'You'll find me in the Ballylawn region. Please make haste – time is of the essence.'

Duncan jotted down the location, assuring the colonel. 'I'll be there. Let me prepare my gear and I'll arrive shortly.'

'*Very well, Mr Saul. Until then.*'

'Goodbye, Colonel.' Duncan ended the call and accessed his contacts, selecting his mother's number. He held the phone to his ear as it dialled.

'*Hello?*'

'Mum, I need to tell you something,' Duncan said.

'*What is it?*'

'I've been assigned a mission,' he explained. 'The Colonel of the Seventh Brigade wants me to investigate the patrols that have gone missing in the Ballylawn region. So, I'll be gone for quite a while.'

'*Okay, I see. Do you have anything you'd like to say to Elisa?*' Sara asked.

'Just tell her I said hi,' Duncan replied.

'*Sure thing.*'

'Okay, I'll talk to you later.'

'*See ya.*'

Duncan hung up the phone and turned his attention to the map of Flora on his desk. 'The Ballylawn region,' he muttered to himself.

With a red marker, he circled the Ballylawn region on the map, his mission location. Duncan then organised his tools, neatly arranging various firearms and explosives on his desk. Among them were an M1911A1 pistol, a Steyr AUG, an SVU and an Astra 357. In addition to these, there were smoke grenades, stun grenades and C-4 plastic explosives. Duncan also grabbed his gas mask, ready to protect himself from potential enemy gases, and donned thermal goggles to aid his vision in darkness.

Once fully geared up, Duncan dressed in his combat uniform. This included a desert camo military jacket, a tactical vest, rugged tactical gloves and sturdy khaki tactical army boots. With his preparations complete, he was ready to embark on his mission.

Chapter XXVII

UNRESTRAINED VALOUR

At seventeen, Duncan had already shed much of his boyish innocence. The softness in his face had hardened into sharper lines, and the weight of vengeance had settled on his shoulders like an iron coat. Out here, on the fringes of civilisation, the world felt quieter. Uncle Konrad's wooded property stretched for miles, a secluded place wrapped in rustling leaves and the scent of pine sap. Birdsong echoed distantly through the canopy, and the wind stirred the tall grass with a gentle hiss.

Duncan stood in a rough clearing, boots planted in the dirt. The air was cool, the kind that bit the fingertips. In his hands, he held a cold steel pistol – heavier than he'd imagined.

Its cold metal pressed into his palms as he stared at it, unsure whether to be afraid or awed. The weight wasn't just physical – it carried something else. Something permanent.

Konrad stood beside him, arms folded. 'A gun, Duncan,' Konrad began, 'is not merely a tool of violence. It's a means to protect those you hold dear. You must learn to respect its power.'

Duncan gave a small nod, eyes still locked on the pistol. His heart was thudding, fingers twitching. The thought of using it – to fight, to avenge his father – felt overwhelming. But necessary.

Konrad noticed the tremble in his hands.

'Steady now. That fire in your chest? It's not a weakness. But you've got to control it. Focused anger can be useful – reckless anger gets people killed.'

Duncan swallowed hard. *Control. Right.*

He tried to still his hands. *Dad wouldn't have flinched.*

'I understand, Uncle. I'll do whatever it takes.'

Konrad offered a faint smile, placing a firm hand on Duncan's shoulder.

'Good. Now grip it – tight, but not stiff. It should feel like an extension of you. Don't fear it.'

Duncan inhaled slowly, then raised the weapon. His palms were still damp, but his grip held. He followed Konrad's finger as it pointed to a glass jar on a table across the clearing.

'That jar is a threat. Nothing more. Lock on. Breathe. Squeeze – don't yank – the trigger. Let the bullet do the work.'

Everything else seemed to fall away. The sound of birds, the wind in the trees, the crackle of the fire behind them – it all faded.

Duncan exhaled, lined up the sights, and pulled the trigger.

BANG!

The bullet tore through the jar, shattering it instantly.

'I got it!' he gasped, blinking in disbelief, a grin tugging at his lips.

Konrad chuckled. 'Told you. Keep that up. Calm mind, sharp shot.'

Pride surged in Duncan's chest. He stepped back, then raised the gun again, lining up another target. This time, there was less hesitation. Less fear.

As he fired again – and again – the clearing filled with the rhythm of gunfire, sharp cracks echoing through the trees. Each hit fed a growing sense of control, of purpose.

But underneath the excitement, something heavier stirred.

This isn't a game, Duncan thought. *This is real. This is what it takes to protect people. To fight back.*

And as Konrad watched from behind, arms still folded, Duncan could feel his uncle's gaze – not just evaluating his form, but weighing something deeper.

Discipline. Control. Purpose.

That's what it meant to carry a weapon.

And for the first time, Duncan didn't just understand it – he believed it.

The military camp in Ballylawn bustled with activity. Soldiers conversed among themselves, military vehicles were parked in orderly rows and numerous tents dotted the area. Duncan stepped into the tent where Colonel Callen was stationed, a middle-aged man with thinning white hair. The colonel eyed Duncan with a hint of impatience.

'Finally, you're here. Took you long enough.'

Duncan approached the colonel and extended his hand. 'Pleasure to meet you, Colonel.'

The colonel looked at Duncan's outstretched hand, then at Duncan, and finally shook it with a firm grip. 'Likewise. Now, let's get to business. You're aware that we sent a patrol out four days ago and we've had no communication from them since. We need someone to investigate, and that someone is you. You'll be working alongside Lieutenant Lansaw.'

Only one person? Why? To minimise casualties? To reduce risk? Does this colonel have that much confidence in me? So many questions swirled in Duncan's mind. He cocked his head in confusion. 'With all due respect, Colonel, why send just one person? Why not dispatch an entire unit?'

The colonel sighed. 'Most of our men are injured from the battle we recently faced. We're short on manpower. That's why we've partnered you with Lieutenant Lansaw.'

'But why not send at least a few more men? Wouldn't it be safer?'

Colonel Callen elaborated. 'I can't afford to risk more lives. The recent battle was brutal and we had severe casualties. Some men even came back with lost limbs, hearing and sight. I won't allow more casualties if it can be avoided. Our duty is to minimise losses in this war, so we've brought you in because you're the best for this job. Your records speak for themselves – you're the Heretic Hunter with unique combat skills that exceed most of our soldiers in this division. Your unorthodox abilities are precisely what we need. Teaming up with Lieutenant Lansaw will yield exceptional results.'

'It appears you have a lot of faith in me, Colonel.' Duncan, who had been grappling with self-doubt lately, had always excelled in his work, and it was a much-needed boost to hear it from this man.

The colonel affirmed. 'Indeed, I do. I had a choice – continue to deplete our ranks or bring in a professional. I believe the latter is the wiser option.'

Duncan couldn't deny the colonel's reasoning. How many lives had this war taken? 'Your analysis is sound,' Duncan replied. 'Don't worry, I will try my best, Colonel.'

Colonel Callen seemed satisfied. 'You're performing a great service for our fallen king. Ensure you return with your findings.'

'Understood.'

'Lieutenant Lansaw is waiting at one of the camps. Goodbye, Mr Saul.'

'Farewell, Colonel.'

With a nod, Duncan exited the military tent to find Lieutenant Lansaw, weaving through the bustling camp. Soldiers worked, engines hummed and orders echoed.

Locating the lieutenant, Duncan stepped into another tent, the sturdy fabric rustling as he entered. Inside, the air was filled with a mix of canvas and the scent of recently brewed coffee. A dim, battery-powered light hung from the tent's ceiling, casting a glow over the utilitarian setup of folding tables and chairs. In one corner, Duncan quickly spotted Lansaw, a dark-skinned man with a shaved head, immersed in studying a digital map displayed on a tablet. Lansaw, dressed in a crisp military uniform adorned with rank insignias, glanced up as Duncan approached.

'You must be the famous Heretic Hunter I've been hearing about. It's an honour to meet you,' Lansaw said, extending a hand.

'Duncan Saul. Freelance Mercenary from Centurion Arms,' Duncan replied, shaking Lansaw's hand.

'Mark Lansaw, Lieutenant of the Floran Armed Forces.' He had an accent – definitely not a local. Flora wasn't known for having many foreigners around. It was refreshing to see a different face for a change.

Duncan asked, 'Not from around here, are you?'

'I was born and raised in Flora, but my parents are from Kalari,' Lansaw explained.

'A Kalarian? So, how do you like it here?' Duncan inquired.

'Indeed ... The difference between here and Kalari is the temperature,' Lansaw replied with a chuckle.

'If you reach the northern part of this country, you'll freeze your arse off,' Duncan added with a grin.

Lansaw laughed before getting serious. 'But we must save the jokes for later. We need to hurry, Mr Saul, because time is of the essence.'

'Yeah, you're right,' Duncan agreed.

Lansaw laid out their plan. 'We will take the military Jeep and head towards the region.'

With that settled, Duncan and Lansaw set off towards their destination.

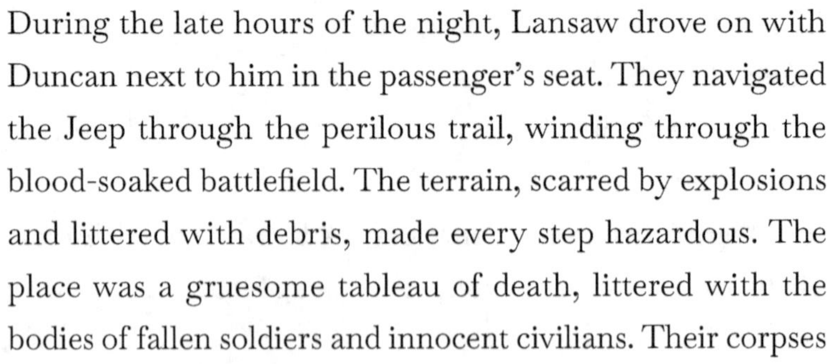

During the late hours of the night, Lansaw drove on with Duncan next to him in the passenger's seat. They navigated the Jeep through the perilous trail, winding through the blood-soaked battlefield. The terrain, scarred by explosions and littered with debris, made every step hazardous. The place was a gruesome tableau of death, littered with the bodies of fallen soldiers and innocent civilians. Their corpses had succumbed to decay, some charred beyond recognition. The once-vibrant grass beneath them was now blackened and ruined. Abandoned vehicles, such as cars and buses, lay in various states of disrepair.

Duncan's companion broke the eerie silence with a sombre observation. 'My God ... Look at the corpses.'

Duncan clenched his jaw, his eyes fixed on the gruesome sight. 'Trust me ... I see that stuff every day. It's war, it's in our nature. Every era, we still see the same shit ... Wait, stop the vehicle ...'

Lansaw obediently released his foot from the pedal. 'What's the matter, Saul?'

Duncan noticed something in the distance, a red flare breaking through the dark. 'See that?'

Lansaw squinted at the signal, his brow furrowing. 'It's a flare, a distress signal.'

Duncan nodded. 'We're at the right place, aren't we?'

Lansaw consulted the map to confirm, saying, 'Yeah, we're at the right place.'

Turning to face his companion, Duncan's expression turned grave. 'Before we go ... we need to be cautious.'

Lansaw raised an eyebrow, prompting Duncan to explain. 'We don't know for certain who launched the flare. They could be allies or they could be enemies.'

Puzzlement coloured Lansaw's voice. 'What are you suggesting?'

'One of us needs to check who sent the distress signal. In my experience, this could be someone conjuring illusionary magic.'

'Magic? I didn't know that would come into play ...' Lansaw admitted.

Duncan's gaze bore into him, deadly serious. 'Trust me, I've dealt with magic users before. They sometimes pull that shit – it's a pain in my arse.'

Lansaw couldn't help but chuckle softly. 'Oh, how observant of you. Good thing we hired you.'

Duncan returned a faint smile. 'Indeed ... The colonel made a logical decision,' he said as he exited the Jeep. 'I will let you know what I discover via the radio. Please keep in touch.'

'Understood. I'll meet you when you're done.'

With a nod, Duncan turned and silently moved towards the source of the distress signal. He put on his thermal goggles to help him see in the dark.

Arriving at the scene, Duncan retrieved his knife, his senses on high alert. As he approached the individuals responsible for the signal, he knew instinctively that they were not what they seemed. He pressed a blade against one of their necks, his voice low.

'Good evening ...'

But as the Night Hawk started to speak, Duncan swiftly silenced him by covering his mouth with his gloved hand. In one fluid motion, Duncan drove his knife into the side of the man's throat. The Night Hawk let out a gruesome gurgle, his body convulsing in shock. Duncan carefully lowered him to the ground and extracted the blade from his throat. As Duncan remained vigilant, another Night

Hawk approached the scene. Upon noticing this, Duncan swiftly hid in the shadows.

The Night Hawk's eyes widened in horror at the sight of his fallen comrade. 'What the fuck!?'

Before the Night Hawk could finish his warning to his comrades, Duncan swiftly lunged forwards. He seized the man's face and slit his throat with the knife. Blood sprayed, staining Duncan's jacket. He reached for his walkie-talkie and urgently whispered into it. 'Lieutenant, Lieutenant. Respond.'

'*Saul, is everything alright?*'

'Yeah, no hostile in sight.'

'*Okay, approaching your location,*' Lansaw replied.

Soon, Lansaw arrived and queried Duncan through the radio. '*Mr Saul, inform me. What do you see?*'

Duncan scanned the area once more, his keen eyes picking out the details in the battleground. His reply came through the radio, his voice low and focused. 'I spot about six men who are Night Hawks. They also have a few people who are hostages, from my point of view. Furthermore, one of them is wearing a Red Lion's uniform. They probably wanted to set up an ambush ...'

'*Oh God ... Good thing you took precautions. I would have blindly gone towards the enemy's trap.*' Lansaw continued. '*So tell me ... what do you have to defuse the situation?*'

'Hm ...' Duncan rummaged inside his backpack and said, 'I can use a couple of things to distract them. I've got smoke grenades and stun grenades.'

'Ah, those could be useful ... We can use them to weaken the awareness of the enemy.'

Duncan agreed, his mind calculating the tactical advantage. 'Yeah. When these guys are distracted, it will be an opportunity to open fire. A good ol' assault rifle would do the trick. They will never know what hit 'em.'

'Good thinking, Saul.'

Duncan grinned. 'Hey, they don't call me the *Heretic Hunter* for nothing.'

Lansaw made his way to Duncan's position. 'Saul,' he whispered, 'I'm here.'

Duncan nodded, gesturing towards the spot he wanted Lansaw to take. 'I need you to go over there.'

Lansaw followed Duncan's instructions. *'I'm in position,'* he confirmed.

As the Night Hawks held their hostages and conversed among themselves, Duncan initiated communication through their radios. 'Alright, when the smoke grenades are deployed, that's your signal to open fire.'

'Understood.'

Wearing his thermal goggles, Duncan could clearly see the enemies highlighted in his display. He initiated the countdown. 'Okay, on the count of three. One ... two ... three!'

Simultaneously, Duncan and Lansaw hurled smoke grenades towards the Night Hawks. Startled by the sudden appearance of the grenades, the Night Hawks shouted in alarm. 'Smoke grenades!'

Coughing and disorientated by the thick smoke, the Night Hawks were caught off guard as Duncan and Lansaw swiftly drew their assault rifles and began to eliminate their adversaries. Panic spread among the Night Hawks.

'Take cover!' one of the Night Hawks shouted, but it was too late for them. Duncan's aim was precise. He took out another of them with a single shot to the head. A Night Hawk cried out in anguish as he witnessed his comrade fall.

'Shit!'

In desperation, a Night Hawk broke from the group, fleeing the scene and leaving behind his fallen comrades. He grabbed a middle-aged woman with grey hair by the arm, using her as a shield.

'No! No! Please!' the woman cried in terror.

The Night Hawk pressed a pistol to her temple. 'Stay back! You better not come near me or I'll put a new hole in her!'

'*Saul, he's got a hostage. What do we do now?*' Lansaw asked urgently.

'Don't worry ...' Duncan replied.

Duncan yanked a stun grenade from his bag, thumbed the pin out, and skimmed it across the ground.

The Night Hawk followed the clatter, realised too late, and swore – then the grenade went off in a white crack. Both he and the hostage folded with a cry, hands clamped over their faces.

'Lansaw – take her!' Duncan barked.

Lansaw didn't hesitate. He slid in, hauled the woman upright, and pulled her with him into cover.

Good. One less thing to worry about.

Duncan swung back to the remaining heretic and opened fire. The Night Hawk threw up a slab of rock with a sweep of his hand – magic – and Duncan's rounds sparked uselessly off the conjured wall.

Duncan hissed under his breath. *Brilliant. A magic user. Just my luck.*

The Night Hawk ripped a boulder from the ground and hurled it. Duncan rolled aside, the boulder smashing into the pavement where he'd been a heartbeat ago. Dust stung his eyes.

'Bloody hell—!'

The heretic bolted.

Duncan pushed to his feet, drew his revolver, and fed rounds into the cylinder as he ran. The chase carried them through the wreckage of a collapsed holding, half its walls still standing like broken teeth. Duncan kept pace, breath steady, mind cutting through possibilities.

He didn't follow the heretic through the main entrance. Too obvious.

Instead, he stopped short, veered left, and slipped into the ruined shadows. The kind of movement Konrad drilled into him years ago: disappear, reappear, strike.

A dark gap above caught his eye – a jagged hole where a window once sat. Best option. He climbed quickly, fingers finding purchase on rough concrete and warped metal, and hauled himself inside. He dropped softly to the floor.

Thermal goggles on.

The world melted into gradients of heat.

There – behind the collapsed sofa – the heretic crouched low, hands glowing as earth-magic pooled between his palms.

Duncan's pulse steadied.

One clean shot before he casts.

He lifted his rifle—

His earpiece crackled. Lansaw's voice cut in, urgent and breathless. *'Saul, do you copy?'*

Duncan hissed back, barely above a whisper. 'Loud and clear.'

'I've contacted HQ. Medevac's inbound. Support helicopter on the way for extraction.'

'Good work. I need something else from you.'

'What's the situation?'

'He hasn't clocked me yet, but he's waiting to spring an ambush the second he does.'

'Do you have eyes on him?'

'Yeah.' Duncan's gaze stayed glued to the glowing hands behind the sofa. 'And he's a magic user.'

'What kind?'

'Elemental. Earth.'

A short, sharp curse. *'Shit. Any ideas?'*

Duncan already had one forming. 'I'll provide cover fire while you move to flank him.'

'Understood. I'll move into position ... bullets won't get through his shield, so I'll use a stun grenade to break his concentration.'

'Careful,' Duncan warned. 'He'll try to crush you the moment you step inside.'

'Acknowledged.'

Duncan sank lower behind his cover, watching the heretic's heat-signature flicker like a furnace. Seconds dragged. Then a faint shift in the thermal haze – Lansaw sliding behind a wall opposite.

'I'm here,' Lansaw said.

Duncan nodded, even though the lieutenant couldn't see it. 'Good. We strike on my mark.'

A breath. Another.

'Three ... two ... one.'

Duncan snapped up and unleashed a controlled burst.

The heretic jerked in surprise, eyes blazing, and yanked a stone wall from the floor. Duncan's bullets smacked uselessly against it – dull thuds on dense rock.

Fine. Stay behind it.

Just stay there.

He kept firing, stitching shots across the barrier – loud, relentless, perfect distraction – while Lansaw slipped into position to strike.

Lansaw didn't waste the chance. He hurled a stun grenade, the metal casing skittering across the cracked tiles.

The heretic clocked it instantly.

'Oh, for–'

He dived aside a heartbeat before the blast lit the room white. The shockwave rippled through the air. The heretic rolled with it, came up on one knee – already gathering magic.

'Lansaw, move–'

Too late.

The heretic slashed his hand through the air, ripping a storm of jagged stone from the floor. The shards lanced across the space, slamming into Lansaw. One buried itself deep in his chest. Lansaw staggered back with a strangled sound, crumpling as blood began to seep through his uniform.

Duncan's stomach dropped.

Shit.

He ducked behind cover as another burst of stone tore past him, chips of concrete stinging his cheek. His heartbeat thundered. Lansaw was down. The heretic was still firing up. And they were running out of time.

The heretic turned towards the fallen lieutenant, attention momentarily fixed on the easier kill.

Duncan moved.

He sprinted up the rusted ladder of an old elevator platform and took aim from the height – just as the heretic's head snapped up. A sharp gesture, a crack. The stone beneath Duncan exploded. The whole platform buckled and dropped out from under him.

He crashed into the rubble, air ripping from his lungs. Stone rained down. Pain flared sharp across his ribs.

The heretic was already advancing.

Panic flickered – then Duncan crushed it. He snatched a grenade from his belt, yanked the pin, and hurled it. The explosive rolled to the heretic's feet.

A shield of rock burst up in front of him.

Duncan was already sprinting.

He closed the distance fast, boots skidding across debris. His fingers brushed the summoned rock – and he channelled his will into it. The stone softened, colour draining as it turned into brittle, glassy translucence.

Before the heretic could react, Duncan drew his pistol and fired. The bullet punched through the weakened glass, shattering it in a burst of glittering fragments.

Time slowed.

The heretic's eyes locked onto his.

The spell in his hands faltered.

Duncan raised his revolver.

No hesitation. No mercy.

The silver round struck the heretic clean through the left eye. His body jerked violently, then folded to the ground. Silence followed – thick and absolute.

Duncan stood over the corpse, weapon trained, breath ragged. When the heretic didn't move, he let out a long exhale and lowered his revolver.

'Target neutralised,' he muttered, voice dry. A grim smile tugged at his mouth. 'Well. That's one way to *kill* the bloody mood.'

He jogged back to Lansaw.

Blood soaked the man's uniform, dark and spreading. Shards of stone jutted from the torn fabric; some had punched deep. Lansaw's breathing was shallow, uneven – pain etching lines across his face.

Duncan knelt beside him and pressed fingers to his neck.

A pulse. Weak, but steady.

'Still with me,' he murmured.

He grabbed Lansaw's radio and keyed it. 'Floran HQ, do you copy? This is Duncan Saul – Lieutenant Lansaw is down. Repeat, Lansaw is down. Requesting immediate medical support.'

Static hissed for a moment.

Then: *'HQ here. What do you need?'*

'Duncan Saul, Centurion Arms. Lieutenant Lansaw is grievously wounded – stone shards have ruptured bone. He needs medevac, fast.'

'Acknowledged. Medical team en route.'

Duncan let out a breath he hadn't realised he'd been holding. He glanced at Lansaw and offered a faint, lopsided smile.

'Hear that, mate? Mission accomplished.'

He stayed crouched beside the wounded lieutenant, gun still in hand, eyes scanning the ruined hall while he waited for the medics to arrive.

The fight was over – but the adrenaline still thrummed under his skin, refusing to quiet.

Chapter XXVIII

CRIME AND PUNISHMENT

Duncan listened to Uncle Konrad who was imparting crucial lessons on heroism. They both sat cross-legged on the basement floor, the weight of Konrad's wisdom settling between them.

'The road you're on isn't going to be easy, Duncan.' Konrad's voice was steady, almost gentle. 'You'll have to do things you never thought you would.'

Duncan absorbed his uncle's words.

'A hero always needs a villain to defeat – without one, they're nothing.' Konrad's eyes locked with Duncan's. 'But remember this: never lose your moral compass. Never let your code slip, no matter how dark it gets. And never, ever give up on your ideals.'

Duncan's chest tightened. Those words felt like a challenge and a promise all at once. He knew what losing his way looked like. It scared him.

'Heroes don't quit. They fall, but they get back up. Again and again. That's what sets them apart.'

Duncan absorbed the lesson, his gaze unwavering. Konrad wasn't just talking about fighting; he was teaching him how to *live*.

'Heroes always face conflict. It's never simple. Whether it's saving people or stopping evil, there will always be something – or someone – standing in their way.'

Duncan scratched his chin, brow furrowed. 'I've noticed that in stories ... But why? Why do people always try to stop the hero? What do they get out of it?'

Konrad's eyes drifted to a distant point, searching for the right answer. 'It's never simple. People act for reasons – motivations deeper than what we see. If they didn't, we'd be nothing but machines, repeating the same motions.'

Duncan nodded, chewing on that thought.

'War, conflict – it's part of human nature. We can't just erase it.'

The lesson ended as Konrad stood and smiled gently, ruffling Duncan's hair like a proud father.

'That's it for today. Remember this, kid – I won't be here forever. You'll have to stand on your own two feet sooner than you think.'

Duncan watched him, heart pounding. The path ahead was daunting, but for the first time, it felt possible.

Duncan found himself reporting back to Colonel Callen. Inside the colonel's tent, he conveyed the status of his mission. 'Colonel, the job is done. I successfully carried out my task.'

Colonel Callen acknowledged, saying, 'Good. Good. It was a wise choice for us to hire you. I find it quite regretful that you are a freelancer instead of military personnel. We would find it most favourable if you were aiding the armed forces.'

'I get your perspective, but I prefer to march to my own beat. I'm not one for taking orders, even if they come with good intentions.'

The colonel seemed to understand, nodding in agreement. 'Alright. So, what went down?'

'The patrols you sent got taken out by the Night Hawks. Turns out, they were scheming to ambush the Floran military. One of those Night Hawks swiped a uniform, thinking they could blend in. They even set off a distress signal, hoping some military unit would stroll into their trap. And, on top of that, I stumbled upon a bunch of civilians they had taken hostage.'

The colonel nodded thoughtfully. 'Mm-hmm ... Okay, okay ... That's good, that is pleasing to my ears. You'll be awarded for your service. We'll deposit the money into your bank account within three working days.'

'Thank you, Colonel.'

'I hope we continue to work with each other in the future. Your skills are efficient, and we could use you to help with the military.'

Duncan agreed. 'I hope so. I look forward to that day.'

'I bid you farewell, Mercenary.'

'Same to you too, Colonel.'

Exiting the tent, Duncan left the military camp of Ballylawn.

Duncan moved through the battered landscape of Flora, boots crunching over broken glass and scattered debris. The ruins around him told the same story he had seen a hundred times – burntout homes, splintered trees, roads split open like old wounds. All of it quiet now. *Dead* quiet.

He needed a place to rest before heading back – somewhere out of sight. Somewhere safe. But safe was no longer something you found; it was something you carved out with vigilance and a loaded rifle.

He climbed a slope of rubble and crouched atop a halfcollapsed tower, lifting his binoculars. The view stretched out for miles – just more of the same. But then, movement.

A group near an old checkpoint: soldiers, armed and tense, corralling civilians like cattle.

Duncan tensed. He adjusted the focus. Four officers, armed to the teeth. Civilians – perhaps a dozen – herded together, fear plain on their faces. He dropped low and climbed down the pile, slipping into shadow, boots silent as he crossed the ruin. A chunk of broken wall gave him cover close enough to hear.

'Can I ask?' one of the civilians said – a man, perhaps in his forties, voice trembling. 'Why are we being held here?'

The officer – probably the captain – answered with a shrug, almost cheerful. 'Oh, no reason at all.'

Then the bastard added, almost offhand, 'You're all going to be executed. For supporting the Night Hawks.'

Duncan's jaw tightened. His grip on the rifle shifted, finger brushing the trigger guard. *Executed.* For what? Supporting the wrong side? He had seen this before – military justice with no justice in it at all.

Gasps and cries rippled through the group. Someone shouted – a young man, barely holding it together. 'So we deserve to die for that? What kind of monsters are you?'

Duncan did not need to hear the answer. He had already heard it too many times in his life.

Duncan quickly contacted his partner. 'Jénmar, I need you to run a recording.'

'*Why? Is something happening?*' Jénmar asked.

'Yeah. I'm overhearing the Floran military having a conversation with some civilians. They're rounding them up to be executed.'

'We're the monsters?' The captain scoffed. 'Some of you were part of the protests that led to a riot. You harmed several individuals in the process, all in the name of defending that murderer.'

Another person stood up and inquired, 'But how are *we* responsible for what transpired? There are innocent people here who had nothing to do with it!'

Duncan couldn't simply stand there: action was imperative. If he didn't intervene, these people would die.

'Jénmar, I've gotta help those people,' Duncan said.

Jénmar disagreed. '*No, Duncan, you can't. Taking on the entire military isn't the solution. Wait ... record a video and inform the colonel.*'

Duncan hesitated. 'I ...'

'*Listen, Duncan. As much as I want you to kill and shit, now's not the time. The smarter move is to contact the colonel and let him know what's happening.*'

'Shit,' Duncan muttered, realising Jénmar was right. Taking on an entire battalion wasn't a viable option. Even if he considered attempting it, the chances of survival remained slim. Sacrificing these civilians was not what he wanted to do, but it was the smart thing to do.

Duncan slipped away from the crowd, his footsteps quiet against the backdrop of anxious murmurs. Finding a concealed spot behind a dilapidated building, he brought out his communication device – a small, sleek device with a dimly lit screen. The urgency of the situation hung heavily in the air as he quickly dialled the familiar frequency for the colonel. The device crackled to life, and a voice echoed through the speaker.

'*This is Colonel Callen. Report.*'

'Colonel, it's Saul. We've got a critical situation here. A Floran captain is rounding up civilians, accusing them of supporting the Night Hawks. He claims they're to be executed.'

'*Executed? On whose orders?*'

'Probably a captain's, sir. He hasn't given any clear justification, just accused them of betraying the monarchy,' Duncan replied.

Silence followed on the other end, punctuated only by the distant sounds of unrest from the gathered civilians. Duncan could almost feel the weight of the colonel's contemplation.

'*Stay calm, Saul. I'm dispatching a rapid response team. Give me your location,*' the colonel commanded.

Duncan quickly relayed his coordinates, eyes darting around to ensure he remained undetected. He could feel the tension building in the air, every passing moment an agonising reminder of the lives hanging in the balance.

'*I need you to keep a low profile, Saul. Do not engage unless absolutely necessary. We'll handle this.*'

Acknowledging the order, Duncan took a deep breath, his gaze fixed on the unfolding scene. 'Understood, sir. I'll await further instructions.'

The communication ended, leaving Duncan with a mix of relief and concern. He knew he had made the smart decision by contacting the colonel, but he feared they might not make it in time to save these people.

Duncan returned to the scene and swiftly activated his body camera, ensuring the unfolding events were recorded. 'Jénmar, I've switched on the recording,' he said.

'*Good. Now just stand there and record ...*'

'Dammit,' Duncan muttered with regret.

One of the captain's subordinates voiced his concern. 'Captain Shane, should we really be doing this? Isn't it a crime to kill civilians?'

So that's the captain, Duncan thought, studying the man more closely. White, closecropped hair. Midforties, by the look of him. The kind of officer who'd seen too many campaigns and lost whatever soul he might've had along the way.

'These *civilians* aren't innocent – they were involved in those atrocities. Consider that they're the ones who killed a few of our men during the riot. They shouldn't go unpunished for their actions.'

'I understand, but ...'

The captain smirked with malice. 'Soldier, think about it strategically. We should view this as a tactical advantage.'

'What do you mean?'

'If we eliminate these people now, we can prevent future recruits. It won't be long before these individuals join the Night Hawks.'

'But Lance Sainglend is already in captivity. What would be the point?'

'Yes, Sainglend has been captured but his other followers are still out there. Just because their leader has surrendered doesn't mean they won't find someone else to replace him. Besides, I simply want to eradicate the supporters of that bastard. It will be a significant problem if they continue to spread like a disease.'

'I'm not sure about this, sir.'

Shane raised his tone abruptly. 'That's an order, soldier. Disobey and it will be considered treason.'

The subordinate hesitated for a moment, then reluctantly replied. 'Understood, sir.'

Duncan's fury simmered as he watched the military officers load their guns and take aim at the terrified civilians, including women and children.

'Men, do not leave a single one alive.' Shane smirked.

The captain raised his hand, and Duncan knew it was time. He heard the sound of gunfire and the horrified screams of the innocent. Blood spattered and lifeless bodies piled up against the wall. It was a massacre. He couldn't believe his eyes: the gunshots, the screams, the brutality firsthand. It was a horrifying scene that would haunt him for a long time.

Jénmar's voice crackled in his earpiece. '*Oh my God ...*'

Duncan quivered. 'J–Jénmar, have you recorded the conversation?'

Jénmar responded. '*Yes, I have ... Shit. I've seen a lot of death, but this was intense for even me ...*'

Duncan's expression twisted into a scowl, his resolve hardening. 'Good – these sons of bitches will have it coming.'

As Duncan listened back to the conversation between the captain and his subordinate, a heavy sense of despair settled deep within him. It was clear that justice had been abandoned in this desolate landscape, and he could feel his heart sinking further with each word exchanged.

'The deed is done,' the subordinate reported to his captain.

Duncan's gaze remained fixed on them, hidden in the shadows, as he strained to catch every word.

'Good job, soldier,' Shane responded. His voice held a chilling indifference that sent shivers down Duncan's spine. 'Now, do me a favour. Burn the bodies. We can't have them as evidence or we may be in trouble.'

Duncan clenched his fists, his stomach churning at the captain's callous instructions.

The subordinate nodded in acknowledgment. 'Understood.'

Duncan's heart ached with the weight of the situation, knowing he had to act carefully. He listened as the subordinate relayed his orders. 'All units, make sure we incinerate the bodies.'

After some time, the boy found himself trapped under a pile of corpses. He wore a blue hoodie, green shorts and blue Converse shoes, the attire of a normal, harmless child.

Panic set in as he struggled to free himself, the weight of the lifeless bodies restricting his breathing. It felt suffocating, but his determination and desperation fuelled his efforts to crawl out.

With each movement, he inched closer to freedom until he finally broke free from the gruesome mound. His small face was drenched in blood, and his breaths came in gasps.

'Oh God ... Oh God ...' the boy muttered, his voice quivering with fear and shock. He stood there, paralysed by the horrors he had just witnessed, unsure of what to do next.

Suddenly, voices nearby snapped him out of his stupor. He strained to listen, his heart pounding in his chest.

'Should we have really done this?' a military officer said.

'It was that or insubordination.'

'But it's a crime to kill unarmed civilians ...'

'Even so, we had our orders.'

The first officer shook his head. 'But what we did was murder.'

The second officer asked, 'Would you prefer if we were thrown in jail instead?'

The boy listened, wide-eyed and trembling, as the two officers discussed their actions. He watched as they eventually moved away from the scene, their conversation leaving the first officer in disbelief.

With the officers gone, the boy seized the opportunity to escape the nightmarish place. Fear propelled him forward, and he ran without any sense of direction, desperate to put as much distance as possible between himself and that dreadful place.

'Okay, Duncan. You need to get out of there. ASAP.' Jénmar's voice came over Duncan's earpiece.

'Agreed ...'

Even though Duncan couldn't save these people, his training had always emphasised the importance of selfpreservation – especially in situations like this. It was instinctive to prioritise his own safety and get out as quickly as possible. The rational part of his mind agreed with Jénmar's advice. He knew he ought to heed the warning and withdraw without delay.

But then something unexpected caught his eye – a frightened young boy, fleeing in panic.

Duncan froze. He couldn't just abandon the child to the horrors unfolding around them.

'Wait, there's a kid,' Duncan said.

'Duncan, it's better to get out of there. You don't wanna take on the entire military. That's not recommended.'

'I'm sorry, Jénmar. There's been enough people that died today.'

'Duncan, don't.'

'I'm sorry.'

'Dammit! Whatever, just don't get yourself killed.'

Jénmar didn't appear pleased with the decision that Duncan made. While preserving his safety seemed logical, morally, it would be better to save the boy. Too many lives had already been lost, and he wasn't willing to let an innocent boy perish that day.

Duncan moved swiftly – his sole focus on reaching and rescuing the terrified boy.

The boy bolted through the chaos, limbs flailing, breath ragged. Duncan caught a glimpse of him just before he collided into his chest with a sharp thud. The kid hit the ground hard, skidding in the dirt, wide-eyed and trembling.

'Please! Please don't kill me! Don't kill me!' the boy shrieked, flinging his arms over his head as though Duncan were a monster.

Duncan froze.

Shit ... he's just a kid.

'Hey. Easy.' He crouched down, voice low and steady. 'I'm not gonna hurt you. Breathe. You're alright.'

The boy peeked out through his fingers, still gasping like a cornered rabbit. Duncan kept still, letting the panic burn itself out.

'A–aren't you ... gonna kill me?' the boy finally croaked, eyes wet and wide.

'No,' Duncan said, shaking his head. 'I'm not one of *them*. Just a freelance merc.'

It meant little to the boy – his trust was cracked, hanging by threads – but at least he wasn't running anymore. Poor sod probably didn't even understand what was happening. Just one more civilian caught in a nightmare.

'What's your name, kid?'

'M–Matthew,' he stammered, voice barely holding together.

'How old are you?'

'Twelve.'

Duncan nodded grimly. 'Alright then, Matthew. I need you to be brave now. Things are gonna get loud. Stick close. Do *not* run. Got it?'

Matthew gave a tight nod, his small hands balled into fists. Duncan led him behind a crumbling wall, crouching low as the footsteps of Red Lions crunched nearer.

'Is the lighter ready?' one of them asked, voice calm – like he wasn't about to commit murder.

'Yes,' another answered.

Matthew flinched beside him. Duncan didn't look – just breathed once, steadying himself.

Then he moved.

Matthew nodded, lips pressed tight, and stuck close to Duncan as they ducked behind a crumbling wall. The lad was shaking. Duncan could feel it—hell, he could *hear* it, each breath a shallow rasp beside him. And then came the voices.

'Is the lighter ready?' one soldier asked, close enough that Duncan could make out the gravel in his tone.

'Yeah.'

Duncan's jaw clenched. *Bastards.*

He didn't need to see the kid's face to know he was terrified. Could almost feel Matthew shrinking beside him. Duncan slipped his knife from its sheath, slow and silent, letting instinct take over. One breath. Two. Then he moved.

A blur – Duncan sprang from cover, knife flashing. He sliced across the first man's throat before the second could react. The first dropped with a gurgle, blood pooling fast.

Duncan didn't hesitate – he grabbed the rifle's muzzle and, with a flick of his magic, the second soldier's gun dissolved into water.

The man shouted in confusion. 'Wha–?'

Too late. Duncan's blade buried in his throat.

The two men fell, their lives gone in a matter of seconds.

Silence.

'Alright, Matthew,' he called gently. 'It's safe now.'

The boy crept from hiding, steps slow, heart still pounding. His gaze locked on the bodies. And then – past them. The civilians.

His mother.

Matthew ran to her, fell to his knees. His tiny hands reached out, desperate for warmth. But her skin was already cold.

'No ... no ... Mum ...' he choked out, voice cracking as he shook her shoulder. 'I wanted her to see me play ... to see me in the Alpha Leagues ...'

Duncan stayed quiet. There was nothing he could say. No way to soften that kind of grief.

'It's not *fair*!' Matthew's voice rose, full of fury now. 'Why!? Why did they have to take my mum away!? Why would the Red Lions do this!? They were *supposed* to help!'

He clawed at the dirt with both hands, his small frame shaking.

'I *hate* them! I hate all of them! I'll kill them! I *swear* – I'll kill them all!'

Duncan stepped closer and laid a hand on the boy's shoulder. Just enough pressure to remind him – he wasn't alone.

Matthew looked up at him, eyes glassy, chest heaving.

Duncan didn't speak.

He just held his gaze – and let the silence speak for both of them.

Duncan's voice softened as he crouched beside the boy. 'Hey ... listen, kid. I'm sorry about your mum. Really, I am. But you've got to keep quiet now. We can't afford to stay here – more soldiers will be swarming in any minute.' He glanced around the ruined street, tension prickling at his skin. 'So, pull yourself together. Think less about revenge and more about getting out alive. That's what she'd want.'

He saw the fight flicker back in Matthew's eyes, raw grief still simmering beneath the surface. The boy's pain was a weight Duncan understood all too well – loss was a poison that could either kill or fuel you. Matthew said little, merely nodded, the silence thick between them.

'Right. Come on. We need to move.'

They pressed forward through the wreckage, shadows swallowing their steps. Matthew kept stealing glances over his shoulder, eyes fixed on the bodies of civilians left behind. His mother's still form haunted his gaze, twisting his heart into a knot Duncan could not untie.

Ahead, a figure appeared – one of them. Duncan froze, then pressed a finger to his lips, signalling Matthew to hush. He crept forward, knife ready. Before the soldier could react, Duncan's hand clamped over his mouth. The man struggled, panic wide in his eyes, but Duncan's grip was iron.

The blade slipped free. A soft, gurgling sound, and the soldier went still. Duncan eased him to the ground, eyes sharp as he looked back to Matthew. A subtle nod told the boy it was safe to move on. Trust was built in small moments like this.

Not long after, another soldier came into view. Duncan raised his hand, halting Matthew's cautious step. The officer turned, oblivious to the danger creeping up behind him. Duncan was on him in a heartbeat – silent, deadly. Blood spilled quietly onto the cracked pavement, and the man slumped away.

'C'mon,' Duncan whispered.

Matthew obeyed, stepping closer now, his shoulders easing as the threats fell away. The tension clinging to them both began to loosen, if only slightly.

Duncan activated his earpiece, connecting with Jénmar. 'Jénmar, can you give me an update on my location – any hostiles?'

'*Yeah, there's one in front of you. Twelve o'clock,*' he reported.

Peering cautiously from behind a ruined wall, Duncan spotted a soldier guarding his post. He quickly retreated into cover and relayed the situation to Jénmar. 'Yeah, I see him.'

But then, an unexpected disturbance in the signal disrupted their communication. '*Ah shit!*' Jénmar cursed.

Duncan's anxiety heightened. 'What!?'

'*Something's up! There's something disrupting my signal!*'

'Oi? Jénmar!?'

Suddenly, a military officer stumbled upon their path, engrossed in a radio conversation with a comrade. 'Something's not right. I don't know why Private Lemur didn't respond on the radi–?'

The soldier's suspicion arose as he noticed Duncan and Matthew. A tense silence enveloped them, broken only by the officer's scrutiny. Duncan noticed that he was looking at his arm – was he checking for the armband?

The officer tried to whip out his pistol. In a split-second decision, Duncan knew he had no choice. He fired several shots at the officer, the deafening noise piercing the eerie silence. The gunshots were loud, alerting other soldiers nearby.

'Shit …! They heard that!' Duncan whispered urgently to Matthew, his heart racing.

'What happened!?' Matthew asked, his fear clear.

'Kid, the military's coming. Make sure you stay behind me!'

'What!?'

Without explanation, Duncan grabbed Matthew's hand and pulled him along, their escape taking precedence over any questions that could wait.

'Hey, wait a minute!'

Duncan's frustration boiled as he spoke into his earpiece. 'Jénmar! What the hell!? I thought you had my back!'

Jénmar's voice crackled through the earpiece, sounding genuinely apologetic. '*I don't know what happened, he didn't show up on my radio. The guy's transmitter must have interfered with my signal. It must've messed up my radio frequency.*'

'Dammit, Jénmar! Argh! Just give me an update on my location!'

'*Uhhh ... Duncan, you have hostiles incoming, twelve o'clock!*' Jénmar reported.

'Okay, got it.'

Two soldiers broke off from the group, heading straight for him and Matthew.

Duncan moved fast, slipping behind what remained of a crumbling wall. Dust clung to his coat as he dropped to one knee, rifle raised. No time to think – just act.

The first soldier stepped into view. *Crack.* A clean headshot. The second barely had time to react before Duncan dropped him too. Both fell without a sound. No hesitation. No remorse. Just two more names he'd never know.

Then – footsteps. Shouts.

Reinforcements burst into the room.

Duncan's hand shot to his belt. He yanked a stun grenade free, flicked the pin, and lobbed it straight into their path.

'Eyes down!' he barked to Matthew, already turning away as the flash lit up the room like lightning.

'Grenade!' one of them yelled, and the air around them exploded in a blinding flash and deafening roar, sending dust and debris flying.

'Argh! Argh! I can't see!'

'Fuck!'

As the disorientated soldiers stumbled, Duncan methodically dispatched them, one by one, until they lay incapacitated on the floor. More soldiers arrived, this time deploying smoke grenades, shrouding the area in a thick haze.

'Smoke grenades! Matthew, get back!'

Duncan, ever resourceful, switched to his pistol and donned his thermal goggles to see through the smokescreen. With rifles at the ready, the soldiers entered cautiously, equipped with their own thermal goggles. Duncan and Matthew took refuge behind a table, and Duncan used his Material Alteration spell to transform the table from steel to concrete, providing them with better cover. The soldiers proceeded with their search, their voices low.

'Do you see anything?'

'Negative.'

'Okay, keep looking.'

With his keen marksmanship, Duncan emerged from cover and began picking them off methodically. One soldier, attempting to close in on Duncan, stumbled over a fallen comrade and fell to the ground, losing his grip on his rifle. Duncan loomed over him, pistol aimed at the soldier's face, and without a trace of emotion, he pulled the trigger. The man's cry was cut short.

Approaching Matthew, Duncan inquired with concern, 'Are you okay ...?' His voice was softer now, a stark contrast to the cold detachment he had just displayed.

Matthew watched with wide-eyed shock. 'Oh God, is this what you do ...?' Duncan remained silent and Matthew continued. 'You're scarier than I thought ...'

Duncan's demeanour had transformed – he now wore a cold and emotionless expression. Still wordless, he couldn't help but feel some regret. He had hoped to shield the boy from the brutal reality of his profession, but it seemed that the truth was unavoidable.

Matthew managed a humourless laugh. 'Hahaha ... Glad you're on my side, right.'

Duncan nodded in acknowledgment. 'Yeah, but you have to know that it's my sworn duty to protect the innocent from evil.'

'Oh ... So, you're like those people, huh?' Matthew remarked.

Just as the soldiers closed in on their position, Duncan heard their approach. 'I'm sorry, but I have no time to explain this!' Grabbing Matthew's hand, Duncan began to run. 'Come!'

Matthew protested. 'Hey!'

The soldiers entered the room filled with lifeless bodies, some pausing to stare while others wasted no time and pursued Duncan and Matthew.

Duncan and the boy raced through the decimated streets, bullets whizzing past them as the soldiers closed in. Desperation fuelled their flight, and they both instinctively lowered their bodies, narrowly evading the deadly projectiles. Amid their frenzied escape, Duncan returned fire with his pistol. Matthew's scream mirrored the intensity of the situation.

Their flight continued relentlessly until their path led them to the edge of a cliff where Duncan and Matthew skidded to a halt, their breaths ragged.

Shit.

'It's a dead end,' Duncan muttered, his eyes scanning for a way out. The approaching military officers left him no time to think. 'Shit, they're coming! We have to jump!'

Matthew's gaze dropped to the perilous height below. 'Are you crazy!? I'm not falling down there!'

'We have no choice!'

'No! I'll die!'

Duncan turned to the boy, urgency in his eyes. 'Kid, do you trust me?'

'Uhh ... A bit, but not to this extent!' Matthew hesitated.

'Good, because it doesn't matter!' Without further ado, Duncan propelled him forward.

'No–no–no–no–no!' Matthew's protests fell on deaf ears. They both leapt into the void, their voices merging into a single, heart-pounding scream.

The two of them crashed into the unforgiving ground below, the impact causing a sharp pain to shoot through Duncan's body. Groans and grunts filled the air as they both struggled to regain their bearings.

'Matthew, you good?' Duncan inquired.

Matthew nodded, wincing in pain. 'Yeah, my arm really hurts.'

Duncan rose to his feet, guilt etched across his face. 'Yeah, sorry about that.'

'Ow, ow, ow!' Matthew cried out as Duncan helped him up, his injured arm causing him significant discomfort.

Duncan continued apologising, remorseful for inadvertently causing the boy more pain. 'Sorry, sorry.'

Taking cover behind a nearby wall, Duncan assessed his remaining arsenal. He retrieved a few grenades from his backpack, inspecting them with a sombre expression.

'Three grenades left ...' A quick check of his ammunition left him disheartened. 'I'm running out of ammunition.' Turning on his communicator, Duncan sought assistance from Jénmar. 'Jénmar, I need intel support.'

Static and interference plagued the connection, making Jénmar's response barely comprehensible. '*S–r–y I ca—'t he– y– bre– up!*'

'Jénmar! Shit, no signal.'

Panic welled up within Matthew, and he clutched Duncan in terror. 'Oh God, why did this day have to come!? I don't know if I can do this ...! I don't wanna die!'

Duncan cupped the boy's face, forcing him to meet his eyes. 'Look at me, look at me! You're going to make it alive. I'll make sure of it. Okay?'

Matthew nodded shakily.

'Now, I need you to be brave. Let's hide here until they go away,' Duncan said.

The two of them settled into their makeshift hiding spot in the ruin, and Matthew couldn't help but voice a question. 'Aren't you scared?'

Duncan met the boy's gaze directly. 'Of course, I'm scared. I'm scared every day, but I don't let it get to me.'

'Do you think I'm really going to live through this?'

Duncan's conviction shone through as he nodded firmly. 'Yes. I swear on my life. You need to live a long life.'

'You say that but what's the point? My mum can't see me become a football player.'

Duncan stood still in thought, averting his gaze. While Matthew was discussing his pain, Duncan couldn't help but empathise with the boy's feelings of loss and despair. He knew firsthand the profound impact that the absence of a parent could have on a young person's life.

'I know how it feels to lose a parent,' Duncan revealed, capturing the boy's attention.

'What?'

'My dad. He left me when I was young.'

The boy struggled to comprehend. 'Left you?'

'He was attacked by someone and that made him leave. I don't know for sure, but he's probably dead. I haven't seen him for about ten years.'

In that moment, Duncan bared a part of himself he rarely shared. The wounds of his past, the abandonment he had experienced and the uncertainty surrounding his father's fate were scars that had shaped him into the person he had become.

'That's a long time ...'

Duncan remained silent. *A long time indeed.*

'So, this person that attacked him, did you get him?' Matthew asked.

Duncan shook his head. 'No. I'm still looking ...'

'Oh ...'

Duncan looked at Matthew and said softly, 'You reminded me so much of my younger self, especially when you talked about hating those soldiers. I felt the same way when that criminal took my father away from me. Hunting down the man was the only thing that kept me moving forward.'

Matthew listened intently to Duncan's story.

'However, looking for the criminal wasn't the thing that gave me hope – it was someone else who came into my life.'

Uncle Konrad was always there when he needed him most.

'That's why you must keep living. Even in the darkest moments, hold onto hope. Your future is promising and life can improve. Even if your mum won't be there to see you as a football player.'

'I didn't really look at it that way ...'

'So I swear that we'll make it out of this. You just need to trust me.' Duncan gave Matthew an assuring smile.

'Should we do a fist bump on that?' Matthew suggested, a hopeful smile on his face.

'What?'

'Fist bump. It's when people give respect to each other. I do it with my friends all the time.'

Duncan chuckled. 'Yeah, fist bump.'

The two bumped fists together, sharing a brief moment of camaraderie, their laughter ringing through the turmoil around them.

Chapter XXIX

THE GREAT ESCAPE

Matthew and Duncan's brief moment of bonding was interrupted when Duncan heard the approaching footsteps of another group of soldiers.

'Dammit,' Duncan muttered under his breath. 'Soldiers.'

He glanced at Matthew. They both knew that their peaceful encounter was about to be disrupted by the presence of the approaching military personnel. Duncan peered out of the window. 'There are two of them coming our way.'

Matthew inquired, 'What's the plan?'

'Right now, we have to make do with what we've got,' Duncan replied. He then turned to Matthew and added firmly, 'Stick close to me, okay?'

Duncan strategically placed several C-4 explosives in different spots, setting up a trap for the approaching soldiers. He also readied his smoke and stun grenades for the impending battle. He motioned to Matthew, saying, 'Kid, stay put right there.'

They listened to the soldiers conversing among themselves.

'Any visual on the target?' one soldier asked.

The other replied, 'Negative. Still no sign.'

'Alright, keep your eyes peeled.'

Duncan didn't hesitate. He yanked a smoke grenade from his belt and hurled it towards the two officers.

'Smoke grenade!' one shouted as the canister clattered to the floor and hissed.

A thick cloud erupted, swallowing the room in grey. The soldiers coughed, fumbling for their masks.

But Duncan was already prepared. Thermal goggles slid over his eyes, and through the haze, two bright figures glowed.

He opened fire – one clean shot, straight through a skull.

'Damn it!' the second soldier shouted, scrambling – too late. Duncan cut him down with a burst from the rifle.

The room fell silent again.

'Come on, Matthew,' Duncan said, voice low but firm as he took the boy's hand.

They ran, boots pounding against tile, until they reached a half-ruined building with no roof. Duncan scanned for cover – too late.

The door burst open.

Soldiers flooded in, rifles up.

'There he is! We've got a visual on the target!' one yelled.

Duncan's heart kicked into overdrive. No time to think. Only survive.

He shoved Matthew aside – hard but careful – and threw himself forward, his body hitting the ground in a controlled slide.

'Stay down!' he barked, skidding towards a nearby table.

He slapped his hand on the table's surface, channelling his magic.

Focus.

Wood shimmered, hardened – turned to solid steel under his will.

With a grunt, he flipped it on its side just as gunfire erupted.

Bullets pinged against the steel barrier, deafening.

Duncan crouched behind it, shielding Matthew with his own body, breathing hard.

I can't fail him, he thought. *Not now. Not ever.*

He checked his ammo, jaw clenched. The next move would have to count.

'A magic user!?' one of the soldiers exclaimed in surprise.

Duncan drew his pistol – one shot, and a soldier crumpled to the floor, blood blooming across his chest.

Without hesitation, Duncan grabbed the nearest table and hurled it at the last man standing.

The edge slammed into the soldier's chest, knocking the wind out of him and sending him stumbling back.

Stunned, he barely had time to react before Duncan closed the distance in a brutal tackle, pinning him to the ground.

His knife flashed, stabbing deep – again and again.

The soldier's fingers clawed weakly at Duncan's arm, trembling as life bled out from gaping wounds in his abdomen.

Each stab drained more strength, leaving him gasping, desperate to hold on.

Duncan's face twisted – rage, desperation, everything crashing down at once.

Blood sprayed, coating Duncan's shirt, splattering across his face. The metallic tang filled his nostrils, mingling with sweat.

The soldier's gurgled cries echoed, haunting.

Then, merciless, Duncan drove the blade home – deep into the soldier's neck.

A spray of blood burst free. The carotid artery severed in an instant.

The body went limp, the blood pooling beneath him spreading like dark ink.

Duncan hauled himself up, lungs burning, muscles trembling.

Around him, the battlefield was stained – his clothes soaked through, his face slick with sweat and gore.

He swallowed hard.

This was far from over.

'Are you okay?' Duncan asked.

Matthew nodded fearfully. 'Y–yeah,' he stammered.

In the distance, they heard the soldiers' voices calling out. 'Gunshots! They can't be far!'

Thinking quickly, Duncan retrieved a C-4 plastic explosive from his backpack and moved towards the room's door, locking it securely. He affixed the C-4 to the door and then took Matthew's hand.

'Okay, come on, kid!'

Matthew, still shaken, asked nervously, 'Why are the Red Lions doing this? Why do they want us dead so badly?'

Duncan retorted with frustration. 'Those aren't Red Lions, they're just psychotic dogs!'

'*Duncan, there are some hostiles approaching your location, but they've stopped*,' said Jénmar, quickly relaying the information to Duncan through their communication device. '*I can see a cluster of dots on my radar that have come to a halt.*'

Duncan realised the significance. 'That probably means they're at the door!'

Outside, some soldiers had indeed reached the door. One of them attempted to open it but found it locked, unaware of the potential explosives.

'Kick it down!' ordered one of the soldiers.

With a forceful kick, the door flew open, and the soldier who had kicked it ended up flat on the ground.

Duncan wasted no time; he pressed the C-4 remote, causing the explosives to detonate, eliminating the soldiers at the entrance.

'Okay, we're almost at the exit,' Duncan said.

Suddenly, a bullet whizzed past Duncan's feet. He came to an abrupt halt, stepping back.

'Stop, fugitive!' Shane of the Floran soldiers shouted. Duncan and Matthew found themselves surrounded by Floran soldiers. Shane continued. 'If you surrender and lay down your arms, both you and the boy will be unharmed.'

'Matthew, stay behind me,' Duncan whispered to the boy. Matthew obeyed, taking cover behind him. Duncan pointed his gun at Shane, his gaze fixed firmly on the man. 'So, you can shoot me in the back, eh? To tie up loose ends, is that it?'

Shane shook his head, his arms behind his back. 'If you keep your mouth shut and forget about all of this, I guarantee my men will safely escort you and the boy. We can then go our separate ways.'

Duncan's eyes narrowed as he exchanged a nervous glance with Matthew, who shook his head in fear. Shane presented Duncan with a choice, leaving him to decide their fate.

'You can't walk away from this,' Shane asserted, sharing his perspective. 'You're weary, resources are dwindling and we have the upper hand.'

Duncan's glare remained fixed on Shane as the man drew his pistol.

'I'm growing impatient with you, Heretic Hunter! I'll count to three!' Shane yelled.

Duncan reluctantly placed his weapon on the floor. 'Alright ... Alright ...'

Matthew whispered desperately, alarmed by Duncan's decision. 'What are you doing!?'

Shane watched Duncan disarm himself and gave his orders to his men. 'Men, escort him. The boy comes with me ...'

The officers seized Duncan, their guns trained on him, while one of them grabbed Matthew by the arm.

Matthew cried out. 'L–let me go!'

'Stop struggling!' the military officer spat.

As Matthew continued to resist, the soldier resorted to violence, slapping him across the face. Matthew held his cheek in silence while Duncan clenched his fists, fighting the urge to intervene. The military officers then led Matthew away.

Duncan was escorted by the soldiers, and one of them whispered to Shane, 'Sir, are we really letting them go?'

Shane shook his head and replied in a hushed tone. 'Of course not. Like he said, he's a loose end and we can't risk having witnesses ...'

Separated from Matthew and flanked by armed soldiers, Duncan felt the trap closing in around him. He wasn't naïve – he'd always known Shane wouldn't simply let him walk away. Not after all this bloodshed.

He was a loose end. A threat.

Determination surged through him like wildfire. Failure was not an option. Especially not for Matthew's sake.

Duncan remained alert, waiting for the first sign of betrayal.

A soldier's finger twitched near his rifle's trigger – aimed directly at Duncan's back. Time seemed to slow.

Duncan snapped his hand forward, grabbing the rifle's barrel.

In one fluid motion, his pistol was drawn. The shot cracked – clean and merciless – striking the head of the officer beside him.

Without hesitation, Duncan jabbed the pistol into the rifleman's throat. The man gasped, clutching at his neck in searing pain.

Duncan dropped low, firing another bullet into a third officer's stomach. The first target swung a savage punch at Duncan's jaw – he barely dodged.

Then came the sweep kick. Duncan's leg swept out, sending the soldier crashing hard to the dirt.

He raised his pistol – steady and cold. One shot to the head. The officer's lifeless body hit the ground with a sickening thud.

The remaining soldiers spun around, eyes wide at the sudden eruption of gunfire.

Duncan's breath was ragged, his heart hammering.

There was no turning back.

'Eh!' one of them yelled in alarm.

Thinking quickly, Duncan grabbed one of the fallen soldiers and used his lifeless body as a human shield. The remaining soldiers opened fire, but their bullets were blocked by the body. Meanwhile, Shane continued to drag Matthew away, the boy's protests growing louder.

'Let me go! Let me go!' Matthew yelled while desperately striking the captain's arm.

Duncan charged forwards, dragging his human shield like a weapon. Two shots cracked through the air – two officers dropped without a sound. He kicked one corpse hard, sending it crashing into the last man. The soldier grunted, falling backwards.

But there was no time to hesitate.

Before the officer could recover, Duncan lunged, wrapping his leg tight around the man's neck like a trap. His fist hammered into the officer's face, stifling any chance of struggle.

Cold steel flashed. Duncan plunged his combat knife beneath the man's throat.

The officer gurgled, blood bubbling as his eyes rolled back, life slipping away in slow agony.

Duncan yanked the blade free and pushed himself upright, every muscle screaming.

The brutality of the fight weighed on him like lead. He swallowed a ragged breath, fighting exhaustion clawing at his chest.

No time to rest. Matthew was still waiting.

Duncan pressed on.

However, his reunion with Matthew was interrupted when Shane shot Duncan in the arm with his pistol, warning him with a shout. 'Stay back!'

Duncan winced in pain, clutching his wounded arm and scowled at Shane. Shane, now holding Matthew hostage, looked at Duncan with defiance. Matthew whimpered in fear.

Duncan couldn't hide his disgust. 'Are you serious about holding a child hostage? How low can you go? But then again, I should expect no less from a vile dog who murders innocents.'

Shane retorted angrily. 'All I was doing was carrying out justice! You know what they were guilty of. They supported the Kingslayer! He's the murderer who plunged this country into civil war. If he never existed, I wouldn't have had to kill those people and nobody would've got hurt!'

Duncan's eyes widened with shock, utterly baffled by the captain's response. 'Justice!? Don't feed me that bullshit! You had a choice to spare those people, but instead, you mercilessly killed them and used the Kingslayer as an excuse.' Duncan's eyes narrowed with hostility. 'You're not a soldier! You're nothing but a fucking murderer!'

Shane's smirk remained in place as he taunted Duncan. 'Oh? And how many people have you killed in your line of work? How many executions did you carry out to keep Flora clean?'

Duncan fell silent, taken aback by the question.

Shane pressed on. 'The military's role is to eliminate the enemy. That's precisely what I did. So, tell me, how are we all that different?'

'*Enemy?*' Duncan repeated, his shock evident.

Shane continued with a smirk. 'Yes.'

Duncan's anger flared, and he growled in rage. 'Did you even listen to what you just said? You murdered innocent people. A boy lost his mother because of you!'

'And what about *you*, eh? You talk of protecting Flora, but can you honestly say that every life you've taken was a direct threat?'

Duncan recoiled in shock, feeling the captain's words strike a chord deep within him. His words forced Duncan to reflect on his own actions, particularly regarding Antonio Brown, who had pleaded for mercy mentioning his daughter. Was Antonio even truly a bad person? Hell, many of those Duncan had killed had begged for their lives.

Shane gave a cruel smile. 'So, I was right. Are you sure that we aren't different?'

Duncan remained silent.

'In reality, we're just pawns following orders that serve the same purpose as mine – maintaining order through bloodshed.'

Shane had a valid point. Yet while Duncan had killed many people before, it was a different situation with that monster. Duncan had only targeted and tortured his enemies. When it came to innocent people or his loved ones, his instinct was always to protect them.

Duncan attempted to shake off the captain's words, grappling with the urge to deny them. 'N–no! Don't you dare compare me to the likes of you. I don't kill innocent people!'

That was it. The breaking point.

Duncan couldn't take any more. Not from this bastard.

This captain – this *monster* – had to pay. Either he died here, or he'd never hurt another soul again. No more.

But the fight wasn't just physical anymore. It was grinding into his bones, dragging him down. After a day of unending battles, exhaustion was a weight pressing hard on every muscle, every breath. He was running on the edge of collapse.

Can't let this go on. Can't afford to lose.

Time was bleeding away, and so was his strength. If he didn't end this fast, he'd be finished.

The question wasn't if he could beat Shane anymore. It was *how*.

But in the roar of pain and chaos, one thing was crystal clear: Matthew's life depended on him.

Everything else faded. Everything else disappeared.

Save Matthew.

That was all that mattered.

'Enough! You'll do what I say or I'll–' Shane began, but before he could finish his threat, Matthew seized the opportunity and bit down hard on the captain's finger. Shane screamed in pain, and his grip on Matthew loosened enough for the boy to break free. 'You little shit ...' the captain grumbled.

Duncan saw his opening – and bolted.

The chaos bought him seconds – seconds he intended to use to end this. He closed the gap in a blink, hands snatching Shane's pistol and wrenching it away just as it fired. The shot tore through the air, harmless.

Now.

He struck fast – one brutal jab to the nose, then a rising kick that cracked against the side of Shane's skull. The captain reeled, dazed.

But Duncan had overcommitted.

He threw a punch, but Shane blocked it with ease and surged forward, slamming his fist into Duncan's jaw. Pain flared behind his eyes. Another punch – low and vicious – drove into his gut. He folded with a choked gasp, the air ripping from his lungs.

Then came a brutal strike to Duncan's arm – the same spot Shane's bullet had grazed. Pain surged through the half-healed wound.

He knows. He remembers where it hurts.

Duncan staggered. A strangled groan escaped his lips as his knees buckled, legs trembling beneath him.

Then came the hook – clean, merciless. Duncan's head snapped sideways, the world tilting. He crashed to the ground, cheek smacking cold concrete.

Blood filled his mouth.

He blinked against the ground, heart pounding, lungs dragging in air through gritted teeth. His entire body throbbed. His limbs felt like sandbags. His vision blurred.

But he wasn't done.

Not yet.

With a snarl, Duncan planted his hand on the ground – and pushed.

'You should've done what I asked. If you had stayed out of this, you would've walked out of here alive!' said Captain

Shane. Duncan grunted as he struggled while the captain continued to berate him, his voice filled with contempt. 'You don't understand what this war means to us, interloper. Winning is everything! It's not about saving, rescuing or protecting, it's about winning! Defeating the enemy is all that matters. You're nothing but a traitor to the army of Flora, siding with those devils!'

Matthew whispered quietly, his hope hinging on Duncan's ability to rise from his losing position. 'Come on, get up ...'

As Duncan struggled to stand, Shane seized the opportunity to pick him up and deliver a final, ominous threat. 'Now, you may die along with these parasites you so desperately want to protect!'

Shane's arm clamped around Duncan's throat like a vice, crushing his windpipe. Duncan thrashed, teeth bared, muscles straining against the iron grip. His vision narrowed, dark spots flickering at the edges. Then – pain. A savage kick to the back of his knee dropped him hard.

His breath hitched. *I'm going to die, if this keeps up.* The thought flared like a match in the dark. *Not like this.*

Fighting the blackness creeping in, Duncan fumbled for his sidearm. His fingers closed around cold steel. He yanked it free and shoved the barrel towards Shane's face.

Shane flinched – just enough. Duncan pulled the trigger. The shot went wide, deafening in the confined space. Another shot – missed again. Shane snarled, knocking the gun aside with a brutal slap. It clattered across the floor.

But the grip on his throat loosened.

Now. Move.

He twisted violently, breaking the hold. Grabbing Shane firmly, Duncan hoisted him off balance and slammed him hard onto the ground. The floor shuddered beneath the impact.

For a moment, neither moved.

Duncan blinked through sweat and blood. His lungs heaved like bellows. Pain bloomed in his ribs; his knee throbbed – but he forced himself upright. Limping, staggering, he fixed his gaze on the pistol, just a few feet away.

Shane groaned. Stirred.

Duncan lurched forward. So did Shane.

They moved at once.

Duncan dived. Fingers scraped metal. He rolled, spun, raised the gun—

BANG!

The shot hit. Shane's body jerked violently as the bullet struck him in the gut. His mouth opened in a silent scream, eyes wide with disbelief – and pain. He stumbled once, then collapsed.

Duncan lay on the floor, chest heaving, pistol still raised. The silence rang louder than the gunfire had.

I lived. Barely.

Duncan lowered his gun, panting heavily, adrenaline coursing through his veins. He dropped to his knees, his face marked with blood and bruises. This gruelling fight had taken a significant toll on him.

'You won!' Matthew said.

Duncan's exhaustion was palpable as he let out a tired smile. 'Yeah, I guess I did ...'

Matthew, filled with relief and joy, exclaimed, 'You were amazing! I knew you could do it!'

Duncan's elation was tempered by the reality of their situation. 'I appreciate the kind words, but let's not start celebrating yet. I need to get you to safety.' Duncan took Matthew's hand and, together, they made their way to a secure spot and Duncan leant against the wall.

Matthew, curious, asked, 'So what happens now?'

'I contacted the colonel earlier ... His team should be arriving here soon.'

Shane was crawling – Duncan didn't notice at first. His focus was on Matthew, whose small frame stood just ahead, unaware of the dying captain behind them.

The sharp crack of a gunshot shattered the moment.

Duncan spun, instincts kicking in too late. Shane was behind them, gun shaking in his bloodied hands. Another shot rang out – and Duncan's heart plummeted.

The bullet didn't hit him.

It hit Matthew.

The boy jolted. No scream, no cry – just a stunned gasp as he staggered. Time slowed.

No. No, no, no—

Duncan's mind reeled. The sight of red blooming across Matthew's side hit him harder than any bullet could. Shock twisted into something feral.

'No!' he roared, voice raw with panic.

Without thinking, he raised his gun. His hands trembled, but his aim was lethal. He fired, again and again, each shot laced with rage.

Shane managed to roll aside, dragging his ruined body behind cover – but Duncan wasn't watching anymore.

He dropped to his knees beside Matthew, breath ragged, ears still ringing from the last shot. His mind couldn't grasp what had just happened – not fully – not yet.

Blood.

So much of it.

Matthew lay sprawled on the floor, gasping, tiny fingers pressed against the wound in his stomach where the red soaked through. Duncan just stared. *No ... no, this can't be happening.*

He pressed down, hands shaking, trying to stop the bleeding. The warmth hit him through the gloves. *Too much. Too fast.*

'Stay with me, Matthew!' he shouted, his voice cracking. 'Stay with me, dammit!'

Tears streaked the boy's cheeks. His chest hitched, breath rattling. His small body trembled ... then slowly went still.

'Come on, kid ...' Duncan choked, barely able to speak. 'Come on, you're alright. You're gonna be alright.'

But Matthew didn't move. His hand slipped from Duncan's grasp like it didn't weigh anything at all. His eyes – wide, frightened – were already gone.

Gone.

Duncan froze. Couldn't breathe. Couldn't think.

I failed him.

Not just anyone – *a child.* This boy. This innocent boy …

Just *died* …

Not because of bad luck. Not even because of the bullet.

Because Duncan hadn't been fast enough.

Duncan stared down at the blood on his gloves, at the stillness that used to be life, and felt something break. Not fast, not loud – just a quiet, permanent shatter in the centre of his chest.

He knelt there, drenched in silence and failure, the weight of it pressing until he couldn't move.

Then suddenly, he slowly rose. His face was blank – too blank. No fury on the surface, no sorrow, just cold stillness, like a weapon being drawn. He turned his gaze towards the fleeing captain, *Shane.*

That bastard was going to pay.

Shane clutched at his bleeding side, barely managing to stay upright as he limped away, dragging one leg behind him. His breath came in ragged gasps. He spotted something on the ground – a grenade, just within reach.

The grenade exploded with a sharp *crack*, and Shane was thrown backwards, landing hard, dirt and smoke clouding the air.

Duncan appeared behind the wounded captain, his voice flat and almost bored as he said, 'I threw the grenade far from you so it wouldn't kill you. Should've accounted for the bloody shrapnel, though.'

Shane tried to drag himself forward using what little strength he had left in his fingers, smearing blood across the dirt as he went. The pathetic sight made Duncan's lip curl.

'Do you honestly think you can escape me?' Duncan's tone was low and dangerous. The captain whimpered but did not answer. That silence snapped something in Duncan.

'Oi. I'm talking to you.'

He did not wait. Duncan raised his pistol and fired into Shane's calf at point-blank range. The leg jerked violently, bone punching through flesh; the captain's scream ripped through the ruins, raw and feral. Duncan did not even blink. If anything, the sound irritated him.

'I'm not going to kill you,' Duncan said, his voice cold as steel. 'But who said you need to be intact when I hand you over?'

He stepped closer, planted a boot on Shane's back to pin him down, and shot him through the elbow. The crack of bone was louder than the gunshot. Shane shrieked – high, broken, animal. Duncan felt the vibrations of that scream through his boot but pressed down harder, grinding the captain into the dirt.

'Oh, shut it,' he snarled. 'You've no idea how much worse I can make this.'

Shane writhed, sobbing, but Duncan was not finished. The next shot punched clean through the captain's other wrist. Blood sprayed up Duncan's arm. Shane's screams dissolved into a wet, choking cry, then into nothing at all.

His body went slack.

Jaw hanging open. Eyes rolled upwards, unseeing. Drool and tears mixed on his ruined face.

'Oi!' Duncan barked, giving Shane's cheek a sharp backhand. No response. Not even a flinch. 'Wake up!'

Nothing.

Duncan crouched, checked the man's pulse with rough fingers, and let out a quiet, irritated huff. 'Passed out.'

He stared down at the mangled limbs – arms useless, legs little better – and felt nothing but disgust.

'That'll keep you from using your arms and legs ever again,' he muttered, turning away. Then, louder, spitting the words over his shoulder, 'Stay right there, you fucking degenerate piece of shit.'

Duncan turned back to Matthew's lifeless body, gathering him into his arms. The boy's weight was too light. Too still.

He gave a broken smile – hollow, bitter. 'Don't worry, kid ... I didn't let the bad guy get away. Even though I couldn't save you ...'

His voice cracked. Tears slipped down his face. 'I couldn't save you ... I couldn't ...'

Grief surged, raw and violent. He clenched his fists and slammed them into the floor. Once. Twice. Again.

'You worthless bastard!' he shouted at himself. 'You couldn't save one fucking child!'

His cries echoed through the silence. His shoulders shook as he bent over, forehead pressed to the bloodstained ground.

Why him? Why did it have to be Matthew – so young, so full of life?

The boy deserved better. A future. A chance.

But all Duncan could do now was weep.

Alone. Helpless.

And too late.

Time passed, and the Floran military eventually arrived at the scene. The ground was littered with the lifeless bodies of soldiers, their blood staining the earth. Duncan's face was a mask of dirt and dried blood as he sat on the ground, his head bowed in guilt. Captain Shane, who had ordered the attack, lay unconscious nearby.

The commanding officer of the military approached Duncan and inquired, 'What happened here?'

Duncan explained the situation. 'The captain over there ordered his men to kill innocent civilians. I stopped him ...' he said as he pointed at the captain.

The officer asked, 'Do you have proof of what you say?'

'My partner, Hendrik Jénmar, recorded the scene with his computer as evidence.' Duncan retrieved a card with Jénmar's contact information from his pocket. 'Here's his number.' Duncan handed the card to the officer and added, 'Contact him and then send it to the colonel.'

The military officer nodded and ordered his men to take the captain into custody. 'He will answer for his crimes when he wakes up.' Then the officer turned his attention back to Duncan. 'And you too.'

Duncan narrowed his eyes in response. 'For what?'

'In case you're lying about the situation,' the officer stated. Duncan's scowl remained, and the officer continued. 'You *did* kill many of our officers. If what you're saying is true, we will take into consideration that you acted justifiably. If you're lying, you will be thrown in prison for murder and treason, likely facing a life sentence. I'm afraid you wouldn't be treated nicely.'

Duncan accepted the gravity of the situation and told the officer, 'Do as you wish, but I assure you that the recording is no lie.'

'Very well,' the officer replied.

Duncan followed the officer and his subordinates, leaving the area behind. He was left to brood and reflect on the harrowing events that had unfolded. The sorrow and regret for not being able to save the innocent boy weighed on him, and he knew that he would never be the same again.

Chapter XXX

SORROW AND REGRETS

Matthew's heart pounded as he stood on the pitch, surrounded by roaring spectators and teammates. The sun cast a warm glow over the field. The school football tournament had reached its final match.

Nerves churned in his stomach. This was his moment – he couldn't afford to falter. He glanced at the stands. His mum sat forward on the edge of her seat, eyes locked on him.

The whistle blew.

The match unfolded fast and tense. The score stayed 0–0. Matthew darted across the field, searching for an opening, but the opposing defence held strong.

Then came the break.

Matthew sprinted towards the goal, feet pounding the grass, weaving through defenders with sharp turns and quick footwork. The ball stayed close. He saw his chance.

With a flick of his foot, he struck. The ball soared past the goalkeeper's outstretched hands.

A beat of silence – then the crowd erupted.

He'd scored.

Cheers thundered. Matthew's gaze shot to the stands. His mum was on her feet, beaming, clapping with pride.

'Nice one, honey!'

Joy flooded him. It wasn't just his win – it was theirs. She'd always believed in him. And now, that belief had carried him here.

He vowed silently: he'd keep going. For her.

Days later, Duncan stood motionless beneath the scalding spray of the shower, arms braced against the tiled wall, steam curling around his head like smoke from a battlefield. The water pummelled his back, but it wasn't enough to drown out the silence in his chest – the kind that echoed.

Matthew.

The name alone felt like a knife twisting in his gut. That stupid, sweet little grin. The way the kid had looked up to him, clinging to every word like Duncan was some kind of bloody hero. And what had he done? Stood there – right there – when the boy was shot. A twelve-year-old. Gunned down in front of him. Too close to stop it. Too slow to change anything. Too fucking late.

His fists trembled against the tiles.

He remembered the moment – the captain's smug, steady aim, the shot cracking through the air, Matthew crumpling at his side. Duncan had already torn through the captain's men by then. They were nothing. But the captain … the captain he didn't kill. No. He made him suffer. And still, it hadn't been enough.

His chest tightened. His breath caught.

And then he snapped.

'Fuck!' He roared, slamming his fist into the wall with a sickening thud. 'Fuck this war! Fuck everything! Fuck Lance! Fuck the Night Hawks! Fuck the Red Lions!'

His voice cracked with fury. 'This is not fair. This is not fucking fair! Why did he have to die? Why couldn't I save him!?'

His knees buckled, and he collapsed onto the cold shower floor. The water beat down on him like rain on a ruined statue. He barely felt it. Hands clutching his head, he trembled – silent, shaken, breaking apart.

'I'm so fucking worthless …' The words spilled out of him like poison. 'I should've protected him … I should've—'

He dug his fingers into his scalp, wishing he could tear the memory from his skull. But it was etched there. Permanently. Like a brand.

'I promised him he'd be safe ...' His voice broke, barely audible. 'I promised ...'

He knelt there as the water poured down, tears mixing with the heat and steam. The weight of it all pressed down on him, suffocating.

'Father ...' he whispered, voice hoarse and trembling. 'I couldn't save him ...'

The silence that followed was unbearable. Duncan stayed there, on the shower floor, drenched and broken, letting the grief bleed out from somewhere deep and hidden.

No mission. No orders. No vengeance.

Just loss.

The hours had blurred into something shapeless. Duncan sat slouched on the sofa, his old slippers scuffed at the toes, a white vest clinging loosely to his frame. The quiet pressed in around him, heavy and unmoving. His arm still throbbed faintly where the bullet had grazed him, and a dull ache pulsed along his bruised cheek. He hadn't bothered with painkillers. He didn't see the point.

When the doorbell rang, it cut through the silence like a blade.

He didn't move. Just sat there, staring at nothing. For a moment, he considered ignoring it. Let them knock. Let them wait. But the sound came again, and with a muted sigh, he forced himself upright.

Each step towards the door felt like dragging himself through fog. Not from injury, though that didn't help – but from something heavier. The kind of weight that settled in the chest and made everything feel like too much effort.

He opened the door slowly.

Sara stood there, her usual spark dimmed, brows drawn tight with concern. She said nothing at first, just looked at him – really looked at him – her eyes flitting briefly to the bruise on his cheek, then down to his arm.

Next to her was Elisa, hands tucked behind her back, eyes flicking nervously to his.

Duncan's gaze lingered on her – on the way she shifted slightly, as though hiding something. His brow creased.

His mother immediately embraced him in a warm hug. 'Oh, Duncan, thank God you're alright. We were so worried. You weren't answering any of our calls, and Elisa and I were panicking.'

'I see …' Duncan's response lacked energy and emotion.

'What happened during that mission?' Sara asked.

Duncan hesitated, averting his gaze. He spoke reluctantly. 'The military took me into custody to answer for what happened in the incident.'

Sara furrowed her brow. 'Why?'

'I … I don't wanna go into detail …'

Sara offered a gentle smile. 'Come on, Duncan. Share it with us. Let it off your chest.'

Duncan's irritation surfaced. 'I ended up having to kill many Red Lion officers. They committed war crimes by murdering Night Hawk followers, and I tried to save a boy named Matthew, but I failed.'

'Oh ...' she uttered.

Duncan's gaze turned distant, his demeanour impassive.

Sara attempted to uplift the mood with a smile. 'At least you're back in one piece ...'

Duncan immediately shot her with a cold glare causing her smile to instantly fade. He was being cold, but who could blame him? After the incident, it had become difficult for him to truly care about his surroundings.

Sara stole a nervous glance at Elisa before speaking up. 'Well, Elisa has something important to say.' Turning towards Elisa, Sara gestured for her to step forward. 'Go on.'

Her hands concealed behind her back, Elisa took hesitant steps towards Duncan. 'I ... I came here to present you with a gift.'

Duncan's expression remained impassive as he dryly replied, 'A gift ...?'

'Y–yes ... It is to express our deep gratitude for your tireless efforts in keeping Flora safe. Your mother and I truly appreciate the risks you've been taking to help the military. It is our way of saying thank you.'

Duncan fixed his gaze on Elisa, taking a moment of silence before speaking sarcastically. 'Oh ... How sweet.'

Unfazed by his lacklustre response, Elisa nervously pleaded. 'Please, open it.'

Duncan opened the gift box to reveal a sleek silver wristwatch.

'A wristwatch?'

'Yes, I hope you like it ...' Elisa smiled.

As Duncan continued to study Elisa's face, silence hung heavy in the air. No number of gifts would help make him feel better. Despite their efforts, he couldn't shake off the sombre mood that enveloped him. He sensed Sara's growing annoyance, her hands finding their way to her hips in a gesture of frustration. It was clear she couldn't contain her irritation any longer.

'I thought you'd show a bit more gratitude, considering Elisa went out of her way to bring you this gift. A little appreciation wouldn't hurt.' Sara fell silent, observing Duncan's expression. Softening her tone, she spoke gently. 'It was meant to cheer you up, especially after everything you've been through.'

Duncan's frustration permeated his cold reply. 'I appreciate both of you coming, but I'd prefer to be alone. Not in the mood for conversation, as you can see.' He moved towards the doorway, attempting to close the door, but Sara swiftly blocked his way with her hand.

'Hold on, Duncan! Please, don't be like that,' Sara exclaimed, her plea escaping in a quick breath. Leaning in closer, she whispered, 'I can sense you're going through tough times, but I ... *we* genuinely want to help you.'

Duncan, returning his attention to Sara, softened at her words.

'I don't want to see you drowning in grief,' Sara continued. 'It just breaks my heart.'

Breaks my heart ...

Her words settled in his chest like a slow-burning ember, stirring something raw. It was a reminder of the depth of their bond, the unspoken connection that bound them together as family. Her sincerity pierced through his defences, chipping away at the walls he'd erected around his heart. In her eyes, he saw not judgment but understanding – a silent acknowledgment of his struggles.

Sara suggested, 'Let's head inside and talk about it in more detail. I'll listen to everything, if that's okay with you?'

Duncan remained silent, contemplating whether he should open up. While he appreciated her willingness to listen, he couldn't shake off what Elisa had told him about suppressing his feelings. After a brief pause, he finally relented, gesturing for his mother to lead the way into the house. Inside, Duncan took a seat on the sofa.

'Okay, tell me everything,' Sara said.

Duncan sank into the sofa, his shoulders slouched. The room seemed to close in on him, the walls echoing the silence that had settled between him and Sara, who was still standing beside him. She exchanged a concerned glance with her son.

Hesitation gripped him as his eyes flickered between Sara and the floor. The room felt charged with unspoken emotions. Finally, he sighed and began to open up. Duncan explained what had happened at the Ballylawn region.

After sharing with her, he was met with a warm hug.

'You did all that you could,' she whispered.

As Sara wrapped her arms around him, Duncan stood stiff at first, his body tense with the remnants of everything he'd held in for far too long. But slowly – almost imperceptibly – his shoulders eased beneath her touch.

A rush of conflicting emotions surged within him: shame, sorrow, relief. He hadn't wanted to let it out, hadn't wanted to be seen like this. And yet ... here she was. No judgment. No demands. Just her.

Her warmth, her scent, the way she held him – it pulled something loose inside him.

And then, without a sound, a single tear slipped down his cheek. Then another.

Not sobs. Not brokenness.

Just tears – quiet, unannounced – falling like the rain that comes after the storm has already passed.

He didn't wipe them away.

He let them fall.

For the first time in a long time, he didn't feel weak for it.

Elisa stood outside, patiently waiting. She observed Duncan and Sara emerging from the house.

'Elisa, I'll hang out with you, but it won't be for long,' Duncan said.

Elisa widened her eyes, surprised by Duncan's agreement. 'Oh, that's incredibly kind of you, Mr Saul.'

'Just bear with me ...'

He retreated into his home momentarily to select an outfit. Soon, Duncan appeared wearing a black hoodie adorned with a flaming football logo on his chest, paired with comfortable jeans and his well-worn Converse shoes.

Duncan announced in a subdued tone, 'I'm ready.'

'Well ... I'll leave you two to it ... I'll head back now, but feel free to give me a call when you're finished,' Sara said.

Elisa nodded. 'Very well. We shall see you later, Mrs Saul.' She smiled warmly and gestured for Duncan to follow. 'Shall we, Mr Saul?'

Duncan grumbled, his reluctance still apparent. 'Ugh. Fucking hell ...'

The two of them left Duncan's house, with Elisa leading him to the playground in the nearest park to his home. Duncan, with his hands tucked in his pockets, questioned the purpose.

'Why are we at the park?'

'I thought it would be good to get some fresh air,' Elisa said, trying to sound upbeat. 'You've been inside all day, and sometimes a change of scenery helps.'

Duncan crossed his arms. 'A playground, Elisa? Really? Of all places?' He shot her a sharp look, his patience thinning. 'You think being around swings and slides is going to make me forget that I couldn't save him?'

Elisa winced at his words, realising how her suggestion must have sounded. 'That's not what I meant, Mr Saul ... I just–'

'I'm not a kid,' he interrupted, his voice tight. 'And this? This isn't helping.' His hands balled into fists in his pockets.

Elisa hesitated, trying to find the right words. 'I did not bring you here to make you feel worse. I just ... thought maybe some fresh air could help clear your head. I did not mean to upset you.'

Duncan let out a weary sigh. 'I think I'll just lie on the grass. Wake me if something important happens,' he muttered, turning away.

'Okay,' Elisa whispered, watching him head towards the grass. She sat down on the swing, her earlier optimism deflated. She only wanted to help, but clearly her attempt had backfired.

As she swung back and forth gently, Elisa's mind drifted to Duncan's pain, her concern for him deepening. *Was he still haunted by the boy's death*? Elisa couldn't help but wonder as she swung back and forth on the playground. She had seen the anguish in Duncan's eyes when he had spoken about not being able to save the innocent child.

Her thoughts turned to his mission, the relentless pursuit of the heretic who had attacked his father. She knew how deeply personal it was for him, but she also worried about the toll it took on his spirit. As she swung higher, her concern for Duncan only grew. She wished she could find a way to ease his burden, to help him find a moment of peace. But for now, all she could do was be there for him.

Duncan lay on the grass, drifting into slumber. Elisa decided to join him, sitting on the grass nearby. While Duncan slept, she listened attentively to his mutterings, catching his words.

'Father, I failed to save him ... I couldn't save him. Just like I couldn't save you ...'

Was the boy's death somehow linked to his father? Elisa noticed that Duncan often got very upset when he failed to help someone, whether it was his father, Ryonil or the boy he had mentioned. She glanced at him briefly, then sat up, grasping a blade of grass and using it to gently tickle Duncan's face. He twitched and opened his eyes.

Elisa spoke with a playful tone. 'Mr Saul, it seems you fell asleep.'

Duncan stretched his neck and replied, 'Yeah, seems like I did.' Duncan furrowed his brow, casting a questioning gaze at Elisa. 'Wait ... Were you watching me sleep, girl?'

Elisa nervously scratched her cheek with her index finger, her face reddening in embarrassment. 'Uh ... Yes, I caught a glimpse.'

Duncan averted his gaze, his eyebrows knitting together. 'Okay ...?'

Putting her hands together, Elisa composed herself and asked, 'So, do you want to head into town next?'

Standing up from the grass, Duncan shrugged nonchalantly. 'Whatever.'

As they made their way towards the town, Elisa skipped along, her joy evident in the sway of her hands behind her back. Turning to Duncan, she spoke up, her tone sincere. 'Mr Saul, I've been meaning to ask you something.' Duncan simply frowned and Elisa asked, 'Why must you continue to work yourself like a machine?'

She couldn't help but worry about Duncan. His dedication was undeniable, but it came at a cost she feared he didn't fully grasp. He was pushing himself too hard. She felt that this question needed to be asked.

Duncan glanced aside. 'It's a requirement. People are in constant need ... I need to disregard my well-being for others, to ensure safety. Uncle Konrad taught me that a hero always needs a villain to defeat or they'll never be called one.'

Elisa sighed in response. 'Mr Saul, while I honour your work, I have to state the flaw in your methods. You disregarding your well-being isn't always the right thing to do. You need to worry about yourself, too, you know.' His determination was admirable, she acknowledged, but it couldn't come at the cost of his own well-being. Elisa sighed, frustration mingling with her empathy. She just wanted to help him find a healthier balance.

Duncan answered strongly. 'I do worry about myself ... I don't wanna die before finding the heretic that attacked my father. I must get that done ...'

Elisa folded her arms and gave him a sullen look. 'You make it sound like the problems you have or the duty you must do is yours alone to handle. You don't have to shoulder this all yourself ... Think about it – why do superheroes have sidekicks to help them?'

Duncan frowned, looking unconvinced. 'I don't see what you're getting at, Kid ... I've got Jénmar watching my back.'

Elisa grumbled, her frustration evident. 'I see you're still using that nickname ...'

'What?' Duncan asked, confused.

'Never mind.' Elisa waved it off. 'What I'm saying is, have you truly opened up to Jénmar? Have you shared your struggles and fears with him?' She challenged him pointedly.

Duncan averted his gaze, his silence speaking volumes.

Elisa firmly looked at Duncan with sharpness in her tone. 'You should realise, Mr Saul, that you're only human. You have limits just like everyone else.'

Duncan folded his arms and retorted. 'I'm aware of that. Don't forget what I said earlier about making the world a better place.'

'I understand your perspective, Mr Saul, but I firmly believe there's more to life than one's duty. Continuously chasing your goals without attending to your well-being may lead to eventual breakdown.'

Duncan argued. 'Yes, but a strong man must be able to carry his own weight, no matter what challenges come his way.'

'But a man cannot do everything by himself.'

Duncan delivered a firm look at Elisa, and he replied, 'I would love to argue with you all day, Elisa, but I don't feel like debating on my method of action right now. So, I politely ask you to leave me alone ...' Duncan's arms remained folded, his demeanour aloof. He maintained his silence, seemingly unresponsive to her words.

Recognising the need to respect boundaries, Elisa spoke softly. 'Very well. Should you feel inclined to share your emotions with me, I would appreciate your openness, though I understand that it's entirely your decision.' Elisa, learning the importance of allowing Duncan the space he required during this difficult time, understood that forcing him to share his feelings wasn't the solution.

Duncan's eyes narrowed further, his silence persisting as he maintained a defensive posture. After a beat, Duncan finally uttered, 'Fine!'

Elisa looked at him, taken aback. She noticed tears welling up in his eyes, a surprising revelation. It seemed that Duncan was indeed grappling with a profound emotional struggle. Was grief affecting him more deeply than she had realised?

Duncan continued. 'It's not fair! I couldn't save that innocent child. Why did he have to die? What was it all for? It's like ... in times of war, people's morality turns to shit! First Ryonil and now him. Why does this have to happen? Is this war ever going to fucking end!?'

Duncan's outburst left Elisa stunned, her eyes wide with surprise. She had never expected him to react with such raw emotion.

His voice cracked as tears streamed down his face. 'I failed to save him. He had a dream ... He wanted to become a football player ... and I couldn't protect him. I'm such a failure.'

Elisa shook her head. 'No, Mr Saul, that is not true. You mustn't blame yourself for what happened. You are not responsible for the tragedies that befall others.'

She watched him, the way his shoulders tensed – as if guilt clung to every inch of him.

'But I was there … I should've done more. I should've done a better job of protecting him. Maybe then he would still be alive.'

Elisa's heart clenched. There was something unbearable about hearing that kind of regret – not from a stranger, but from someone like Duncan. Someone so strong. So unrelentingly guarded.

'You cannot carry the weight of the world on your shoulders, Mr Saul. It is a heavy burden that no one should bear alone. We all have our limits, our vulnerabilities. You did what you could with the resources and knowledge you had at the time.'

For a moment, Duncan didn't speak. Then, quietly, he wiped his tears with the back of his hand – a small, aching gesture.

'But it wasn't enough,' he said. 'I let him down. I let myself down. It's too hard to be a hero … I don't want to see anyone suffer … Anymore.'

Elisa's breath caught. She had always known there was pain behind his hardened exterior, but seeing it – raw and unguarded – struck something deep within her. The mercenary she'd come to admire, known for his unwavering strength, looked fragile in that moment. Human. Achingly so.

Tears welled in his eyes, and Elisa found herself momentarily stunned. She had never seen him like this – vulnerable, fractured. The suddenness of it, the way his voice cracked under the weight of grief, unravelled every preconception she had of him.

Without thinking, her hand reached out, resting gently on his arm. She didn't speak. There were no perfect words, nothing that could erase his pain – but in that quiet gesture, she hoped to share just enough of it to ease the weight he carried.

Her fingers trembled slightly against the fabric of his sleeve. Her heart ached not just for his sorrow, but for how long he must have carried it alone.

She looked at him then – truly looked – and her eyes softened, reflecting something beyond sympathy. A deep, unspoken understanding.

He didn't have to be a hero for her. He just had to let himself be seen.

'It is natural to feel that way, but you must remember that you are only human. We all make mistakes and we cannot change the past. What truly matters is how we learn and grow from our experiences.'

'I just wish I could've saved him. He deserved so much more.'

'You cared for him deeply, Mr Saul, and that speaks volumes about your character. Sometimes, despite our best efforts, circumstances are beyond our control. It is important to acknowledge the love and care you gave rather than dwelling on what you cannot change.'

Duncan's tears slowly subsided.

Elisa beamed with excitement as she responded. 'Allow me to take you to a place that will cheer you up.'

'And where's that?'

With a mischievous smile, Elisa shook her head playfully. 'I'm not telling ... it's a surprise.'

Chapter XXXI

SALVATION

Duncan wondered where he was going as Elisa tugged at his arm, leading him towards a place he hadn't expected: the Ocean Cinema.

Duncan glanced at the sign and asked, 'The movies?'

Elisa raised her hands in the air enthusiastically. 'Yes!'

'Elisa, what're we watching?'

With a delighted expression, Elisa replied, 'A sci-fi movie called *Galaxy Ranger*.'

Duncan couldn't help but express his confusion. 'Really? I thought girls like you were interested in romantic movies.'

Elisa let out a small hum, pondering Duncan's statement. She then shared her opinion. 'Romantic movies …? That's a bit of a cliché. I prefer to watch anything, as long as it's not horror. However, if you so desire, we can explore alternative options.'

Duncan shook his head. 'No, it's okay. Let's go in.' At this point, he simply wanted to get through the event, even if it meant embracing an unexpected movie choice.

Together, they entered the Ocean Cinema, and Duncan couldn't help but reflect on the day so far. He was grateful for Elisa's efforts to lift his spirits, even if he struggled to fully engage in the experience.

The two entered the cinema suite and settled into their seats amidst a modest crowd. Elisa wore her glasses, protecting her eyes from the screen's glare.

As *Galaxy Ranger* began, Duncan's attention was drawn to the screen where a space adventure was unfolding. The protagonist, in his space suit and helmet, ventured onto an unknown planet filled with peculiar creatures. *Sci-fi*, Duncan noted with a hint of curiosity. It was a welcome departure from his usual routine.

Elisa's offer of popcorn surprised him, and he momentarily hesitated before accepting. It had been a while since he'd been to a movie, let alone with someone as enthusiastic as Elisa. But then, their hands brushed against each other and Duncan couldn't help but react.

'What the ...?'

The unexpected contact had caught him off guard. Elisa's swift withdrawal left him with mixed feelings. Her blush and shy, apologetic demeanour made him momentarily unsure of how to react. Studying her for a moment, Duncan slowly averted his gaze, and they resumed watching the film in silence.

As the movie concluded, the two emerged from the cinema suite. *That flick was a bit different from the usual rubbish,* Duncan thought as they exited the cinema. He appreciated the imaginative world of *Galaxy Ranger* where futuristic technology and extraterrestrial life took centre stage.

Elisa shared her thoughts on the film. 'The movie's setting was truly fascinating. A world unfamiliar to us yet with glimpses of familiarity. The technology they portrayed has the potential for realisation in our modern era. We simply require the necessary resources and funding.'

'I reckon our world's gonna shape up like *Galaxy Ranger*. Over time, we've seen weapons change, from blades and bows to guns and knives. Gotta admit, the idea of laser guns or laser swords as weapons is pretty cool.'

Elisa concurred. 'I agree ... The utilisation of solar energy as a power source adds an innovative touch. Additionally, the exploration of extraterrestrial life forms caught my attention.'

'Their physical appearance looks weird in comparison to the non-humans we see here on Earth.'

Elisa agreed. 'Yes, the non-humans there looked quite different. It piques my curiosity to discern the difference between extraterrestrial and the non-human creatures.'

Duncan, deep in thought, tried to unravel Elisa's question. 'That's simple, I think? The creatures in our world are often associated with magic, while those from outer space ...' He paused, his brow furrowed in perplexity. 'When I really think about it, what *is* the difference between the beings from outer space and those found on Earth?'

'Maybe the technology they use?' Elisa asked.

'Maybe.'

Shaking off his contemplation, Elisa redirected their attention. 'Regardless, would you like to venture towards the hills? There's a sight I wish to show you.'

Acquiescing, Duncan said, 'Okay ...'

The sun began its descent, painting the sky the colour of vibrant orange as clouds scattered across the horizon. The two found themselves at the village harbour, guided by Elisa to a vantage point that overlooked the picturesque village and the vast expanse of the sea. Elisa walked towards the barricade, her hands gently resting on the bars. She turned to Duncan with a warm smile.

'It's a splendid view, isn't it?'

Duncan couldn't deny the beauty of the scene unfolding before him. The sun's descent, the picturesque village and the vast expanse of the sea. It was a sight he rarely allowed himself to enjoy, and he found himself appreciating it more in Elisa's presence. Her enthusiasm and the nostalgia she shared added a layer of warmth to the moment, making it all the more precious.

Elisa walked around the barricade and stepped onto the grassy hill, seeking an even grander perspective of the village. Duncan followed suit, joining her, and softly spoke with dryness.

'Yeah, the village appears so beautiful. It's nothing short of a miracle that it has remained untouched by the war.'

Elisa's smile widened as she nodded in agreement. 'Indeed, I concur. This place reminds me of the family vacations we used to take. We often encountered sights like these ... They were truly breathtaking ...'

Duncan remained silent, his attention focused on Elisa.

'Mr Saul, may I ask you something? Do you believe that attaining your goals is the sole source of happiness?'

Duncan folded his arms, his tone firm. 'Of course, that's been the driving force behind my entire existence.'

Elisa's eyes sparkled as she delivered a bright smile. 'Mr Saul, I believe that happiness can be found in the present moment. You should embrace the joy of the journey. If you believe that happiness will only come once you achieve your dreams, it becomes a futile pursuit. What if that dream never materialises? Will you spend your life unfulfilled?'

He listened to her speak – about happiness, about purpose – and for once, didn't immediately dismiss it as naïve. Her words struck something in him, something quiet and long-neglected.

Could happiness really be found in the present moment? The thought felt foreign. Alien. His life had always been a mission – a chain of objectives, each one darker than the last. There had never been room for anything else.

Duncan looked away, a scowl etched across his face, more from discomfort than defiance. He couldn't argue with her – not because she was wrong, but because deep down, he feared she might be right.

Elisa's voice remained soft, unwavering.

'I firmly believe that you can find happiness, Mr Saul, even without capturing the culprit. If you solely fixate on your goals, you risk becoming nothing more than a machine. Your purpose in life extends beyond your aspirations. There are other things worth living for ...'

He kept his gaze fixed on the horizon. The sun bled orange across the clouds, casting long shadows over the field. He said nothing. He didn't know what to say.

The silence stretched, not cold – just full. Then, from the corner of his eye, he caught the motion: Elisa, cheeks tinged pink, slowly reaching towards him.

Her fingers brushed his, tentative at first, then curled around his hand with a quiet certainty. Duncan blinked, looking down at their joined hands – slender and warm in his calloused grip. Then, slowly, he met her eyes.

Still he said nothing. But he didn't let go.

Elisa tucked a strand of hair behind her ear and offered him a small, sincere smile.

'Let us cherish this moment together ...'

Something in him cracked – not in pain, but in release. He hadn't realised how tightly he'd been wound until that moment. A smile crept onto his face, hesitant and unpractised, but real.

As they sat together beneath the fading sky, Duncan let the stillness settle around him. The pain of the past was still there – it always would be – but for once, it didn't drown everything else. Her hand in his was a quiet anchor. Her presence, a balm.

It was just a moment. A simple, human moment. But it reminded him that there was more to life than grief and vengeance.

And as the light faded into dusk, Duncan held her hand just a little tighter.

After their date, the duo found themselves walking through the town at night. Duncan gingerly slid his hands into his pockets as he turned towards Elisa.

'Thanks. For cheering me up ... I really appreciate it ...'

But the memory of the boy's death still lingered in the background, a reminder of the harsh realities of his world. It wasn't something he could easily shake off, and the pain it caused was still raw. Was he feeling better? He wasn't sure.

Elisa had certainly brought a moment of respite, but the wounds ran deep.

Elisa's smile widened. 'You are most welcome, Mr Saul. You must never doubt yourself. I know deep down that you will find the heretic one day. I believe in you, truly.'

Duncan's weary expression softened slightly, touched by Elisa's faith in him. He locked eyes with her. 'You know, Elisa,' he replied, his voice steadier now. 'You're right. I couldn't save that boy, but that doesn't mean I should give up.'

Elisa smiled and nodded.

'Well, that's enough for today. I'll inform Mum that you're ready to be picked up.'

After what felt like an eternity of waiting, Duncan's ears perked up as he heard a faint noise nearby. It grew louder and closer, piquing his curiosity. He turned to Elisa and asked, 'Wait, what's that noise?'

Elisa seemed equally curious. It echoed through the air, much like a motorcycle's roar.

Finally, the source of the sound revealed a figure in a stylish bike jacket and an open-faced helmet with dark goggles. The person braked the motorcycle and quickly took off their helmet, letting their hair fall free. Duncan saw that it was his mother, who greeted them with a cheerful, 'Hey, kids!'

Duncan's surprise was evident as he furrowed his brow and exclaimed, 'Mum?'

Elisa mirrored Duncan's reaction, exclaiming in disbelief. 'Mrs Saul?'

Sara's smile widened as she dismounted the bike. She addressed the two with enthusiasm. 'Check this baby out!'

'You finally bought a motorcycle. When did it arrive?' Elisa questioned.

'Just recently, while you two were away,' Sara replied proudly.

Duncan, inspecting the impressive machine, asked, 'Oh, what type is it?'

Beaming with pride, Sara provided a detailed explanation. 'It's a two-wheel straight-three engine that can reach speeds of up to a hundred and twenty-five miles per hour. It even comes with an open-face helmet, and best of all' – she gestured towards her jacket excitingly – 'they got me a jacket, too. How cool is that?'

'Great, now you can go far without having to take the car,' Duncan said.

Sara hummed in agreement. With contagious excitement, she gestured with her thumb towards the backseat, inviting Elisa to join her. 'So, Elisa, want to hop on the back? I can take you for a ride around the streets if you'd like.'

'Certainly, Mrs Saul.'

'You two have fun, okay,' said Duncan.

'Okay. Bye, Mr Saul.'

Sara, preparing her engine, yelled back over the revving sound. 'Okay, see ya, Duncan! Thanks for taking Elisa out today. You're a true gentleman.'

As the motorcycle roared to life, the two riders set off, leaving Duncan alone. He couldn't help but smile, appreciating the joy on their faces, before continuing on his own path.

Chapter XXXII

A RISING UPSTART

Jeremy sat alone at the sturdy wooden table in the dimly lit confines of his home, the soft glow of the lamp casting elongated shadows across the room. The air was heavy with the aroma of aged whiskey mingling with the faint scent of cedarwood from the rustic furnishings.

A gentle knock echoed through the room, drawing attention to the entrance as a female Night Hawk stepped in. Her blonde ponytail swayed with each step, complementing her brown eyes.

'Hi, Anna. What brings you here?' Jeremy inquired.

'Jeremy, the leaked video is here. It's horrifying ... It shows the Red Lion army ruthlessly executing our followers,' Anna replied.

Jeremy nodded, his expression growing sombre. 'Show it to me.'

Anna handed Jeremy a tablet, and a chilling video began to play. The footage portrayed the Red Lion army's brutality as they mercilessly killed innocent civilians associated with the Night Hawks. Jeremy watched, his jaw tight and his fists clenched.

'Those monsters!' he shouted. His initial reaction was one of anger and righteous indignation. Anger at the inhumanity displayed by the Red Lions, anger at the senseless loss of innocent lives and anger at the injustice of it all. 'These atrocities can't go unanswered, Anna. The Red Lions will regret crossing us,' Jeremy declared.

Anna nodded.

'Do you know who recorded the video?' Jeremy asked, his tone sharp.

'One of our scouts identified him as Duncan Saul. The Heretic Hunter,' Anna replied.

Duncan Saul ...

The name struck a chord. Jeremy's brow furrowed as the memory resurfaced – the man who'd helped that woman deliver the letter. The same man who'd once head-butted him. The memory still stung – more to his pride than anything else.

He leant back slightly, mind churning. *What the hell is he playing at?* Duncan had aided Elisa. That much was certain. And yet ... he also handed them a tool powerful enough to sway public opinion. Why? Out of principle? Sympathy? Or was he playing both sides?

The thought didn't sit well. Jeremy hated uncertainty – and Duncan Saul was fast becoming a walking question mark.

Still, he shelved the unease. There were bigger priorities now. They had something far more valuable in their hands – truth, caught on camera. Proof that could shake the Red Lions to their foundations.

'We have the power to shift the tide in our favour, Jeremy. Let's expose their true nature to the world,' Anna urged, eyes gleaming.

He met her gaze, resolute.

'Yes. We'll release it – but it needs to spread everywhere. Cities, wastelands, borders. No one gets to look away.'

After a while, Jeremy stepped into Anna's house, the click of his boots echoing faintly against the hardwood floor. The place was dim, quiet – save for the soft hum of machines and the rhythmic tapping of keys. His eyes landed on Anna, seated in front of a wall of monitors, her face bathed in blue light, sharp and focused. She didn't look up, didn't need to. Her fingers moved with a speed and certainty that came from years of doing this.

'Jeremy, it's finished,' she said without turning. 'I've encrypted the video. No one can alter it. Once we send it out, it'll be everywhere – news outlets, socials, darknets. They won't be able to bury it.'

Jeremy gave a small nod, a slow breath leaving him. *Good.*

'Credit it to the Night Hawks. Make it clear – this is us pulling the curtain back. No more hiding. We're naming names and burning the façade they've lived behind.'

This wasn't just vengeance. It was messaging. It was identity. The Red Lions had built their narrative on control, honour, unity. Jeremy would gut it with truth.

Anna leant back, eyes still scanning the data. 'It'll be a rallying cry. People are angry. Lost. They'll come to us for direction. This'll bring new blood.'

Jeremy stood straighter, tension humming beneath his skin. He could already feel the shift coming.

'It's time they saw what the Red Lions really are. Butchers, cloaked in virtue.'

This wasn't only about justice. It was about power. Legitimacy. No more hiding in the wastelands like outlaws. If they were going to win, they needed to be more than a rebellion – they needed to become a movement.

He turned towards the door. 'Gather everyone at the bar. Tonight. I want them all there.'

'Understood,' Anna said without missing a beat.

Jeremy didn't reply. His mind was already ahead, racing through the next steps. The world was about to watch.

And he'd make damn sure they remembered the name *Night Hawks.*

The bar was packed – every table taken, every wall lined with Night Hawks. The stale scent of sweat, smoke, and tension filled the air. Jeremy stood before them, the flickering light of the video screen casting shifting shadows across the room. The leaked footage played out in harsh clarity. No edits. No filters. Just raw, brutal truth.

He watched their faces as they watched it. Stunned. Angry. Grieving.

Jeremy raised his voice, letting the fury in his chest bleed into every word.

'See, my comrades? See how those animals took our people's lives away from them?' He gestured sharply at the screen. 'And what does Reiman do? Tells us to wait. To sit on our hands like scared children. To hell with that!'

Murmurs rippled through the crowd – not just agreement, but frustration. It was building, and Jeremy could feel it. The same restlessness that gnawed at him had spread like fire in dry brush. They were tired of patience. Tired of orders that led nowhere.

They needed someone willing to act. He could be that man.

No – he *had* to be.

'Somebody new has to be in charge,' he said, voice ringing out. 'And that should be me.'

The shift was immediate. Interest, doubt, suspicion. They didn't hate the idea – but they weren't sold either. Not yet. Jeremy knew this would come. Respect wasn't enough. Not anymore.

'Why should we make you the leader?' someone challenged from the back.

Jeremy's jaw tightened. No hesitation now.

'Because if I'd been in charge, I would've acted. Just like I did when I gathered you all to rescue Lance. I didn't wait. I moved.'

That landed. Heads nodded. People remembered. He could see it – the way their eyes flicked towards each other, silently recalling that moment. When no one else stepped up, he had. But being bold wasn't the same as being *ready*.

Giovani, always the calm one, spoke next.

'Leadership means more than just taking action in the heat of the moment, Jeremy. It's about guiding us through the hardest choices. Are you ready for that responsibility?'

The words cut deeper than Jeremy expected. He paused.

Was he?

He took a breath, steadying the knot in his chest.

'I won't pretend to have all the answers,' he said honestly. 'I haven't led like this before. But I'll be damned if I stand by while more of us die. I'll fight for us with everything I've got. I swear it.'

He locked eyes with them – one by one – holding their gaze, daring them to see his resolve.

'We've suffered too much already. But we've always come through, together. I believe in this cause, and I believe in every one of you. Let's stop surviving in the shadows and start shaping the future we deserve.'

Silence. Then nods. Slow, but sure.

'You have our support, Jeremy,' someone said, firm and clear.

Voices followed. A chorus of trust. Of unity. Of rebellion.

Jeremy exhaled, steady but burning inside. This was just the beginning. The crown was heavy, but he was ready to bear it – for all of them.

The streets of Gothenburg were filled with worried whispers as anxious citizens gathered in small groups. The recent capture of Lance had left a void in the hearts of resistance fighters and instilled fear among the people.

Reiman strolled through the hallways of the Night Hawks' mansion. Inside, it offered an intriguing blend of renaissance-era aesthetics and modern technology. Cream-coloured, patterned walls adorned with fancy paintings gave it a unique charm. For security, the mansion had several CCTV cameras.

As the doors swung open, Reiman stepped outside, his stern expression becoming resolute. The assembled citizens turned their weary gazes towards him, and he stood before them with squared shoulders.

'My fellow citizens,' he said. 'I understand your fears, your anger and your frustration. The recent events have shaken us all, and I share your concern for our safety and the future of Gothenburg.'

A murmur rippled through the crowd as some nodded in agreement and others remained sceptical.

'But let me assure you,' Reiman continued, 'that the Night Hawks will not falter. We are planning our next move. The capture of Lance has not weakened our resolve.'

A voice rose from the crowd with bitterness. 'What good is your resolve if it only lands our leader in cuffs? What assurance do we have that the Night Hawks can protect us from the Red Lions!?'

Reiman locked eyes with the citizen who had spoken, acknowledging their pain. 'I understand your doubts. But know this – Lance knew the risks and he chose to take them for the greater good of Flora. We need to have faith in Lance so that he can bring peace between us and the Red Lions. We must be patient.'

'To hell with that! Why should we have peace with the Red Lions after they slaughter our followers in cold blood!?'

'What?' Reiman asked, his voice betraying genuine shock.

Another man chimed in. 'The Red Lions executed Night Hawk followers during the battle of the Ballylawn region. The news showed what they did! What's stopping them from doing the same thing to us!?'

Reiman's mind raced. He had not been informed about this, and yet the anger and fear in the crowd were undeniable.

How did this happen without my knowledge?

He needed to regain control, to calm the unrest.

'I … I was not aware of the full extent of what happened during the Battle of Ballylawn,' he admitted. 'But I can assure you, those responsible for such atrocities will not go unpunished. What the Red Lions did is unforgivable. The pain and loss suffered by our fellow Night Hawk followers is a wound we will carry together. But we must not let that anger blind us to the need for strategy.'

Reiman took a deep breath before continuing, trying to gather his thoughts. 'We have to be smart. Lance took these risks for a reason – to create the possibility of peace. We will not forget the bloodshed, but we must use it to fuel our resolve, not our rage.'

The tension in the courtyard was palpable as the citizens listened intently, their gazes fixed upon Reiman, seeking reassurance.

'But let me assure you,' Reiman continued, 'that we are not defenceless. The Night Hawks have endured hardships before, and we have learnt from them. We won't allow our people to be silenced or subjected to further acts of brutality.'

'How can we be so sure of your word?' the man asked.

'Yeah!' the people shouted in unison.

'Please, fellow citizens, remain calm. We are exerting our utmost efforts,' Reiman reassured.

'What efforts!? You waiting around while Lance is in jail!?'

Reiman stepped forward, addressing the people with a calm voice. 'I understand your doubts and concerns,' he acknowledged. 'Words alone may not be enough to quell your fears. But let me assure you that the Night Hawks are fully committed to this cause. We have dedicated our lives to fighting for justice, freedom and the safety of every citizen in Flora.'

Yet, despite his assurances, the citizens' faces remained etched with anger, scepticism lingering like a typhoon on the horizon. Reiman felt the mounting pressure, a sense that the Night Hawks stood on the precipice of a critical moment that would define their relationship with those they vowed to protect.

'I only ask for your trust and patience,' he said, meeting the eyes of each concerned citizen. But the citizens were not happy with that response.

'Trust and patience, my arse!'

'We need more than words, Reiman! We need action!'

Reiman couldn't deal with this anymore. He swiftly closed the mansion's gate, and in the midst of the uproar from the citizens, a man in the crowd hurled a can of fizzy drink at the gate. Ignoring the commotion, Reiman immediately made his way towards his office.

Reiman sank into his chair. His office exuded quiet authority, a reflection of years of discipline and strategy. The dark wooden desk stood at the centre, its polished surface flanked by stacked files and a softly humming monitor displaying intelligence reports. Behind him hung a large map, dotted with pins marking past victories. Framed commendations lined the walls, and a bookshelf of military history and leadership texts filled one corner – a room built for command, not comfort.

Thoughts of Lance stirred mixed emotions within him, challenging his faith. Doubt crept in, questioning the cost of their actions.

He said to himself, 'Lance. I hope that what you're doing is worth it.'

He leant back in his chair, his gaze drifting towards a framed photograph on his desk – a snapshot of happier times. Lance stood beside him, smiling with an arm around Reiman's shoulder.

'You always believed in the power of our cause,' Reiman mused. 'But the risks we're up against ... They're weighing heavily on all of us.'

Chapter XXXIII

RIFT IN LOYALTIES

Following the revelation of the Red Lions' involvement in war crimes during the battle of the Ballylawn region, Jeremy experienced a significant surge in his number of followers. The shocking news not only tarnished the reputation of the Red Lions but also served as a catalyst for Jeremy's growing support base.

Reiman was engrossed in a series of important documents in his office, the rhythmic scratching of his pen the only sound in the dimly lit room. The tranquillity shattered when the door burst open. A man strode in – one of Jeremy's people.

Reiman tensed, his instincts flaring. 'What's the meaning of this?'

The messenger stood firm. 'Sir, we've been ordered to take control of the Night Hawks.'

Reiman's eyes narrowed. 'Ordered? By whom?'

'Jeremy,' the man replied evenly. 'He demands the Night Hawks' loyalty to the new regime – and your arrest.'

Silence hung between them. Reiman studied the man carefully, searching for any sign of deceit or hesitation. This wasn't a mercenary or a hired thug; this was someone who had once fought alongside him, a *Night Hawk*. Jeremy hadn't sent a stranger – he had sent someone Reiman might still listen to.

Reiman exhaled slowly. 'Why would Jeremy do this? We bled together for this cause. We fought for the people. Now, he turns on me?'

The man's expression remained unreadable. 'I don't have all the answers, sir. But you know as well as I do that Jeremy isn't the kind to leave loose ends.'

Reiman's stomach tightened at the implication.

He glanced at the documents on his desk – plans, supply routes, intelligence reports. If Jeremy had truly taken control, then everything Reiman had built was at risk. His men were at risk.

He straightened. 'I understand.'

The soldier blinked. 'Then you'll come quietly?'

'No. But I won't be reckless, either.' He locked eyes with the man. 'I still have people who believe in me. If Jeremy is doing this of his own will, I need to know why. If he's being forced into it, I need proof.'

The soldier's jaw tightened. 'Sir, I have my orders–'

Reiman exhaled, his fingers drifting subtly under his desk. Beneath the polished wood, he pressed a concealed button – an old failsafe for situations just like this.

Before the soldier could finish, the door behind him burst open with a loud crack. Armed Night Hawks stormed in, moving like a well-oiled machine. Weapons were drawn in an instant, and their commands were sharp.

'On your knees! Hands where we can see them!'

The soldier froze, hands rising instinctively, his face pale as he realised he was caught.

'Dammit,' he muttered under his breath.

Reiman stood slowly, straightening his coat. His eyes flicked over to the Night Hawks, all focused and ready. He then turned back to the messenger.

'I appreciate the message, but I can't have you running back to Jeremy just yet.' He nodded towards his men. 'Secure him. Unharmed.'

As the soldier was swiftly restrained, one of the Night Hawks spoke up. 'What should we do with him, sir?'

Reiman's gaze never wavered. 'Take him to the holding cell. He'll stay there until further notice. We need him alive for now.'

Once the man was led away, Reiman turned back to his desk, his mind already whirring with the implications of this sudden turn of events.

A Night Hawk stepped forward, his face tense with concern. 'What's next, sir?'

'Gather the rest of the Night Hawks,' he ordered. 'We'll meet at the safe house. We need to regroup and make sense of all this.'

Reiman's mind raced – Jeremy had pushed him into a corner, and the situation was now out of his control. But he wasn't about to back down. He'd faced worse odds before.

Reiman sought out Jeremy, his steps purposeful as he entered the room, accompanied by his men. The space was dimly lit, the soft glow of overhead lamps casting long shadows on the walls. The air carried a faint scent of aged wood and a trace of tension, as if the very walls were privy to the weighty conversations that had unfolded within.

The room was furnished with weathered wooden tables and chairs, evidence of the many discussions that had taken place within its confines. Faded maps pinned to the walls marked the territory of alliances forged and battles fought. A large, worn-out Night Hawk flag hung in a corner, bearing the emblem of a once-united cause now fractured by ideological differences.

Reiman's gaze swept across the faces of those who had once been his comrades, finally settling on Jeremy who was seated in a chair. Anna and Giovani stood faithfully beside him, flanked by several individuals who had also chosen to align themselves with the new regime. Jeremy's gaze met Reiman's for a moment.

Reiman's voice broke the silence. 'Jeremy, why have you done this? We were brothers, fighting for the same cause together. How could you turn against everything we stood for?'

Jeremy's expression remained stoic, devoid of the friendship they had once shared. 'Times change, Reiman,' he replied coldly. 'The Night Hawks aren't what they once were. The new regime promises results. They believe that the Night Hawks' passivity has caused more harm than good. They demand your loyalty, and your arrest is a necessary step in their plan.'

What is this new side of Jeremy? He's different ...

Jeremy didn't look at him as a friend – more like an obstacle standing in his way. 'Jeremy, what happened to you? What happened to the friendship we once had?'

'You're being naïve, Reiman. The world has grown darker and sacrifices must be made for the greater good. I chose to create the new regime because I believe it's the only path forward.'

Reiman stepped forward, his voice firm. 'You may have chosen a different path, Jeremy, but I won't abandon the Night Hawks. I won't betray the ideals we once had.' Reiman extended a hand, not in surrender but in an offer of reconciliation. 'Jeremy, it's not too late to make amends,' Reiman said. 'Cease this treachery.'

'No,' Jeremy declared. 'If you don't stand with me, then you stand against me.'

Jeremy's men, loyal to their leader, aimed their weapons at Reiman whose men mirrored the hostile gesture. In a tense standoff, both factions faced each other, locked in a dangerous stalemate. Reiman's eyes widened in disbelief, his heart sinking at Jeremy's words. The friendship they once had seemed shattered. The weight of betrayal pressed upon him, but he refused to let it consume him entirely.

'Jeremy.' Reiman's voice quivered with hurt. 'I understand your concern, and I do worry for Lance's as well. But removing me from leadership will only weaken us further.'

Jeremy's expression remained unyielding. 'Reiman, you've been an admirable leader, but we can't afford to be tied down by past ideals. The Night Hawks require decisive action.'

Reiman's voice resonated with a plea as he addressed his comrades, hoping to break through the turmoil that had engulfed them. 'Listen to reason, my friends. We are the Night Hawks, guardians of justice. Lance, our founding member, would never condone this path of violence and chaos. He sought to end the bloodshed, not perpetuate it.' He looked at Jeremy with disappointment. 'Jeremy, remember what Lance stood for. He would have wanted us to find a peaceful solution.'

Jeremy's gaze hardened. 'Reiman, Lance's absence has left us in despair. We can't wait idly for him to return. We must take action and fight for his freedom. It's our duty as Night Hawks.'

'But at what cost, Jeremy? If we abandon our principles, if we turn against one another, what will be left of the Night Hawks? We risk losing not only our integrity but also the very essence of what made us a force for good.' Reiman's eyes darted around the room, searching for any sign of hesitation, any sign of doubt. 'My comrades, remember the oaths we took when we joined the Night Hawks. We swore to protect and serve with honour. Let us not forget the values that have guided us thus far.'

As Reiman spoke, a silence settled over the room, broken only by the heavy breaths of the Night Hawks, their internal struggles playing out.

Jeremy retorted. 'Consider the news we've witnessed, my comrades. Where the Red Lions mercilessly executed our followers. What would stop them from doing the same thing to us? We can't stand idle and risk being extinguished one by one.'

A murmur of agreement rippled through the room. It seemed like Jeremy was winning this argument. Reiman didn't have a counter to the recent event. His words alone wouldn't convince the traitors.

One voice rose above the rest. 'He does make a valid point. If we don't take action, who's to say we won't suffer the same fate?'

'But violence and bloodshed will only perpetuate the cycle of destruction. We need to rely on Lance,' Reiman replied.

Jeremy retorted. 'Don't be naïve, Reiman. Do you honestly think that the Red Lions would let Lance have his way? I'm willing to take action, to fight and even die for our cause. If it means freeing Lance and ensuring the safety of our fellow Night Hawks, then it's a sacrifice I'm prepared to make.'

A sombre expression crossed the faces of the Night Hawks, their loyalty now divided. With a heavy heart, they turned towards Reiman, their former leader.

'I'm sorry, sir,' one of them murmured.

Reiman's eyes widened in disbelief as handcuffs were placed around his wrists, his heart heavy with a mix of sadness, frustration and betrayal. The Night Hawks he had once led who now stood before him had turned against him.

'Now, seize him!' Jeremy commanded.

'You're making a mistake, Jeremy!' Reiman pleaded. 'Our principles. They're being torn apart!'

Reiman's plea hung in the air, but it seemed to fall on deaf ears. The Night Hawks who had sided with Jeremy remained resolute in their decision, their loyalty firmly aligned with the new regime. They had chosen a different path, one that Reiman could no longer sway. Reiman was taken away.

Chapter XXXIV

UNVEILING SECRETS

Duncan stood at the door of Jénmar's house, waiting patiently for the man he had come to see. Finally, Jénmar opened the door.

'Jénmar, you called?' Duncan asked.

Jénmar nodded, his expression serious. 'Yeah, I wanted to speak with you. Come with me.'

They made their way towards Jénmar's work room, and Duncan settled into a comfortable chair as they entered.

'Duncan, I may have found a way to help you find your father and the culprit ...'

Duncan couldn't believe his ears. The opportunity to help find his father and the heretic seemed too good to be true. His eyes widened with anticipation, and he couldn't help but step closer to Jénmar, his excitement bubbling to the surface.

'Really? Tell me! Tell me!'

Jénmar raised his hand. 'Easy, easy!'

Realising his enthusiasm had got the better of him, Duncan stepped back, embarrassed, and sheepishly rubbed the back of his head. 'Sorry ...' Collecting himself, Duncan inquired eagerly, 'What information did you find?'

Jénmar leant back, sipping his coffee. 'During my research, I stumbled upon something that the AMOB had uncovered. They've come across a ruin at the far Northpoint of Syrida. They dispatched a missing agent named Richard Dickenson on an espionage mission to infiltrate the place.'

Duncan leant in, intrigued. 'How did you manage to uncover this information?'

Jénmar glanced away, hesitating before revealing his illicit actions. 'Yeah, so I had to do something illegal. I hacked into the AMOB's database. It was the only way to access the highly classified information.'

Surprised, Duncan commented. 'Well, well, well, Jénmar. Engaging in illegal activities ... apart from gambling, this is a new side of you.'

'Shh ... This is important, especially for you. This is a once-in-a-lifetime opportunity, and you mustn't waste it, kid.'

Duncan chuckled softly. 'I understand. I'm grateful.'

Returning to the main topic, Jénmar continued. 'Anyway, while Dickenson was there, he reported encountering a Jötunn guarding the place.'

Duncan's eyes widened in surprise at the revelation. 'A Jötunn?'

'Yeah.'

'What does this have to do with Dickenson?'

'His mission was to gather information about the place. It's rumoured that the ruin is guarded by a Jötunn eagle and you need to go inside to retrieve a certain item. You must beat the AMOB to it because they're keen on furthering their research.'

Jénmar played the recording he had obtained, and as the audio filled the room, the sounds of stuttering and rattling indicated a man's footsteps echoing through an unknown location. The recording continued on the computer, the voice speaking with a sense of urgency and discovery.

'Report, 19 August. Time, 12.37 p.m.

The Jötnar are very intelligent creatures with a mastery of magic that transcends most humans. They have acquired knowledge and written encrypted texts on the walls. These walls contain books written in their language.

Perhaps this is what Professor Levi hinted at in his publications, although he didn't provide full details about what had occurred.

I encountered a Jötunn who took the form of a dark eagle. In that form, he can speak the human language. The Jötunn identified himself as Hraesvelgr.

We engaged in conversation, and he possesses knowledge about the last individual who came here.

I didn't reveal much personal information to him, nor did I disclose my affiliation with the AMOB. He remains unaware that my purpose is to retrieve the artefacts and bring them back to headquarters.

I intend to keep it that way.'

Jénmar clicked on the next file, deciding to fast-forward through parts that were irrelevant to Duncan's immediate concerns. He continued the audio file.

'Report, 19 August. Time, 3.29 p.m.

As I further explore this place, I discover countless items and knowledge that remain unknown to humanity. I asked the Jötunn to provide descriptions of the effects of these artefacts.'

Jénmar skipped ahead, anticipating Duncan's interest. 'Let me fast-forward this bit …' The audio continued, revealing another piece of valuable information.

'A mask that can pinpoint the location of something or someone through the person's mind.'

Duncan's eyes widened with hope as he processed the implications. 'Really? So, there's a magical artefact that can pinpoint the location of my father and the culprit?'

Jénmar nodded. 'It seems so.'

A sigh of relief escaped Duncan's lips, his tension easing. 'Well, shit. That makes things a lot easier for me. Could you play towards the end of the recording?' Duncan asked.

Jénmar complied, clicking on the appropriate section. The audio file played, revealing the final entry.

'Report, 20 August. Time, 9.16 a.m.

This is my last day in this place. I will attempt to retrieve an artefact without alerting the Jötunn to my actions. Caution is of utmost importance.'

'Seems like it ends here,' Jénmar said.

Duncan pondered the new information. 'So, Professor Levi was there before?'

Jénmar nodded. 'Yeah, his findings were never made public. The AMOB kept the information he gathered for their own research purposes.'

Duncan's brows furrowed as he voiced his next concern. 'What I want to know is what happened to Dickenson? You mentioned he's missing, so the only logical conclusion I can come to is that he either deserted or was killed.'

'That's a high possibility.'

A smile crossed Duncan's face. He was not just happy, he was ecstatic. After years of searching, the possibility of finally uncovering the truth about his father's disappearance filled him with an overwhelming sense of joy and relief. The prospect of bringing the heretic to justice added to his happiness. It was a moment of triumph that he had long yearned for, and the happiness he felt was deeply satisfying.

'Okay, this is good. This is perfect. After all these years, I can finally find the culprit. There's so much to take in. I can finally bring an end to this and bring the heretic to justice ...'

'Well, good luck with that. Just to let you know, I'll be right behind ya.'

'Yeah. However, it seems like this is a job for two people. And you can't help me because of your arm.'

Jénmar sighed. 'Sorry, I wish I could. With the state of my arm, I can't even scratch my own stones, let alone assist you.'

'Damn. Okay, maybe Abraham?'

'Abraham? Really? Sure, he has military training, but he hasn't been involved in that line of work for years. Got a family to look after, you know? He could hook you up with weapons if that's what you're after, but don't expect him to be pulling any crazy shit.'

Duncan scratched his head, searching for alternatives. 'Ugh. Who else can I rely on?'

Jénmar shook his head. 'I dunno. Perhaps you could consider hiring someone?'

'Hire? No thanks.' Duncan shook his head. 'I can't just hire anyone. There's always a risk of them taking the artefact for themselves or betraying me out of greed.' Duncan contemplated the options before him and eventually made a bold decision. 'I'll go myself.'

'Are you sure about that?'

Duncan nodded. 'Yeah, what's the worst that could happen?'

Jénmar's tone grew serious as he reminded Duncan of the risks. 'You know you'll be facing a Jötunn. They wield magical powers that'll leave most humans in the dust. You need to be on your toes, mate.'

Unfazed, Duncan asserted his confidence. 'Ah! But I'm not like most humans. I'm the Heretic Hunter, remember?'

Jénmar chuckled. 'That's true. You've earned that title for yourself. Just make sure you're fully prepared because there's not much I can do to cover you.'

Duncan nodded. 'I understand.'

Jénmar rose from his chair and extended his hand, shaking Duncan's firmly. 'Fair enough. Good luck on your journey, kid.'

Duncan returned the smile. 'Thanks, Jénmar. I'll see you later.'

With their farewells exchanged, Duncan departed from Jénmar's house. Yet, doubt began to seep into the depths of his thoughts. Was he making the right choice? Despite what the captain had said – no, he firmly believed that he was doing the right thing. And he began his journey back home to prepare for the task that lay ahead.

The next day, the room was filled with anticipation as Duncan sat on the sofa, flanked by Sara and Elisa. Sara broke the silence with a smile, her eyes shining with excitement.

'So, you're going on a mission next week?'

Duncan nodded. 'Yes, I am.'

'Will you be gone for a long time, Mr Saul?' Elisa inquired.

Duncan nodded again, his eyes meeting Elisa's. 'Yeah, I'll be back before June.'

Suddenly, Sara's face lit up with an idea. 'Hmm ... Since it's the spring break and Duncan's going on his mission next week, why don't we visit an amusement park?'

Duncan's brows furrowed, and he asked, 'And do what exactly?'

Sara chuckled. 'Why do you think? To have fun!'

Elisa nodded in agreement. 'That sounds like a good idea.'

Duncan sighed. 'What Park are we talking about?'

Sara's response was immediate. 'Rush Peak Amusement Park.'

Duncan's silence hung in the air. 'Really, that place?' he said, finally breaking his silence.

A strange mix of nostalgia and disbelief swept through him.

Rush Peak. He hadn't thought about it in years. As a kid, he used to beg to go – convinced it was the most magical place in the world. Not that they ever had the money for it. His parents were always working, always scraping by. But he remembered the posters, the cartoon mascots, and the stupid jingle he'd hum under his breath. He'd wanted to meet *Peter the Tiger* more than anything.

And of course, Sara couldn't let that memory rot quietly in the past.

Sara's eyes sparkled. 'Yeah. Duncan always wanted to go to that place when he was a kid. He always said, "Mummy, Daddy! I wanna go! I wanna go! I wanna meet Peter the Tiger. I wanna feel his cute little fur! I wanna hug, and squeeze him."'

'Yes, yes. By all means, Mother, find new and creative ways to embarrass your only son. It's not like I have a reputation to maintain or anything.'

Sara pouted playfully, folding her arms. 'Ah, lighten up, gloomy git. Don't you have a sense of humour?'

Duncan narrowed his eyes, arms crossing in perfect sync with his mood.

'Yeah, I do. It's just dry enough to be mistaken for sandpaper.'

Sara's pout deepened, her disappointment evident. 'Ugh. Way to kill the mood ...'

When Sara mentioned that he had wanted to visit that specific park, Duncan couldn't help but avert his gaze, lost in the flood of nostalgic memories. It had indeed been a long time, and he had grown into a different person since then.

'But why that park specifically? We could go somewhere else,' Duncan said.

'I know, but you always wanted to go,' Sara replied.

Duncan averted his gaze, memories flooding his mind. 'That was a long time ago ...'

'So, what do ya think, Elisa?' Sara asked.

'It would be a good idea. The more the merrier.' Elisa then turned her attention back to Duncan, her eyes searching his. 'Right, Mr Saul?'

Sara bounced on her seat, cuddling Duncan with exuberance. 'Whatcha think, Duncan? Wanna come?' she exclaimed, her voice reaching a childlike pitch. She couldn't contain her excitement any longer.

Ugh. My mother can be so embarrassing ... Duncan took a moment, contemplating the proposal. He picked up a biscuit from the plate beside him, nibbling on it as he weighed his options. Finally, he spoke, his voice measured.

'As long as it doesn't hinder my mission.'

Sara's joy overflowed, and she threw her fist in the air, letting out a triumphant shout. 'Yay, we're going to Rush Peak Amusement Park!'

'Get off me, please ...' Duncan muttered, trying to disentangle himself from his mother's exuberant embrace.

Sara's enthusiasm remained undiminished as she continued to celebrate.

Chapter XXXV

HELD BY KIND HANDS

Sara was clad in a grey trench coat, her ponytail neatly tied into a bun. She paired the ensemble with white trainers and blue jeans. Elisa sported her newsboy cap alongside a cream-coloured coat, complemented by blue jeans and trainers. Duncan donned his black hoodie with a red shirt featuring a phoenix logo. He completed the look with blue jeans and black trainers.

The three found themselves on their way to the amusement park, but their journey was riddled with obstacles.

As they drove, they encountered yet another roadblock marked by a sign reading *NO ROAD AHEAD*. Construction workers were busy repairing a damaged motorway, causing parts of the road to be missing. A worker motioned for them to change their course.

Frustrated, Sara let out a complaint. 'Oh, come on!'

Elisa, ever the voice of reason, reassured her. 'Calm down. We will just find another way there.'

'I won't let us miss this day,' Sara said, determined.

Undeterred, the three continued their journey, seeking an alternative route. Along the way, they passed a crowd protesting in the streets, holding signs: *FREE LANCE!!!*, *LANCE IS JUST!!!* and *LANCE HELPED US!!!* The demonstrators chanted, 'Free Lance! Free Lance! Free Lance!'

Sara expressed her exasperation. 'Jeez, they really want Lance out of prison ...'

Duncan glanced at the protest and felt a deep sense of unease. After Matthew's tragic death, anything related to the civil war was the last thing he wanted to see.

As they drove on, Sara's car was abruptly halted by a checkpoint manned by security officers. One of them wore thermal goggles, suggesting heightened security measures. Approaching the car, the officer requested their passports or IDs. Everyone promptly produced their identification, handing them over to Sara who then handed them to the officer.

Reading through the documents, the officer muttered to himself. 'Okay. Okay.' Satisfied, the officer returned the IDs and informed Sara, 'Okay, good.' Turning to the gate security, the officer relayed his permission. 'Let them through.'

The gate officer nodded and lifted the bars, allowing the trio to proceed. Sara manoeuvred the car past the checkpoint and, finally, they reached their destination.

Parking the vehicle, they stepped out and began walking through the bustling streets, only to be met by a gathering of people. A man stood on a makeshift stage, addressing the crowd. His voice carried as he spoke passionately.

'The Kingslayer may be behind bars, but what about Flora and its people, eh!? What about the destruction that the civil war has brought upon us? What about the homes we've lost, the jobs that have disappeared and the loved ones we've had taken from us?' The man continued. 'During this civil war, the government directed all their powers and forces towards the military. They neglected their own people!'

The crowd listened attentively to his words, nodding in agreement.

'Worst of all, they've gone and let loose a video showing those Red Lions committing war crimes in the Ballylawn region.'

Duncan froze mid-step, his eyes snapping wide with disbelief. *They released that video?* The question hit him like a punch to the gut. *How? When?*

He stood rooted to the spot as the memories surged – brutal and uninvited – crashing over him like a relentless tide. Screams echoed in his mind. The images were vivid:

the chaos, the blood, the faces of the dying. It was all still there, rotting just beneath the surface.

'Is everything alright, Mr Saul?' Elisa's voice cut gently through the haze.

He blinked, his chest tightening. *No. It's not.* But all he could say was, 'Can we please move on?'

'Of course, let's keep going,' Sara said quickly, her tone understanding.

But the crowd around them didn't move on. Supportive voices rose, feeding off the speaker's outrage.

'They did what?' someone shouted.

'Yes,' the man at the front affirmed, voice thick with fury, 'they slaughtered our followers in cold blood!'

Gasps and murmurs swept through the gathered listeners like a spark in dry grass.

'Are we going to let this violence continue with our people?'

'No!' came the sharp reply.

The speaker raised his fist. 'Then what should we do?'

The crowd's answer came without hesitation:

'Fight! Fight! Fight! Fight!'

Their chant echoed through the park, slicing through Duncan like a knife.

'We need to raise our voices and make them hear us!' the speaker shouted.

The crowd roared its approval.

Duncan's fists clenched at his sides. His nails bit into his palms. That chant – that fire – it stirred something ugly inside him. Something he'd buried. He wanted to tell them they were wrong, that this path would only lead to more blood, more loss. But his throat was tight. Useless. He couldn't get the words out.

They don't know what it costs, he thought bitterly. *They don't know what it takes.*

The memory of Matthew's face flashed unbidden. The cities turned to rubble. The children who never got to grow up.

'Let's go *now*,' Duncan said abruptly, his voice clipped and sharp.

Elisa and Sara exchanged a quick glance, then nodded.

As they walked away, Duncan said nothing. The cheerful music of the amusement park played on, bright and oblivious – but it didn't reach him. The noise faded into a dull hum beneath the roar of old ghosts in his head.

Sara turned to the two with a mischievous glint in her eyes. 'Do you two wanna try the rollercoaster?'

Duncan shrugged his shoulders, his expression casual. 'Sure, I wouldn't mind.'

But as soon as Elisa heard the word *rollercoaster*, her face turned pale and anxiety coursed through her veins.

She blurted out desperately, 'Th–the rollercoaster? Uhhh ... I'm not really up for it.'

Undeterred, Sara grabbed Elisa's arm and pulled her towards the rollercoaster queue. 'Come on, don't make a big deal out of this, you big baby.'

Elisa protested nervously. 'Mrs Saul, I truly do not wish to go on the rollercoaster!'

Sara reassured her with confidence. 'Scary? Pffth! No. Rollercoasters are thrilling. You might be nervous at first, but once it's over, you'll feel amazing.'

Elisa hesitated, seeking further reassurance. 'Are you certain?'

Sara nodded emphatically. 'Yep! Mama knows what she's talking about.'

Duncan frowned at the playful banter between Sara and Elisa but kept his thoughts to himself. He quietly followed them towards the queue.

Soon enough, the three of them were strapped into the rollercoaster, the safety bar pressing against Duncan's chest a little too tightly for comfort. As the ride began its slow ascent, the click-clack of the chain filled his ears, tension coiling in his stomach with every passing second.

He glanced around, the wind brushing his face as the city unfolded beneath them. From this height, Flora looked almost peaceful – houses, cars, and streets all reduced to tiny, toy-like shapes. But the tranquillity didn't last.

Just as the ride reached its peak, Duncan felt Elisa latch onto him, her fingers digging into his sleeve. She let out a high-pitched squeal, the sound piercing, and he winced, caught between alarm and discomfort. *Great.* He shifted slightly, trying not to seem too bothered, though his arm was definitely being crushed.

Then Sara's voice rang out beside him, unmistakably panicked.

'Oh my God! Oh my God!'

Duncan barely had a moment to brace before she grabbed his shoulder like it was a lifeline.

He let out a resigned sigh. *Of course they'd both grab me.*

The drop was coming. Fast.

'Mum, you're squeezing my–!' He attempted to speak up, but his words were drowned out by the rush of wind as the rollercoaster plummeted downwards.

The rollercoaster plunged, and all three of them screamed – a chaotic mix of fear, exhilaration, and sheer survival. The wind tore past Duncan's face, whipping his hair back as the ride hurled them downwards. He clenched his jaw, baring his teeth, his stomach lurching with every twist and drop. A part of him hated this – but damn, it was thrilling.

Out of the corner of his eye, he saw Sara – her face twisted in a blend of adrenaline and sheer wind resistance, eyes wide with manic delight.

Beside him, Elisa's scream cut through the air. High-pitched. Uncontrolled. Tears streaked down her cheeks, whipped away by the wind. She clung to him with a desperation that made his heart twist.

The ride finally slowed, grinding to a stop, and the restraints released with a loud click.

Sara flung her arms up, still riding the high.

'Phew! That was a blast!'

Duncan exhaled, catching his breath – and then looked down.

Elisa was curled against his chest, whimpering softly.

He blinked. 'Elisa ... you can get off me now.'

She didn't respond right away. Her grip lingered. He noticed the wetness on her cheeks, her breath shaky and uneven.

'Are you crying ...?' he asked quietly.

His tone softened as he reached up, rubbing her head with careful fingers. 'Shhh ... It's okay. It's alright.'

She didn't say anything, but her body slowly began to relax.

The three of them got up and started walking through the amusement park again – neon lights flickering, kids laughing in the distance, the smell of fried food lingering thick in the air.

Then Sara turned to them with that mad grin of hers. 'So? Whatcha think, everyone? Wasn't that *fun*?'

Duncan winced as he rolled his shoulder, pain flaring under his shirt.

'Argh, my bloody shoulder ... You're squeezing like you want to snap it.'

He shot Sara a look.

Sara cackled. 'Oops. Got a little *excited*, I suppose!'

She turned on Elisa then, eyes glinting with mischief. 'You should've seen your face! Absolutely priceless!'

Before either of them could stop her, Sara clasped her hands together and adopting a ridiculous, high-pitched princess voice, she mocked, 'Oh, Mr Saul, please hold me, Mr Saul! Save me from this monstrous contraption!'

Elisa's cheeks turned scarlet.

'No-no-no, please, Mrs Saul, stop!' Elisa begged, flustered beyond belief.

Sara took a step back, her giggles stifled as Elisa clapped a hand firmly over her mouth.

Duncan didn't laugh. He didn't even smile.

He just drifted back into his thoughts, barely hearing them now.

What do I tell them?

He was on the verge of locating the culprit, and the weight of the situation bore down on him. He had been tracking this individual for so long, and now he was close to finally apprehending them. However, doubt and uncertainty crept into his mind.

What if I don't make it back? What if this mission's the one that finally gets me killed? What if the bastard I'm chasing is worse than I ever expected?

Sara noticed the pensive expression on Duncan's face and inquired, 'Duncan, what's the matter?'

Shaking his head and breaking free from his contemplation, Duncan replied, 'No, it's nothing ...'

Sara chose to ignore his response and cheerfully suggested, 'Well then, let's head over to the Ferris wheel. Who's up for a ride on that majestic pony? But first, I wanna grab some ice cream,' Sara exclaimed, her eyes sparkling with anticipation. She turned to Duncan and Elisa, asking, 'Is that okay?'

Duncan shrugged nonchalantly and replied, 'Who am I to say?'

With a nod of agreement, Sara led the trio to the ice cream stand where they indulged in sweet, cold treats.

Duncan couldn't bear it any longer. He had been pushing his thoughts of the tragic events in the Ballylawn region out of his mind, trying to repress any memory associated with Matthew's death, but he had reached his limit. He couldn't help but dwell on what the captain had said to him. He found himself questioning his role after Shane's words had planted doubt. The idea that they might not be so different challenged his self-image. The clear aspiration to be a hero now wavered under self-reflection.

Can I really call myself a hero?

The question lingered, casting a shadow over his purpose. Shane's words resurfaced, reminding him of the moral complexities in his actions. *You talk of protecting Flora, but can you honestly say that every life you've taken was a direct threat?*

Maybe revenge fuelled him more than protecting Flora. The thought crept in, realising his motivations might be tainted by personal vendetta, the line between heroism and vengeance blurred, making Duncan question the purity of his intentions. The conversation between him and Elisa about his methods of violence and killing not always working also made him ponder.

Could she be right?

Duncan struggled as he acknowledged his desire to kill the heretic who attacked his father. If he killed the heretic, would he just become a murderer?

No.

Duncan refused the label of a mere murderer. The pursuit of justice fuelled his conviction. The heretic posed a threat that needed to be eliminated to save lives.

As they strolled through the amusement park, Sara noticed Duncan's distant expression and decided to bring him back to the present. She spoke up, catching his attention. 'What's up with you?'

Duncan snapped out of his thoughts, somewhat bewildered. 'Huh? What d'you mean?'

Frowning, Sara confronted him. 'You've been lost in your own world since we arrived here. You don't seem engaged when I talk to you, and during the rides, you act like you're somewhere else entirely.' She gently grabbed Duncan's cheek, her concern evident in her eyes. She asked, 'What's on your mind, kiddo?'

Duncan tenderly removed her hand from his cheek and confessed, saying, 'I've been thinking about the future.'

Sara furrowed her brows. 'That's odd. You don't usually dwell on the future unless it's connected to your father.' Duncan remained silent. 'This again?' she asked.

Quick to reassure his mother, Duncan explained. 'Hey, Mum, don't get the wrong idea. I'm closer than ever to tracking down the heretic. But now, I'm grappling with what comes next if I actually find him. When I reach my goal, I can't help but question if what I'm doing is right. Remember how you disapproved of me being a mercenary? The people I've killed – was it for the right reasons? Do you think I'm nothing more than a cold-blooded murderer?'

Sara took a deep breath before responding. 'Duncan, you're not a cold-blooded murderer. I may not agree with your choices sometimes, but I know you have a strong sense of justice. You've always tried to do what you believe is right, even if it means taking on dangerous missions.'

'But when it came to that captain ... I can't shake the feeling that I'm not all that different from him. It's like, I ended those lives out of revenge and now I'm questioning if I was ever a good guy to begin with. I wanted to be a hero, but I'm not sure I am.'

Sara sighed, her eyes searching Duncan's troubled face. 'Duncan, being a hero is not about being perfect or never facing doubts. It's about confronting those doubts, questioning yourself and striving to make the right choices. Everyone has moments of uncertainty, especially when facing moral dilemmas. What's important is that you're aware of these feelings and that you're willing to reflect on your actions.'

'But what if my motivations are selfish, Mum? What if I'm just using the guise of justice to satisfy my own need for revenge?'

Sara gently cupped Duncan's face in her hands, forcing him to meet her gaze. 'Duncan, the fact that you're asking these questions shows that you're different from those who never question their actions. Self-reflection is a strength, not a weakness. It's okay to have doubts, but it's crucial to stay true to your core values. Your desire for justice might be fuelled by a personal vendetta, but that doesn't necessarily make it wrong. What matters is how you channel that energy and whether you're making choices that align with your principles.'

Duncan pondered his mother's words, uncertainty in his eyes. 'I just don't want to become the very thing I'm fighting against, you know?'

Sara smiled softly, her thumb brushing against his cheek. 'I know, sweetheart. It's a fear that many who walk the path of justice carry. But remember, it's not about the absence of fear, it's about facing it head-on. If you ever feel lost, talk to those who care about you. We'll help you find your way back.'

Duncan sighed. 'I just want to make a difference, Mum. I want to protect people and make the world a better place.'

'And you can, Duncan. But don't forget to protect yourself along the way. Being a hero means caring for others but it also means taking care of your own well-being. Trust your instincts, stay true to your values and remember that you're not alone on this journey.'

Duncan's face brightened, a genuine smile crossing his lips. 'Thanks, Mum.'

Sara then wrapped her arms around both Duncan and Elisa, pulling them close in an affectionate embrace.

'Alright, kiddos, let's head to the bumper cars or the arcades, your pick!'

Elisa chimed in. 'Bumper cars.'

Duncan agreed eagerly. 'Bumper cars sounds exciting.'

Sara released them and took off ahead, excitement radiating from her. 'Let's goooooooo!'

Elisa chuckled. 'Wow, your mother is quite flamboyant.'

'Yep, it's one of her best qualities.'

The three continued to revel in the wonders of the amusement park, enjoying the exhilarating ride on the bumper cars and laughing together. However, when it came time to go on the Ferris wheel, Duncan hesitated and ultimately declined.

The trio found themselves walking, with Duncan lost in his thoughts, contemplating what he should say to them. Sara and Elisa exchanged concerned glances as he suddenly halted, his gaze fixed on the ground. Sensing the seriousness of the moment, Sara and Elisa stopped in their tracks, giving Duncan their full attention.

'Guys, the place I'm headed to holds an artefact that might lead me to my father and the culprit,' Duncan said, his tone serious. 'I'm gonna find this culprit, and when I do, I have to do it alone.'

Silence hung in the air as Sara and Elisa absorbed Duncan's words.

He continued, his voice laden with vulnerability. 'I can't let you two get tangled up in this … I don't want either of you to get hurt.' Emotions welled up within him, and he opened up further, admitting, 'You two mean everything to me, more than anything else …'

Sara and Elisa remained silent, grappling with the weight of Duncan's confession. He had never been this open before. Sharing such feelings with his mother was normal since they were family. But with Elisa, a friend he'd grown close to over the months, confessing that she meant something special to him was unexpected.

Elisa, finally breaking the silence, inquired, 'Do you truly mean that, Mr Saul?'

Duncan nodded meekly, his gaze still downcast. Sara, though her irritation surfaced, approached it playfully, resting her palm on Duncan's shoulder.

'You idiot … What did I say earlier? You have us.'

'Mrs Saul is right. Who says you have to face this alone? We can support you,' said Elisa.

'Remember, Duncan, we're all in this together.' A smile graced his mother's face as she began to sing a song. '*We can do anything as long as we're together.*'

'This isn't a joke. I've been chasing this culprit for the past several years, and it ends when I get my hands on this artefact.'

Elisa and Sara both gave firm nods.

'I'll be away for a bit. When I return, I will make sure that the culprit's been brought to justice. Got it?'

'We understand, Duncan,' Sara said.

'Good,' he said, a smile on his face.

'Now. Let's head home and I'll order some pizza!' Sara suggested cheerfully.

Elisa quickly interjected, reminding Sara, 'Vegetarian.'

Sara's face lit up with realisation. 'Oh shit, I forgot.' She playfully corrected herself. 'Veggie pizza it is, then!'

A smile spread across Duncan's face as the three resumed walking. Together, they made their way home, cherishing the bond they shared. The day at the amusement park had come to an end.

Jeremy's boots echoed sharply as he stormed into headquarters, flanked by his men, every nerve taut with purpose. The dull rustle of papers ceased abruptly as Rainer looked up, startled, confusion clouding his pale eyes. Jeremy could almost taste the fear beneath that façade – the same fear he himself had once felt before deciding that action was the only path forward.

'What's the meaning of this intrusion? Have you lost your senses!?' Rainer's voice cracked with disbelief.

Jeremy's pistol was steady, trained on Rainer's chest. 'We've come to reclaim what rightfully belongs to us, Rainer. Your paralysis has cost us enough.'

He saw the flicker of surprise, maybe even doubt, cross Rainer's face, but Jeremy's resolve did not waver. He had long wrestled with the chains of hierarchy – loyalty twisted and strained by the slow rot of inaction. The old order had failed. It was time for new blood, for decisive hands.

'Jeremy, do you understand the grave consequences of your actions? You are defying your superiors!'

Jeremy allowed himself a faint, cold smirk. 'I understand perfectly, Rainer. I've realised you no longer serve the cause – only your own safety.'

There was no room left for hesitation. No more waiting.

'Gentlemen, it's clear Rainer is a hindrance to our mission. It's time for decisive action.' His voice brooked no argument. 'Men, seize this milksop.'

The word hung heavy in the stale air – a bitter epithet that carried years of contempt. Jeremy felt a surge of grim satisfaction as his loyal followers closed in, strong hands gripping Rainer's arms.

'You'll regret this, Jeremy! Our principles cannot be forsaken!' Rainer's protests were frantic, but Jeremy's expression hardened, steeling against the old man's bluster.

'Our principles were forsaken the moment you chose inaction over duty,' Jeremy said quietly, voice cold as iron. 'The people suffer while you turn a blind eye. Protection and guidance demand courage – something you lack.'

Rainer thrashed, desperation igniting wild eyes. 'No! I won't be taken by you!' But it was futile. Without hesitation, a Night Hawk swung the butt of his rifle hard against

Rainer's jaw. The sickening impact silenced him instantly, and he collapsed, limp and unconscious.

As the heavy silence settled, Jeremy felt the weight of the moment. With the old guard removed, the path was clear. Lance would be freed. The Night Hawks would rise. And Jeremy would no longer be shackled by cowards.

Epilogue

REVELATION

The morning sun cast a warm, golden light over Lancefield, but the brightness did little to lift the heaviness settling in Duncan's chest. At twenty, standing on the doorstep of his home, he felt the sharp edge of this farewell. Konrad was leaving – the man who'd been more than a mentor, more than family.

Duncan's eyes found Konrad, luggage in hand, backpack slung over one shoulder. The older man's gaze held a flicker of nostalgia, as if he was seeing not just Duncan but the boy he once was.

'You've grown into a remarkable young man, kid,' Konrad said quietly. 'Couldn't be prouder.'

Duncan's throat tightened. 'None of this would've been possible without you, Konrad. You've been my mentor, my confidant ... my family. I can't thank you enough.'

Konrad's smile softened. 'It's been my honour, Duncan. Watching you grow has given my own life meaning.'

The words settled around them like a fragile warmth. Konrad reached into his backpack and pulled out a baseball, weathered but well cared for, his signature scrawled across its surface.

'This holds our memories, Duncan – our fights, lessons, every damn step. Keep it close. Let it remind you of what you've learned.'

Duncan took it, fingers brushing over the faded ink. A small smile cracked his face. 'I'll cherish it, Konrad. And I'll carry everything you taught me forward.'

Without thinking, he wrapped his arms around Konrad, holding on tighter than he wanted to admit. The hug said what words couldn't – thank you, goodbye, I don't want this to end.

Konrad pulled back, voice low but firm. 'I'm leaving for Citra today. There's a war there, and I have to help. But remember – this isn't the end. It's the start of a new chapter.'

'I'll miss you. But the world's wide. There's more out there for you to discover.'

Konrad's hand rested on Duncan's shoulder. 'Stay true to yourself. Chase your dreams. Never forget the values we built. You've got the power to make a difference.'

Duncan met his eyes, determination flaring. 'I promise. I'll make the most of what you gave me. One day, I hope to be as wise as you.'

Konrad smiled, pride shining through. 'No doubt you will, kid. Farewell – for now.'

And with that, he turned and walked away, shrinking into the distance. Duncan stood rooted, clutching the baseball tight, feeling the full weight of the lessons, the history, the future pressing down on him.

This was his journey now.

As the three of them approached home, Elisa hesitated for a moment before gathering the courage to speak up. Turning to Sara, she politely asked, 'Mrs Saul, would it be alright if I had a quick conversation with your son?'

'Sure, sure. Take all the time you need,' Sara said happily.

Elisa wasted no time and gently took Duncan's arm, leading him away to a secluded spot where they could speak privately.

Duncan, perplexed by her urgency, furrowed his brow and asked, 'What's the matter? Why're you dragging me away like this?'

Taking a deep breath, Elisa met his gaze and asked directly, 'I wish to help you on your endeavour.'

'About my mission?'

Elisa nodded.

'Why?'

'Because you have done so much for me,' she explained earnestly. 'You provided me with a home, supported my journey into university and even saved my life. I feel a deep desire to repay your kindness.'

Duncan sighed. 'Listen, Elisa, this isn't an easy path. It's dangerous and I can't guarantee your safety.'

Elisa stood her ground. 'I understand the risks, Mr Saul. I want to join your cause, to assist you in locating your father and, more significantly, to prevent any future tragedies akin to what occurred in Pete's Fort.'

Duncan's expression softened, but he still had reservations. 'Elisa, I really appreciate your offer to help, but this is a seriously risky move. The AMOB may be involved and they don't take kindly to people who interfere with their mission.'

He was not wrong. Elisa knew about the AMOB all too well. Disappearances, acts of violence and the utter obliteration of anyone who crossed their path were common themes in the AMOB's dark history. Despite the fear that even mentioning the AMOB brought, Elisa's determination remained unshaken.

'Mr Saul, I simply cannot remain idle and observe. If there exists an opportunity to enact change and safeguard the lives of the innocent, I am compelled to seize it. My aspiration to serve within the ministry can be postponed. Right now, I wish to help you.'

Duncan rubbed his forehead, clearly conflicted. 'You're putting your future on the line for this. What about your education, your dreams?'

'I hold belief in my own abilities. Place your trust in me and I promise I will not falter. I am determined to prove myself and prove that I am capable of exceeding your expectations.'

She needed to convince Duncan. She had to. She couldn't bear the idea of feeling useless to him, of missing the chance to make a meaningful impact in the face of the impending danger. She kept hearing the voice in her head: *You have to help him. You have to help him. You have to help him* ... Over and over, like a broken record.

Duncan remained sceptical, his arms folded across his chest. 'Elisa, I value your confidence, but this ain't a walk in the park. It could get dodgy. How can *you*, a nineteen-year-old who hasn't even begun her semester, possibly support me?'

He had a point. When it came to life experience, there was a significant gap between them. Duncan had experienced adulthood while Elisa, at nineteen, was on the threshold of it. She was still at the stage where the world held youthful optimism and idealism, yet to be shaped by the tough lessons that often came with growing up.

'Well, for starters, I may be young but I have a way with words. I'm an eloquent speaker and persuasive in negotiations. If we encounter any obstacles, I can use my skills to help us overcome them.'

Duncan considered her point but still expressed concern. 'Elisa, this adventure comes with some serious risks. What about my mum? She worked so hard to make sure you got into university. Taking you into such a dangerous situation would go against her wishes.'

Right. His mother. What would we tell her? Elisa pondered for a moment, searching for a solution. 'Perhaps we might frame it as an academic excursion. We shall inform her that our purpose is merely to retrieve an artefact, not to embark upon some suicide mission. We can further assure her that every measure will be taken to ensure our safety.'

Duncan sighed, his frustration evident. 'You don't seem to understand, Elisa ...'

'Mr Saul, please hear me out. I understand your concerns, but I genuinely want to help. I believe in your cause and I believe in my ability to contribute. Together, we can find a way to make this work while keeping ourselves safe.'

'Why're you so fixated on this? I can handle it myself.' Softening his tone, Duncan sighed and said, 'Go live your life, girl. Don't get yourself involved with me.'

Once again, the voice insisted – this time, dark and menacing: *You think you can walk away? You worthless girl. He sacrificed so much for you, and you would repay him with cowardice? You'd better help him, or you'll prove how truly useless you are.*

Elisa then desperately grabbed his hands and looked into his eyes, her expression pleading. 'Please, Mr Saul ... I *need* to do this.'

Duncan gave her a serious look. He frowned and asked, 'Need to?' A reluctant smile formed on his face. 'I understand ...'

Abruptly, Duncan's hands clenched Elisa's shirt, his grip tight and forceful. With a sudden burst of aggression, he hurled her down to the cold, unforgiving grass. The impact sent shockwaves of pain through her body, leaving her trembling with fear. Beads of sweat trickled down her forehead, mingling with the tears welling up in her eyes.

Elisa didn't expect Duncan to be so physical with her. This was the first time he had been aggressive. Duncan had been her mentor, her protector and the one who had offered her guidance and support in times of need. She had never expected him to react with such violence.

As Elisa mustered the courage to look up, she found herself staring into the abyss of Duncan's anger. A deafening silence filled the atmosphere, only broken by the sound of her rapid, shallow breaths. Duncan's cold gaze pierced through her, his eyes burning with an intensity that sent shivers down her spine. With a chilling calmness, he uttered words that reverberated in her ears.

'Are you willing to die for me?'

Elisa's mind raced, panic coursing through her veins. Her voice caught in her throat, rendering her speechless, powerless, leaving her to gaze back at Duncan, her eyes wide.

After what felt like a long time, Duncan finally released his grip on her shirt. He stepped back, his face etched with caution. His voice carried a stern warning as he spoke.

'Do me a favour, Kid, and *stay* out of my way. It's for both our sakes.'

With those words, he turned and left, leaving Elisa in stunned silence.

After a few days, Elisa arranged to meet Duncan in the park, and as he approached, she sat patiently on a weathered wooden bench, her gaze fixed on the path ahead. Duncan settled down beside her. Sensing his reluctance, Elisa took a deep breath. 'Mr Saul, I wish to speak with you.'

Duncan let out a weary sigh, stealing a glance at Elisa. He knew she harboured a persistent desire to join him on his mission, and he braced himself for another attempt. Resigned, he leant back, preparing himself for the discussion.

'If this is about joining me, please save it.'

Elisa moved closer to Duncan, and the look in her eyes confirmed his assumption.

'Seriously?' Duncan frowned. 'I already said no.'

Elisa took another deep breath, her eyes fixed on the ground as she gathered her thoughts. 'Mr Saul, I understand your concerns and respect your decision. But please, hear me out. This isn't just about joining you anymore. It is about acknowledging the impact we've had on each other's lives and the potential we hold together.'

Duncan raised an eyebrow, his curiosity replacing his initial resistance. He remained silent, allowing Elisa to continue.

'I know I've already mentioned how you've helped me in the past, but it goes beyond that. You've taught me to be brave, to step out of my comfort zone and seize opportunities. I've watched you face challenges head-on, and your resilience has inspired me to do the same.' She paused, giving Duncan a moment to absorb her words before pressing on. 'By rejecting my offer to join you, you are not only dismissing my desire to help you, you are dismissing the growth we could both experience through this journey.'

Duncan's mind churned beneath the quiet surface. He'd been digging in his heels, pushing Elisa away, but now that resistance was starting to crack. Maybe he did need her.

The faces of Ballylawn's civilians flashed before him – the screams, the blood, the bodies left in the mud. And then Matthew ... the boy who had trusted him, who had deserved better, lying cold and lifeless.

Finding his father was clear enough – but putting an end to the war would require something greater. The civil war. All of it had to stop – once and for all. And he couldn't do that alone. He would need help. He would need Elisa.

Still, Duncan's gut twisted with doubt. What was driving her? Was she repaying some kindness he barely remembered giving, or was this about her own fight – trying to prove she mattered, trying to grow stronger beside him? He'd tried to scare her off, to keep her safe, but she wasn't backing down. That stubbornness both annoyed and intrigued him.

And yet, the thorn in his side was still there. How the hell was he supposed to explain this to his mum? Letting Elisa in would open a can of worms – complications, questions, maybe even trouble. Duncan clenched his jaw. Whatever he decided, nothing was going to be simple.

Lost in his thoughts, Duncan finally broke the silence. 'Fine, but I'm not gonna let you become a liability. I'm going to teach you how to survive.'

Elisa's eyes lit up with joy, a wide smile spreading across her face. 'Yes! Thank you, Mr Saul. I won't let you down.'

Duncan watched Elisa celebrate, but inside, a tight knot formed in his chest. Her reckless desperation unsettled him more than he cared to admit. How could she be so calm, so unfazed by the risks staring them in the face? It didn't make sense. Anyone with a shred of sense would have said no and gone back to their books, safe and sound. But not her. Not Elisa. That stubborn recklessness rattled him more than he wanted to admit.

As the evening sun began to set, casting an orange glow over the horizon, Jeremy stood at the centre of a small gathering of his trusted comrades. They were stationed outside a safe house on the outskirts of the city of Gothenburg. Giovani stepped forward and addressed Jeremy.

'I'm sorry I ever doubted you, Jeremy. Perhaps with your plan, we can truly save the Night Hawks from the Red Lion military.'

Jeremy's piercing grey eyes met Giovani's, and a faint smile tugged at the corner of his lips. 'No apologies are needed, my friend,' he replied. 'We all had our doubts, but now is the time for action. The passivity we've embraced for too long will only lead to our demise. We can't allow the Red Lion military to hunt us down and extinguish us.'

His words resonated with the new Night Hawk regime. They had witnessed their brethren fall one by one, their voices silenced, their sacrifices in vain. Jeremy's plan offered them hope, a chance to turn the tides and reclaim their power.

With a firm nod, Giovani took a step closer to Jeremy. 'I stand with you, Jeremy, as do many others. We believe in your vision and your leadership. The time has come for us to rise, to show the world the strength of the Night Hawks.'

Jeremy's gaze swept the group, measuring their loyalty, their hunger for change. *They need to believe. They need to believe in me.*

'Tonight, we'll free Lance, our leader, from the Riverdam's prison! He embodies our spirit, our resilience, and we owe it to him and to ourselves to fight for his freedom. The trial they have set up is nothing but a mockery of justice!'

As Jeremy spoke, the Night Hawks' determination grew, their faces etched with a renewed sense of purpose. 'Yeah!'

'The Night Hawks will rise and Riverdam will witness our strength! Together, we'll defy the oppressors, strike fear into the hearts of those who would seek to subdue us and pave the way for a brighter future!' Jeremy's voice raged out with conviction, punctuating the air as he delivered his impassioned declaration to his fellow Night Hawks.

'Yeah!' The collective shouts echoed through the still evening air, rippling with energy.

'Wings of Courage, carry us beneath the moon's watch. Night Hawks – take flight!' Jeremy raised his fist in the air as he spoke.

In response, his loyal comrades raised their voices in unison, their unified shouts echoing through the air, chanting the battle cry of the Night Hawks.

'Night Hawks, take flight! Night Hawks, take flight! Night Hawks, take flight!'

Their approval was not merely a vocal agreement but a manifestation of their unyielding loyalty and belief in the cause they fought for. It was a rallying cry, an affirmation that they were ready to march forward as one, prepared to face the perils that lay ahead.

As the group prepared to set their plan into motion, the sun finally dipped below the horizon, casting the world into twilight.

To Be Continued

Acknowledgments

Editor: Gillian Baines
Book Cover Designer: Yulia from Miblart
Book Cover Artist: CHAWAK

Writing *Tenets*, the first instalment of the Vagabond series, has been an extraordinary journey, one that would not have been possible without the support and encouragement of many remarkable individuals.

First and foremost, I would like to thank God Almighty for his blessings and guidance throughout this journey.

To my family, for their unwavering love and belief in me. Your constant encouragement kept me going even when the road seemed long and arduous – thank you from the bottom of my heart.

I am grateful to my editor, whose keen eye and dedication to excellence helped refine my manuscript into the polished novel it is today.

To my beta readers – thank you for your time, enthusiasm and honest feedback. Your perspectives have been incredibly valuable.

Finally, to my readers – thank you for embarking on this journey with me. Your support and passion for storytelling fuel my desire to continue writing. I am deeply grateful for each and every one of you.

This book is a labour of love, and I am honoured to share it with you. Here's to many more books in the Vagabond series.

With gratitude,
A O Ambali

About the Author

A O Ambali is a British Nigerian author based in London, UK. With a love for crafting intricate, character-driven fantasy, Ambali has dedicated their writing to exploring the complexities of human relationships, layered characters, and the intertwining of intense action with romance as a subplot.

When not writing, Ambali enjoys spending time with his family, playing video games, and reading manga, comics, and books.

To learn more about A O Ambali and stay up to date with upcoming works and news, visit:

Website: https://www.aoambaliauthor.com/

Instagram: @a.o._ambali

Goodreads: https://www.goodreads.com/user/show/166868674

www.ingramcontent.com/pod-product-compliance
Lightning Source LLC
LaVergne TN
LVHW020646110826
845149LV00012B/1923

* 9 7 8 1 0 6 8 1 5 4 8 1 2 *